Upstaged by Betrayal

Books by Virginia G. McMorrow

The Mage Trilogy
Mage Confusion
Mage Resolution

Novel
Upstaged by Betrayal

Coming Soon!
The Mage Trilogy
Mage Evolution

The Firewing Trilogy
Firewing's Journey
Firewing's Shadow
Firewing's Hunt

For more information
visit: www.SpeakingVolumes.us

Upstaged by Betrayal

Virginia G. McMorrow

SPEAKING VOLUMES, LLC
NAPLES, FLORIDA
2023

Upstaged by Betrayal

ISBN 978-1-64540-967-0

For Kevin

Acknowledgments

Special thanks to my literary agent, Cherry Weiner, as well as Kurt Mueller, Erica Mueller, and the staff of Speaking Volumes.

Chapter One

"Want the good news first, boss?"

Nevis Conarkin, mage extraordinaire, eyed the middle-aged manager of her sorcerous theater across the cluttered desk, her empty stomach flipping with a strong sense of unease. "Before I've eaten one measly bite of my sweet and sticky breakfast roll, Simon?"

"I wouldn't pester you," Simon Masters hedged, sliding a rough hand over his thinning gray hair, "if it weren't important."

Precisely what had set the mage's instinct jumping furiously up and down. The somber, organized, and utterly reliable manager ran Nevis' seldom-placid theater troupe with expert efficiency, handling more problems in a day than the mage ever dreamed could possibly exist. And wasn't paid nearly enough.

Nevis sighed, hating to take advantage of a man who loved the chaotic world of the stage as much as she did, but profits had never come easy for them. Not like the playhouse run by her prosperous rival, Barry Faddle, whose traditional, non-sorcerous theater entertained the elite crowds of Port Jambi. Of her own desire, Nevis catered to the working class and merchants.

Barry Faddle disdained the lower class audience who flocked to the mage's performances. Yet he simultaneously looked down his very elegant nose at his elite audience, proudly charging them outrageous sums for tickets to his theater, sums that would have made Nevis ill had she been forced to charge the scandalous fees. She'd rather shut the playhouse down than charge so much that a laborer couldn't share a performance with his family.

The fact that her ill-paid manager disturbed her daily morning ritual of devouring that sweet and sticky, sugar-coated nightmare meant that trouble was brewing for Nevis Conarkin's Sorcerous Theater.

"The simple fact that you said it's important is the only reason I haven't changed you into a squealing piglet."

Simon's smile was tight. "Nevis—"

"All right, old friend." Nevis heaved a melodramatic sigh that would have been the envy of her leading actress and prima donna, Gabriella de la Morsage. Before hearing the news, the mage reached for her sweet breakfast cake and paused, one hand hovering over the treat, but still refusing to touch the cake.

"Boss?"

"Simon, there's a raspberry star on top."

"There's a new baker in the neighborhood. Didn't I tell you? The owners sold the shop to an old woman, made her promise to bake those horrible concoctions just the way you like them or they wouldn't give her the keys. Is the raspberry a problem? Will it make you sick or something? If it will, don't—"

"No." Nevis kept her voice exceptionally calm, expression deadpan. "Her name, Simon? The new baker?"

"Clari. Clari's Sweet Shoppe. Boss, you feeling sick or something?"

"I'm fine, Simon." Nevis took a deep breath, forced her trembling fingers away from the raspberry-star-topped cake, a special decoration she hadn't seen in ten long years. Was it possible that Clarissa was still alive? And only three blocks away from her cursed theater? And, by the gods, Nevis thought numbly, how long had she been this close, watching in the shadows?

"Should I go call Doc Esteway? You look a little pale."

Nevis shook her white-haired head, clearing away old memories, doubts, and unending guilt. "I said I'm fine, Simon. So, good news first. Tell me the king finally listened to my groveling and agreed to cancel this horrendous performance."

"Wish I could. But the wondrous and all-knowing Devlin Graham is eagerly awaiting the opening night of the 'Doom of Bambari'."

"Damn that thick-headed fool. I've been trying to bribe him for weeks. Nothing's worked." Green eyes darted to the wall behind the stage manager in open annoyance, alighting on a brilliant poster that proclaimed the "Doom of Bambari" in stylized lettering. Triumphant over Adrian Bambari, rogue and treasonous mage, was none other than the white-haired owner of the theater, Nevis Conarkin. "I wish Dev would reconsider and let me cancel the performance."

"You did save Devlin's life and his kingdom of Montbasso a decade ago, and he wants people to remember. Hence, the ten-year anniversary re-enactment," Simon said diplomatically, daring his employer's irritation, which would occasionally erupt in magefire.

"I'd rather they forgot." For a lot of reasons Simon and the townspeople of Port Jambi didn't need to know, Nevis reaffirmed to herself. Why re-enact the destruction of Adrian Bambari when Hugo San Rossi, Adrian's former apprentice and current mage adviser to the king, remembered that humiliating fact every day? And by the gods, what if Clarissa Bracken really was alive?

"I'm no longer the royal mage adviser, Simon. That's old history. At the moment, I'm just the owner of an unprofitable playhouse in Devlin's capital that allows me a blissful escape into make believe. And this doomed play isn't an escape. It's a nightmare. I like being a nobody, Simon. It keeps people off my back."

Simon's thick eyebrows inched skyward as he considered his employer's disgruntled mood, hearing the pain of old memories. And so he tried to bring a smile to her lips, in light of the other news he was bringing her this morning.

"So humble, boss? You're one of a rare bloodline, since you're a genuine mage. Not too many of you oddities around, are there? And besides, you're the most envied woman in the prosperous city of Port Jambi, not to mention the entire kingdom of Montbasso."

"For sharing the king's bed?"

"People are shallow, if that's all they think. As a—"

"Tell me the good news, Simon."

The manager shifted his argument, knowing when it was best to follow her lead. "Gabriella grudgingly agreed that she would wear the white wig Verdi Casporet created for her."

"If Gabriella is playing my part in the play, then she's supposed to look like me, and she doesn't have a choice."

Simon scrutinized his employer's prematurely white, short-cropped hair, a legacy from the sorcerous battle in which she barely escaped with her life, courageously and single-handedly preventing Adrian Bambari from bringing foreign invaders from Cashogi, across the Percy Sea, into Devlin's unsuspecting kingdom.

The brightness of Nevis' hair was a vivid contrast to the ebony garments she'd always worn, regardless of the season or time of day. The only other lightness to her appearance was the ivory-handled stiletto at her waist or the occasional diamond that Devlin forced her lovingly to accept, despite her lack of desire or need for jewels, as a sign of his affection.

"Gabriella's agreed to wear the wig only in the last act."

"It was only in the last act, when I was only thirty years old, that my hair turned prematurely white. As for Gabriella, if that plump-headed, sack-breasted, egotistical windbag—"

"Calm down. Gabriella meant no offense. As a matter of fact, she told me just last night after rehearsal, right after you left the theater, that you're a stunningly attractive woman—"

"Who pays her wages, not that they're exorbitant, mind," Nevis admitted with genuine regret and honesty. "The gods save me from actresses with fat heads."

The gods being whatever deities the people chose to worship in private, so declared by Devlin Graham's great-great-great-great grandmother who tired of continual religious fighting and bloodshed, and officially closed all seven houses of worship. And privately, Nevis kept on the far left corner of her desk a carved likeness of Janni, the mother goddess, a dozen children playing at her feet, one suckling at her breast, yet another, head resting on her lap in peaceful sleep. The carving had been a gift from Nevis' long-dead mother, and the mage kept it there, not for worship, but for the sense of serenity it always provided.

"Are there any other kind of actresses?"

"A joke, Simon, so early in the day? From you?"

"In light of the other news," the manager mumbled, eyes darting to every corner of the cramped office, past the locked cabinet in which Nevis kept her inventory of prepared spells, out the back window overlooking the Basol River and the busy merchant activity sliding past, anywhere but at Nevis Conarkin.

"Simon."

A sigh escaped. "I've had to send word to the Port Jambi constable just now. We need an official presence."

"Constable?" Nevis lurched to her feet, sticky roll, and its haunting baker, forgotten. "Did the carpenter use those drugs again? I told that irresponsible idiot only the other day that if he messed up the scenery one more time—"

"Nevis."

"Stupid fool. What's he done?"

"Not a thing. Nevis, listen, it's about the royal box."

"What about it? No, don't tell me. You'll take all day. I'll see the trouble for myself."

Simon didn't argue, thought it best, though cowardly on his part, not to say anything further and let Nevis find out the problem with her own eyes. He watched in grim silence as Nevis drew the ivory-handled stiletto from its sheath at her leather belt and faced the cabinet that held her inventory of spells. Two round knobs, allowing her to pull the doors open, worked their own special sorcery. The left provided a perfect view of any room in the sorcerous theater, the other let Nevis glimpse the orphanage that she and Lily Frascat, a successful brothel owner and Nevis' oldest friend, operated from their own limited funds.

Green eyes cool, Nevis tapped the left sphere with the stiletto, watching through narrowed eyelids as the interior of her theater came alive in all its bright colors. She couldn't hear anything, but saw all as she spun the transparent crystal gently with her stiletto, allowing the stage to slip past.

"No one's working. By the gods, what are they staring at?" she murmured, more to herself than Simon, as the sphere revolved again, tilted slightly toward the ceiling, until the mage had a crisp, clear view of the private box overlooking the right side of the stage; the box reserved for his majesty, Devlin Graham, and any special guests her lover might bring to the theater. "Simon, there's a—"

"Aunt Nevis!" A scarlet-faced, ten-year-old whirlwind slid through Simon's skinny legs and crashed into the desk. "Aunt Nevis, there's a dead body in the king's private box."

The mage turned from the crystal sphere in shock, stared at Simon, green eyes unblinking, across her nephew Teddy's unruly curls. "Please tell me that Hans Takat is practicing his death scene."

"Wish I could, boss. Wish I could."

* * * *

Stepping silently first down the narrow stairs, then across the prop-laden stage, and up the center aisle toward the back of the theater, Nevis scanned the curious, wary faces of her subdued cast and crew, wondering what unfortunate soul was missing, and why. "Simon, who told them there was a dead body?" Nevis questioned the manager in a low voice.

Simon leaned closer to the mage. "There was an, ah, unfortunate odor that they complained about. I went up to investigate and found a stranger who wasn't breathing." He shrugged, looking a little sheepish as he added, "I fled back down quickly, warning them all to stay away, and sent for the constable."

"All right. Go back up to the box and wait for me. I want to be sure no one sneaks up there before the constable arrives." Nevis studied the silent, gathered crowd. All were present, even Hans, actors, stagehands, designers, and clerks, for which Nevis immediately breathed a silent, heartfelt prayer to the gods of all seven nonexistent houses of worship. So who was dead in her theater?

By the time she reached the front door, heading for the side stairway that led back upstairs to the private royal box, the Port Jambi constable had arrived. It was a woman Nevis didn't recognize, having little interaction with the city enforcers unless absolutely necessary.

"Mage Conarkin?" Brea Kilganor, short, stocky, and well-fit, studied the mage's tense face through calm dark eyes framed beneath a tangle of short-cropped black hair heavily sprinkled with white. The constable's gaze was placidly professional, in harmony with the crisp folds of her deep blue uniform. "I'm Constable Kilganor."

The mage met her gaze without wavering. "I'm afraid I don't know you. Are you new to Port Jambi?"

"Not in the least. Only new to your neighborhood." The constable's smile left Nevis uneasy for reasons she didn't dare consider at the moment. "I was enjoying this fine summer morning—"

"Is it?"

"The murderer might think so."

"We don't know there's been a murder, only that there's a dead body in my theater. And for the gods' sake," Nevis grumbled, raking hair back from her forehead, "I don't even know who the poor soul is."

Brea Kilganor spun on her well-polished heels. "Then let's go have a look, shall we?"

Nevis stepped a half pace in front of the constable, found her movement blocked by Brea's stocky figure and courteous smile. "Me first. For security, mind," she added dryly, "in case the murderer is still on the premises."

Nevis' protest died on her lips. "Simon found the body. He's already been up there. He's there now, waiting for us."

"Not touching anything, I hope."

"He knows better."

Brea grunted before taking the plain wooden stairs at an easy pace. The two women, one short and muscled, the other lean and tall, emerged into the narrow corridor that ran behind the balconies along the two sides and back of the theater. The royal box was directly opposite Nevis' own private box, from which she nightly released the extravagant sorcerous spells that so enchanted her working class and merchant audience, not to mention her curly-haired nephew.

Waiting anxiously at the door, Simon nodded at the constable with genuine respect.

"Touch anything?"

"Of course not."

"Recognize the dead person?"

"Possibly."

One dark eyebrow inched upward as the constable crossed her arms, eyes not on Simon, but rather Nevis' surprised expression.

"Can't be sure, boss, which is why I didn't say anything," Simon addressed the already-rattled mage, "but from the peek I took, without touching anything," Simon directed at the constable, who simply stared back, "I think it's Adam Museo."

Nevis' curse was loud and eloquent.

"The same Adam Museo who's hauled you into court because of the orphanage building across the park?"

Unsettled at her knowledge of Nevis and Lily's legal tangle, Nevis snapped, "Is there any other? Why'd he have to die in my theater?" She moved to step inside the royal box, but Brea gripped her wrist, surprising Nevis with her strength. When the mage sighed, Brea slipped past Simon.

"Does our glorious king come here often?"

"When he's in the mood. Look, constable—"

"And his daughter?"

Nevis eyed the constable through narrowed lids, trying to determine the purpose and tone of her query. "Rarely."

"Doesn't she approve of your relationship?"

"Listen to town gossip if you're out for information like that, Constable. It has nothing to do with the dead man in my theater."

"Maybe. Maybe not. One never knows what information comes into play later on when all the scattered pieces are gathered together. The corpse is in your theater, Mage Conarkin, and there are people who don't like you very much. Not many, I'll grant, but a few. And in return, you don't like those people either."

"For someone new to the neighborhood, Constable, you're rather well informed," Nevis muttered.

"When the theater and orphanage in my territory is operated by the king's lover, I'd be pretty stupid not to be well informed, don't you think?" Brea Kilganor started ticking off names on her sun-browned hands. "Adam Museo, our corpse, for one. Alana Graham, Devlin Graham's only daughter and heir to the throne of Montbasso. Hugo San Rossi, Alana's lover, who also happens to be Devlin's mage adviser. Anyone else I might have missed?"

Nevis kept her face exquisitely neutral, betrayed only by a sharp glint in her somber green eyes.

The constable nodded. "That particular mutual feeling between you and Mage San Rossi is open knowledge in Port Jambi, too, though no one quite understands the reason for the hostility."

"Listen, constable—"

"As your immediate successor to the position of mage adviser to Devlin Graham, Hugo San Rossi is jealous of the great and famous Mage Conarkin, who stepped down from the position ten years ago, of her own free will, so the gossip runs. That jealousy is one reason tossed about in the taverns."

"He should be jealous," Simon snarled from the doorway. "Hugo San Rossi is a despicable pig who won't accept the fact that Nevis is superior in every way, and I'm not just talking about sorcery or power. She—"

"Simon—"

"She—"

"Simon," Nevis chided gently, grabbing the manager's wrinkled cotton sleeve, "hush." When Simon nodded, stymied protest still visible in his eyes and his stance, Nevis turned back to the other woman. "What's between me and the king's mage adviser is none of your affair, constable."

Brea Kilganor held her gaze for a long, silent, and uncomfortable heartbeat. By the gods, Nevis brooded beneath that unrelenting scrutiny, could the corpse really be connected to Hugo San Rossi in any way? Is that why Clarissa returned to Port Jambi and sent a signal this morning? And if so, whose side is the old woman really on? With utter care, Nevis wiped all traces of anxiety from her face.

The constable spun on her heels and approached the body, revealing a young man in his thirties, sprawled across the front row of cushioned seats. Oblivious to the unusually subdued and silent crowd gathered below on the stage, Brea studied the motionless figure. The front of the scarlet velvet shirt was soaked with an odd-smelling, overpowering liquid. On the seat next to the corpse, a sealed letter and an empty flask were cast aside.

Nevis cursed again, sharply enough to gain the constable's attention. "My flask," Nevis explained in response to a raised eyebrow.

Brea knelt beside the chair, eyes fixed on the ebony flask, engraved with the mage's initials in ivory. "Gift from Devlin?"

Nevis mumbled an assent as the constable picked up the flask and sniffed, sending another whiff in Nevis' direction. "Firespark?"

"Familiar with it, Mage Conarkin?"

Old memories assaulted the mage, bringing unwanted grief from its hiding place in her heart. Not memories of Firespark, but another poison, no less compelling, that destroyed Adrian Bambari's sense of reality and very nearly destroyed Devlin's kingdom of Montbasso. "Adam Museo was selling Firespark to my cast and crew until I asked him to stop."

"Did you ask politely?"

"No." Green eyes met dark ones over the corpse. "Adam Museo was selling the drug to Lily Frascat's girls, too." The mage leaned against the sturdy railing, ignored the whispered voices down below. "I hadn't heard it was fatal, or I would have threatened my troupe with more than a tongue lashing."

"Fatal only in a severe overdose taken in a very short period. It was popular with Lily's whores, you said?"

"Until she caught on. You'll probably hear it in the taverns, Constable, so I might as well tell you myself. Adam physically abused one of her sweet girls, and Lily warned the bastard to keep his distance." Nevis stared at the constable, green eyes dark with anger, daring her to point a finger. "Neither of us did anything wrong. We were only trying to protect our people from harm."

"Fiercely enough to murder the man?"

"I didn't murder Adam and neither did Lily."

"Lily Frascat shares an interest in the orphanage you both run on the other side of Alvaron Park, and Adam was threatening to take back the building his father supposedly donated to you before he died."

"There was no 'supposedly' about the matter."

"Maybe from your perspective. I understand you and the madam were unable to provide documentation to support that generous contribution. Seems reasonable to assume you both have some decent motives for getting Adam Museo out of your hair, at least sufficiently convincing for a judge to find credible."

The stage manager tugged uneasily at his thinning hair, eyes darting back and forth between Nevis and Brea Kilganor. "Constable—"

"Hush, Simon. Listen, Constable, what I see in this theater right now is an overdose of Firespark, not a murder."

Brea Kilganor's dark eyes stayed fixed on Nevis' face for a long, tense moment before she snatched up the sealed letter and ripped it open. "Your personal stationery, too, I presume?"

"Yes."

Brea uncoiled in an unexpectedly graceful motion and got to her feet, leaning on the arm of a neighboring chair. She scanned the contents of the note, eyes unreadable, then handed the letter to Nevis. The mage's face was a jumble of emotions as she read the damning words beneath Brea Kilganor's unwelcome scrutiny.

"I've nothing to live for, thanks to Nevis Conarkin. With the king's inevitable support of her claim against me, the Montbasso court will never grant me a fair hearing. Without the funds that Mage Conarkin legitimately owes me for the purchase of the orphanage building, the funds she never paid my father, I'm bankrupt. And in truth, I'd rather die than face bankruptcy and shame.

Adam Museo"

Nevis took a deep breath before meeting the constable's eyes. "Devlin would never interfere and pressure the court's decision. Not that he'd need to," she added, allowing a dash of righteous anger to show. "My claim, and Lily's claim, regarding the building is legitimate. Adam's father donated the structure when Lily and I first discussed opening the orphanage. We didn't even ask the old man, but he had a decent heart. Heard someone talking about our plans and immediately told us we could have the building to use at our discretion."

"Lily's idea, wasn't it? Starting an orphanage for the underprivileged? Tough childhood, so I heard, orphaned herself as a very young child, and grew up on the streets. And just see what's happened to her, Mage Conarkin. She's running the whorehouse next door to your theater."

"A very respectable and enjoyable brothel. And yes, it was her idea to keep the children off the streets."

"And then train them to be prostitutes as they matured?"

"By the gods, Constable, if you ever so much as think something that filthy and vile again—" Nevis took a step back, shoved her hands deep into the pockets of her black breeches, and retreated from the very tempting idea of smashing her fist into Brea Kilganor's smug face. "Adam Museo is—" Nevis flushed, trying to get her anger back under control. "He was nothing like his father. All Adam cared about was his own personal gratification."

"I heard," Brea smiled, her teeth not as crisp and regular as her uniform, "that Adam didn't believe his father would ever make a charitable donation to a madam in a whorehouse—"

"Whose very prostitutes presented the old widower with hours of simple, pleasurable, uncomplicated delight. Someone stole the documents from Lily and me. We both had copies for safekeeping, and they're gone."

"Conveniently."

"Damned inconveniently."

"You blame Adam."

"Seems logical, doesn't it?" Nevis' thin hands flew out of the pockets of her black breeches, waving in frustration. "Look, even if the royal court decided in his favor, and Lily and I had to pay for the orphanage building, it wouldn't have saved Adam from bankruptcy."

"Because?"

"Gambling debts. Damned heavy ones, too."

"Were you privy to his financial status? Did Finlay Oscram make you privy to Adam's financial status?"

"No." Nevis flushed with anger that the constable knew her banker's name. "The entire town of Port Jambi was privy to Adam Museo's financial status. And he was sinking fast. What doesn't make sense," Nevis ran one hand absently across her hair, "is that he'd kill himself."

"He didn't."

Nevis' green eyes went wide as Simon gasped behind her. "How do you know that for sure?"

"His shirt."

"That shirt is the villain's shirt. Hans Takat will be livid when he sees his costume destroyed," Nevis murmured, approaching the corpse with despair, counting the days until opening night.

"Verdi Casporet will be worse," Simon said quietly, inching closer into the room. "She'll have to embroider another shirt."

"The villain's shirt," Brea murmured to no one in particular. "The doomed mage, Adrian Bambari."

"I'm doomed if Verdi can't create a new one by opening night."

"You're doomed, Mage Conarkin, if you don't have an alibi," the constable declared. "Do you?"

Green eyes met dark ones in utter silence until Nevis slowly shook her head. "No."

"You weren't with Devlin Graham?"

"I have my own life, Constable, and my own responsibilities. I'm not always with the king. And I'm never with Devlin on audience day. He spends the evening with Alana, with his heir, going over the administrative and diplomatic decisions he's made that day. It's good training for her to rule in his place."

"What about Hugo?"

"What about him?" Nevis lost her patience. "I don't keep track of Hugo San Rossi's movements. What's he got to do with this murder, anyway?"

What does he truly have to do with this, Nevis fumed silently. *And why did Clarissa Bracken send a signal now after ten long years of silence, ten long years in which I believed her dead? Ten long years of grief.*

"You tell me."

"You said Adam was murdered. How do you know that?"

Unperturbed, the constable pointed. "Look at the shirt. Here." She tapped the velvet with the point of her dagger just beneath the last button, directly over Adam's heart. Certain she had the mage's attention, Brea slipped open the lavishly embroidered garment, revealing a tiny slit in the cold flesh where a minimum of blood had escaped. "A skillful thrust to the heart by a very fine weapon." The constable's dark eyes strayed casually to the ivory-handled stiletto at Nevis' waist, the only bright spot among her ebony garments.

"Don't be ridiculous," Simon exploded, ready to throttle the constable. "If you're accusing Nevis—"

"I'm just pointing out the obvious," Brea said reasonably, resheathing her own dagger. "Everyone in Port Jambi knows Mage Conarkin uses the stiletto to trigger her spells, particularly the special effects during the performances that create bone-rattling earthquakes and fires and fierce thunderstorms." The constable met the manager's angry gaze with supreme indifference. "I haven't attended one of the performances yet, so I can't agree or disagree on whether the performances are extraordinary."

"There are other possible weapons," Simon protested, face growing scarlet. "Verdi uses thick needles for sewing leather. Someone could have easily borrowed one. Someone who—"

"Someone who hates me enough to set me up," Nevis said quietly, sorrow in her eyes, swiftly replaced by anger. "Constable, I've no time for this problem. I'm sorry Adam's dead, but I didn't do it. Opening night is less than two weeks away. We're in the middle of final rehearsals, and I've got a life's worth of work to do."

Brea's grin sent a shiver down the mage's back. "Since you may be doing it from a prison cell, maybe you should include a jail scene in the next rehearsal."

Chapter Two

"I'm far too overwrought to rehearse!"

"Gabriella—" Simon sidestepped the leading lady's wild gestures and jutting breasts with practiced familiarity and a roll of the eyes. "Opening night is less than two weeks away, and we need to achieve perfection."

"I'm not an amateur, Simon Masters." Gabriella de la Morsage sniffed in disdain, tossing auburn hair over one shoulder at the stage manager. "I know my lines. I've known them for weeks. Let the others practice."

"Gabriella—"

"No one's got a clear head today. Cancel the rehearsal." Nevis slipped quietly into the discussion and shot a warning glance at her manager. "Send everyone home, Simon, until tomorrow."

"Everyone but me." A female voice piped up from beneath bolts of scarlet velvet in the far corner of the stage. "Why did that idiot have to die in one of my richest, most extravagant costumes?"

"Sorry, Verdi," Nevis murmured wholeheartedly as the bolts of velvet quivered with indignation.

"It took weeks to embroider that shirt for Hans."

"I know. Make a simpler one—"

The bolts of material went flying as a young woman swept free of the material, head encased in a white wig. "I take pride in my needlework, Nevis, just as you take pride in your explosive storms and drenching seas and—"

The mage rolled her eyes at Simon, who coughed delicately and looked away before the costume designer threatened him with a sewing needle.

"Take my wig off your ugly, lice-ridden head this minute." Gabriella launched her feminine curves at the costume designer with a snarl, tackling the wigged woman, and sending the velvet cloth flying into the wings.

Watching the leading lady's fevered antics, Nevis calmly plucked a sphere from the bottomless leather pouch at her waist that frequently had the crew wagering on how many spheres their employer could really hide away in the sorcerous wallet. Within the sphere that Nevis held up to the flickering magefire lamplight lay a miniature cannon. Sliding the ivory-handled stiletto from its sheath, the mage pierced the sphere, triggering an ear-splitting explosion that shook the stage beneath her feet.

Cast and crew, so often forgetting their employer was a powerful mage, swiftly fell silent.

Sliding the stiletto back in its sheath, Nevis patted the worn leather with fondness. "As I was saying, no rehearsal today. But I'll expect everyone to show up an hour after daybreak tomorrow. We'll use the entire day if we have to so that everyone knows their lines to perfection. Verdi," the mage eyed the costume designer as she disentangled her short legs from Gabriella's voluminous silk skirts, "work at your own pace, as long as Hans has a shirt by opening night."

"Tell that lice-ridden bitch to take off my wig."

"Gabriella," Nevis towered over the kneeling actress. "Verdi has a reason for whatever she does. Since she's never worn any of her wigs before, I'll assume she has a purpose that eludes even your crafty little mind."

"But—"

With a whispered incantation, more reminiscent of a crude oath than a sorcerous spell, Nevis vanished from sight, without benefit of a sphere, leaving Gabriella slack-jawed and wide-eyed. It was rare that

Nevis performed sorcery without her spheres, particularly in front of her cast and crew. Invisible, the mage walked softly to the side of the stage and headed for the front entrance, simultaneously reappearing as a flamboyant middle-aged woman entered the subdued theater, floral-print silk gown flowing gracefully around her shapely legs, matching feathers perched in her fashionably coiffed scarlet hair.

"By the gods, Nevis, I wish you'd stop doing that."

"Sorry, Lily."

"Well, it's not quite as shocking as that contemptible pig dying in your theater. Why couldn't he die in Slick Hands' playhouse?" the brothel owner grumbled, referring to Nevis' theatrical rival, Barry Faddle, or Slick Hands Barry when he was close to Nevis or any other attractive female.

"Barry couldn't handle the bad publicity."

"That swine would turn it to his own advantage."

Nevis laughed and took her friend's arm, guiding Lily back outside into the bright sunshine, where a man-high transparent sphere dominated the front of the theater. The sphere was cupped within two immense wooden hands that the owner of the Ruskin Shipyard, just upriver, had donated from a discarded figurehead. Every evening, when the last rays of the setting sun had vanished, the sorcerous sphere came to life, with fantastical images of ships and mythical creatures and storms appearing throughout the night. Maintained by a spell that Nevis reinforced every few weeks, the sphere proclaimed the theater's unique attraction.

Nevis led Lily toward the lush green expanse of Alvaron Park that separated the sorcerous theater from the small orphanage financed by the two women. May Quiddle, Nevis' younger sister and ten-year-old Teddy's mother, ran the orphanage, keeping herself busy while her sea-faring husband captained his merchant vessel to Montbasso's other major trade cities, upriver to Port Cordillero, around the southern cape to Port Magista, or skirting the northern shore to Port Neeri. Theo Quiddle's runs depended on the season and how far north he could journey before winter storms trapped him in the harbor.

Across the park, Nevis and Lily could see nearly a dozen children just emerging for a bit of play under Teddy's reluctant shepherding. It was a well-known fact that the boy would rather spend his days in his aunt's theater, a fact that contributed to his mother's never-ending affectionate despair.

"The constable stopped by to tell me the news," Lily explained, pushing back a loose strand of flaming red hair set free by the river breeze, still cool despite the onset of summer. "She'll be back to speak with some of my girls."

"She's a sharp one."

"Don't I know it? Remo had some dealings with her in recent weeks. She'll find some stupid little detail and work it mercilessly."

"Then she should be able to find the murderer and put this nightmare to rest." As the madam of the most beloved and successful whorehouse in Port Jambi gracefully sat on a wooden bench in desperate need of new paint, Nevis made a mental note to send one of her stagehands around with a brush. "She'll be back to speak with some of my cast and crew, too, particularly the ones who bought Firespark from Adam."

Lily studied the mage's somber expression as Nevis restlessly paced in front of the bench. A stranger watching would have wondered at their odd friendship, at the contrast in lifestyle, appearance, and interests. Anyone, that is, who didn't understand the core of decency and genuine affection that had drawn them together as very young children and kept them close despite the passing years, and the passion with which they desired to create the orphanage, a desire that ran from Lily's own lonely childhood and Nevis' great heart.

"Is there a connection to the missing documents?"

Nevis rested one black boot on the bench. "Damned if I know."

"Nevis, whoever's behind this murder knows that you weren't with Devlin last night."

The mage turned away from her friend's unsubtle expression.

"Alana Graham—"

"Has no cause to set me up for murder."

Lily's expression was eloquent.

"That's a little extreme, even for Devlin's heir."

"Is it?" When Nevis' boot started to slip from the bench, Lily grabbed it and held on tight. "Just listen for a minute."

With open reluctance, the mage stood still, face empty of all emotion, bringing a sigh of fond exasperation to Lily's lips.

"Sometimes, Nevis. Sometimes, truly— Yes, fine, I'll stop. But just listen first. When you defeated Adrian Bambari ten years ago, you saved Devlin's life, along with his queen. Alana doesn't know that her mother betrayed her father and fell in love with Adrian. And the girl doesn't know," Lily added with emphasis, "that her mother, by supporting the traitorous mage, nearly let Cashogi foreigners invade Montbasso in return for their support, taking what they wanted and leaving the throne to Bambari and his lover, once Devlin was assassinated and no longer an obstacle."

Lily paused, studied the mage's stony expression, and still Nevis remained coolly silent.

"The girl doesn't know the truth," Lily continued, "that her royal mother was a whore and a traitor."

Nevis refused to bite. "Old history, Lily."

"You promised to listen." Lily sighed once more as the mage stifled a half smile. "When Devlin's queen committed suicide some months after you destroyed Adrian Bambari, Alana blamed her mother's death on a broken heart because Devlin had fallen in love with you."

Nevis turned her face toward the Basol River, shoulders tense beneath the black shirt. "We never pursued each other, not while his queen was alive."

"Doesn't matter to Alana. She blamed you unfairly. Her mother did die of a broken heart, but it was for the wrong man. Maybe the girl should know the truth. She's old enough." Lily's smile was wicked. "Certainly old enough to take a lover to her bed. A pitiful choice if you ask me, sharing her bed with Hugo San Rossi, who, mind you, is ten years older than the girl, but nevertheless, she is old enough."

Nevis shook her head fiercely, short hair blowing gently in the breeze. "I agreed with Devlin ten years ago, and I still agree. It serves no purpose to tell Alana that her mother betrayed him and her own people."

"Doesn't it? You've been paying for that ignorance ever since." Lily took a deep breath and spoke her mind. "The girl thinks you've been whoring for her father before she was even born. It's not right."

The mage shrugged, her profile like granite.

"Hugo San Rossi doesn't help the situation."

Nevis' slender body radiated tension, and it was all Lily could do to bodily grab the mage and prevent her from walking away or vanishing from sight through sorcery. But the madam kept her jeweled hands in her lap and took a chance.

"Devlin could have chosen a more neutral mage to take your place when you stepped down as mage adviser."

"Not many of us around, Lily."

"He didn't look very hard."

"Hugo was Adrian Bambari's duped apprentice, or so we thought at the time. We were fools, Lily, taken in by skillful acting. I was just as much to blame."

"Hugo knows too much."

"He knows, for the most part, how to behave in front of Devlin."

"Yes, but what does he whisper in Alana's ear at night? Surely not the truth about her treasonous mother." When Nevis didn't answer, Lily sighed. "Some days, old friend, I wish Clarissa Bracken were still alive."

Nevis tensed, green eyes narrowing, every instinct alert. "Why are you even thinking about Clarissa now?" she asked quietly, trying desperately to keep the edge from her voice.

Lily shrugged, oblivious to her friend's apprehension. "Talk of old history, I suppose. Look, Nevis, I know it's a sensitive topic for you, but no one really knows what happened to your mentor. There were all those rumors about Clarissa helping Adrian to betray Devlin—"

"No one cares about old rumors. By the gods, Lily, I don't want to talk about Clarissa. Not today. Not tomorrow. Not ever." Nevis stormed away, prompting her very worried friend to scurry after, feathers bobbing in rhythm.

Lily eyed the mage with speculation. "Why was Adam killed in the royal box of your theater? And why was he wearing the shirt that Hans would wear in his role as Adrian Bambari?"

"How should I know?" Without warning, Nevis stopped and spun around to face her friend, nearly causing the other woman to collide with her. "What do you want me to do?"

"Watch your back." Lily gripped her sleeve and held on tight. "I know you'll try to ignore everything I've just said because you adore Devlin Graham, for which I thank the gods every day, and because you don't want to upset his cozy relationship with his no-longer innocent daughter. But you can't ignore the truth. Alana hates you for no good reason, and she's standing between you and Devlin."

"We—"

"Do just fine. I know." Lily shook her head in fond exasperation. "I adore Devlin, too. But you're the king's mistress when you could, and should, be his queen."

A crooked smile escaped Nevis' lips. "Who's been filling your feather-tipped head with sorcerous tales?"

"You're the one who refuses to wed him."

"For good reason. I won't have Alana point her finger and accuse me of lusting after her father's power or influencing his state policies."

Lily's laugh was richly affectionate. "Pardon me, old friend, but if Alana only believes you can influence your father in a council chamber—"

"And not between the sheets— I know, Lily. I'm not as naïve as you sometimes think. But still," the mage drew herself straight, despite the turmoil in her head, "I won't be the cause of trouble between father and daughter."

"Honorable."

"Nothing wrong with it."

"Nothing wrong with Alana considering you no better than one of my lovely prostitutes?"

"Nothing wrong with your girls, Lily. They're honest and decent, and they work hard."

"Nevis—" The madam started to protest, but shook her head in resignation. "Then listen to one more piece of unwanted advice. Don't scold, Nevis." When the mage waited impatiently, she said, "Have a chat with Remo."

The mage blinked in confusion, then understood all too clearly. "Don't you think Remo Savanak's tired of me as a client? He's already defending my plea, and yours, I might add, against Adam for the or-phanage."

"And now that Adam's a rotting corpse, and Brea Kilganor has made it very clear that you're a suspect—" The madam shrugged. "I'm a suspect, too, so I've surmised. I'll set up a meeting for the three of us."

"Together? A threesome?" Nevis forced a grin to her lips, earning a mock scowl from her friend.

"I share many things with you, Mage Conarkin, but not my Remo."

* * * *

Nevis waited outside the stately brick house that had been in a dire state of disrepair ever since the older Museo had died a few months back and left the property to his only son, Adam. Biding her time, Nevis kept watch until Brea Kilganor had finally departed before using her stiletto to trigger a spell plucked from her bottomless pouch, encasing her tall, slender body in the illusion of invisibility. The spheres, many of which Nevis used nightly to create the spectacular effects in the the-ater, were not only prepared beforehand for her convenience, but to preserve the mage's energy during the performing season. And believ-ing that she needed energy more than ever at the moment, Nevis de-cided to use the sphere rather than the incantation to disappear as she had in front of her cast in the theater earlier.

Taking a deep breath, she approached the residence, boarded and sealed with the constable's official notice, then headed for the ill-kept and overgrown backyard. Itching simply from the sight of the profusion of weeds, Nevis grunted and groaned until she managed to slide open a back window leading into the pantry.

Adam Museo had been a pig, not only in spirit, but in social manners and housekeeping as well. Filthy, crusted dishes and half-eaten meals littered the kitchen, and Nevis wondered, not for the first time, what his father must have thought. Maybe the old man had died without knowing the truth.

Careful to leave no trace of her presence, she stepped warily over mounds of trash and piles of wrinkled clothing in the parlor, eyes scanning the dusty chamber for potential hiding places. The constable had left her own trail beckoning up the stairs, particularly in the main bedchamber, judging from the wooden safe skillfully cracked open and the scattered remnants of Firespark sprinkled on the furniture. Nevis glanced at a discarded wrapping that had fallen behind a footstool, surprised to see words penned in the Cashogi language, words she couldn't decipher, though the stylized lettering was easily identifiable.

The sight left Nevis cold. Had Adam been dealing with Cashogi criminals? If that were possible, Nevis thought in confusion, then he was doubly breaking the law. First by dealing in illegal drugs, and second, by trading with Cashogi merchants. There'd been no friendly trade relations since Adrian Bambari's failed treason, though Devlin Graham was heavily steeped in recent weeks trying to revive the age-old agreement between the two kingdoms.

Trade Minister Mikaline Nashat had arrived only weeks earlier, representing the first official trade delegation from Cashogi in ten years. His two ships were docked in the harbor, blue banner with its brilliant white rearing stallion, flying proudly from their masts. The Cashogi were an island people and depended on the sea for trade. But their limited supplies of lumber had grown scarce in recent years, a fact that had initially prompted Adrian Bambari's alliance with them. Montbasso's lake regions were plentiful with oak and pine used in the Ruskin Shipyards not far upriver from Nevis' sorcerous theater.

Devlin was trying to negotiate a reasonable trade arrangement that would allow the Cashogi access to the fine vessels produced by the Ruskin Shipyard without creating an aggressive navy. In return, Montbasso would benefit from the excellent crafts of Cashogi artisans, particularly from the artists of Kolmari, a city along Cashogi's northwest coast. But Cashogi drugs, the poison that had first weakened Adrian Bambari's loyalty to his king, and to all that Clarissa Bracken had taught both him and Nevis a lifetime ago, were forbidden.

By the gods, what did it all mean? And did it mean anything at all?

Nevis glanced over at the safe, saw it was empty, but for a note propped up against the crumpled door:

"Mage Conarkin,

No documents in the safe. Sorry to disappoint you. If you find them elsewhere, please let me know.

Brea Kilganor"

Nevis growled a rude comment, then laughed, half in desperation. She stepped slowly through the remnants of the chaotic bedchamber, found a lovely portrait fallen face down on the ground. The young woman's face was striking, her hair long, rich with glossy black curls, the image somehow very familiar, yet beyond Nevis' immediate recall. The mage had lived in Port Jambi all her life, and the girl could be any one of the young women she passed on the street every day or in her theater audience. Thinking the portrait might have been someone dear to Adam, she set it gently on the low table beside the bed.

Alert for any peculiarity that might betray a hiding spot, Nevis slowly searched the entire house, from the dust-covered attic to the dank cellar below, finding only a door that led to the weed-grown gardens. The young woman, if she was indeed a close acquaintance of the deceased, had left no trace of her feminine presence or influence. If she had had any sense, the girl wouldn't want to be anywhere near this pig-sty, Nevis thought in disgust.

Focusing on her fruitless search, the mage couldn't make sense out of anything. If Adam didn't have the documents proving that his father donated the orphanage to Nevis and Lily, then who did? Or had he destroyed the evidence? The mage thought back, with open reluctance, on Lily's insinuations about Hugo San Rossi. Did Hugo despise Nevis enough to risk putting himself out of favor with the king? In his eyes, he surely had cause; for her destruction of his own mentor, Adrian Bambari. Or did Hugo think he could simply let Nevis sink deeper into trouble, little by little, knowing she'd refuse to ask Devlin for help?

And by the gods, what did the message from Clarissa Bracken mean? If it had truly been from Clarissa—

Frustrated and confused, Nevis headed back toward the rear entry, so lost in tangled thoughts she nearly fell flat on her face when a tiny shape darted out from beneath the faded sofa in Adam's parlor. Catching her balance, Nevis stood motionless, listening hard, until she successfully traced the source of whimpers. On her knees, she pushed aside a pile of discarded clothing and found a white-tailed, black kitten, shivering with fear and hunger.

"Poor, pathetic ball of fur. Come on. There."

Nevis gently scooped the quivering body in her hand and continued speaking in hushed tones, unwittingly sending the poor creature into shrill protests. Only then did she realize the kitten couldn't see her. Releasing the invisibility spell, she stroked the soft fur, finally calming its shattered nerves.

"I suppose I can't make you suffer just because your owner was a contemptible pig. Let's go see if I can find a new home for you."

Leaving through the rear entrance of the residence, Nevis cradled the ball of fur as she made her way quietly through the middle-class merchant neighborhood, grateful that the streets were apparently empty.

The theater was situated not very distant, past the merchant homes and their neighboring shops, not far from the outskirts of the business district. On the far side of town, where wealthier visitors to Port Jambi came to stay in the more elite, posh inns, Barry Faddle had strategically built his traditional, non-sorcerous theater. Slick Hands catered to an audience that Nevis had never been interested in wooing, instead preferring the hard-working middle and lower classes, the underlying reason for her lack of overflowing profits, according to her banker, Finlay Oscram, who often threw up his hands in mock despair.

Nevis headed purposefully past her own theater and through Alvaron Park to the orphanage, where May was busy tutoring the older children, including a reluctant Teddy, while the little ones were soundly napping. Or so Nevis thought.

Just approaching the neat, fresh-painted wooden structure, Nevis glanced up to find auburn curls bobbing in the window. The mage raised a hand in greeting, then placed a finger to her lip, unable to restrain a smile as three-year-old Kimmi vanished from the window. Bracing herself for a sisterly scolding, Nevis slipped into the building and glanced distractedly at the never-ending minor repairs her crew hadn't yet had time to work on, before following the sound of her younger sibling's voice to rap sharply on the door of the crowded schoolroom.

"Yes? Who— Oh." May Quiddle raised one hand in warning at the rush of eager voices greeting her sister, the two women dissimilar in appearance but for matching green eyes. May's soft brown curls were so unlike Nevis' straight, short-cropped white hair that no one ever thought they were siblings, even before Nevis' hair had turned its distinct shade. "Mage Conarkin, the children are in session, and they—"

"I thought you might want to teach them how to care for a kitten." Nevis held out her arm, the black kitten curled inside her hand, soundly asleep. "Unless, of course, they're not interested." Nevis laughed as she found herself beseeched by enthusiastic boys and girls, ranging from six to about eleven, pleading with May to let them keep the kitten, no less an orphan than themselves.

"It looks like you, Aunt Nevis," Teddy grinned, elbowing his mother politely aside. "All in black, with a white tail."

"My tail," Nevis told him sternly, to the delight of the children, "is not white. My hair is white."

Unfazed, Teddy reached out to gently stroke the kitten. "Looks just like you. Shall we call him Nevis?"

"I think you should call him Rascal. The little rascal nearly tripped me on my face." She held out the kitten for the others to see. "I'll only leave him here if I know someone will care for him."

With their fervent promises ringing in her ear, and May's resigned headshake, Nevis left the kitten at the orphanage. Heading across the park, she stopped when May ran after, calling her name.

"You can't give him back."

"I wouldn't dare. The children would report me to the king for torture. Nevis, listen, Teddy told me about the body. Are you in trouble?"

"Me?" The mage swiftly cloaked her expression in her skilled, I'm-the-older-sister-don't worry-about-me look, not surprised when May snorted in disgust. "Of course not."

"Nevis—"

"I'll come back when I have something solid to tell you, all right?" Grateful for the shriek of delight from inside the house, Nevis inclined her head in that direction. "You'd best go save that kitten."

"Nevis, sometimes you're impossible."

"Lily had the same thought this morning." Nevis squeezed the younger woman's shoulder. "I'm fine, really. Do you mind about the kitten?"

"What's one more orphan?"

* * * *

One more visit and then Nevis could crawl into her beckoning bed, throw the covers over her head, and escape the relentless demands brought by the unusual day. But unless she actually made this last un-inviting stop, dreamless slumber would never come. And even then, she wasn't sure she could escape the old nightmares brought about by Adrian Bambari's death at her hands.

Standing across the street from the tiny bakery shop on the corner, three blocks south of the theater, she waited. Green eyes watched as the old woman, long silver braid centered down her spine, locked the door and headed slowly around the back of the building to narrow stairs that led to a tiny set of rooms above the bakery.

Nevis studied her careful walk, thinking she might have been mistaken and that it might not be Clarissa Bracken, but knew that appearances were deceiving. It was only when her attention fell on the rhythmic clicking of the wooden cane, the sorcerous wooden cane, that the mage acknowledged the truth. Remembering the walking stick that had been ever-present throughout her apprenticeship under Clarissa Bracken's tutoring, Nevis mentally revived a clear, detailed image of the carved wood at its head, the carved head that held a different image for each onlooker.

For Nevis, it had always been a flame-breathing dragon; for Adrian Bambari, a fork-tongued snake, and later, for the young mage who had become Adrian's apprentice, for Hugo San Rossi, it had been a fox. Clarissa had allowed Lily Frascat and Devlin Graham their own glimpse ten long years ago, with Lily's image that of an elegant, stunningly graceful horse, and Devlin, a proud and fierce hawk, the very same creature emblazoned in scarlet on the tunics of his guard and that flew from his banner high atop the fortress walls.

Clarissa had never confided to Nevis the creature revealed by the sorcerous cane for Clarissa's own eyes, and Nevis wasn't sure she wished to know. Though if Nevis had known, it might have put her troubled emotions to rest.

The old woman halted at the top of the rickety stairs, placed a gnarled hand on the doorknob, and slowly turned her head, silver braid swaying gently. "Are you coming in, child?"

Nevis took a deep breath and followed. The scent of cinnamon tarts wafted up the stairs as Nevis' long legs took the steps two at a time. She entered the dim lit parlor and shut the door behind her with a soft click.

Clarissa Bracken set her walking stick aside, letting Nevis see the dragon's image on the cane's head. The older woman said nothing, waited for Nevis to speak. But the grueling day caught up to Nevis, and she simply sagged back against the shut door.

"You're angry with me."

Nevis shrugged, careful to keep her expression empty, knowing it was useless. Clarissa had always been able to read her with barely an effort. "I thought you were dead. I thought—" Nevis took a calming breath. "I thought you hated me."

"I did." The woman sank onto a worn and faded sofa, plumped fraying pillows behind her back. "For a time."

"Adrian would have destroyed the peace."

"There were other ways to control him. Death wasn't necessary," Clarissa's dark brown eyes studied the fatigue on Nevis' face, "so I thought at the time. Maybe it was. I still haven't decided."

"I didn't know what to do," Nevis whispered, letting old grief escape from a hidden core of her soul. "Adrian was dangerous, out of control. The Cashogi drugs had eroded his ability to reason. I destroyed Adrian more in self-defense than anything else. By the gods, Clarissa, do you think I wanted to kill him?"

"Peace, child." The older woman patted the sofa, waved Nevis to sit beside her, and still Nevis refused. "I trained you both side-by-side for half your lifetime. I know his betrayal was as much a blow to you as to me. But still, when I heard he'd been destroyed, and by your hand—" She shut her eyes, lamplight sending shadows across her wrinkled cheeks. "Did you think I had helped him, had betrayed Devlin, too?"

"Some people did."

Dark brown eyes slid open. "That's not what I asked."

"I didn't want to believe it of you." Nevis shrugged, tired of being on the defensive after the earlier session with Brea Kilganor. "I didn't know what to think. You left Port Jambi without a word." *You left me without a word.* Nevis pushed away from the wall, her shadow slicing the tiny room in two. "Why did you come back? To torment me with old memories?"

Clarissa ignored the barb. "I've been planning to come back for some time. You've done well, capturing the heart of the king."

Nevis turned to leave.

"Child, forgive me. I don't know how to speak to you."

"Fair enough." Nevis' hand rested on the doorknob, her rigid back to the old woman. "Shall I keep your presence a secret?"

"I would like that for the moment. Nevis—" Clarissa grabbed her walking stick, fumbled slowly to the door. "Child, don't hate me."

"I don't."

"Can you look me in the eye and say that?"

Disheartened, Nevis shut her eyes, leaned her weary head against the door. "I don't know."

Clarissa stroked the younger woman's hair gently, then stepped back. "Good night, Nevis. Sleep well."

* * * *

"After our last delightful evening together, I didn't quite get the idea that you'd grown weary of me. Did I miss my cue?"

Nevis turned from the window, so engrossed in distracting thoughts that she hadn't heard Devlin arrive in her parlor on the second floor of the theater, behind the stage. The monarch of Montbasso stood just inside the doorway, uncharacteristically uncertain of his welcome. Tall, Devlin had a shock of thick brown hair flecked with gray, blue eyes that studied the mage's reaction as his fingers strayed to the short dark hairs of his beard.

"I also thought you might have sent along that prettily worded note suggesting I stay away because you didn't want me tangled in your affairs." When Nevis flushed, in sharp contrast to the brilliant white of her hair, Devlin laughed softly. "Don't you think it's a little late for that?"

"You're so damnably infuriating when you're right."

"Am I ever wrong?" Devlin shut the door with the worn heel of his boot. In a heartbeat, he'd crushed Nevis to his chest, allowing her a brief illusion of safety. "I had a little chat with Lily before coming here," he murmured in her ear, warm breath tickling her skin.

"Lily?" The mage pushed Devlin away, green eyes wide. "What will all your subjects think?"

"That I've grown weary of you in my bed?"

"For the gods' sake, Dev, Lily does run a whorehouse. Your people might be scandalized."

"Lily Frascat happens to be my friend, not to mention a wonderfully decent woman. Besides, I knew I couldn't rely on you to give me the whole story," he grinned, "unless of course I pulled it from your lips, word by word."

Nevis crossed her arms against her chest and stared him down. "What precisely did that woman tell you?"

Devlin pulled her down beside him on the soft, pillow-strewn sofa. "The essentials. Don't waste my time."

But the mage kept her distance on the couch, hugging bony knees to her chest. Wearing an innocent expression, Nevis rested her chin on her knees, reminding Devlin of a white-headed, ebony cat with soft green eyes. Had he known about the kitten Nevis had rescued, it would have greatly amused him.

"What are you plotting, Mage Conarkin?"

"Let me cancel the play."

"Absolutely not."

"If—"

"If whoever's set you up has timed the murder to coincide with the play, it's too damned bad. I want people to remember precisely what you did for them ten years ago. As my mage adviser, then, not now," he added grumpily, never having completely forgiven Nevis for resigning after saving Montbasso from Adrian Bambari's treachery. Not that he didn't have access to her advice, but with magery so rare, it was a completely trusted mage he preferred in that visible public position.

Nevis stuck her tongue in the hollow of her cheek and studied her lover. Then she shook her head and asked, "Isn't that a bit pushy? Telling your subjects how great your lover is, or was? Not to mention that I'm a prime murder suspect."

"You are not."

"According to Constable Kilganor—"

"I'll talk to the constable."

"You'll do no such thing." Nevis grabbed his thick hands and gripped them tight. "Let the woman do her job without the king peering over her shoulder. If you poke that handsome nose where it doesn't belong, no one will ever believe my innocence." As Devlin reluctantly digested the truth of her argument, Nevis' grinned. "Sometimes I'm right, too."

Devlin's hands flew to her sides, swiftly and unerringly finding her vulnerable ticklish spots until the mage begged for mercy. "Admit I wasn't wrong, only considering the alternatives."

"You have an ego the size of your— Oh, never mind."

Blue eyes lit with mischief. "Go on. Things were just getting interesting. What about the size of my—"

"Oh, hush."

"Appalling way to speak to your monarch."

"Not when I've seen him naked."

"Don't distract me with flattery, Mage Conarkin, before I forget why I originally came here."

Nevis' expression subtly changed, and Devlin grew wary. "Some people think there's only one reason you come here."

Devlin caressed her cheek, tangled his fingers within hers. "They wouldn't if you'd wed me—"

Nevis jerked away.

"If you won't marry me," Devlin swiftly changed tactics, knowing the present wasn't the time to press his argument, "the least you can do is promise to attend the merchants' dinner tomorrow night."

"Not a good idea."

"You're the owner of Port Jambi's sorcerous theater, not to mention a well-respected mage." When Nevis snorted in a very unladylike manner, he added, "your banker will be there, as well as your attorney. Consider it a rather necessary business meeting."

"Dev—"

"Madam Frascat will be there."

"Lily?"

"She's the co-owner of the orphanage, isn't she?"

Nevis stared long and hard at Devlin, trying to determine whether he was serious. "Lily didn't say she was going."

"Must she tell you everything?"

"No, but—"

"Isn't she your partner?"

"Sure, but—"

"Then what she does in her spare time is of no concern to me. Nor should it be to any of the other attendees."

"You've got it backward," Nevis smacked his wandering fingers away, before they could distract her. "Operating the orphanage is what she does in her spare time. Running the whorehouse is her main obsession."

"And she does a splendid job of it. Now say you'll come tomorrow night, and I'll leave you in peace. Besides, I'd like you there for reasons other than being able to adore you in public and make all those other women jealous."

Nevis grabbed back his wandering fingers and held them close to her lips. "Such as?"

"The Cashogi trade minister will be there."

"Should he be?"

"If we're to initiate trade relations after years of keeping our distance, I think he should get a close look at the merchants who will be providing the goods. He's not just interested in ships and lumber. There are other, less important, though attractive items Montbasso can offer his country. And I'd like you to get a close look at Minister Nashat," he added, holding her gaze. "I very much want these trade negotiations to succeed. And I want your thoughts about the man."

"I'm no longer your mage adviser."

"That's your own damned fault. Besides," he added swiftly at the sudden flash of anger in her eyes, "Hugo San Rossi was Adrian Bambari's apprentice when that rogue was flirting with the Cashogi. We never really determined just how duped Hugo was. And furthermore," he freed his fingers and gently pushed back a lock of her hair, "I don't care whether you're my mage adviser. You're an intelligent woman with excellent instincts, whose opinion I greatly value. Please do this favor for me."

"Those instincts failed you when I couldn't see through Hugo's false appearance," Nevis said quietly.

"Hugo San Rossi was, and is, a good actor. The man played an exceptionally convincing role. No one could have seen through his performance, especially you, a woman whose heart had just been broken after destroying a long-time friend. Hugo played on your grief, Nevis, and I was deceived as easily as you were. And by that time, Clarissa Bracken had disappeared, leaving you to pick up the pieces, and we had no one to depend on but ourselves. I've never stopped depending on your judgment because you learned a lesson as severely as I did that day. I have no reason not to trust you." He ran his fingers down her cheek, sending a shiver along her body. "Now, will you come to the merchants' dinner as a favor to me?"

Nevis took a breath and shoved him back playfully. "What do you expect me to say after that pretty little speech?"

"Say yes, so we can get on to the rest of my business here."

"What other—"

But Devlin covered her lips with his own, wisely removing the stiletto from its sheath, placing it carefully out of reach.

Chapter Three

A heartbeat after the ivory-handled stiletto slid neatly into the sphere that housed a tiny bolt of lightning, all hell broke loose in the sorcerous theater as thunder rumbled, lightning crackled, and the very stage shook beneath the feet of Nevis' acting troupe, not to mention the solid wood flooring beneath the audience seats. Nevis watched serenely as the cast flung themselves into position to weather the tempest and then, satisfied, popped the last morsel of sticky breakfast cake into her mouth, refusing to think about whose gnarled hands had baked it expressly for the mage.

When the fierce storm finally subsided, Nevis tapped the stiletto against the railing of her private box. "Hans?" Nevis leaned over, addressing the young actor who appeared, to her eye and unexpectedly, ill at ease. "You're supposed to be Adrian Bambari, a wicked, ill-tempered rogue mage. If you tremble in fear at thunder and lightning, you're not going to be very convincing to the audience. And if the audience isn't convinced, the season is ruined."

"I told you he was a poor choice," Gabriella de la Morsage announced, patting both her disheveled tresses and heaving bosom into place.

"Gabriella, I don't think—"

"Admit it's true, Nevis."

"Hans is just a little shaken after yesterday's murder."

"We all are," Gabriella flounced across the stage. "But we're professionals and know how to conduct ourselves. Most of us, anyway." She eyed the young man with suspicion, delicate arms crossed beneath her well-endowed breasts.

"Do I detect a hidden meaning in your snide comment?"

"Nothing hidden about it, Nevis. Someone stole one of my rings, the ruby encased in a gold heart. Maybe that's what's making Hans Takat jumpy, too."

"When did this happen?" Simon demanded from the front seats where he'd been keeping an eye on the troupe antics.

"I came back to the theater last night. In all the confusion, I forgot my lace gloves. We were all distraught over what happened." Gabriella's jutting breasts indicated the royal box overhanging the stage. "That's when I remembered the ring."

"Any chance that you misplaced it?"

"You know how careful I am, Simon, particularly about things I hold dear." With a sniff, Gabriella turned her back on the stage manager, who rolled his eyes at Nevis in disgust.

"If anyone knows anything about the ring, I'd appreciate a word," Nevis studied the various expressions below her, adding, "in private. And Gabriella, whatever you might think of your fellow actors, and I don't need to know at the moment," she said swiftly, as the actress' eyes flashed fire, "I wouldn't be so quick to make accusations. Hans—"

"Hans is nervous, isn't he?" Gabriella addressed the cast and crew at large, focusing all eyes on the young man, who did, unfortunately, in both Simon and Nevis' opinions, look rather ill at ease.

Nevis interceded before Gabriella launched another accusation at the young actor. "Was it the spell I just triggered? Noisier than the others? Was my timing off?" the mage graciously tried to give Hans an excuse.

"The spell was perfect, Nevis. It was my timing." Hans pushed back a rebellious lock of brown hair, avoiding her watchful eyes. "I expected the storm a few moments later. My timing is the problem, not yours."

"I'll wager his timing is off between the sheets, too," Gabriella murmured, loud enough, certainly, for both Nevis and Simon to hear.

"That's enough, Gabriella," Nevis snapped, green eyes signaling her annoyance. "Don't tempt me to waste another spell to make you all disappear for eternity. Now," Nevis stepped back from the railing, "let's assume the storm is over, Adrian Bambari has just slipped into the tower beneath the cover of wind and rain—" Nevis waved them on to the next scene, distracted when Simon appeared at the door to her private box.

"Nevis?"

"Weren't you just in the front row?"

"That was before I saw the constable."

"She's here?"

The manager nodded. "Wants to talk to some of the stage crew."

"I thought she might." Nevis bit her lower lip. "Did she say why?"

"You won't want to hear her reason." Simon shifted his weight from one foot to the other. "Seems our carpenter and playwright both bought drugs from Adam Museo. Recently, anyway, since most of them at some point or other might have dabbled in Firespark, at least until you declared it off limits."

"How does Brea Kilganor know?"

"She didn't say. I don't know, boss, maybe she found their names at Adam's house. Or maybe she knows more about Adam Museo and his bad habits than she's letting on." Simon glanced over his shoulder to be sure the constable hadn't crept up on him. "Who knows what she knows? Look how much she's dug up about you. It's not right."

"I suppose it's her job," Nevis muttered. "Do the boys know that Brea wants to talk to them?"

"Yes."

"Do they mind?"

"Not if it will save your hide." When Nevis frowned, ill at ease as he quite expected, Simon scolded, "They're a pair of egotistical, arrogant, insane artists, but they know the difference between a good boss and a tyrant. And you, Mage Conarkin," the stage manager's usual solemn expression melted into a grin, "are definitely a tyrant. Where should the constable take them for her private chat?"

"My office, I suppose, you disrespectful idiot. Let her think I don't mind her snooping through my things while she tortures my employees."

"Done." Simon disappeared down the hall, leaving Nevis in a distracted mood. So distracted, she forgot her cue.

"Does anyone hear the earth-shaking thunder of the advancing royal cavalry? Have I gone deaf? Have I missed my cue? Or, perhaps, has our resident mage muffled their sorcerous hooves with silk?" Pepo Daken, playing the part of Devlin Graham, combed thick black hair from his forehead with a flourish, directing his impertinent questions to cast and crew. "Or are we, perhaps, being compassionate and considerate of our faint-hearted villain's queasy temperament this morning?"

Nevis lurched to the railing and glared at her leading man. "Would you like to hear the earth-shaking thunder of advancing cavalry every minute of your miserable, cursed life?"

Sapphire eyes glittering with amusement, Pepo strutted his tall, well-built body from center stage until he stood beneath the mage's private box. "I can take my vastly unappreciated acting talent to the sorcerous theater upriver in Port Cordillero. I hear their mage never misses his cues and always takes his own performance quite seriously. Or maybe, Mage Conarkin, I should hire a carriage to take me to the richer part of town, knock on Barry Faddle's door, and star in his traditional theater," the actor paused for dramatic effect, blue eyes fixed on his employer's face, "where my considerable acting talent will not be overshadowed by extravagant sorcerous tricks."

"Simon, see that Pepo gets any back wages we owe him," Nevis immediately said so matter-of-factly over her shoulder to a nonexistent stage manager that Pepo blanched. "Great, Simon, thanks. Hans, would you prefer to play the role of Devlin Graham? Seems we have an opening."

"I don't think so," Pepo squeaked, raising both hands in a theatrical gesture, nearly slamming into Gabriella's jutting breasts as she edged closer to him, fingers flying to her mouth. "That won't be necessary."

Nevis kept her face astonishingly blank. "Sure?"

"Absolutely. Go on, Nevis, trigger the damned cavalry spell."

The mage complied without blinking, slipping the ivory-handled stiletto into the next sphere set along the shelf just inside the railing, releasing the thunder of galloping horses that set the theater vibrating. They reached the intermission without major incident, and Nevis called a break, though it was her ill fortune to be interrupted. Stretching her long limbs to ease the kinks in her muscles, she found Brea Kilganor watching in silence from the doorway.

"Constable."

"Have you a minute?"

"Sure." Nevis waved Brea to a seat, watched as the older woman slung a muscled leg over the velvet-covered arm without creasing the fabric of her uniform.

"Both your carpenter and playwright made me promise to put in a good word for them."

"Why?"

"They don't want you to scold them for still dealing with Adam after you warned them not to go near Firespark."

"I'm not their nursemaid, but I'm not pleased that they were indulging in that poison. By the gods, why do they bother?" Nevis murmured in disgust, not really expecting an answer.

"I suspect your stage designs and scenery might be rather tame without your carpenter indulging in some poison." When Nevis didn't answer, Brea added, "And your playwright claims it helped him write heart-stopping dialogue."

"That's no excuse," Nevis sighed, shaking her head.

"They don't want you angry at them," Brea said quietly, "not because they were indulging, but because Adam Museo had taken you and Lily Frascat to court over the orphanage building." When the mage's expression stayed genuinely blank, the constable explained, "they'd rather you didn't think them disloyal to you."

"Idiots. Maybe I should retire."

"You're a young woman, Mage Conarkin, forty or so, by my reckoning. I can't imagine you not keeping busy. Despite their juvenile antics, you love this place and the people in it."

"Keeps reality at bay," Nevis murmured, meeting the constable's gaze. "For the audience."

"And you, I'd guess. Nothing wrong with that, unless you've got something to hide."

Annoyed that she'd let Brea Kilganor so easily regain the upper hand, Nevis sat straighter, brushing white hair from her eyes. "Did they tell you anything useful, constable, or am I not allowed to ask?"

"Did you find my note?"

"Along with a hungry, frightened kitten, yes. Satisfied?"

A sly, crooked grin was all the answer Nevis received. "By the way, what happened to the kitten? Did you abandon the pathetic little creature?"

"He's at the orphanage."

"Kind heart, Mage Conarkin. Too kind-hearted to kill?"

"I've killed before, constable, when I've needed to do so." Though Clarissa Bracken seems to think I could have handled Adrian's betrayal differently, Nevis thought, uneasy at her bitterness. But the old woman hadn't been there to see what had become of her once-beloved apprentice.

"Adrian Bambari? Or were there other victims?"

"Adrian alone, and he deserved it. By the gods, Constable—"

"Adam Museo kept raising the prices on his drugs, claimed they cost him more. But the word on the street is that he was in heavy debt."

"To whom?"

"I don't know the answer to that, not yet, anyway. There was something else about the Firespark, according to your boys. Seems that the shipments were getting stronger. You needed less of a dose to get the same effect."

"Is that a good thing?"

"Getting high is one thing, getting reckless is another, quite foolhardy. The new shipments were coming in from a different source," Brea removed her leg from the arm of the chair and smoothed her uniform. "A foreign source."

"I saw the package at Adam's house."

The constable studied Nevis' carefully neutral expression. "I thought you might. Is that a problem for you, Mage Conarkin, that the drugs came from Cashogi?"

If there was anything more behind the question, the constable didn't give any sign to Nevis. Cashogi drugs had been Adrian Bambari's downfall, and the mage loathed anyone selling them. For those using any form of the poison, she had more sympathy because of the drugs' attraction, but little tolerance. "It might be a problem for Devlin, if the shipments came from either of the two ships docked in the harbor, flying the blue stallion flag."

"I'd imagine they would use other ships, hiding somewhere off the coast, rather than navy vessels. The trade minister would be foolish to bring such blatantly illegal goods into our waters while maneuvering his way into a trade agreement. But then again, he might not even be aware of the cargo."

The mage grunted an assent, but didn't say anything further.

"I must tell you, I'm quite impressed."

"I'm afraid to ask why."

"It's been more than a full day since Adam Museo's body was discovered, and Devlin Graham hasn't come knocking at my door."

Nevis didn't blink. "I told him to keep his royal nose out of your affairs or people would never believe I was innocent."

The constable discarded the cocky remark poised on her lips, said instead, "I'm glad someone's thinking clearly."

* * * *

"Magic! Magic! Magic!"

The moment she stepped within sight across the lush, springy lawn of Alvaron Park, Nevis was immediately surrounded by a dozen children, ranging from the three-year-old redhead to those near Teddy's age.

"Children, hush. Mage Conarkin is too busy to perform silly tricks for your entertainment," May Quiddle scolded gently, uncertain of her older sister's mood and unforeseen presence.

"I am?" Nevis winked at the three-year-old with the riotous head of curls who had peered out the window the previous day when she should have been napping. With Kimmi clinging possessively to her black breeches, Nevis dropped to the grass in the midst of them all, the little girl tucked right beside her thigh, thumb positioned, as usual, in her mouth, despite May's unending efforts to dislodge it.

Teddy stood at the fringe of the eager crowd, the black kitten cradled in his elbow. His pleasant face broke into a huge grin when his mother sighed and turned away in mock despair.

Nevis crossed her long legs beneath her and opened the bottomless leather pouch at her waist, pretending to search for a spell. Not one child, down to the youngest, was fooled. The day Mage Conarkin appeared without a magic sphere in the sorcerously bottomless pouch was well near impossible.

White hair gleaming in the sunlight that filtered down through two leafy river oaks, Nevis plucked a perfectly round sphere from the pouch, its center filled with a miniature three-masted ship. The mage held the sphere aloft to the open delight of the children and carefully drew out her stiletto, pricking the sphere and triggering the spell. Nevis met May's smiling eyes over their heads as the children watched in astonishment as a brilliant scene unfolded in the air above them.

Gasps of awe were intermingled with laughter as the graceful ship sailed from isle to isle, discovering treasure, flying fish, and mermaids until finally, after a wild escape from pursuing pirates, the ship faded gracefully beneath a rainbow arch.

Having already sheathed the stiletto in anticipation, Nevis braced herself for the onslaught of hugs and kisses until May finally shooed them all away to let Nevis catch a breath.

"A lot of effort for these spoiled hooligans," May gently admonished her sister, whose attention was focused on getting the three-year-old back on her feet, though not before Kimmi threw skinny arms around the mage's neck and hugged her hard.

"Worth it, don't you think?"

"You spoil them, and I'm left to discipline them."

"Wouldn't be fair if you had an easy job, now, would it?"

May grumbled something inaudible, earning a rap on the knuckles.

"Mind the children. You know how they pick up the slightest curse."

"You mind yourself," May chided the older woman, suddenly frowning. "Nevis, are you really as untroubled as you appear to be?"

"Sure."

"Sure," May repeated, crossing her arms in disbelief, smaller shadow flung across the seated mage. "I had to get the whole ugly story from Lily."

"So did Devlin." Nevis let a grin escape.

"You're impossible. Just because you're older than me, doesn't mean I don't worry about you." May stared hard at the mage until Nevis flushed and turned away. "When will you ever learn?"

"You've enough worries, with a houseful of children and Ted not due back for some weeks."

"Makes the homecoming all the sweeter," May laughed, pinching her sister's arm. "You know how those ship captains get when they've been journeying so long away from willing ladies."

"Keeps Lily in business."

"Thank the gods for her business and yours or these spoiled hooligans would be wandering the streets."

Getting to her feet, Nevis waved away May's earnest words, stopping when May coughed delicately behind one hand. "What?"

"I got the story from Devlin, too."

"He's going to drive everyone mad."

"No, he won't. Dev's just worried. He needs to know what's going on, since he can't get much from you. I told him," May swiftly added, as indignation flared in her sister's green eyes, "not to interfere."

"Well, that's good. He usually takes your advice pretty seriously. Maybe he'll listen just this one time." Nevis brushed twigs from her breeches. "I know he wants to help, but he'll only make things worse for me."

"That's why he feels so helpless."

"Devlin Graham?"

"Yes, Devlin Graham, mighty and powerful monarch of Montbasso, is feeling helpless. Not hard to understand, when the woman he adores is tangled in something he can't untangle."

"I thought only older sisters like me had wisdom."

"Nevis—"

"Only teasing," Nevis apologized, hugging the shorter woman briefly. "I do appreciate all you're doing."

"I'm not doing anything."

"Sure you are. I'd best get back to the theater and see whether the lunatics have taken Simon hostage."

"You're very well suited to that madhouse," May laughed, brushing brown curls behind one ear. "And I'm very well suited to shepherding these hooligans back inside. Go on. Just promise to be careful."

"I promise." Nevis watched her sister gather the younger children with the help of the older ones and turned back toward the theater.

Slightly downstream, Brigadier Bridge spanned the Basol River, connecting the major districts of Port Jambi with the fertile farmlands and racing stables across the river. Beyond that, no more than a mile, the river opened into the broad harbor of Port Jambi. The deep channels at the mouth of the river and easy access to open water made Port Jambi perfectly suited to shipbuilding, with the Basol River leading straight upstream to Rohan Forest, where sturdy oak for planks and pine for tall, slender masts grew plentiful along the shores of Lakes Giornot and Dellaran, and even further north to the Boudin Forest across the Bardene Mountains.

The trees were cut in winter, then floated downstream in the spring thaw, a wild ride that brought a cheering audience all down the length of the river until the logs safely slid beneath Brigadier Bridge and into the eager hands of the Ruskin shipbuilders. And once there, the whole town celebrated, including Nevis. Lily's girls and Nevis' troupe had helped May set out a picnic for the children as they watched the frantic activity on the river some weeks ago.

A lifetime ago, Nevis thought with a sinking heart.

Halfway through the park, Nevis heard noise and turned to find Teddy dogging her heels, slipping behind a tree, keeping his lanky body out of his mother's hawkish sight.

"I'm afraid to ask what trouble you're in, Teddy boy."

"Not me." The boy grinned, fingers gently stroking the kitten, whose paw reached out toward the mage, then abruptly shifted into a more somber manner. "Aunt Nevis? I need to tell you something."

Instinct awake, Nevis nodded, toying with the kitten's black paw.

"One of the boys saw something yesterday morning, something I think you should know about."

"Is he afraid to tell me himself?"

Teddy's firm headshake set loose brown curls bobbing, reminding Nevis of Lily's ever-present feathers. "No, but he'd rather you didn't know. Ma might scold him for sneaking out of the building."

"And I won't?"

"I heard you and Ma talking one night about how you'd sneak out of the house to find Lily when Grandma and Grandpa were still alive and you were a little girl." Teddy shoved his free hand into the pocket of his dusty, patched breeches.

"You eavesdropping—"

The kitten chose that precise moment to launch itself at Nevis, landing against her chest, and scrabbling for a firm hold.

"You did that on purpose," Nevis scolded the boy, settling the kitten into a more secure position.

"Did not."

"What did the boy see?"

"It was near dawn, and—"

"Near dawn? For the gods' sake, Teddy, what was the boy doing out of bed at that uncivilized time of day?"

"You promised not to yell."

"I'm not yelling, not yet. I promise you'll know when I am." Nevis started to cross her arm, remembered the kitten in residence. "Teddy, what was he doing out at that time? It was dangerous."

"Fishing."

Nevis narrowed her eyes. "You can do better than that."

"It's true, Aunt Nevis. Everyone knows there's good fishing for trout down by the theater right before dawn. Something to do with the currents, I think," Teddy added, trying to sound convincing. "It's true, I swear."

Nevis studied the boy's anxious face and nodded. "Did he catch something besides trout?"

Breathing in relief that his aunt hadn't changed him into a squealing piglet, even for a heartbeat just to scare him, Teddy explained, "He saw two people leaving the theater by the side door."

Nevis carefully considered his words. The theater had four entrances, the main entrance that faced McOsley's Road, a side entrance that led to the alley adjacent to Lily's whorehouse, the rear entrance along the riverbank that led to Nevis' private rooms, and the fourth entrance. "The door near the park?"

Teddy nodded.

"Two men?"

The boy flushed, eyes darting everywhere but at his aunt's face.

"Teddy boy, it's important."

"I know." Teddy looked up, saw beyond her stern expression to the genuine worry. "There was a man and a woman, talking. But he couldn't understand what they were saying. They weren't close enough. Aunt Nevis, there's something else you need to know."

Nevis handed the kitten back to Teddy, surmising he needed the comfort more than she did. "Go on."

Grateful for the distraction, the boy took the kitten, stroking its soft black fur, staring at its bright white tail. "The woman, Aunt Nevis, she had short white hair just like yours."

* * * *

Lost in thought, Nevis wandered through the silent theater building, lit by ever-burning magefire in sconces spaced evenly along the walls, surprised to find Simon bent over her desk, thinning hair visible on the top of his head as he busily scratched out a note.

"Why is it, boss, that anytime I start leaving you a note, you walk in and I end up throwing away the paper, thereby wasting desperately needed supplies that we can't afford?"

"Sorcery, plain and simple," Nevis grinned, sinking into the worn leather chair behind her desk, idly scanning the paperwork scattered in neat piles. One finger ran along the smooth wood of the carving of Janni, tracing the goddess' all-embracing arms. "Why are you still here, anyway?"

"A stage manager's work is never done."

"A good stage manager's work is never done because he's too busy solving everyone's problems. What's in the note you just tossed away?"

"Another minor problem, of which you should be aware."

"You did say minor, didn't you?"

"Sure, boss, but I don't like it on top of Gabriella's accusation this morning about the missing ring."

That caught Nevis' complete attention. "Something else missing?"

"Coins from the petty cash box."

The mage frowned. "Everyone knows we just keep a little bit in there for emergencies."

"Yes, but sometimes there's more than just a little bit, when we replenish the contents."

"And this time there was more than just a little bit."

"Sorry, boss."

"Not your fault."

"Sure it is. I keep it locked away, but I guess maybe I was careless and left it out without thinking. I had to give Teddy some coins to pay for the face paint I promised Gabriella." Simon shrugged unhappily. "After he left, maybe someone saw the box open and decided to take advantage of my absentmindedness."

"Maybe someone just picked the lock."

"Maybe." The manager hung his head, still blaming himself. "Since we opened the theater ten years ago, nothing has ever gone missing."

"We've never found a dead body either. Let's keep our eyes and ears alert. Oh, and Simon, why don't you make a trip to Finlay's and withdraw some funds to replenish the coins, and then," Nevis paused, to be sure she had Simon's full attention, "make a point of telling me at the next rehearsal?"

The stage manager rubbed his chin and thought for a moment before nodding. "Sure. Good idea."

"And then go home, will you?"

"I've got work to do."

"And I need you alert."

When Simon left Nevis alone, the mage pushed back her chair and unsheathed her ivory-handled stiletto. For triggering most spherical spells, which would work only that one time, Nevis needed to thrust the stiletto into the transparent shell. For the viewing spheres on her cabinet, which worked indefinitely, a simple tap would first trigger the spell, followed by other taps to guide its eye. Nevis tapped the stiletto point against the left sphere on the cabinet door, rotating the sphere until she determined that the costume designer was still hard at work.

"I don't pay Verdi enough either," Nevis murmured, resheathing the stiletto as the image faded. She headed down the stairway in the direction of Verdi Casporet's closet-sized costume room, crammed with fabrics, finished costumes, and wigs, surprised to find Hans Takat standing in the doorway. He hadn't been there a moment ago. "I thought sure you'd escape once rehearsal had ended."

"I wish he had," Verdi shouted through the half-open door. "He's driving me mad about the damned shirt."

"I feel responsible," Hans admitted, scarlet spots appearing on his cheeks. "It was my costume. I should have kept an eye on it."

"Why? Verdi keeps everyone else's costumes together. Don't see why you should take it on yourself," Nevis said quietly, watching the young actor's uneasy expression. "Someone's been busy making free with my theater, and I'm not very happy about it, Hans. But that doesn't mean it was your fault. Unless of course you handed it over to the murderer for some mysterious reason—"

"Don't even say that in jest!" Hans' flush grew deeper, and Nevis worried that he had a fever. Or, perhaps, that Gabriella de la Morsage was correct in implying that the young man was edgy.

"If he did hand it over," Verdi threatened, waving a fist, "I'd personally take your stiletto, Nevis, and flay the skin from his bony little body." A spool of green thread flew through the narrow opening, just missing Hans' handsome nose.

"And I'd hold him down while you did." Nevis bent down to retrieve the spool of thread, one eye on the actor. "Go on, Hans, get some fresh air."

When Hans eagerly agreed, she watched him leave, then peered cautiously inside the open doorway. The crowded room was dizzy with color and fabric, crammed with costumes and wigs for past and present performances. And one exceptionally bright object stood out like a beacon.

"Verdi, why are you still wearing that wig?"

The young designer scowled, but kept on with her delicate embroidery of Hans' new velvet shirt. "Because someone was fooling with it."

Nevis leaned against the doorframe, a dark silhouette broken only by the startling shock of white hair, a perfect match to the wig on Verdi's head. "How can you tell? By looking at it?"

"I leave the wigs on the dummy heads." Verdi nodded in the direction of the shelf on the opposite wall where a half dozen other wigs of various colors, textures, and lengths sat waiting. "Someone touched this wig. It wasn't set properly on the dummy head, and ended up being stretched in the wrong spots."

"All right," Nevis agreed softly, green eyes puzzled. "But why are you wearing it instead of the dummy? You know how to set it properly."

"My head size is pretty close to Gabriella's, except on those days when it's as fat as a pregnant cow," Verdi grinned. "I can't use the dummy head, Nevis. Whoever toyed with the wig, dropped the dummy head and dented it, destroying its shape."

"I'm sorry for all this extra work right before opening night. Can I do anything to help?"

Verdi immediately glanced up at the mage's genuinely apologetic tone. "Don't mind me, Nevis. I'm always griping. You're the one in trouble. Wish there was something we could do to help you."

"Thanks."

Verdi shrugged off her gratitude. "If the members of Nevis Conarkin's Sorcerous Theater don't look out for each other, they don't belong here. They belong with Slick Hands Barry and his oh-so-boring theater troupe." Verdi flashed her employer another grin, before returning to a more serious mood. "That's why I was so cranky with Hans just now."

"I don't understand."

"The constable was here today. You know all about that, right? That she spoke to some of the boys?"

"Yes."

"Yes, well she should have spoken to Hans, too." Verdi held the mage's gaze for a heartbeat. "But he never said a word, even though he's had recent dealings with the corpse, too, buying Firespark. You gave that boy a really good chance to make something of himself, Nevis, playing a major role. The least he could have done was be honest with the constable. I'm disappointed in him."

"He was jumpy in rehearsal today."

"No excuse for being a coward. Damn it, Nevis, if any one of us was in trouble, you'd be shoving people out of the way to get to the front of the line to save our pathetic hides. We've all seen you in action." Verdi ignored the mage's embarrassment. "Hans was afraid to get involved, when it meant that maybe he could say something to get you off the hook. And maybe he couldn't have told the constable anything of value, but it's the principle. I'm damned upset with him and told him so."

"I suppose he had his reasons," Nevis said softly. When the costume designer only grumbled, Nevis forced a smile to her lips. "Maybe he doesn't deserve such a lavish costume, Verdi. Don't stay too late."

"Don't you go telling me what hours to keep, Mage Conarkin. You'd never be able to pay me for all that work, anyway."

Nevis flinched. "Verdi—"

"Someday, Nevis, your theater will make an astounding profit, so astounding it might kill us all from shock. But until that time," the younger woman grinned, "I'll continue to work at poverty level."

"You could make more up north in Port Cordillero's theater," Nevis said casually, pushing away from the doorframe, "or at Barry Faddle's."

"Twice as much in Port Cordillero and almost twice as much at Barry's, but I'd be fighting off Slick Hands' roving hands day and night. Besides, I wouldn't be working for Nevis Conarkin, then, would I?" Verdi's grin turned into a scowl as she yelped. "Damned needles—"

"Needles. By the gods, I forgot why I came looking for you in the first place. Verdi, maybe you can help me." Nevis tucked her hands in the deep pockets of her black breeches. "The corpse had a slit in his chest precisely as wide as a thrust from my stiletto." She unsheathed the ivory-handled weapon at her waist and held it out for Verdi's inspection. "Do you have any needles that could mimic this weapon? Something you use for leather, maybe?"

Verdi scratched the tip of her nose, thinking, before raising the lid of a wooden box on a nearby shelf. She pulled out the largest needle. "It's not as flat, see, there, at the end, where it's rounded."

"Nor big enough."

"Wouldn't seem to be. I didn't see the body, but if you're saying the wound suggested a stiletto—" Verdi shrugged, lost in thought until something occurred to her. "Gabriella uses a false stiletto in the last scene, doesn't she, when she destroys Adrian Bambari?"

"It's made of wood."

"Sure, but it's the same size. Maybe someone borrowed it." The designer set aside the velvet shirt and grabbed Nevis' sleeve. "Come on. You won't be satisfied, and neither will I, until we've taken a look." She led the mage to the adjacent room where all the props were stored and pulled open a squeaky drawer.

Nevis removed the sheathed stiletto, the false ivory handle a close match to the one Nevis had replaced at her waist. She slid it free, examined the smooth wood of the false weapon, unstained with blood or any other substance. Without expression, she set it down and shut the drawer. "Thanks."

"Shouldn't you be getting dressed for dinner?"

Nevis blinked.

"You forgot the merchants' dinner."

"That cursed dinner," Nevis grumbled, looking sheepish. "By the gods, Verdi, I did forget."

"I'll wager Devlin would have sent someone around to remind you." The costume designer smiled, waving her employer upstairs.

But before she went to change her clothes, Nevis made one more stop for no other reason than to keep her sanity. She shut the door to her office to avoid interruptions and unlocked the cabinet that held all the spells waiting for release. Taking a swift inventory, she counted spells for wind, rain, thunder and lightning, cannon fire, and a host of other extravagant effects, with a few extra spheres for the children. These she examined carefully, and thought about a different scene.

With a half-smile, she remembered the first sphere she'd ever created under Clarissa Bracken's sharp eyes. It involved sugar-coated cakes, a vice Nevis had never been able to shed. Sighing, she shoved aside that particular memory and sat at her desk, eager to create another sphere and gain a measure of calm.

Across the blank writing paper in the center of her desk, she sketched a seal pup, then another, bouncing a laughing child between them. Chanting softly over the figures, she traced their lines, until they lifted from the paper, hovering over her desk. With a whispered command from the mage, the three figures coalesced into a single black miniature figure in the shape of one seal. Cupping her hands around the seal, she murmured softly, creating a transparent sphere that encased the figure.

Calm and content, Nevis smiled, locked the spell inside the cabinet for the right opportunity, nodded a farewell to Janni and her brood of children, then headed upstairs to dress for Devlin's dinner.

Chapter Four

"Aren't you a bit overdressed for a visit to the local constable?"

Short legs stretched across her desk without disturbing the crisp lines of her uniform, Brea Kilganor tilted back her worn chair. She appraised Nevis' black silk gown, ebony broken only by the ivory handle of her stiletto, attached to a thin ivory-colored leather belt, and a shimmer of diamonds, interspersed with onyx, roped delicately around the mage's neck. And, of course, Nevis' brilliant white hair.

"Merchants' dinner."

"Oh, yes. Devlin forcing you to go?"

"No," Nevis replied, taking the cracked leather chair opposite the desk. "I'm going to prove I've got nothing to hide."

"Shocking liar," Brea said, adding dryly, "about not being forced to attend, that is. And, of course, if you're innocent—"

One white eyebrow shot towards the ceiling. "If?"

"If you're truly innocent, Mage Conarkin," the constable continued smoothly, dark brown eyes fixed on the other woman's face, "then surely you have as much right to be at the dinner as any other legitimate merchant in Port Jambi."

"If I'm not," Nevis pressed, letting her fingers run along the silky fabric in her lap, finding comfort in the smooth, cool material.

"Then you've got sorcerous balls, I'd say." Brea let her muscled legs drop to the floor with a thud. "Now tell me why you're here. Come to plead guilty?"

Nevis sat back, away from the constable and felt the cracked leather bite into her shoulder. "One of May's children saw two people leave the theater just before dawn, the night that Adam Museo was killed."

"Before dawn? Must have been fishing for trout."

Nevis nodded, not surprised anymore at the constable's knowledge. "May doesn't know the boy crept out of bed."

"I'll wager she doesn't. Could the child identify anyone?"

"No. But he did see a man and a woman. The woman—" Nevis paused for breath, determined not to let the constable rattle her. "She had white hair like mine."

Brea stared at the mage for a long, tense heartbeat.

"I don't have an alibi, Constable, and for all the boy knows, it was me. But it wasn't," Nevis said simply.

"Sometimes guilty people enjoy playing games like this, Mage Conarkin. Giving up evidence to show how cooperative they can be."

"By the gods, Constable, I didn't kill Adam Museo. And there's something else. Verdi Casporet told me that someone messed around with the white wig she created for Gabriella to wear in the last scene."

"Convenient. Making your costume designer think someone used it to impersonate you."

"Believe what you want, Constable. I'm just telling you what I know." Nevis stood up, paused behind the chair.

"You don't lie very well for a mage. You should take lessons from Hugo San Rossi." Brea Kilganor got to her feet, crooked smile predatory. "You'll be late for your dinner, Mage Conarkin. I wouldn't want Devlin Graham to come blaming me when his lady," she said the word mockingly, "arrives unfashionably late."

* * * *

"How utterly appropriate. First the madam makes a grand entrance down the marble stairs into the ballroom, then the whore."

Nevis spun slowly to face the black eyes that shone with malicious contempt beneath a head of thick black hair, set in a handsome face that didn't suit the owner's heart. "Hugo, it's a very good thing you're not seeking employment as a playwright for my troupe. Your lines are getting stale."

"Good, Nevis. Very good." Hugo San Rossi, mage adviser to the Montbasso monarch, forced a smile to his lips that never reached his eyes.

"You make it so easy."

Hugo sighed, as though he were exquisitely bored. "You may not need another playwright, but the Nevis Conarkin Sorcerous Theater may soon need another owner. I hear Barry Faddle is always looking to buy your theater, Nevis. Maybe you should take him seriously. Unless, of course, Devlin steps in to save you, proclaiming to the people of Port Jambi that his lover is innocent of murder charges."

"I'm quite capable of doing that myself. Speaking of innocence, and lost innocence, you must be proud of how jaded Alana has become since she started sharing your bed."

"Oh, but I am." The mage smoothed the front of his forest green silk jacket as he caught Alana's watchful eye across the crowded chamber. "But you're wrong about her. Alana's not jaded. She's quite realistic, something you'd never be able to understand, not with your false morality."

"You've drained the idealism from her soul."

"A whore preaching of souls?"

"At least I have one."

"Hugo—" The blonde, blue-eyed heiress to the throne of Montbasso signaled her lover to her side.

"Pardon me, Nevis. Duty requires my presence."

"Do you consider making love to the royal heir as part of your duties as mage adviser?" Nevis had trouble restraining her smug expression as Hugo muttered something inaudible but definitely unpleasant.

"You started this private chat. Don't blame me. Best go see what your employer desires." She turned her back on the mage adviser and headed straight for a safe harbor.

"I wondered whether I'd be defending you against a charge of cold-blooded murder just now." Remo Savanak, a suave middle-aged gentleman, whose fine light-wool jacket matched his gray eyes to perfection, smiled at the approaching mage. Fashionably cut blond hair framed a pleasant, smooth-shaven face. Beside him, Lily was resplendent in a subdued pale blue and lilac floral print gown from beneath which lilac slippers peered out.

"Awfully tempting."

"Too many witnesses," Lily remarked, tucking a lilac feather in place at the back of her neck.

"There is that," Remo agreed, offering Nevis a glass of champagne from a passing servant. "Nevis, my love, you're keeping me awfully busy. I hope you've come here to reassure me of your innocence in the ghastly deed."

Nevis sipped from her glass, catching Devlin's eye at the far end of the ballroom where he was speaking with the royal treasurer and a gentleman she didn't recognize. "I am innocent, but one of May's boys saw a man and a white-haired woman leaving the theater near dawn. And May doesn't know," she warned Lily, "so don't snitch on the boy. Not that you would do it on purpose," she added swiftly when Lily looked faintly hurt.

"I take it that wasn't you."

"Right again, counselor."

"Want some ideas?" Lily refused to be intimidated by Nevis' glare. "What did that arrogant bastard say to you, anyway?"

Surprising her friend, Nevis laughed. "Only that first the madam made a grand entrance, then the whore." Too late, Nevis caught the warning in Lily's eyes and wished she hadn't repeated Hugo's welcoming remark.

"Whore?" Devlin whispered in Nevis' ear, his neat-trimmed beard tickling her exposed neck. "Did someone use that word in your presence?"

"Dev—"

"If that someone was Hugo San Rossi, I'll hang him by his sorcerous balls from the flagpole outside my window."

Nevis spun slowly to face the king, eye to eye with his barely controlled anger. "Your daughter wouldn't appreciate a lover with damaged balls, sorcerous or not. Let it go. Besides," she gave him a crooked grin, knowing it would make him laugh, "I gave him a decent parting shot."

"Did you?" Devlin's face lit like a child who'd just opened a marvelous gift. "Good for you!"

The mage laughed and squeezed his arm, playfully pushing him away. "Surely you don't doubt me, majesty. Now be a good boy and mingle with your guests, or there'll be even more talk. Not that you don't enjoy it. You sometimes take a pitiful delight in gossip, my lord."

Devlin's eyes searched her face hungrily, ignoring her jest, ignoring Remo and Lily, too. "Later?" he said quietly.

"Yes, of course."

"Promise?"

Nevis placed one hand on his chest, held her fingers there for a moment over his heart, felt his tempting warmth. "Yes."

Satisfied, Devlin took his leave, prompting a sigh of fond exasperation from the mage.

"He's right to be worried."

"You're supposed to reassure me, counselor."

"Give me something solid with which to reassure you. Nevis, seriously, what Lily said earlier—"

"Hugo wouldn't be that stupid to show up at my theater himself."

"I agree, but what if he's the mastermind behind the evil plot?"

"Sounds like one of my plays."

"I'm serious." Remo took Nevis' thin elbow and guided the mage closer to Lily so he could speak with both women in privacy. "You and Lily had separate copies of the document from Adam Museo's father, granting you ownership of the building, free of any charge."

"We should have given you a copy," Nevis admitted, even though Remo had never once scolded them.

"Easy to say now, Mage Conarkin," the attorney said graciously. "After all, who expected harassment from Adam the very moment his father died? The old man wasn't even buried before Adam sent a lawsuit your way." Remo glanced from one woman to the other. "Why?"

"He's a greedy bastard. Was."

"No, Nevis. Why did he start harassing you then? Wouldn't it stand to reason that he knew the documents were missing?"

Nevis set her empty glass on a side table. "Sure."

"And that leads to my theory about Hugo." The attorney set his glass beside the mage's, gave her his full attention. "Isn't it possible that Hugo whispered in Adam's ear that he could make the documents vanish, either through theft or sorcery, so Adam would be free to harass you in the courts?"

"I suppose," Nevis admitted reluctantly, not meeting Lily's eyes, already knowing what her expression would be.

"She supposes," the madam grumbled. "Nevis, he's wanted to embarrass and discredit you ever since he assumed your position as Devlin's mage adviser. He stopped playing innocent apprentice mage to Adrian Bambari within an hour of Devlin's public announcement. Unfortunately, he fooled us all."

Nevis turned away, stared across the ballroom to where Alana had just slipped her arm through Hugo's, brushing her fingers over his forest green jacket. Her young face had lost all innocence in the last two years, ever since the older mage had openly pursued and captured her attention. Nevis still had hopes that Hugo had no unbreakable claims on the girl's heart.

"My problem with all of this unpleasantness," Remo leaned closer, interrupting Nevis' distracted thoughts, "is that it's highly unlikely we'll ever be able to prove a connection."

"Maybe there is none." Stubborn, Nevis met Lily's equally determined expression.

"Maybe not," Remo interceded in a reasonable tone, running his fingers lightly over his jacket front, gray eyes amiable, "but I intend to explore every possibility, including information from our friendly banker, Finlay Oscram." Remo smiled a welcome as an elderly gentleman, bald head gleaming in the bright lamplight, approached their group.

"Private party?"

"Of course not, Finlay." Lily kissed the banker's flushed cheek. "You're always welcome."

"Being nice to the man who holds the mortgage on your business, Mistress Frascat?"

"And my theater. I'd better follow her manners," Nevis laughed, kissing the banker's other cheek. "Speaking of loans, how about negotiating a lower rate in case I have an empty theater on opening night?"

"That's not a worry, trust me. Your theater will be jammed with the curious and the degenerate, wanting to see with their own eyes how Mage Conarkin is handling the pressure of the murder investigation."

Oscram winked at Lily. "You're not as convincing as the villain, my dear."

"Should I be insulted?" Nevis asked, not quite sure whether to be annoyed or amused at the fickle public.

"Not at all. The gossipmongers of Port Jambi always have something to say about the woman who's ensnared Devlin Graham's heart and soul. They forget that you saved their hides from treachery and invasion."

"Finlay—"

"It's true, Nevis, and it's a disgrace. I know you've been vehemently opposed to running this particular play, because you're ridiculously modest, but I agree with Devlin. I don't always agree with some of his damn fool policies, but I do agree completely with this decision."

"By the gods, Finlay—"

"If your banker is upsetting you, my dear, I'd be happy to buy your theater at an outrageous price and put those worries from your mind." Lecherous eyes danced in a face that was exquisitely sculptured beneath a mop of tight black curls. Perfect dimples balanced each other across a ridiculous drooping moustache that would have looked foolish on any other face.

"Master Faddle." Nevis stepped out of reach as Slick Hands Barry sought to envelope the mage in a hug. "A pleasure."

"For me, always. For you, well, Nevis, I know you're just being polite." The theater owner smiled at the others, preened in his scarlet velvet jacket, and turned back to his original topic. "I'm serious, Nevis. If you ever want to leave the nasty, boring, and dreadful business of running an unprofitable theater, what with all those appalling egos to please—"

"Weren't you an actor when you were younger?" Lily enquired sweetly, eyes tracking Slick Hands' fingers as they ached to touch feminine flesh.

"So kind of you to remember."

"Hard to forget," Lily said dryly, swiftly adding, "You were so popular with the ladies," when Remo pinched the small of her back in warning.

"Were?" Barry's gray eyes were mournful. "Surely, I still am. If I can only snatch Nevis from Devlin—"

"You'd stand a better chance of buying her theater," Finlay cut in, unimpressed with Barry, watching his fingers skillfully attempt to maneuver Nevis closer. "Which, incidentally, isn't for sale."

"My loss."

"What would you want with another theater?" Nevis asked, suddenly suspicious of everyone and everything that crossed her path, even as she slipped away from Barry's wandering fingers. "You run a highly respected traditional theater. With music and drama and exceptional acting—"

"You're not supposed to compliment the enemy," Lily chided, ignoring Remo's second pinch.

"Enemy? Lily Frascat, how can you say such a thing? Nevis and I are artistic competitors, though I must confess, her special effects are astounding. If I were to buy her theater, and my interest is solely in expansion, you understand, then of course, I'd hire her as my house mage." Barry Faddle declared this last item in such a matter-of-fact manner that no one dared fault him for his audacity.

"Perhaps," Nevis said carefully, not risking a glance at Lily, for fear of breaking into unrestrained laughter, "you might suggest your idea to Devlin and see what he thinks."

"Splendid idea. Nevis, you're special, truly." With a flourish and a last effort to embrace the mage, Barry wished them a fond good evening and went in search of Devlin Graham and his never-ending quest, the scarlet jacket vanishing in the crowd.

"Tell me, please, he isn't serious," Remo laughed. "If he suggests that very thing to Devlin—"

"It will surely make Devlin laugh," Nevis smiled at the image that encounter would present. "Dev knows how I feel about Slick Hands Barry. Still and all, though he appears a buffoon, the man does run a tidy and profitable theater." The mage stared off into space, thoughtful. "He can pay his cast and crew decent wages."

"Barry caters to a different audience and charges outrageously more for his tickets. He's never in debt, Nevis, because his family is wealthy," Finlay said quietly, exchanging a disturbed glance with Lily when the mage frowned. "Did you know that Adam Museo was in serious debt?"

"To you?" Remo asked, snatching another glass of champagne, this time for the banker.

"No, thank the gods. I only transact business with respectable people like Nevis and Lily."

"A madam and a whore," Nevis muttered, earning a stern look of disapproval from both gentlemen. "But you did handle old man Museo's business dealings, didn't you?"

"Yes, though when he died, and Adam continued to act like a spendthrift, I cut my losses and ran as far from the idiot as possible. Adam came to me several times, asking for loans, sometimes begging, but I refused. I couldn't risk another unpaid loan. The boy was getting desperate, in my opinion."

"To whom did he owe money?"

"Gambling houses. Drug merchants, too, Nevis. I heard Adam borrowed a large sum—" Finlay glanced unobtrusively in Hugo San Rossi's direction, where he and Alana were speaking to a small, dark-haired woman Nevis didn't recognize.

"Why?"

"He needed money."

"Why Hugo? Isn't that odd that he would go to Hugo for a loan?" Nevis kept her expression remarkably bland. "I wouldn't think the two men spent time together or even knew each other."

"Serious gamblers cross each other's paths frequently in a town like Port Jambi." Finlay studied the mage's expression. "Does that surprise you?"

"I didn't realize Hugo was a serious gambler."

"Quite serious. Horses. No street dice for a man like Hugo San Rossi. He prefers the racetrack across the river, with its princely horses and prancing fillies."

"And delicate princesses," Nevis murmured, brushing hair from her eyes. "Did Hugo ever borrow from you? Or is that an illegal question to which you'd be unable to answer in front of an honorable attorney?"

"Counselor, cover your ears," Finlay suggested when Remo started to answer. "I told you earlier, Nevis, I only do business with respectable customers. Adam Museo and Hugo San Rossi don't meet my criteria, though Hugo did in earlier days before he showed his true colors with respect to you."

"Then you'd better watch your back," Lily warned, ignoring Nevis' look of irritation.

"Oh, but I do. By the way, Nevis, though I don't transact any loans with Hugo San Rossi, he still keeps funds in my bank from those earlier, more carefree days. Not a large account, but a respectable sum."

Finlay ran his free hand over his bald head. "Frankly, I'm surprised he hasn't taken his funds elsewhere."

"Were Hugo and Adam friendly?" Remo put his arm about Lily's waist, though whether to keep her from growing more emphatic in her opinion about the mage or from simple affection, Nevis couldn't decide.

"My last recollection of the two was at the races. I'm not certain you'd call their interaction friendly. They were arguing about a woman."

That caught Nevis' attention from its slow meandering in Devlin's direction, where he was skillfully and charmingly playing host, and deftly avoiding Barry Faddle's scarlet jacket. "There was a portrait of a woman in Adam's house."

"How do you know that?" Remo demanded, smooth-shaven cheeks turning pink. "No, don't tell me. I probably don't want to know."

"I won't. And you don't."

"It's not what you're thinking, Nevis," the banker replied to her expression. "Hugo told Adam he should just go after the woman, that she deserved it, had it coming to her."

"It? Dare I ask?"

"Adam had a heavy hand when it came to women," Lily said unexpectedly. "I barred him from my brothel after the recent incident." She looked at Nevis and shrugged apologetically. "Sorry. You were busy with final rehearsals, and we never had a chance to really discuss what happened in detail."

"Hugo San Rossi's no better," Finlay said in disgust. "Not that he has a heavy hand, at least not to my knowledge, but he's no gentleman. I often wonder that Alana is so taken with him. He's at least ten years older than the girl."

"He has a certain reptilian charm," Lily murmured, earning a scowl from both men. "Well, he does."

"I wonder, too, that Devlin doesn't step in," Finlay said cautiously as Nevis' expression went carefully bland. "It's not a criticism—"

"Sure, it is, old friend, but that's not what troubles me." Annoyed that she was wearing a gown, Nevis ached to slip her hands into the pockets of the breeches she'd left back in her bedchamber. "Alana has a right to take a lover. Dev can't forbid his daughter to see Hugo simply because the man doesn't like me. After all, Hugo is the royal mage advisor."

"I know you're right," Finlay conceded, "but I'd just like to take that girl over my knee and— Stop looking so scandalized, Lily. Don't tell me you haven't thought of it yourself. Oh, and Nevis, one other curious point about your friend Hugo," the banker continued, his bald head flushing scarlet beneath Lily's scrutiny. "I did see the mage at the racetrack, over across the Basol River, deep in private conversation with the Cashogi trade minister's bodyguard."

Oscram nodded in the direction of the tiny, delicate woman with thick black curly hair, dressed, like Nevis, completely in ebony, the same woman with whom Alana and Hugo had been speaking.

"That's the trade minister?"

"That's the bodyguard."

Nevis nearly choked. "Then who— Ah, that's the trade minister," she said, staring at the man with the closely cropped dark hair who'd been speaking with Devlin earlier in the evening.

"Don't let her appearance fool you."

"How deep and private was their conversation?"

"Very. As a matter of fact—" Finlay's expression swiftly transformed into a warm welcome. "Minister Nashat! Have you met my friends?"

The banker waved the approaching foreigner into their midst, Devlin Graham and the minister's bodyguard trailing along in his wake. Mikaline Nashat, the visiting trade minister of Cashogi, was a pleasant-looking man in his prime. Unlike the other men present, he wore his dark hair cut very close to his scalp, quite fitting to his unremarkable features.

Bowing to Nevis and her gathered companions, the minister held out his hand in the direction of his bodyguard, "Shayna Kashi, my companion. Mage Conarkin," he caught Nevis' eye and smiled pleasantly, "I've been anxious to meet you, having heard so very much about you."

"All pleasant, I hope. I do need your exquisite fabrics for my theater or my costume designer will never forgive me."

"It will be my pleasure to personally deliver a multitude of samples to your door, Mage Conarkin, once your monarch and Master Oscram and the rest of the trade council succeed in negotiating favorable rates. Perhaps you can persuade them."

"I'll try my best," Nevis smiled, finding the minister far more charming than expected, though she wondered about his trustworthiness. "I think both our countries would benefit."

"As do I."

"Trading between our northern and southern ports, from Port Neeri to Port Cordillero and down to Port Magista allows us a marvelous selection of goods from within Montbasso, while sharing our natural wealth," Nevis said quietly. "But trade with a foreign kingdom, such as the isle of Cashogi, would enrich us further. You would benefit from our lumber. We would benefit from your artisans." She shrugged, stole a glance at Devlin, who listened intently. "If handled intelligently, the balance of trade between Montbasso and Cashogi should profit all of us."

"I find your willingness to trade with Cashogi quite surprising," Shayna Kashi broke her silence, expression unreadable, though her fingers strayed to the stiletto at her waist, reminding Nevis of her lethal position.

"Why, may I ask?"

"You defeated Adrian Bambari, the renegade mage who allied with the Cashogi dissidents to invade your country. They, too, lusted after Montbasso's rich forests and other plentiful resources that would have made Cashogi a more powerful, seafaring nation."

"The Cashogi dissidents, as I recall from ten years back," Nevis said carefully, treading on delicate ground in front of Devlin and the minister, both of whom were watching her closely, waiting for her response, "only represented a small number of individuals. My recollection of that turbulent period is that they were punished. Isn't that true, Minister Nashat?"

A glimpse of old sorrow shadowed the gentleman's face, puzzling Nevis, before he replied. "Indeed they were, as reparation to your monarch. You must forgive my companion," the minister said quietly, squeezing Shayna's arm in a paternal gesture, his expression a mixture of concern for the younger woman and anxiety, lest he anger his receptive hosts.

"It's all right."

"No, please, let me explain. Shayna's parents were falsely accused ten years ago of involvement in the plot. Their innocence was determined too late."

"I hope you don't hold their false accusation against me," Nevis said quietly. "I never knew the conspirators, barely remember hearing their names, only that Adrian Bambari had made a treasonous alliance with some of your countrymen." The mage peered at Devlin, who absently stroked his trimmed beard, blue eyes thoughtful. "But that's old history," she added quietly, "and I can see no reason that our two kingdoms shouldn't move beyond that terrible period."

"No bad feelings toward you, Mage Conarkin," the young woman replied, smile not quite convincing as her fingers lightly gripped the stiletto at her waist. "Under the circumstances, considering your difficult role at that point in time, I just wondered at your willingness to trade."

"Don't be surprised," Nevis laughed good naturedly. "With my banker standing at my heels, I have to prove quite willing to purchase top quality goods at the best prices. And frankly, minister," she turned back to Nashat, who appeared far more relaxed, "my costume designer will kiss my boots if I can bring her some of your fabrics to use in our performances."

"Thank you."

"That's not flattery, my lord. It's simple truth. Your fabrics enjoy quite an excellent reputation in Montbasso. I've been itching to get my hands on them for the last ten years. So has my theatrical rival, Barry Faddle."

"Your theater has quite a reputation in Cashogi, as well, Mage Conarkin. Forgive my saying this, but your troupe is highly regarded in my country, whereas the sorcerous theater in Port Cordillero and Master Faddle's theater here in Port Jambi are, sadly, not as favorably regarded. And I don't say this now because of your personal relationship with Devlin Graham," the minister added unexpectedly, eyes darting in the king's direction. "You do run an excellent theater."

"And both Barry and the Port Cordillero mage have excellent troupes, too. You should see them perform."

"You're gracious as well as lovely, Mage Conarkin. I look forward, at least, to viewing one of Master Faddle's performances, but far more eagerly anticipate a superb performance at your theater. Your monarch has provided tickets. Both Shayna and I will be there for opening night."

"If there is an opening night." Hugo San Rossi, hand in hand with Alana Graham, sauntered toward the group, smiling at Devlin. "Only a jest, my lord. Only a jest." Then slid a glance at Shayna Kashi, who bowed her head, letting long black curls hide her expression.

"Not a very diplomatic one."

Nevis smiled at Devlin. "As long as he's an excellent mage adviser to you, he doesn't have to be diplomatic. I recall being rather undiplomatic myself from time to time when I assumed that role."

Blue eyes met hers in a private exchange, and Devlin laughed. "You were. Quite undiplomatic. Well, Hugo, I'll not bite off your head in public as long as Mage Conarkin isn't insulted."

"Wouldn't dream of it," Nevis smiled, grateful when Alana tugged Hugo away from the group on the pretense of mingling with her father's guests. As they left, Nevis took careful note of Shayna Kashi's dark, brooding eyes, watching the two walk away, arm in arm.

"If you'll pardon me, Nevis, but I did wish to introduce the trade minister to several other of my guests." Devlin eyed her warily as she took the Cashogi minister's arm, trying to decipher her thoughts at Hugo's departure.

"Minister Nashat, I look forward to seeing you and your companion in my theater on opening night."

"I hope I shall see you before that," Nashat murmured, taking the mage's hand and bringing it to his lips. "I know how busy you are with opening night so close, but if you could find an evening free to dine with his majesty and me, I would be honored. Mistress Frascat," he repeated the gesture, placing a soft kiss on Lily's hand, to the madam's pleasure. "Gentlemen." Slipping his bodyguard's arm comfortably through his, Nashat followed Devlin to another group of merchants that included Ivan Ruskin, the grandfatherly owner of the Ruskin Shipyard.

"Smooth."

"Why, Mistress Frascat, you're blushing," Nevis laughed, enjoying her friend's unexpected reaction. "You'll have to kiss her hand from now on, Remo."

"Indeed I shall," the attorney said, placing his arm around Lily in genuine affection. "But not here, unless the gentleman thinks we're mocking him. He does have rather nice manners."

"So do you," Lily declared fiercely, prompting laughter from both Nevis and Remo.

"Pardon the interruption—"

Nevis froze at the familiar voice, and the sound of a walking stick on the marble floor. Before she could say anything, Finlay Oscram took the lead, bewildering Nevis even further.

"Clari, welcome. You're not interrupting. Here, have you met everyone yet? Nevis—"

"Mage Conarkin and I have already met, Master Oscram. I bake her sugar-coated monstrosities, or so Simon Masters calls them with appropriate disgust every morning." The old woman smiled, nonplussed by the rigid control on the younger mage's face and the tense set to her jaw. While Finlay introduced Clarissa to Remo and Lily, Nevis watched Lily's face, saw no apparent recognition. "I won't intrude," Clarissa was saying, "I just wished to thank you again for all your assistance in transferring ownership of the bakery without any trouble."

"It was surely my pleasure, as well as my business." Finlay smiled, oblivious to Nevis' unease.

"And my fortune to find such an honorable banker. My business forces me to rise well before anyone else in my neighborhood, so I'll bid you all a pleasant evening and—" Clarissa stumbled, dropping her cane so that it fell at Lily's feet.

The madam knelt gracefully to retrieve the wooden stick for the older woman, stared in astonishment at the carved head, revealing a beautiful, spirited horse, the cane nearly slipping from her fingers.

"I'll take that, my dear," Clarissa said quietly, dark eyes watching Lily's face, saw the recognition, and smiled. "Thank you, and enjoy the evening."

Lily ignored the murmured wishes of Remo and Finlay, eyes fixed on Nevis' unreadable expression. "It's a trifle warm in here. Nevis, would you like some fresh air before supper?"

"I gather the gentlemen are being dismissed," Finlay sighed in mock despair as Lily made a forced attempt at humor.

Nevis reassured the banker and the attorney that they'd return soon enough, and followed Lily's retreating back through the open balcony doors into the comfortably warm night air. Lily waited until they were alone, at the farthest end of the balcony, before turning on her lilac slippers.

"How long have you known?"

"About the same time that I discovered a dead body in my theater."

"Nevis—"

The mage placed a quieting hand on Lily's arm. "Hush."

"Have you spoken with her?"

"Briefly."

"And?"

Nevis shrugged, her face a mask. "I don't know. We didn't say much."

"Why did she leave Port Jambi without word?"

"She was shaken by Adrian's death, by her hatred of me for destroying her other apprentice."

"You had no choice." Lily peered carefully at Nevis' shadowed expression as the mage turned away. "Don't you dare start second-guessing what you did all those years ago, Nevis Conarkin. Adrian was a traitor."

"Adrian was my friend."

"Only insofar as he could use you."

Nevis started to walk inside, but Lily grabbed her silk sleeve and held on tight. "Let me go, Lily."

"Let the guilt go, old friend. We don't talk about it much, you and I, but I know it's still there after all these years." When Nevis shut her eyes, the madam said quietly, "I don't know why Clarissa chose this moment to return. But if she's here to cause trouble for you, I'll take that skinny little walking stick and—"

Nevis laughed gently. "Hush."

Skin flushed to match the flame of her hair, Lily shook her head in disgust. "Tell me one thing before we go back inside. Do you trust her?"

Nevis thought for a moment, sought the truth. "I don't know," she finally admitted. "I really don't know."

* * * *

"Nevis, your shoulder muscles are appallingly tight."

"That's why I need you to massage them." Nevis leaned back against Devlin's warm chest and sighed.

"So now I'm reduced to the level of servant." Devlin slid his fingers down her sides until he found her vulnerable ticklish spots.

"Dev, no—" The mage shot up from the bed and planted her knee in a very threatening position.

"I surrender."

"Coward." She slid willingly into his embrace and tried to relax, but the more she tried, the more she tensed.

"You're never easy when we're together here."

"Too many possible interruptions, my lord." Nevis idly scanned the masculine bedchamber, its dark, massive furniture arranged functionally with very little regard for aesthetics. The bed was huge, the chamber spacious, and the whole effect left her utterly unsettled.

"I told everyone to leave us alone."

"If a matter of state—"

"You're my matter of state." Devlin slid his fingers across her flat belly. "The only matter of any importance at the moment." Blue eyes studied her profile. "Hugo San Rossi upset you tonight."

Nevis shrugged.

"He's jealous of your influence on me." When she didn't respond, he added, "Hugo also believes you're just waiting for him to do something wrong, so you can take back your position."

"I don't want it. I gave it up ten years ago."

"Because of Alana." Devlin held the mage still when she tried to disentangle her legs from the sheets. "Because my daughter blames you unfairly for her mother's death. She's old enough to know the truth, including the fact that her mother wasn't ill, but committed suicide."

"No. Don't say anything to Alana." Nevis turned to look at him and cupped his face within her icy hands, sick with fear, the bristle of his beard soft against her skin. "Promise me."

"Why?"

"Under Hugo's influence, she won't believe you. It will only make matters worse for all of us."

"Then I'll damn well get rid of Hugo."

"No."

"Nevis—"

"Dev, listen to me, please. Listen carefully. If Hugo is offering you sound advice, if you trust what he's told you, then he's fulfilling his duty to you, his monarch, as mage adviser."

"His duty—"

"Whether or not he hates me, whether or not he persuades Alana to hate me, whether or not he dismisses and insults me in public, doesn't matter. What does matter is that he hasn't told Alana the truth about her mother and Adrian Bambari."

"He doesn't dare. It would only make you look the heroine you are, and Hugo the villain he is. Damn it, Nevis—"

"All that matters is that he advises you well, and that your daughter loves and respects you."

"That's not all that matters."

"Yes, it is," Nevis said softly, caressing his cheek, tracing the borders of his neat-trimmed beard. "And that's the end of it."

"Doesn't a king have any power in his own bed? Nevis, I could have him thrown out of office just for the comment he made in front of trade minister Nashat about your opening performance."

"That would make you look a tyrant in front of a man with whom you're trying to negotiate delicate trade relations, a man who, I might add, does seem genuinely interested in making progress."

"You think so? I do, too, but his bodyguard leaves me unsettled."

"That's her job." Nevis paused, thought a moment, and decided to tell Devlin what Finlay Oscram had told her. "She was seen cozying up to Hugo at the races just the other day."

"Diplomatic relations?"

"I hope so. Not only for your sake, but Alana's."

"Do you think Hugo is involved in Adam's murder?" When Nevis shook her head in fierce denial, disheveling her white hair, Devlin laughed softly. "Thank the gods, my love, you're not an actress in your own theater. You're not very convincing."

"I don't believe he's involved. I don't," she repeated, frowning. "But Lily and Remo do." Nevis bit her lip, looked away, resolved not to mention Clarissa Bracken. "I don't have the right to think him guilty."

Devlin straightened up, blinking, the sheets slipping down to his waist. "Care to explain that ridiculous statement?"

Nevis shrugged and considered her words. "If Hugo hates me, for whatever reason, for whatever poison Adrian Bambari poured into his mind, for my destroying his mentor when Adrian turned rogue, does it seem fair to suspect him of a crime simply because he despises me?"

"When that crime so closely involves you, by setting you up as the murderer, fair play doesn't enter into the discussion."

"You're prejudiced."

"I'm worried." Devlin pulled the mage closer until she was eye-to-eye with him. "And so are you."

"What you should be worried about is Barry Faddle."

The complete change of topic made Devlin blink and sit back. "Nevis, what are you talking about? That preposterous idea about buying your theater and hiring you as a house mage?"

"I told him to discuss it with you."

Blue eyes narrowed. "Imp. One of these days, Mage Conarkin—"

"If you don't satisfy this lustful body, my lord, I may have to visit Slick Hands tonight, after all." When Devlin responded as expected, Nevis sighed with relief at successfully taking his mind off Hugo San Rossi. But for all Devlin's loving caresses, Hugo San Rossi remained in the back of her own thoughts.

Chapter Five

Not long before dawn, while it was still dark, Nevis gracefully stepped from Devlin's carriage and thanked the driver with a murmured farewell. Standing before the theater on McOsley's Road, she stared up at the bright, dazzling sphere that was busy creating its final scene before daylight arrived. The thunderous cascade of water roared down a near-perfect re-creation of Casim Falls, the birthplace of Basol River, nestled in the Bardene Mountains.

Pausing beneath the sorcerous sphere, held cupped in huge carved hands, Nevis tried to decide just how weary she was. More restless than sleepy, she headed for the river walk rather than going directly upstairs to her rooms, thinking about May's orphan boy and what he could have seen in the pre-dawn gloom. At this distance, even Brigadier Bridge, a short distance downstream, was lost to sight. But no matter, a shock of white hair would be all too visible, even in the deepest part of the night.

Nevis stepped softly along the path and paused, not surprised, really, to find the boy fishing again on the rocks, less surprised to find that it wasn't one of May's orphans but Teddy, curly hair disheveled from sleep. A heartbeat before Nevis stepped out of the shadows, another figure, clad in a crisp dark uniform, stepped onto the path. The mage held back and listened.

"Teddy?"

The boy jumped, nearly dropping his makeshift fishing pole into the river current. "Constable Kilganor." His eyes went wide as she unexpectedly took a seat beside him on a smooth rock face.

"I thought I might find a fisherman or two along the river. That's best at this time, right in this spot, isn't it? For trout, anyway?" Brea's smile was charming and pleasant as the boy nodded. "Been lucky?"

"Not yet." Teddy scratched his head, letting slip an easy grin. "I wish I were, though. At least I'd have something for dinner if Ma were to catch me."

"Smart." Brea stretched her short legs as far as they would go. "Your aunt told me one of the boys saw two people coming out of the theater. I don't suppose you're that boy, the one who saw those people."

Teddy squirmed beneath the constable's confident stare. "Sure it was me. I just didn't want Aunt Nevis to scold me for sneaking out of bed."

"Understandable." Brea looked out across the river, the land opposite all but invisible in the pre-dawn fog, good solid farming land that supplied most of Port Jambi's fresh produce and meat, side by side with the racetrack and stables. "Can you tell me what you saw the other morning?"

"It wasn't Aunt Nevis."

"How do you know that?"

"Because it wasn't."

"Teddy—" The constable held the boy's determined gaze, kept her voice and her stance nonthreatening. "If you're going to help your aunt, I need to know everything you saw and heard. Deal?"

"I guess." Teddy nodded, shifted his fishing pole against his leg. "A man and a woman left the theater on this side, near the park. The woman had white hair, short and shaggy like Aunt Nevis. I couldn't hear what they were saying, but they were in a hurry. At least, it seemed that way to me. The man—" Teddy squinted up at the constable. "I couldn't recognize anything about him, but before they left, he walked down toward the river and stayed there a minute or two."

"Why?"

"I don't know. It was still pretty dark. By the time I set aside my fishing pole to go see, he'd walked back up the path, and the two of them left."

"By carriage or horse?"

"On foot."

"Did you follow them?"

"I wanted to." Teddy shook his head sheepishly. "My pole started jumping, and I figured I'd caught a trout. Instead, I caught nothing." He looked down at his hands, shame evident in the drooping of his shoulders. "No fish. No proof to help Aunt Nevis. I should have followed them."

"No, you shouldn't have, Teddy boy," Nevis said softly, stepping free of the shadows, her long ebony silk gown waving gently around her legs in the pre-dawn breeze.

"Aunt Nevis!"

"Aren't you overdressed for fishing, Mage Conarkin?"

"I wasn't planning to gut the fish myself. Morning, Teddy." Nevis made her way carefully over the slippery rocks. "Catch any breakfast?"

"Not yet." Teddy rubbed the tip of his nose, uncertain of her mood. "I didn't mean to lie about it being me."

"Sure you did. But you didn't mean any harm." Nevis ruffled the boy's thick brown curls and turned back to the constable. "Why would the man go down by the river?"

"One might think that a murderer would toss the murder weapon into the river," the constable said slowly, getting to her feet. "Not a bad idea to dispose of the evidence, to my thinking."

"Actually, the same thought crossed my mind." Green eyes challenged the constable. "Care to have a look?"

"Can you bring a lamp?"

"I'll do better than that."

Nevis opened the slim, bottomless pouch at her waist and pulled out a sphere. Encased inside was a miniature lamp. With one swift prick of her ivory-handled stiletto, Nevis held aloft a ball of magefire. "Coming, Teddy? I need your sharp eyes."

The boy lodged his fishing pole carefully between two rocks, eagerly following his aunt and the constable back to the theater, then along the path that led from the door to the riverbank. Nevis leaned over the rocks, hand stretched forth, peering into the shallow water.

"If he were smart, he would have tossed it far out and let the current take it." Brea steadied the mage as one foot slipped on seaweed-covered rock.

"If he were smart and calm. If he were nervous, he might have dropped it closer to shore." Nevis stretched her arm, swinging the magefire light in a graceful arc. "Wouldn't be surprised if—What's that? Teddy, can you take a look?"

"Be careful, boy." Brea guided Teddy's confident steps in the direction Nevis was pointing. "If we bring you home drenched to the skin, we'll really have some explaining to do with your ma."

"I won't slip. I always walk these rocks."

"Are you supposed to admit that in front of me?"

"Sorry, Aunt Nevis. Oh, wait. I see it." The boy knelt along the rocks, rebellious brown curls falling into his eyes as the constable clung to his breeches, keeping firm hold when Teddy slipped his hand into the cold water. "It's stuck."

"Careful, Teddy. If it's a weapon, it's bound to be sharp." Nevis knelt beside her nephew, carelessly pushed back the sleeve of her silk gown, and plunged her hand into the water. "By the gods, that's cold. Never amazes me that it stays so damned cold until the summer is over and done. Let me see if I can loosen it. There." With an undignified grunt, the mage sat back, pulling a stiletto from the rocks.

Just as the first rays of sun broke through the fog, the constable took the weapon from Nevis' outstretched hand and examined it closely. The ivory handle was a perfect replica of the stiletto's handle at Nevis' waist, the only difference lay in the jagged edge along one side. When she started to speak, Nevis signaled her silent.

"Teddy? Is that fishing pole shaking again?" Nevis squinted against the early sunlight, pointing toward the boy's pole. "If that's a hungry trout caught on your line, you don't want to lose it."

"Be right back." The boy dashed off toward his pole at a pace that made Nevis bite back a hundred warnings.

"Now then, constable, you were about to say something."

"Always thinking, aren't you, Mage Conarkin?" When the mage didn't respond to the barb, the constable laughed, a sound that surprised the mage with its apparent sincerity. "Don't give me that damning look. I know that Lily Frascat believes Hugo San Rossi set you up, though I haven't had a chance to talk privately with her yet, with the exception of a few stolen moments yesterday. I'm heading over there right now."

"Now? You know the hours they keep."

"Same as you, it seems."

Nevis flushed, though whether from anger or embarrassment, the constable wasn't quite certain, though her tone was decidedly chilly when she asked, "Anything more I can do for you, Constable?"

"Does Hugo San Rossi use a stiletto to trigger his spells?"

"He prefers melodrama, incantations, and an awed audience. Hugo should be running the theater instead of me."

"He speaks so highly of you, Mage Conarkin."

"Then you haven't been paying attention. Only last night, he insulted me in front of Devlin and the Cashogi trade minister." When the constable raised one eyebrow in query, Nevis chose not to comment any further. "To answer your question, Hugo can trigger spells as I do, but usually doesn't. All legitimate mages have that potential, so I've been taught."

"Why do you use spheres?"

"Because I'm practical. During the theater season, I go through an awful lot of spells for every performance. If I used that much sorcery every day, I'd be exhausted and useless."

"So you create them a bit at a time to conserve your energy?"

"Precisely."

Brea glanced over to where Teddy was holding the pole, disappointment on his dirt-streaked face. "But you can cast spells without spheres?"

"Sure."

"Then why not create a trout for the boy?"

"Won't taste as good as the real thing. But I can guide a few fish in the right direction."

Nevis knelt again beside the riverbank, slipped her fingers into the water, and murmured an incantation. Before she stood upright, Teddy was shouting in delight, pulling a sleek shape from the river.

"If the stiletto is the weapon used to murder Adam Museo, it's obviously meant to implicate me, and not only because it looks like mine. I'm not saying Hugo's involved," Nevis emphasized her point by tapping her sorcerous pouch, "but he's kept his magery distinctly different from mine."

"Convenient."

"Possibly."

"As convenient as you finding a similar stiletto at your back door to show me evidence of your innocence?"

"Believe what you want, Constable. I'm going upstairs."

"I intend to, Mage Conarkin. Trust me on that. And—"

"Aunt Nevis! I've caught another! Two trout." Teddy shouted, ecstatic at his good fortune. "Won't Ma be happy?" He carefully unhooked the fishes from his line and scurried back to the orphanage, waving at the two women.

"I suppose," Brea Kilganor drawled, as she stepped away, heading for the road, "it's awfully easy conjuring up trout. Likely as easy as conjuring up a murder weapon. Enjoy your day, Mage Conarkin. I assure you, I plan on enjoying mine."

* * * *

"Two sticky, sugar-coated breakfast buns? Two, Simon? Why?" Nevis eyed both raspberry-star-topped cakes, wondering how she could avoid the daily reminder of Clarissa Bracken's presence only three blocks away.

The stage manager shrugged. "Just in case your prima donnas get outrageously out of control, I thought you should be well fortified."

"Should I peek at my theater through the sphere?" Nevis narrowed her eyes when Simon shook his head. "Know something I don't know?"

"Not a thing, boss."

"All right, thanks. I think." The mage broke off a wedge of the first bun, offered it to Simon, who shuddered. "Is everyone here?"

"All but Gabriella. She—"

"Take my wig off your lice-ridden head!" The shrill voice echoed eerily along the empty corridor. "Take it off this instant, Verdi Casporet, or I'll see that you never work another day in your life in Port Jambi or anywhere else."

Nevis grabbed the two raspberry-topped breakfast cakes. "Sounds like Gabriella's arrived."

With a despairing glance at the carved image of Janni, the only serenity left in her office, Nevis headed for the private box that opened along the corridor. Glancing down at the stage, she saw Verdi, white wig tight on her head, busy repairing a loose button on Pepo Daken's shirt, and placidly ignoring Gabriella's shrieks. Chest heaving with melodramatic intent, Gabriella's jutting breasts nearly shoved Hans Takat off the stage as she stormed straight for the costume designer.

"Gabriella—"

The leading lady stopped in her tracks, auburn hair awhirl as she spun her head to stare at Nevis, daring her employer to question her behavior.

"Verdi has to wear the wig for a day or two. Believe me, it's not her choice. So please leave her alone."

"I refuse to wear it after it's been on her lice-ridden head."

Verdi made false scratching motions behind the actress' back, rolling her eyes at Nevis, who had trouble restraining a smile.

"Verdi is wearing it at my express command."

"Why?" Two hands landed on very slender hips as the actress glowered at Nevis, well-endowed breasts thrusting out so far the mage was astonished that Gabriella didn't tip over.

"Because someone borrowed it and then damaged the dummy head before the wig was completely and correctly stretched." From the corner of her eye, Nevis caught Hans' abrupt movement at the edge of the stage. When she turned her head to study him more closely, the young actor looked away, jamming his hands in the depths of his pockets.

Gabriella followed Nevis' gaze, saw where it landed. "You filthy pervert, dressing in women's clothes—" Shifting her rage from Verdi to Hans, Gabriella launched herself at Hans, chasing him backward into Pepo, who moved aside, unwittingly allowing Hans to trip over Verdi and land flat on his back. "You probably stole my ring, too."

"I didn't wear the wig, and I didn't steal your ring." Hans whimpered, his eyes unexpectedly vulnerable, as he protected his body from Gabriella's stylishly pointed leather boots.

Nevis watched, reluctant to stop Gabriella until Hans had his say, wondering what was really going on with him. Acknowledging that Gabriella was far more effective at the moment, Nevis remained silent.

"Liar."

"I didn't wear the wig, and I didn't steal your ring," Hans repeated, as though trying to convince himself.

"I don't believe you, Hans. You've been nothing but unending trouble the last few days, performing like an amateur, missing even your easiest lines, jumping at shadows, and now this insult—" Gabriella kicked the actor hard, turning back toward the mage. "Nevis, I demand you fire Hans right now and get another actor to play the important role of the rogue mage, Adrian Bambari."

Nevis crossed her arms, listening, taking note of Simon's quiet emergence from the wings of the stage, mimicking Nevis in the act of cramming two sticky buns in her mouth.

"Your honor and the greatness of your deeds in saving the people of Montbasso from the Cashogi invaders demand a quality actor to represent your greatest adversary." Gabriella swept auburn hair from her forehead, eyes fixed on Nevis' placid expression. "Or, Mage Conarkin, would you prefer your audience to see you, through my true-to-life performance, defeat a man who in reality is a whimpering fool, gutless thief, and pathetic liar?"

Nevis craved the rest of her sweet breakfast, but preferred to enjoy it in peace and quiet, with only Janni smiling up at her in maternal blessing. "Gabriella," she leaned her hip against the railing, black-clad leg swinging free, "be reasonable. Even if Hans really did borrow the wig—"

"I didn't."

"Hush, Hans."

The mage dared a glance at Simon, who rolled his eyes. Verdi caught the private exchange and snickered.

"Gabriella, even if Hans is lying, it's not a crime to wear a wig. As for your ruby ring, we don't have any idea what happened to it. For all we know, you could have been careless, and—" When Gabriella's face grew heated, Nevis added, "I'm not saying you were careless, mind, but we've all been genuinely preoccupied with opening night only days away, and truthfully, we don't have proof of any wrongdoing by anyone. As for the white wig—"

"Would you wear a wig that's been worn by Hans, then Verdi? And the gods know who else played with it?"

"I should be flattered to think someone wanted to look like me." Nevis studied Hans' uneasy expression, though he refused to look at her. Sighing, she pushed back from the railing. "Gabriella, if I promise to cleanse the wig by sorcery before opening night, will you wear it? And stop tormenting Hans?"

"Damn it, Nevis—"

"Gabriella, I don't think I'm asking that big a favor. Please."

Something in the mage's voice struck a chord in Gabriella's conscience, and she nodded. "Deal."

"Thank you." Nevis sank into one of the chairs and broke off a morsel of sugar-coated cake just as the stage manager drew closer, standing just below her private box. "I don't think two of Clari's buns are going to be enough, Simon."

"Then I'll get some petty cash and buy you some more. Just filled the box, so—" Simon made as though to get the coins, but Nevis waved him back, acknowledging his mention of the replenished coin box.

"We don't need to keep increasing the baker's profits at my expense. All right, my slaves, let's get started." Nevis munched contentedly, finding it difficult to deny that Clarissa's baking was as tempting as ever, while Simon got the rehearsal underway. By the end of the first act, Nevis had triggered spells for fire, storm, earthquake, and cannon fire, and thought that maybe the rest of the rehearsal might, just might, go smoothly if the cursed cast would continue to cooperate.

A knock on the door to her private box brought Verdi inside, the younger woman's expression beneath the white wig clearly unhappy.

"Dare I ask?"

"Got a moment?"

"Sure. The children seem to be behaving."

"All but one."

"Gabriella again?"

"Hans." Verdi adjusted the wig on her head and sighed. "I don't know what's wrong with the boy, but he's awfully jumpy."

"I noticed. Was he lying about the wig? Or maybe about the ring?"

"Don't know, Nevis, but I wouldn't swear he was telling the truth. Something's got the boy spooked."

"Does Firespark do that to you?"

"Sometimes, but he claims he hasn't used it in weeks. Look, Nevis, Hans is a decent boy, and he's damned appreciative of the opportunity you gave him to play the role of Adrian Bambari."

"I wouldn't have hired him if he didn't have talent."

"I know, but he didn't have that much experience. Slick Hands wouldn't even consider him."

"Slick Hands runs a very different theater troupe."

Verdi sat on the arm of a chair. "I'm worried about opening night."

"I'll have a private chat with Hans."

"Let me try first. He's coming backstage to try on the embroidered shirt again after rehearsal."

"Don't tell me you finished the damned thing already?"

"Not quite. Sometimes heavy embroidery pulls too much and ruins the fit. Just making sure."

"Good thing I hire experts," Nevis smiled, finishing the last of the second sugar-coated cake. "You try first. Then—"

"Has anyone heard the rumble of approaching thunder in the far-off distance? Has anyone even," Pepo Daken's deep voice crept closer to Nevis' private box, "seen our resident mage lately? Perhaps she's fallen asleep because of the extremely late hours she's been keeping at the king's side."

"Cursed fool I am," Nevis murmured to the costume designer, "missing my cue again."

"My fault. I distracted you."

Nevis peered over the railing, found Pepo standing directly below, arms crossed. Before she could defend herself, the leading actor winked.

Nevis narrowed her eyes, triggered the ear-splitting storm, sat back in the chair, and wondered about dead corpses, frightened actors, arrogant mages, and people who turned up when least expected.

* * * *

Resplendent on stage in the last scene, Hans Takat radiated raw power and rediscovered confidence, a despicable adversary for leading lady Gabriella to destroy, as he waited for the tidal wave that threatened the city. Accompanied by the crimson dragon that Nevis had created from a hard-to-dislodge memory of the creature Adrian Bambari had conjured ten long years earlier, Hans was struggling unsuccessfully to defeat the mage, a re-enactment that troubled Nevis every time she witnessed the performance. For the sake of her own sanity and peace of mind, and because Devlin truly didn't want Nevis to relive too many unwelcome and overwhelming memories, Devlin agreed that the play needn't stick to strict historical fact.

But Clarissa Bracken's reappearance had only served to heighten those old emotions, particularly the most prevalent, guilt. And remind Nevis of far too many scenes that the public, and Devlin's daughter, didn't know had ever happened, particularly those involving Devlin's queen.

And though the "Doom of Bambari" showed Adrian's defeat at the hands of Nevis in full view of the city's defenders, the truth was rather different. Nevis had faced Adrian alone, destroyed the renegade mage when he tried to kill her, lost in his drug-induced illusions of power and greed. Devlin had found her, weeping, huddled beside the slain body of her traitorous friend. But the Nevis Conarkin portrayed by Gabriella de la Morsage stood triumphantly over the fallen body of the renegade mage.

Releasing a deep sigh, Nevis picked up the last sphere that encased the miniature tidal wave. She held it in the palm of her hand, stiletto ready, yet hesitated, without first understanding why. While her cast waited, perplexed, Nevis held the sphere up to the magefire lamp.

Pepo's voice roared across the stage. "The dragon is getting frisky, Nevis. Where's our tidal wave?"

Nevis stood slowly in her seat, white hair rising above the railing in full view from the stage, one hand raised to keep the cast silent. She peered intently into the sphere, trying to discern what was tugging at her instinct, until finally she saw, all too clearly, what was missing. The low wall that would keep the unleashed tidal wave in control was no longer in place.

"Contemptible bastard," she hissed, green eyes flashing with the need for violence.

"Boss?" Simon called out from the opposite balcony, troubled by the unsettling expression on her face as Nevis looked up.

"Finish the rehearsal without any more spells." Nevis abruptly turned her back on the stage without explanation and stormed into her office, slamming the door shut behind her. Frantic and furious, she unlocked the wooden cabinet that held her inventory of prepared spells, checked each and every one carefully. Not surprised, she found three more spheres that would have made her hair white had it been its original shade of chestnut brown.

"Nevis—" Simon rapped sharply at the door, unwilling to barge in when the mage was furious, having unwittingly walked into magefire a year ago that nearly singed his hair. "Boss, let me in." Simon raised his hand once more to knock, staggered back when the door flew open.

"Contemptible bastard."

"I'm sorry for whatever I've done," Simon babbled to keep her from striking him. "But what have I done?"

"By the gods, Simon, not you. That—" Nevis spun on her heel and stormed back into the office. "If I had triggered that last spell, releasing a tidal wave, the water would have flowed uncontrolled through the theater and into the street. A tidal wave that would have destroyed this entire sector of the city, not to mention the people in it."

Simon's jaw dropped.

"I found three others. An uncontrolled fire, lightning, and tornado, any one of which would destroy the theater, kill an innocent audience and bystanders in the vicinity, and then—"

"Ruin your reputation as a mage."

Nevis sagged back against the desk, staring at the manager's confident expression as though she'd never really looked at Simon.

"Hugo—"

"I don't want to hear his name in my theater. Ever." Nevis abruptly replaced the malevolent spheres in the cabinet, separating the dangerous ones from the safe, untainted spells, and reset the locking mechanism.

"Maybe you should."

"Maybe you should watch the rehearsal."

"Boss—"

"By the gods, Simon—"

The stage manager raised both hands to stop the torrent of words, braving the dangerous anger in Nevis' green eyes. "Just listen, please." When the mage crossed her arms, expression stubborn, Simon pressed on, "No other mage in Port Jambi, or all of Montbasso for that matter, hates you the way Hugo San Rossi does. He'll do anything to make you look bad."

"Why now? He's had ten years to do it, Simon."

"He's been hostile for ten years, sniping at you a little bit at a time. With the anniversary play reminding everyone how you saved Devlin's life and his kingdom, why not now? Maybe he just jumped on the chance to make you look bad by setting you up for murder."

"And maybe Hugo didn't murder Adam or replace my spells with lethal ones. There are other mages in Port Jambi and throughout Montbasso."

"A handful. Mages are rare, remember? And the ones I know are quite pleasant if a little eccentric. Just like you, boss," Simon added, hoping to make his employer laugh, relieved when she did.

"Simon, there are some days—"

"I know. Look, just be careful."

"Sure." Nevis slipped past the very worried stage manager and headed out the side door into the bright afternoon sunlight, following the river path to Lily's adjacent whorehouse. She was greeted by Lily's sometime bodyguard and resident tough, Chappy Markos, who politely welcomed her inside. A flurry of waves from the bright-eyed, classily dressed prostitutes entertaining their clientele in the elegant parlor greeted Nevis as she made her way along the corridor to Lily's ground-floor office at the back of the building, with a view of the Basol River. Nevis paused in the doorway, and started to edge back when she realized Lily was deep in serious conversation with Remo Savanak. Her movement caught Lily's eye, and the madam raised a hand to stop the mage from leaving.

"You look as miserable as I feel," Lily murmured, gesturing Nevis inside the sunlit room filled with the scent of fresh summer wildflowers.

"More bad news?"

"You first."

"Lily—"

"You first, Nevis." Lily sat back in the padded chair behind her elegant desk, ready to listen, leaning away from Remo, the attorney sitting nearby on the small couch beside the desk. The feathers in her auburn hair were silhouetted against the afternoon sunlight.

Resigned to an unpleasant discussion, the mage perched beside Remo, absently removing the pillows stuffed behind her back and tossing them in a neat pile on the floor. "Someone replaced some of my spheres. The new spells have uncontrolled effects. I nearly unleashed a tidal wave only moments ago."

Lily started to speak, fell swiftly silent at the mage's peculiar expression and utterly flat voice.

"Your turn."

"Can't I even—"

"No."

The mage shook her head, reading all too clearly the thoughts running through Lily's mind, the possibility that it wasn't Hugo, but perhaps Clarissa, or perhaps, both. By the gods, had the woman who mentored both Nevis and Adrian betrayed Devlin and helped Adrian with his treason ten years ago? And was she helping Adrian's own apprentice ten years later?

"Tell me your news. Or you tell me, counselor," Nevis said quietly, responding to Remo's unusually somber expression.

The attorney smoothed the front of his gold brocade vest.

"Remo—"

"Don't nag. The court has decided that with Adam Museo dead, you and Lily need to come up with the funds equal to the value of the orphanage."

Nevis blinked in confusion. "Why?"

"As a good faith measure until they make their decision."

"We didn't have to do that when the cursed bastard was alive. Remo, I don't understand. The value of—" Nevis whispered, her words faltering as the reality of what the attorney said sunk in. "Neither Lily nor I have that much currency available. Finlay can float us a loan, can't he?"

"Impossible."

"Why?" The word was a whisper that pained the attorney.

Remo studied the ring on his right hand, sapphire encased in gold, a gift from Lily for his most recent birthday. "It's beyond his bank's limit per client. Don't scowl, Nevis, and don't turn him into a braying mule. Finlay's not the villain. He may run the bank, but he's got to follow the rules or bring trouble down on his head. The man's awfully heartbroken."

Nevis staggered to her feet, paced for a second, then stopped. "I'll put the theater up for sale. Barry Faddle would just love to snatch it up. He'd probably let me stay on as mage, keep the troupe—"

"You can't sell it."

"It's my theater, Remo. Don't tell me I can't sell it."

"You can't."

"Why not? By the gods, Remo, tell me why not." When the attorney didn't immediately reply, Nevis turned to Lily, who looked away. "Tell me," Nevis whispered, her face unusually pale, "why I can't sell my own theater."

"For one thing," Remo said quietly, meeting her eyes across the empty space between them, "you won't get enough to pay off your mortgage on the theater and provide an equivalent value for the orphanage. Lily's brothel is, unfortunately, just as heavily mortgaged. That's why Finlay can't help you. But there's another difficulty in this whole mess."

"Difficulty?"

"The court has made the requirement effective at midnight. I'd only gotten word a short while ago. If you hadn't arrived here, I would have come to find you. The truth is that you don't have time to sell your theater and come up with gold currency, even if you wanted to do so."

"That's got to be illegal. Remo, how can they do that?"

The attorney's expression was so unsettling that Nevis gripped the back of the couch, braced for more bad news. "They've managed to come up with some loophole in the law that was enacted right after Adrian Bambari betrayed the kingdom. The courts can move swiftly against a mage if they feel justified in taking action."

"Meaning?"

"You're a prime murder suspect, and they're invoking the obscure law." Remo's gray eyes held compassion as he watched the play of turbulent emotions on her face. "Nevis, I'm afraid there's more." At her rigid nod, he said softly, "If you can't come up with the funds, and if the court makes its final decision against you and Lily so that you have to pay for the orphanage, your theater and all that you own will belong to Hugo San Rossi."

"I don't understand." Nevis' skin was as colorless as her short-cropped, shaggy hair. "How is that possible?"

"Adam owed San Rossi gambling debts. Apparently, Hugo made a deal, a loan, in exchange for the rights to the orphanage."

"Bastard."

"However," Remo's voice held such hesitation that Nevis was immediately and legitimately suspicious, "you're out of danger for the moment."

Nevis narrowed her eyes. "Care to explain that?"

"Devlin's putting up the funds."

"Oh, no, Remo, he—"

"Insists." Remo held the mage's gaze for a heartbeat, willing her not to argue. "Devlin told me to tell you, and I quote, 'tell that stubborn woman it's not a gift, it's a loan, which she can start repaying when all this is settled. And tell her, too, that if she even so much as thinks to sell the theater to Slick Hands, she'd better be prepared to deal with me.' That's what he said, Nevis." The attorney bit back the smug remark that nearly slipped out, restrained only by the fire in her eyes.

"If Hugo finds out that Devlin's taking funds from the royal treasury," the mage countered, green eyes flashing, "he'll use it against Dev."

"Not to worry. Devlin's using his own funds. It's personal, Nevis, and he'll be damned if Hugo San Rossi ruins you or Lily."

"He can't, damn him. Dev's not thinking clearly. He's—"

"Devlin is thinking very clearly, and happens to be quite a success-ful and popular monarch. The people of Montbasso enjoy a far better quality of life than a decade ago when the kingdom was in turmoil. When it comes to you, Nevis, he tends to overreact when you're in trouble, I'll admit, but after a short while, he comes back to his senses. And then he thinks very clearly indeed."

"Not in this case. Remo—"

A sharp rap came at the door, and all argument came to a screeching halt as Lily called out permission to enter. The brawny monster that was Chappy Markos peered into the bright office.

"Problem?"

"Sorry to interrupt, ma'am, but the constable's here. She wants to talk to some of the girls. Especially the one—" His eyes flickered to-ward Remo, then Nevis.

"The one beaten by that hideous pig, Adam Museo?"

"Yes, ma'am."

Lily's feathers bobbed as she gave curt orders. "Take the constable to the back parlor, please, Chappy. And send Fani first. She's the only one he roughed up. Then," Lily shut her eyes briefly, thinking, "maybe Melissa. She should be able to handle the constable's questions."

"Yes, ma'am." Chappy left them to their discussion, expression somber and respectful.

"Why can't I ever get Dev to be that polite?" Nevis grumbled, scratching her head absently as an elusive thought stayed just out of reach.

"Waste of time," Lily sympathized. "Most men don't know how to be subservient these days." She blew a kiss at Remo. "Though some do learn quickly how to gallantly kiss a woman's hand and be gracious," she teased.

"Didn't I do well last night?" Remo asked, unaware of Nevis' affectionate regard, pleased as she was for the two of them.

"Quite." Lily caressed his cheek, returning abruptly to the business at hand. "Fani told me—"

"Fani." Nevis sank heavily onto the couch beside Remo, thinking hard. "Fani Sneddle."

"You know the girl. She's been with me nearly two years."

"Dark hair?"

"Long black curls, yes, why?" When the mage shut her eyes trying to snatch the elusive thought, Lily lost patience, feathers quivering as she abruptly pushed back her chair. "Nevis, what—"

"I think it was Fani's portrait I found in Adam's bedchamber."

"Yes," Remo said into the sudden silence, "I've been meaning to ask you about that little adventure."

"I don't know what it means, but we've no time to waste." Lily came around the front of her elegant desk and pulled Nevis to her feet. "Be right back, Remo."

"Lily—"

"Hush, Nevis. Just come along, like a subservient little mage."

The madam led Nevis down the corridor, past the large sunny parlor, still filled with noisy patrons, through the delicious aromas of the kitchen where fresh bread was baking, and down the stairs into the cellar. Checking to see that no one was following them, Lily led her friend to the far end of the dim lit chamber, where her special wines were kept. Stepping carefully into the alcove, lit by slanting rays of fading sunlight that filtered through a nearby window, Lily reached up to the low ceiling and carefully slid aside a well-oiled wooden panel. To Nevis' utter amazement, Brea Kilganor's voice came clear through the rug. The madam took one moment to arch an eyebrow in triumph at the mage's surprise, then turned her attention to the voices overhead.

"I won't take much of your time, Fani, I understand you have a client waiting to see you."

"Thank you, Constable," Fani's voice was a soft contrast to Brea's authoritative tone. "I wouldn't want Lily angry with me. Not that she would be. She hardly ever gets angry with any of us, unless we do something foolish."

"I'd guess, then, that she was gentle with you, took care of you, when Adam Museo beat you."

"Sure she was gentle with me," Fani's voice shook a bit at the memory, "but not with Adam. She made Chappy throw him out on the street, warned him never to show his face here again."

"Had he been here before?"

"Sure."

"For you?"

"Sometimes." The girl's voice was hardly persuasive.

"Sometimes?"

Fani sighed. "Constable—"

"I need to find out about his habits, Fani. If you didn't do anything wrong, you've nothing to worry about. Now tell me, did he come to see anyone else?"

"At first," the girl said softly, both eavesdroppers straining to hear. "But then he kept coming to see me. It was nice at first, made me feel good, you understand, but then he started to get rough, a little bit at a time."

"Did you tell anyone?"

"No. It was little things, so I didn't bother anyone. But the last time—" Fani must have stood up because her steps sounded on one side of the parlor over their heads. "He wanted to play rough, and I said no. Lily always told us we didn't have to give in and play rough with our clients unless we wanted to do so."

"But she'll let it go on?"

"No." Fani stopped pacing. "She said there's pretense and there's real. Pretense is not a problem, but real is dangerous. And it's stupid. She won't let anyone do what Adam did to me."

"So she threatened him?"

Fani must have suddenly realized where the questions were leading because she stamped her foot, surprising both eavesdroppers at the vehemence. "Lily never touched that man. Chappy threw him out, and that was all. She didn't murder him, if that's what you're thinking."

"It's not impossible."

"Sure it is, if you knew Lily Frascat. That's a terrible thing to say, Constable, and I resent it."

"Just doing my job, Fani. It's what I get paid to do. When was the last time Adam stopped by to see you?"

The girl started pacing again. "About a week before he was found dead. I couldn't work for a few days. When I started again, Lily told me I didn't have to work yet, but I thought it only right to earn my keep for her kindness." The footsteps stopped. "Is there anything else, Constable? My client's waiting."

"Just one more question, Fani. Are you seeing any gentleman on a regular basis on your own time?"

"I have regular clients."

"No, I meant a lover. Surely you have relationships with other men?"

"No," Fani said quietly, heading toward the door. "I don't have a lot of free time, Constable, and—" Another sigh escaped, this one full of sorrow and regret. "What man would want a whore to raise his children?"

The constable had no immediate answer to that, only, "Go on, girl. I don't have any more questions for you at the moment." Brea Kilganor's voice held a note that Nevis couldn't interpret, not until she heard the footsteps fade and the constable mutter, "She's lying about something, and I'll be damned if I know what it is."

Chapter Six

"You're not having a very good day, Mage Conarkin."

Nevis didn't bother to glance up, kept her eyes fixed on the river and the distant shoreline as gaily striped sails and the more practical fishermen's white canvas slid past. "Are you going to make it worse, Constable?"

"I could." Brea Kilganor sat on a smooth rock not far from Nevis, where she could watch the mage's expression. "I could say I suspect you of creating those nasty spells and blaming it on Hugo San Rossi."

"You could." Nevis' voice was a whisper, barely heard above the shrieking cry of the seagulls. "Word gets around, doesn't it, Constable? Did Hugo tell you about those nasty spheres or did you bully my cast and crew?"

"I've got sharp ears when it comes to murder," Brea answered calmly. "News like that doesn't take long to spread."

Nevis shrugged. "I didn't tell anyone to keep it secret."

"Why would you? Anything to make Hugo San Rossi look bad. But even you couldn't fake Hugo's claim on the orphanage when Adam died. That would be too much, even for you."

Nevis clenched and unclenched her fists, movement not unnoticed by the vigilant constable, who didn't comment on her reaction. "Do the courts inform you of every little move they take?"

"Only in cases where the individual involved is a prime murder suspect. However, I'm not even sure the two items are related to each other or to the murder of Adam Museo. I'm not even sure that Hugo San Rossi has done anything more than harass you." Brea picked up a stone and tossed it carelessly in the river, where it landed with a clumsy plop, setting off ripples that eventually reached the riverbank by Nevis' boots. "You're within your rights to petition the crown if he is indeed harassing you."

"I can fight my own battles." I learned that particular lesson, Nevis thought angrily, when I had to destroy Adrian Bambari alone.

"That's not what I hear. Word on the street is that Devlin Graham is putting up the loan—"

Nevis lurched to her feet, towered over the calm, unmoving constable, who refused to be intimidated, despite recalling the incredible tales she'd heard rumored about what this mage could do.

"By the way, it's true about Adam abusing one of Lily Frascat's girls. I was just over there, talking to the girl."

Nevis blinked at the change of topic. "Fani."

"I wouldn't think Lily was the vindictive type—"

"You cursed bitch, parading your righteousness in your perfect, properly creased uniform. Don't you dare set me up against Lily Frascat. Don't you dare try to create a wedge between us."

"Just doing my job, Mage Conarkin. One of you, or both perhaps, is on awfully dangerous ground as far as my investigation is concerned. And I keep hearing Hugo San Rossi's name as the villain when you and Lily—"

Nevis grabbed a handful of wool uniform and pulled the constable up from the rock. "I didn't kill the bastard. Neither did Lily. And I haven't a clue who did. That's your job, Constable, so by the gods, go and do your lousy job and leave me and Lily the hell alone."

With one swift shove, Nevis pushed Brea away, nearly toppling the shorter woman into the river. But the constable was braced for such a move and easily regained her balance. Unflustered, she straightened the folds of her jacket.

"For the record, Mage Conarkin," Brea Kilganor said quietly, "I don't believe either of you guilty. And if you were, I'd be damnably disappointed and disillusioned." When Nevis simply stared at the other woman as though she had sprouted fangs, the constable turned to head back up the path toward McOsley's Road, though she paused briefly. "Aren't you dining with the king tonight? You're bound to be late, and I don't want Devlin Graham angry at me."

Nevis watched the short, stocky constable walk away, and shook her head, murmuring, "Maybe I'm losing my mind."

The mage brushed off her breeches and started back along the river path toward the theater and her own private entrance. She nearly made it to the door when she saw a couple strolling arm in arm along the path by Alvaron Park. Not an unusual sight by any means, two lovers walking near twilight, looking for privacy. What made the sight unusual, and brought a startled oath to Nevis' lips, was that the man was unmistakably Hugo San Rossi, and the woman, Shayna Kashi, the personal bodyguard of trade minister Nashat.

Befuddled, Nevis watched the pair turn away from the riverbank and cut through the green expanse of the park, heading back toward the main street. Were they lovers, seeking privacy away from Alana Graham's jealous eyes? But why come here to Alvaron Park, so near Nevis and her friends? She paralleled their progress through the park until she reached McOsley's Road and the front of her theater and saw the two hire a carriage to take them elsewhere. Unsettled, she turned to go back to her apartment when she stared in shock at the huge sphere. Scrawled across the front of the transparent sphere in red letters, probably some poor animal's blood, was the word, 'murderer'."

"I was just coming back to tell you."

Nevis turned at the sound of Brea Kilganor's voice. She started to mention Hugo San Rossi's unexpected appearance in the park, but held her tongue.

"Your expression tells me you know who might have done this insult."

Nevis shook her head, and raised her left hand. She murmured a brief incantation under her breath and watched as a swift shower of rain washed the scarlet letters from sight, not a moment too soon as darkness fell. When her hand dropped wearily to her side, the rain ceased and the sphere came to life, erupting in a profusion of shrill trumpets and booming cannon fire.

* * * *

"Perhaps if you stopped pushing your venison feebly around the plate and placed it successfully in your mouth, my chef wouldn't be completely insulted."

Nevis eyed Devlin Graham across the spotless white-linen tablecloth in his private study. "I'm eating."

"One spiced potato does not constitute a meal, even for a scrawny mage with bony knees. You ate nothing at the merchants' dinner, causing Mikaline Nashat to ask whether the food had been poisoned."

"Dev—"

"I assured the minister that the food was untainted, and that you had a rather peculiar and horrendous desire for sweets. Thankfully, you managed to nibble some desserts or my trade negotiations would be in mortal danger, despite the fact that the minister found you quite charming."

"Because I didn't punch Hugo San Rossi in the balls?"

"He did admit you had admirable restraint." Devlin appraised her plate in despair beneath the soft candlelight. "I hope, at least, you're eating those appalling sweet and sticky monstrosities in the morning." Blue eyes stared at the mage, waiting for some lame excuse.

Nevis grinned, forgetting for a moment precisely who baked them. "Simon brought me two of those marvelously sugar-coated cakes this morning to fortify me to face the lunacies of my troupe. They weren't enough to tide me over. It was pure chaos on stage."

"At the rate your week is going, you'll need a dozen every day. I know you're upset about the orphanage—"

"I'm more upset about the loan. Dev, even Brea Kilganor knows you're backing us. She implied I can't fight my own battles."

"Words, Nevis, harmless words to anger you." At the rising annoyance in her green eyes, the king sighed and set aside his silver fork. "It's her job to poke and prod at you since she hasn't got a solid clue as to the identity of the murderer. But listen to me, Nevis, and pay very close attention. This loan has nothing to do with your ability to defend yourself."

Nevis turned away. "It's not that I don't appreciate it," she said softly, white hair falling loosely in her eyes.

"Appreciate?" Devlin abruptly pushed his chair back, rattling the crystal glasses, nearly upsetting the bronze candlesticks and setting the cloth afire, to crouch beside the mage. "I don't need your appreciation or your gratitude. Damn it, woman, I love you, and I don't want to see you hurt. And Hugo San Rossi is determined to hurt you, whether or not he's involved with the murder. Ever since you destroyed Adrian Bambari while Hugo stood by, afraid and helpless to rescue his mentor from your hands—"

"At the time, we thought him a coward for not helping me."

"I was a fool."

"I was a bigger fool." Before he could continue protesting, Nevis reached out a shaky hand and traced the line of his jaw, took comfort in the tiny hair he'd missed when trimming his beard. "Dev—"

"Don't sweet talk me and then—"

Loud knocking broke into his gentle threat.

Grumbling, Devlin got to his feet. "Yes?"

"Sorry, my lord, your daughter and Mage San Rossi are here." The young guard's apologetic eyes darted to Nevis, then away, his face flushed. "They say the matter is very urgent, otherwise they wouldn't have dared interrupt your supper."

Devlin's expression turned cool. "It's—"

"Urgent." Nevis placed a hand on the muscles of his arm, felt their tenseness through the light wool. "I'll go."

"You'll stay."

"I'll go." Nevis smiled at the young guard, caught between the lovers. "Please tell her highness and Mage San Rossi that the king will be with them in just a moment. Thank you."

The guard's eyes slid to Devlin's glowering expression, heaved a sigh of relief when he nodded his approval, and fled.

"Nevis—"

The mage stopped his protest with a soft teasing kiss that subtly changed to something deeper. Devlin held her tight as she wrapped her arms around his neck, wanting nothing more at that moment than to spirit Nevis away to safety. When she finally pulled free, hands resting against his chest, he hugged her once more, fiercely and possessively.

"Dev—"

"They can wait," he whispered, warm breath ruffling her hair.

"No, they can't." Nevis gently, but firmly, disentangled herself from his embrace. "Whether or not it's truly urgent, you have to see them, or they'll accuse you of shirking your duty and me of distracting you from that duty."

"And my duty to you?"

Nevis' laugh was rich with affection. "Duty? I thought it was pleasure." She kissed the very tip of his nose, playfully slapping his hands away. "Tomorrow."

"Tonight."

"Tomorrow. If I don't get some sleep, I'll have Pepo Daken breathing down my neck for missing my cues again." She touched his face once, the caress eloquent, and slipped from the room, coming face-to-face with Alana and Hugo in the anteroom.

"Do you only charge Devlin half your fee if all you do is dine with him?" Fingers entwined with Alana's, Hugo graced Nevis with a smug smile.

"Even the most desirable and skilled whores occasionally offer a free evening to their exclusive clients," Alana responded before Nevis could frame an intelligent answer, her thoughts jumping not to her own defense but back to Alvaron Park and the message scrawled across the front of her theater. "I'll wager my father gets a free evening the next time they're alone together, undisturbed."

Hugo slipped an arm around Alana's slender waist. "Because of the loan he's just agreed to give her?"

"He's got a soft spot in his heart for whores."

Only the nearly impossible desire to one day erase Alana's hatred kept a horrendous insult from escaping. Instead, Nevis said quietly, "Your mother taught you more tolerance and better manners." She tracked the play of emotions on the younger woman's face, saw briefly the innocent, bewildered child of ten years past, the same child who had once considered Nevis Conarkin a friend.

"My mother—" Alana shoved Nevis roughly against the wall, grabbing a handful of the mage's black silk shirt. "Don't you dare speak of my mother. Don't you ever dare speak of my mother."

"Alana." Devlin had opened the door, approaching the trio without any of them aware of his quiet movement. "You may not wish to hear about your mother from Nevis' lips, but you will hear about her from mine. Your mother did teach you more tolerance and better manners." His blue eyes slid over Hugo's neutral expression, then back to his daughter's flushed face. "Now come inside and tell me what's so very urgent that you disrupted a very pleasant supper."

Devlin held out a hand to his daughter, who accepted it, shooting one final silent warning at Nevis. Hugo followed, though not without a parting insult that brought Nevis' fists deep into the pockets of her trousers to avoid strangling him. When they'd all gone into Devlin's study, and Nevis was left alone, she shut her eyes and leaned her head against the wall, trying to decide what to do next.

* * * *

"Come in, child. I've been expecting you."

Nevis paused at the entrance to the cozy parlor above the bakery, eyes adjusting to the soft lamplight, seeking without conscious thought the wooden walking stick whose carved head held a dragon's fiery image to Nevis' eyes. "And why is that?" she quietly challenged, shutting the door behind her with one boot, not turning her back on the older woman.

"Shopkeepers in Port Jambi hear all sorts of rumors about people in the public eye. And when careless people let secrets slip, such as Mage Conarkin's dire financial troubles—"

"They're nonexistent."

"Would you feel less threatened if I offered my shop as collateral rather than taking a loan from Devlin or having you even consider selling off your theater to that pompous parrot?" Dark brown eyes watched

Nevis as the younger mage refused to answer. "I meant that as a genuine offer."

Nevis stood motionless in the doorway "Why?"

"As a measure of good faith, for what you and I once shared."

"You were my mentor and refused to believe me when Adrian turned rogue, and I have to wonder why," Nevis whispered, her tone deadly in its gentleness. "Was it because you already knew the truth, had indeed been leading him down that path of betrayal and greed?"

Clarissa's eyes held honest pain. "How can you say that to me after twenty years of my teaching, guiding you to follow your heart and tap into your sorcery? How can you accuse me of such appalling behavior?"

"How can I say anything else when you refused to believe me, turned away in dismissal, treated me as though I had gone mad—"

"I turned away from your words because it hurt too much to see what Adrian had become," Clarissa whispered, her rough voice trembling with the threat of tears, "to admit that he had rejected my teaching. I didn't help him, Nevis. I swear that." When the younger woman turned away, leaned her head wearily against the door, she repeated, "I didn't help him."

"You didn't try to stop him either. You left that for me."

"I've no answer for that," Clarissa admitted, surprising Nevis. "It's haunted my dreams for the last ten years. My biggest regret, for Adrian's sake and yours, was that I didn't help you. If you've anger still raging at me, let it be because I failed to be there when you faced the worst decision your young heart had ever faced. Let it be because I was a coward, and failed horribly at being your mentor."

Nevis groaned, pushed back from the door, and fled back into the sweet-scented night, putting distance between her grief and Clarissa's.

* * * *

"Should you be walking along the riverbank in the dark by yourself, Mage Conarkin?"

"Should I be walking along the riverbank in the dark with Lily Frascat's attractive and seductive lover?"

"Considering the fact that Lily sent me out here to drag you back inside, I'd say it's not a problem." Remo Savanak smiled, moonlight reflecting on his nearly even white teeth.

"Don't the two of you have better things to keep you occupied than peering out the window looking for wandering mages?"

"We get inspired by the moonlight. Now come along, please, or Lily will make my life fiendishly hellish. And you know that's no lie."

"Remo—" Nevis paused, stuck her hands in the pockets of her ebony breeches. "Tell Lily I'm fine. You need some time alone with her and—"

"She already warned me that if you said any such thing, I should shut you up quite effectively."

"By tying your silk cravat around my mouth?"

"By dangling another loose thread related to the murder of Adam Museo in front of your quite insatiable need for justice."

"That cursed meddling woman—"

"Is as worried about you as Devlin is. Come and soothe her nerves. Let her see you're fine with her own eyes," Remo said, adding softly, "even though you're so obviously not."

"I so obviously am."

The lawyer snorted and offered Nevis his arm. "Shall we?"

"Oh, for the gods' sake, Remo."

But Nevis didn't argue any further, took the attorney's arm, and walked along the path that led past the whorehouse. They entered the well-lit building through the side door, where Chappy Markos waved them past a lively group playing cards in the main parlor. Remo escorted her up the carpet-covered stairs to Lily's private apartment, where the restless madam stopped pacing and stared at the mage.

"Why aren't you with Devlin?"

Nevis slid the attorney an amused glance, crossed her arms, and met the other woman's narrowed eyes with a defiant pose of her own. Biting her lip to hold back a laugh at the flamboyant sight before her, Nevis appraised the bold scarlet gown, trimmed with beads that glittered like diamonds, complementing the very real diamond clip that held Lily's upswept auburn hair in place.

"Are you my nursemaid?"

"I'm your partner and your friend. Why aren't you with Devlin?"

"His heir, in the company of his mage adviser, interrupted our dinner with a very urgent something or other."

"That arrogant—"

"Could have been worse," Nevis let a grin escape, abruptly relaxing for the first time in hours. "Dev could have been enjoying his dessert."

"If Hugo San Rossi overheard that answer, Mage Conarkin, he'd suggest I hire you to work in my establishment." Lily scowled at the mage, then matched her grin. "But it's the kind of answer I love. Now sit."

"Lily—"

"Sit down, Nevis."

"Not before you tell me why you were spying on me. Especially when Remo could have been enjoying his own dessert."

"Don't be cute. I wasn't spying on you. Remo thought it would be romantic to watch the moonlight on the river and—" Lily glanced at her lover, avoiding Nevis' arched eyebrow.

"There's more to the story, old friend."

"Nevis, you might be my dearest friend and partner, but I've no intention of sharing the details of my intimate moments with Remo."

"Lily—"

"Some things are personal."

"If you don't admit there's more to the story, I'm going to bed."

"Yes, since you're being such an obnoxious pest. There is more. Now sit down, and stop looking like the wrath of the gods."

Laughing, Nevis sank onto the couch, propping her black leather boots on a tapestried footstool. "Confess all."

"We had been enjoying the moonlight nearly an hour ago," Lily smiled. "We were, Nevis, so wipe that cynical expression from your face."

"That was about an hour ago."

"Yes. I thought—" Lily's hands jumped to her hips, setting her feathers quivering. "Stop staring at me like that."

"Sorry."

"Liar." Lily released a sigh, her expression becoming more serious. "We saw two people walking along the rocks down by the theater."

Nevis sat up straight, her lighter mood swiftly evaporating. "What were they doing, exactly?"

"Searching. That's what it looked like, anyway," Remo explained, trying unsuccessfully to wave Lily quiet when he caught the interest in Nevis' eyes, but he lost the battle.

"It could have been Hugo and Alana."

"Absolutely not. They were busy harassing me." When Lily protested, Nevis cut her off. "They were. Believe me, they caused a bit of a scene."

"Maybe they were thugs hired by Hugo, searching for the stiletto."

"Maybe they were two lovers tossing stones into the river. Lily, stop, it wasn't them. Not that time," Nevis murmured, getting to her feet.

"What do you mean?" Lily glanced at Remo, signaling him to grab the mage if she made the slightest attempt to leave. "Nevis?"

"I saw Hugo and the Cashogi minister's bodyguard in the park at twilight. They were walking close together."

"How close?"

"Quite. But I don't know why they were there."

"You said it earlier," the attorney suggested. "Two lovers looking for a bit of privacy."

"Maybe."

"And maybe he was looking for the stiletto earlier and sent others to look again while he was interrupting your dinner. Nevis—"

"We've got nothing to prove Hugo's involved with the murder, Lily. Enough of this talk. Frankly, the only reason Hugo may have been in the park was to paint the word 'murderer' in animal blood across the sphere atop my theater."

Lily's protest died as she stared at Nevis, though not for long. "That bastard is trying to drive you mad. Nevis, if he's guilty of murder—"

Nevis suddenly lost all patience. "I've another rehearsal early tomorrow morning, Lily, and I need sleep. I've no time for this ridiculous speculation." She pulled the door open and slammed it forcefully behind her as she left, shaking the paintings along the wall. The mage didn't see Lily's wounded expression, didn't need to, felt the hurt all the same in the heavy silence beyond the shut door. Before she'd even reached the stairs, Nevis stopped, slammed her fist against the velvet-covered wall, and retraced her steps, slowly opening the parlor door with a slight queasiness in her stomach that Lily might throw her out. "I'm sorry."

"If you'd had time to share Devlin's fine body," Lily remarked dryly, shoving aside her relief, "your mood might be sweeter."

"Is that all you think about, madam?"

"What else matters?" Lily's laughter followed the mage down the hall, bringing a smile to her weary face.

* * * *

"I know it's not tomorrow yet."

"It's near enough," Nevis murmured in exasperation. "Dev, it's the middle of the night."

"I couldn't stay away."

Tying her black silk robe around her waist, Nevis shook her head in affectionate resignation and slid the door open, lack of decent sleep evident in the fatigue lines of her face and the shadows beneath her eyes.

Brushing dark brown hair from his forehead, Devlin looked no older than Teddy Quiddle, except for the beard that lined his chin. "Don't be angry. I have a marvelous plan." He kicked off his boots and walked into her bedchamber, tugged back the blankets, sprawled on the bed, fully clothed, and waved her to follow.

"Dev—"

"You need your sleep. And how can you sleep peacefully if you don't feel secure? Now come lie down." Devlin patted the soft mattress, watched her graceful movements as she slipped off her robe, standing beside the bed in a long gown of black silk. When she lay down beside him, Devlin gathered the mage close, kissed the top of her white, short-cropped hair, and whispered, "now sleep."

"Dev—"

"Hush." He stroked Nevis' back, felt the muscles beneath his fingers go slack, and smiled as she fell immediately into a deep asleep. Resting beside the mage for a bit longer until he was certain she wouldn't wake, Devlin rose from the bed with minimal noise. He stood in the shadows, watching Nevis' pale face, the rise and fall of her chest with even breathing, and turned to find his discarded boots.

A scratch at the window, open to the ever-present river breeze, arrested his stealthy movements, and he watched, in horror, fascination, rage, and heart-breaking disappointment, as a blonde head poked through the open window, followed by the rest of the all-too-familiar slender body.

Eyes focused on the sleeping mage, Alana Graham never noticed her father as she gripped a dagger tight in her trembling hand. The young woman stepped closer to the bed, Devlin mimicking her footsteps in his stockinged feet, and paused, the dagger held aloft, blue eyes determined to fulfill her purpose.

"Alana," he whispered her name.

The young princess jumped, heart near stopping, as guilty blue eyes searched the shadows. "Poppa?"

"Put down the dagger."

"Poppa—"

"Dev?" Groggy from deep sleep, Nevis stirred on the bed, eyes half open for a moment or two until she took in the nightmare scene. "For the gods' sake, Dev, what's going on?"

"Magefire light, please."

Nevis scrambled from the bed, away from Alana, who still hadn't relinquished the dagger. With her stiletto, she triggered a magefire sphere from her pouch and set it within the bedside lamp, banishing the shadows. And wished she'd left the room in darkness when she saw the expression on Devlin's face.

"Dev—"

"Drop the dagger, Alana. Now." His voice was a murmur, fraught with cold warning and pain. When the girl finally obeyed, he practically flew across the chamber and grabbed her thin shoulders, shaking her hard, sending blonde hair whirling around her face. "Damn you, girl, what were you thinking?"

"Poppa—"

"Nevis was your friend."

"Nevis was never my friend. She is, and always was, a fraud." Alana pushed her father away with a fair amount of bravado that impressed the mage. "Everyone thinks she's respectable and honorable. But it's all a lie. Don't you believe what Hugo told you this evening?" When her father turned his back in disgust, Alana swiveled to face Nevis. "We know you're dealing secretly with the Cashogi minister, trying to break the truce between our two kingdoms. Hugo saw you meet with Mikaline Nashat aboard one of the ships in the harbor."

Nevis glanced at Devlin, took comfort from the disgust on his face that he didn't believe the lie. "Whoever he saw, it wasn't me."

"Liar."

Nevis shrugged. "You may call me many things, Alana, but I'm not lying about this matter. The first and only time I met Mikaline Nashat was at the merchants' dinner. I should think," she added, horrified at the thought, "that if the minister heard about your accusation, he'd be highly insulted, which would threaten your father's trade negotiations even more."

"Hugo saw you."

"If you believe everything he tells you—"

"He told me that my mother died of a broken heart because of you," the girl spat, blue eyes flashing with spite.

"Your mother—" Devlin went very still, his empty expression warning the mage of his intent.

"No, Dev."

He raised one hand to keep the mage silent, determination clear in every tense muscle of his body, and Nevis knew she couldn't win this battle. Devlin stared at his daughter, blue eyes cold. "Sit down."

"Poppa—"

"Sit down. And listen to what I'm going to tell you."

Unnerved by his manner, the young woman sat on the unadorned bench against the wall.

"Your mother died of a broken heart, that much is true. But not because of Nevis. Not because I loved Nevis Conarkin. We never betrayed your mother though I had ample cause."

"That's a lie. You were lovers before mama died."

"Never. We were friends only. And if Hugo San Rossi is the one whispering that malicious tale, he knows better. He knows the truth of what I'm going to tell you now. Your mother betrayed me, Alana, and the very people she had sworn to serve. She died of a broken heart because her lover died. When Nevis destroyed Adrian Bambari, she destroyed your mother's lover," Devlin said coldly. "And some months later, your mother committed suicide, though everyone believes she took ill and died."

"No." Alana's whisper was filled with horror as she inched back along the bench away from her father. "I heard her cries. I heard her words of hate for Nevis and for you, at your betrayal."

"You heard wrong. Your mother had a passionate affair with Adrian Bambari and very nearly destroyed the peace I'd worked so hard to keep. With her assistance, Adrian planned to let the dissidents from Cashogi into Montbasso, letting them free to spread havoc and rape the countryside and my people. If not for Nevis—"

"You're lying."

"I have proof."

Her laughter surprised Devlin. "Did Nevis conjure the proof for you? Did Nevis make you so blissfully happy in her bed that you believed all her lies and deception?" Alana's voice rose higher with every question. "Had her whoring for you night after night become more important than the truth?"

Nevis was no less startled than Alana by the slap that sent the young woman from the bench to her knees. Devlin had never once touched his daughter in anger, his own wounded expression stabbing at Nevis' heart.

"Get out of my sight."

"Poppa—"

"Pray to the gods I don't drag you before the courts for attempted murder and have you executed. Not to mention slander against a well-respected mage and a foreign diplomat."

Alana struggled to her feet, holding the arm of the bench for support. "Poppa, I love you. I—" When Devlin turned away, Alana started to weep. She fled the chamber, stumbling down the stairs into the darkness, the far-off sound of a closing door the last sign of her presence.

It was only when his daughter was truly gone that Devlin Graham sank to his knees and wept against Nevis' chest.

Chapter Seven

Nevis stared, unseeing, at the raspberry star topping the breakfast bun waiting on her desk, thoughts so impossibly far away that Verdi Casporet nearly went running to fetch Simon. When the mage finally acknowledged the costume designer's presence, Verdi released an audible sigh of relief. Nevis shook her head to clear the remnants of dismal thoughts and eyed the white wig Verdi placed on her desk. "Finished?"

"Yes. As soon as you set a cleansing spell to work on the creature, I'll put it back where it belongs."

"On Gabriella's head?"

"On the dummy head. Same thing." Relieved to bring a smile to her employer's face, Verdi leaned against the doorframe, blocking the entry. "I managed to repair the dummy head, too."

"And finish Hans' shirt? Thank the gods you work for me and not Slick Hands. I could use a few more miracles around here." Eying the suspicious worry on Verdi's face, Nevis stopped her questions with a distracting change of topic. "Have you spoken to Hans yet?"

Verdi ran her fingers through straight black hair, taking the hint. When Nevis Conarkin, an overall even-tempered mage, refused to discuss something, a smart person didn't argue. "Last night, yes."

Nevis waited patiently as the costume designer shifted her weight, knowing full well that Verdi was uncomfortable.

"He told me why he's been so unsettled," Verdi finally admitted. "Hans has been seeing one of Lily's girls." When that comment brought one white eyebrow skyward, Verdi added, "It was news to me, too. By the way, Lily doesn't know, and he'd rather she didn't, at least for the moment."

"Why the big secret?"

"Lily, like you, isn't fond of her employees using Firespark."

"The stuff is poison."

"I know. Hans finally admitted to me that he was ashamed and sorry for not speaking with the constable, but he didn't want word to get out that he'd recently bought Firespark from Adam Museo. Wanted to be sure no one knew about his past purchases before letting Lily know about the girl."

When Verdi shifted her weight again, the mage tipped her chair back so that it rested precariously on two legs. "There's more?"

"His girl is the one Adam beat up."

"For the gods' sake," Nevis murmured, tipping the chair forward again. "That puts him in an awkward position, doesn't it?"

"That's why Hans wanted to keep things quiet, at least until the investigation was over."

"Can't blame him. All right, Verdi, thanks." Nevis picked up the wig, examined it closely. "I'd better cleanse this monstrosity with sorcery, even though it doesn't need it, before Gabriella has a heart attack."

"Make sure you get rid of my lice." Verdi pushed away from the doorframe, preparing to leave.

"And hair."

"Shouldn't be any. I wrapped my hair in a scarf before putting the wig on. So does anyone who wears a wig. Or they should."

"Then whoever borrowed it never bothered to wear a scarf," Nevis said quietly. "Take a look."

Verdi edged closer to the desk, studied the strands of hair caught within the inner webbing. "Curly."

"Looks like Teddy's. If that little imp—"

"It's not brown." Verdi took back the wig and held it by the window, taking full advantage of the sunshine. "Black, like mine."

"But curly."

"Seems like it."

"Seems like possible evidence."

Both women turned at the unexpected, unwelcome voice.

"Constable."

"Good morning, ladies."

"Do you always eavesdrop?"

"Only on murder suspects."

"Now see here." Verdi prepared to launch her slight figure at the constable but Nevis grabbed her arm and squeezed hard.

"Constable's just doing her job," Nevis murmured. "Aren't you?"

"I am." Brea took the wig from Verdi's hand, examined it carefully under the light, and tucked it under her arm, the strands of curly hair safe inside.

"Give that back."

"Verdi—"

"Gabriella needs the wig for opening night. Nevis, you can't let her just take it away."

"Constable?"

"You're a mage. Conjure up another wig." Brea's grin was predatory as Verdi spouted a string of curses at the constable. "Such language, Mistress Casporet. Shall I arrest you for disorderly behavior?" When neither the mage nor costume designer answered, the constable kept her eyes fixed on Nevis' angry expression, spun on her heels, and departed down the stairs.

Nevis waited until Verdi finished growling the unending string of curses. "I'm really sorry."

"Not your fault."

"I could have argued with her."

Verdi raked straight black hair from her eyes, her question one of curiosity, not challenge. "Why didn't you?"

"Selfish reasons. If it's evidence, Verdi, it'll help me, seeing as I don't have curly black hair."

"You're right. And that's not selfish, it's smart." Verdi sagged back against the wall, thinking. "Who does have curly black hair?"

"I don't know," Nevis lied, as three people came immediately to mind. Fani Sneddle, Shayna Kashi, and Slick Hands Barry Faddle. "Listen, Verdi," she said, to distract the younger woman, "if you find me a wig you don't need, trim it down to the right length and shape. I'll bespell it white."

Verdi placed both hands on her hips in disgust. "Why didn't you just do that in the first place?"

"Can't have you thinking I don't need you, now, can I?"

* * * *

The only joy Nevis took from the immensely successful rehearsal was the sight of ten-year-old Teddy Quiddle, sleeping kitten nestled in the crook of his arm, leaning over the balcony in the royal box. The boy's eyes were wide with awe at his aunt's bone-rattling sorcerous effects.

As the controlled tidal wave flowed back toward the drainage system set in the rear of the stage, Pepo Daken, portraying Devlin Graham with his usual flourish, along with Gabriella de la Morsage, playing the part of Nevis Conarkin with far more drama than Nevis ever did, bid a fierce and final good riddance to Hans, expertly playing the role of the treacherous and ill-fated Adrian Bambari.

The tidal wave swept away the renegade mage and his conjured dragon, setting Nevis' nerves on edge once more. Adrian Bambari hadn't died from drowning, but a fatal burst of magefire from Nevis' trembling hand. Shoving aside the heavily guilt-ridden memories, and the image of herself huddled over his body, weeping, Nevis checked that the spell worked as it should. Elaborate costumes, stage sets, and wigs were safe from storm, fire, and flood, thanks to Nevis' protective spells, a matter of both practicality and safety for both the cast and crew and the audience.

"Bravo! Well done! Very well done!"

Nevis peered over the railing as Lily Frascat's saffron-tipped feathers bobbed at the back of her fiery hair in perfect rhythm with her graceful steps up the center aisle. "Think so?"

"How can you ask? Pepo was dashing, Gabriella courageous, and Hans convincingly wicked. The costumes are superb, the set frighteningly realistic, and Gabriella, that wig! I thought sure it was Nevis on the stage."

Lily chatted happily with cast and crew as Nevis tucked her stiletto back in its sheath, waved Teddy down from Devlin's private box, and headed for the ground floor. As she emerged from the corridor into the side aisle, Verdi caught her eye, pointed to Gabriella's head, and grinned. Hans Takat reappeared on stage, safe and sound from his traumatic and rather melodramatic demise.

"Gabriella, you play the role of Nevis Conarkin with great integrity," Lily assured the lead actress, whose expression showed the slightest doubt. Lily, who excelled in smoothing ruffled feathers and soothing tense egos, had the prima donna's self-esteem well in hand. "With your inspired performance, Port Jambi will be reminded how Nevis saved their city and their king. A fact they so easily forget," the madam murmured with genuine feeling.

"A fact they will as swiftly forget again when I come to arrest Nevis Conarkin for the murder of Adam Museo."

A silence fell over cast and crew as Brea Kilganor strode purposefully up the center aisle, dark uniform crisp, stern eyes scanning the stage, ignoring Nevis' presence as the mage joined Lily at the foot of the stage.

"Constable, you're making a rather tedious habit of harassing innocent citizens." Lily's saffron feathers quivered as she spun to face the constable.

"When I'm not convinced they're innocent, I find it advantageous." Brea's eyes roamed the stage, stopped casually at Gabriella's indignant expression, then Pepo's arrogant scowl, and settled, finally, on Hans' scarlet face.

"You have no proof." Lily prodded the constable's perfectly unsullied uniform jacket. "Now unless you do, kindly take your business elsewhere. I find your presence tiresome."

Eyes shifting from Hans' fidgeting fingers to Nevis' blank expression to Verdi Casporet's fighting stance, Brea shrugged. "I have all the proof I need at the moment to see that Nevis Conarkin is trying very hard to convince me that someone framed her for the murder of Adam Museo."

"She didn't do it," Hans blurted, face scarlet, and openly uneasy beneath the stares and whispers.

"Convince me."

"If you knew Nevis as I do, as we all do, you wouldn't need to be swayed, Constable."

"Fine sentiment, boy, but it won't convince a judge."

"Damn you, she's innocent."

"Know something I should know, boy, to persuade me that Nevis Conarkin is indeed innocent?"

"That's enough, constable," Nevis intervened, smiling her thanks to Hans for his fierce defense. "You know you've got nothing to tell yourself that I'm guilty." She turned her back on the woman and spoke to her cast. "She's trying to rattle me, and you all know I don't rattle easily."

"And when you do, best watch out." Verdi grinned from the wings, where Simon watched alongside her, frowning.

"Precisely." Nevis wondered at Simon's expression as she glanced over her shoulder at Brea. "Go bother someone else, Constable."

"I'll be back."

"I wager you will. Shall I save you a seat for opening night?"

"Charge her double," Verdi shouted.

"Good idea." Nevis smiled as the constable departed amid a flurry of catcalls and insults. "Settle down, children, settle down. Lily was right. You were all incredibly wonderful and deserve a day or two off. Go home and play. You earned it fairly. But be back the day before opening night for one more run-through from start to finish. And you, Teddy Quiddle, get yourself and that nuisance kitten back to work next door before your mother comes to skin me alive."

Dismissed, they good naturedly jostled each other off the stage. Simon headed her way, still frowning, as Hans lingered nearby, took a deep breath, and caught Nevis' eye. When she came closer, he knelt on the stage so that his voice wouldn't carry. Nevis shot a warning to Simon, signaling him back to give the actor privacy.

"Thanks for the defense, but I'd rather you didn't make an enemy of Constable Kilganor. She's not a pleasant adversary."

"I don't care," Hans grumbled, pushing brown hair from his forehead, still damp from his exertions. "She's wrong. You didn't murder Adam."

"Know who did?" Nevis kept her eyes fixed on his face, saw the flush creeping upward from his neck when he shook his head.

"Wish I did, Nevis, truly, so we could end this nightmare for you. Nevis, listen," Hans stole a glance at Lily, who was busy complimenting the carpenter for the fortress set in the last scene, "Verdi talked to you, didn't she? I mean, it's fine. I thought she might."

"I asked her to talk to you first."

"Lily doesn't know anything about—" Hans refused to say the girl's name with Lily so near.

"No. And she won't unless I have to tell her. But you stay off Firespark, and I'll do my best. Deal?"

"Deal. Thanks, Nevis. You're something special." He shot to his feet and fled as Lily turned in their direction.

Nevis waved her friend over, and caught Simon's eye. "Trouble?"

"Some."

"Need some privacy?" Lily asked, joining them as Nevis grabbed her arm, preventing the madam from leaving.

"I might need some moral support. What's wrong, Simon?"

"Coin box is empty again, boss."

Nevis leaned back against the stage, arms crossed as she thought of the implications.

"Who?" Lily asked, glancing at Simon Masters for a clue.

"Wish we knew." Nevis shut her eyes, thinking. "We've had two thefts from the petty cash box and one ring from Gabriella's drawer. Someone needs funds, and seems willing to take it in small amounts."

"We're not exactly overflowing with profits, boss."

"All the more reason why your cast and crew should be the last to steal from you," Lily murmured, studying her friend's disheartened expression. "Come outside and breathe fresh air. It'll help you think."

"I have work to do."

"It'll be waiting when you get back, right, Simon?"

"Absolutely. Go on, boss. You told the children to play. Don't you deserve some free time, too?"

"Don't even ask, Simon. Just command. Come along, Nevis. Don't argue. You look like hell, and I want to know why."

"I'll be upstairs if you need me." Simon winked at Lily and left his reluctant employer in the madam's capable and persuasive hands.

Nevis sighed and pushed away from the stage, grumbling as she led her friend out the side door toward the park. Lily waited, just barely, until they were outside before pouncing.

"Devlin canceled an important meeting today with trade minister Nashat, then he canceled his meeting with the legal guild. He gave no excuse for either action, according to Remo."

Nevis caught sight of Teddy running across the park toward the orphanage building, kitten cradled carefully in his arms. "He doesn't have to give any excuses to anyone for his behavior."

"True, but then that would make him a tyrant. Devlin's far more enlightened and polite than that. Unless he's awfully upset," Lily added, practically shoving the taller woman onto the nearest park bench.

"I'm not in the mood for an interrogation."

"I don't give a damn whether or not you're in the mood. You're troubled, exhausted, and heartsick."

"I'm tired."

"I've seen you tired before. Damn it, Nevis, what's going on? Devlin's been so careful in handling the Cashogi delegates for weeks and then just brushes them off as though they were meaningless. Doesn't make sense. Same with the legal guild. They're not so important, but he enjoys arguing with the contentious bastards, and yet he canceled them, too." Lily's saffron feathers quivered as she crossed her arms, towering over the seated mage.

Nevis shut her eyes.

"If I have to torture you by holding sticky, sugar-coated cakes just out of reach, I will. Even though that means giving Clarissa Bracken a fair amount of business that she doesn't deserve."

"By the gods, Lily, shut up. Sit down."

"Will you escape?"

"I'm too tired."

"Probably the truth," Lily muttered, taking a seat within easy reach of the mage, should Nevis decide to slip away. "Tell me."

"Dev came by last night."

"No wonder you're so tired."

"He came to tuck me in, thinking I'd only fall asleep if I felt safe."

"And wearied out from hours of love making."

"Not even a minute. Believe it or not, he came to tuck me in and keep watch until I fell asleep."

Lily blinked, green eyes softening at the genuine affection between the two lovers. "That was sweet."

"Yes." Nevis shut her eyes again, reliving the previous night's horror. "It was. It was also fortuitous," she added quietly, daring a glance at the brothel owner, "because he saved my life."

"Nevis, what happened?"

At the horrified look on her friend's face, Nevis explained, "Alana crawled through my window and tried to murder me."

Lily started to speak, fell silent, tried again, shook her head, and gaped, her saffron feathers motionless.

"That's about how we felt, too."

"Poor Dev."

Lily stared past the mage, where traffic on the river flowed swiftly past, sending and receiving goods to and from Port Cordillero. Brigadier Bridge yawned wide, its middle section open and lifted to allow the last of three large vessels to sail through. If the trade negotiations with Cashogi were successful, three-masted ships would again be sailing back-and-forth, heavily laden with lumber, works of art, leather goods, colorful fabrics, and so much more, between every one of Montbasso's eager ports and the Cashogi mainland.

"What did he do?" When Nevis didn't answer, Lily stared at her friend's grim expression, and guessed. "Devlin told Alana the unadorned truth about her mother, didn't he?"

"The whole cursed story."

"She denied it."

"Sure."

"And broke her father's heart."

"Not for thinking him a liar, you understand," Nevis said sadly, "but for trying to kill me."

Lily sighed heavily, tucked a loose feather into place before the river breeze sent it flying. "Will he ever forgive her?"

"That's the question, isn't it, old friend?" Nevis watched Brigadier Bridge swing slowly shut again. "Alana also told me their urgent news."

"That necessitated interrupting your dinner?"

Nevis nodded. "Hugo claims to have seen me aboard one of the Cashogi vessels in the harbor, plotting some treason with Minister Nashat."

"That lying swine."

Nevis shrugged, green eyes thoughtful. "Makes you wonder where he would get an idea like that, doesn't it?"

Lily never got a chance to answer, as an unwelcome voice intruded into their private conversation. "What a glorious sight on such a marvelous sunny day. Two of Port Jambi's beauties— Whatever am I saying? The two most beautiful ladies in the entire kingdom of Montbasso are here before me, enjoying the early summer's breeze along the river, brightening the day even more for my fortunate eyes."

Nevis slid a glance at Lily, then away, afraid she'd be unable to stop laughing. "Master Faddle, what brings you to Alvaron Park?"

The theater owner tugged at his drooping mustache, carefully taming his perfect dimples into a somber expression that had both women curious. "I came to scold you, Mage Conarkin."

"Me?"

"Indeed." Slick Hands edged closer to Nevis' side of the bench, fingers itching to touch her shoulder. But Nevis deftly got to her feet and faced him, eye to eye. "Yes, indeed. I came to scold you. There you are, in dire financial straits, and you don't have the decency to ask me for help."

Nevis had an exceedingly difficult time keeping her expression as somber as Barry's. "It wouldn't have been right."

"Right? What's wrong with you, woman? You and I, Nevis, have been friendly competitors ever since you opened your sorcerous theater. If I were in trouble, I'd come straight to you."

"Not for funds, I hope," Lily said dryly, "seeing how Nevis barely has enough to keep her cast and crew from poverty."

"Of course not," Barry agreed, stroking one side of his drooping mustache. "But I would have come knocking on her door for sympathy and advice."

"And I would have gladly given it," Nevis replied, tucking her hands in the pocket of her breeches as Barry's hands sought hers to demonstrate his search for advice. "But coming to you with my money troubles wouldn't have been appropriate, Barry. And though I know you'd dearly love to purchase my theater—"

"Devlin talked me out of that," Barry admitted, looking exceedingly ill at ease, though he brightened up almost immediately. "For the moment, anyway. He suggested that purchasing your theater when you were down and out, and certainly not in the market anyway, might give the public the wrong impression. Under the circumstances," the peacock shrugged, raking black curls from his eyes, reminding Nevis uneasily of the wig, "I believe Devlin's judgment is correct."

"Thank the gods," Lily murmured, her words unheard as Barry tried to maneuver Nevis back against the bench.

"Though I'm not certain that his generosity in extending you a loan is giving the right impression either. One might say his interest is too personal. If I had loaned you the necessary funds," he frowned as Nevis managed to put the bench between them, under Lily's bemused scrutiny, "the message would have been clear."

"Message?" Nevis blinked.

"That Port Jambi merchants help each other. What a marvelous message to send, not only to the public, Nevis, but to the Cashogi delegates."

"Good point."

"Then you'll take the loan from me?"

"No," Nevis smiled, squeezing his arm while keeping her distance, "but I'll always remember your generosity."

"But Nevis—"

"Devlin will be impressed at your thoughtfulness, Barry. He thinks so highly of you, as do I. So highly, in fact, that I told the Cashogi trade minister that he and his companion would be disappointed if they didn't attend one of your performances while visiting Port Jambi."

"You did?" Perfect dimples reappeared. "Thank you."

"It's the least I can do, Barry."

"For what?"

"For not selling you my theater."

* * * *

"Did you see Devlin last night?"

Nevis glanced up, distracted, from the ledger book she'd been gloomily perusing, her still-untouched sticky breakfast cake pushed off to the side, near the carved statue of the goddess Janni, as Lily Frascat swept into her office the next day near noon. Fiery hair unbound and suspiciously without a feather, the madam perched on the cluttered desk, green eyes dangerous.

"Well, did you?"

"No."

"Then come along. You'll see Devlin today, though he won't recognize you. Just as well." Lily reached across the desk, snatched the accounting ledger from the mage's hand, and snapped it shut. With a charming smile, Lily slid the book neatly into place on the shelf behind the desk. "Let's go. The races are starting in less than one hour."

"Races?" Nevis stared at her friend as though the brothel owner had admitted her deepest desire to become a priestess of the unofficial gods in any one of the defunct seven houses of worship. "That's not quite how I intended to raise the funds to repay the loan from Devlin."

"We're not going to wager."

"Then why are we going to the races?"

"To spy."

"By the gods, Lily—"

"Stop wasting my time with meaningless, unconvincing arguments." Without waiting to see whether the mage followed, Lily flowed gracefully from the office, down the stairs, and along the corridor in search of the costume designer. "Ah, Verdi, just the woman I need to see. Though you do work far too hard."

"Tell Nevis, won't you?" Verdi grinned as the mage appeared, a dazed expression on her pale face.

"Nevis, did you hear? Now Verdi, we need your assistance."

"Lily, for the gods' sake—"

"Hush, Nevis, Verdi and I have work to do and very little time in which to do it. So, Verdi, let's get down to the business at hand."

"Which is?"

"I need some clothes to fit Nevis and me. For Nevis," the madam murmured, emerald eyes scanning the hanging costumes, "a skirt, something bright. Ah, yes, just the thing. Not too heavy for this time of year. We're in luck." Lily pulled out a fine light wool crimson skirt and plaid vest, holding both against Nevis' tall figure. "You're not using this costume at the moment, are you, Verdi?"

"No, but—" Verdi darted a wary glance at her employer, fully aware of the mage's disapproval and reluctance, as well as Lily's power of persuasion. Instinct warned her to follow Lily's lead rather than wait for the mage's approval.

"Lily—"

"Hush, Nevis. Go see if it fits."

"It's scarlet."

"Precisely why it'll disguise your appearance. Now go and try the skirt on. Now. This very minute. Verdi, have you a wig you don't need? Ah, there, the blonde one. That should do. Here, Nevis, take this along." Without pausing for breath, Lily tossed the wig at her friend. "Verdi, have you still that costume you made for the elderly dandy in last season's play?"

Verdi Casporet's mouth opened and shut. "Sure." Not daring to look at the mage any more, particularly since that same mage hadn't budged, Verdi rummaged through the clothes rack in the back of the claustrophobic room and pulled out a black-and-white-checked jacket with matching breeches.

"Your character was bald, wasn't he?"

"Wore a skin-tone wig. Here."

"Perfect. Add a feathered cap, Verdi, and Nevis and I are off to the races. Come along, Nevis. Stop grumbling. It's rude." Arms clutching various items of clothing, Lily winked at Verdi, swept past the mage, and headed for the adjacent dressing room. She paused at the open door. "I've the carriage waiting outside, Nevis. Come along. Time is swiftly passing."

The mage released a heavy melodramatic sigh of despair that fluttered the blonde strands of the wig she held and preceded Lily into the tiny dressing room. Nevis tossed the clothes on a chair and slid out of her black boots and breeches, keeping the stiletto and bottomless pouch in sight. She pulled the skirt over her head and fastened the buttons beneath Lily's appraising eye.

"Use your belt to tighten up the waist, tuck the pouch under the vest, and do something with that appalling weapon."

Several suggestions nearly leaped from the mage's tongue as to what Lily could do with the stiletto, but Nevis obediently slid it into the top of her boot. Already stuffing her shirt into the gaudy checkered breeches, Lily eyed the mage as she slipped into the plaid vest.

"For the gods' sake, Lily, why are we doing this?"

"Devlin has invited the Cashogi trade minister and his bodyguard to the races, an event he hasn't canceled, so Remo told me by way of Finlay Oscram. Devlin's favorite white filly, Royal Champion, is in the first race. And Hugo San Rossi and Alana Graham are tagging along because the Cashogi minister asked that they be invited. Finlay will be there, too."

"I can't go, Lily. Dev hasn't invited me."

"He hasn't invited Carmelita either, but she's going." The madam grinned, lowering her voice into a gruff approximation of a man's baritone. "You have to go, Nevis. It's a chance to eavesdrop. And since you probably shouldn't use sorcery because Hugo would sense it, a disguise is the next best thing."

"Lily—"

The madam ignored her friend's plea, fastened her checked breeches, tugged the jacket over her shirt, and threw a scarf at the mage. "For your hair, Carmelita. Makes it easier to slip the wig over your head."

Resigned to being manipulated, Nevis mimicked Lily's determined movements and soon had a long blonde wig covering her hair. Lily, as a balding gentleman, was quite convincing as long as she left the jacket unbuttoned and tucked in her breasts.

"Incredible," Verdi breathed, when both women re-emerged. "No one will recognize you."

"As long as we keep our voices indistinct and play our roles, that's the idea. Nevis, let's go. Verdi, many thanks, but you never saw us."

"Saw who?" The costume designer's grin faded. "Look, Nevis—" She flushed, a bit embarrassed. "I don't know what you're up to, but be careful, will you? I don't fancy myself working for someone else."

"No one else would let you get away with the shoddy work you're always doing," Nevis tossed back lightly. "Stop frowning, we'll be fine. Lily— What's your name, anyway?"

"Eldridge."

"Right. Eldridge will protect me." Nevis led the way out the side door by the brothel, where Lily's trusted driver waited patiently, not bothering to blink as his male passenger helped the female one up the steps.

Neither woman spoke as the carriage rattled along the cobblestone road toward Brigadier Bridge, and over it, to the far side of the Basol River and the open farmlands beyond that kept the city alive. Nearing the crowded racetrack, which was set at a lovely scenic point along the softly curving riverbank, Lily scrutinized Nevis' glum expression and attempted to talk her out of it.

"You're not doing anything wrong."

"It feels like it."

"That's because you're always trying to be honorable. I'll tell you this much, old friend, regardless of whether or not Hugo San Rossi is guilty of any involvement in Adam's murder, we've got to get him away from Alana. She'll never see reason as long as he whispers in her ear."

"Not my place to tell the girl who to bed."

"It is if you're to be her stepmother." Lily's fiery expression dared the mage to argue. "Sooner or later, she'll have to accept your place beside her father. And she'll have to accept the truth, and the truth includes your innocence of whatever lies Hugo has told her about your part in her mother's fate."

Nevis shrugged and declined to answer as the carriage passed through the stately wrought iron gates that opened onto a circular drive leading to the clubhouse. Beyond the huge stone building, the racetrack and paddocks were well situated with a lovely river view. When the carriage rolled to a halt, the driver opened the door, listened politely to Lily's instructions, and watched as Eldridge helped a grumbling Carmelita negotiate the narrow steps.

"Come along, dear. Watch that last step."

Nevis muttered something rude that brought the driver's eyebrows skyward. He dutifully returned to his seat and drove the carriage away as his two passengers strolled, arm in arm, through the clubhouse entry, filled with noise and crowds waiting in line to place a wager at the ticket windows or discuss the changing odds.

Lily steered the mage through the building and back out into the bright sunshine where the glitter of sunlight on the river made Nevis instinctively shade her eyes. They wandered down to the track and casually leaned against the railing, as Lily's cool green eyes scanned the private boxes above the rows of common seats.

"Devlin's upstairs. Don't look."

"Is he alone?"

"Apart from the two half-clad, bosomy ladies on either side—" Lily chuckled as the mage started to peek, caught herself, and flushed. "As though he would even look at another woman when he so obviously adores you. Now, Carmelita, stop grumbling. The Cashogi trade minister is sitting with him, and Alana is as far away from her father as public appearance will allow. She's talking to our friendly banker." Lily coughed into her hand. "Dev seems distracted."

Nevis dared a swift glance to the upper gallery, her heart nearly stopping as Devlin's restless blue-eyed gaze scanned the noisy crowds, and passed her right by. "Where's Hugo?"

"And the Cashogi's bodyguard?"

"Right. I'll wager they're off in a quiet little private spot out of Alana's sight. And he has the nerve to implicate me in clandestine meetings."

Lily grunted and escorted the mage toward the paddocks where the restless horses were on display for their proud owners and prospective gamblers. "Remo never wagers before taking a close look at these beauties."

"Smart man." Nevis stumbled over a nonexistent stone, purposely bringing Lily closer as the madam helped steady her. "Over there, in the shaded corner, by King's Champion."

"Shall we take a close look at that white-maned beauty?" Lily suggested, adding in Nevis' ear, "And see why the two lovers are arguing?"

"Are they?"

"Apparently." Lily draped an arm over Nevis' shoulder and pointed out the fine snowy features of King's Champion, both women within easy hearing range of a very distracted Hugo San Rossi and Shayna Kashi.

"No more Firespark," the Cashogi bodyguard hissed, her voice quivering with anger and impatience. "Not until you pay for what I've already supplied you. My sources won't deal with a man who holds back."

"But you like a man who holds back." Hugo ignored the animated conversation of the two prospective, gaudily dressed gamblers standing nearby. "So you said the other night."

"I'm talking business, Hugo. Cashogi drugs are expensive because they're potent and better than the trash your countrymen distribute. Pay me first for the last supply of drugs, then I'll get you more."

"I can't. Not yet. If I withdraw funds at the moment from Finlay Oscram's bank, he'll be suspicious."

"Why? Have you done anything but harass that white-haired whore?"

"She's got friends watching me. I have to be careful."

"Surely you can withdraw your own funds whenever you wish. There's nothing remotely suspicious—"

"Shayna, you don't understand." Hugo caressed the strands of her long black curls with a sensuous motion that appeared to calm the angry woman. "I have to watch every move I make."

"You should have thought of that before you ordered expensive goods." The petite bodyguard looked past Lily's gauche feathered cap, her expression pensive. "I can't quite believe," she said quietly, "that the mage adviser to the king of Montbasso doesn't have his own supply of riches tucked away."

"It's true."

"Hugo, please. I'm not a fool. If you want the Firespark as desperately as you protest, so you can sell it for profit, then take your gold or jewels or whatever treasure you have stashed away in your private hideaway and go to a broker."

"And get less than half the value?" The mage blurted, caught back further words that might only serve to confirm Shayna's suspicions, and ran his fingers down the side of her velvet-clad arm, seeking to distract the woman. "Really, Shayna, I'm no fool. Only wait a few days more, and I'll have the funds from the orphanage."

The Cashogi bodyguard tossed her long dark curls as she spun back to face him. "And how will you accomplish that feat? Have you bespelled the judges?"

"Surely not. Just a simple matter of knowing some tidbits about their personal backgrounds, and—"

"Blackmail."

"Must you be so crude?" When the woman didn't answer, Hugo's voice took on an unexpectedly pleading note. "I have people willing to buy the drugs at your exorbitant foreign prices."

"Then they should be willing to give you the money."

"Shayna, be realistic. They may be willing clients for the Firespark, but they're not gullible."

"You mean they don't trust you."

"I mean they don't trust my Cashogi contacts." Growing impatient, Hugo grabbed her slender, muscled forearm, but the woman pulled away. "Don't make a scene. Listen, I need to rebuild my business. With my most reliable customer dead and buried—" Hugo shrugged as though Adam Museo didn't matter. "The pathetic bastard never had enough money, anyway. Adam always owed me something."

"Sounds familiar."

"That's not fair. He didn't have people watching every little step he took. I do. And I need to rebuild my business," he repeated. "My reputation—"

"Is well on its way down river and out to sea, Mage San Rossi. I have eyes and ears on the streets of Port Jambi, too. I've no patience to get involved with a man who can't handle his adversaries. By now," she turned her back on him, stared out at the white filly, "a potent and fearless mage would have dealt with Nevis Conarkin as successfully as she dealt with Adrian Bambari."

Hugo said nothing for a long tense heartbeat, then, "Your personal feelings about Nevis and her role in your family's troubles shouldn't come into play with our business transactions." Hugo turned the Cashogi woman slowly around to face him.

"But they do. You're afraid to move and pay me what you owe, all because of a white-haired bitch who has the king wrapped around her littlest finger. If she hadn't destroyed Adrian, my countrymen would have succeeded, and there would never have been any question of my family's innocence or guilt." Shayna's eyes flashed fire. "And you, Mage San Rossi, could be rich and far more potent if you were better at using your intelligence and your position to proper advantage. But the people of Port Jambi don't like you very much. That's where you went wrong. Nevis Conarkin—"

"I'm trying to convince the ignorant people of Port Jambi to despise Nevis as much as they despise me." Hugo's voice held undisguised bitterness. "Have a little bit of faith in me, Shayna, and patience. You won't be sorry. Set a meeting with your supplier two nights from now. In Alvaron Park, as always. We don't know how long the ship will stay in port before it returns to Cashogi with courier messages. I need to take advantage of that hidden cargo." Hugo leaned over to whisper in her ear, prompting a grudging laugh from the Cashogi bodyguard.

"Lovely idea."

"But first, here's an offering of good faith. Watch the first race. Watch what happens to King's Champion."

The two conspirators contentedly slipped away, and Nevis muttered beneath her breath, moving instinctively to trail them. Lily's arm snaked around her shoulder and pulled her close, pointing at the nearest roan.

"Carmelita, your wagering is ill advised. Look at this beauty." Feeling the mage struggling beneath her grip, the madam hissed in her ear, "Don't you dare move. We've got company. Don't even look up."

From the corner of her eye, Nevis caught sight of the constable emerging from the shadows, not very far from where Hugo and Shayna had been standing. Brea was out of uniform, dressed no differently than most of the working-class gamblers. Nevis drew a deep breath as the short, stocky woman swept past, following the other two, her dark, white-speckled hair ruffled by the breeze. "Close."

"Very."

"Come on."

"Nevis—"

"Hugo's planning something nasty for that unsuspecting white filly." Determined, Nevis pulled Lily along, back toward the clubhouse. They saw the mage and his foreign companion place a huge wager on the roan that had been standing in the paddock beside King's Champion.

Lily dug into her pocket. "If you're going to help that beauty win, I might as well take advantage."

"Oh, no." Nevis slapped Lily's hand away from her pocket. "That's completely unethical."

"Nevis—"

"Carmelita," the mage corrected absently, watching Hugo and Shayna head back toward the stairs that would bring them to the upper gallery. "Come on."

She guided Lily back outside toward the racetrack, down by the railing, as close as possible to the curved track. As they watched the fidgety horses being led to their posts, Nevis idly glanced upward in the direction of the gallery, unconsciously matching the smile on Devlin's face as he caught sight of the white filly. When his eyes scanned the other horses, distractedly turning in her direction, Nevis froze as his sapphire eyes narrowed and locked on her face beneath its blonde wig.

"Cursed idiot." Slowly, she broke free of his gaze and intently studied the restless horses.

"Carmelita, my dear, what have you done?"

"Somehow attracted the attention of a sharp-eyed monarch. Don't scold. I didn't do anything on purpose."

"I'll wager his lust led him to spot you."

"Hush, don't distract me. I need to concentrate."

When the horses leaped forward at the blare of the starter's horn, Nevis leaned along the rail, eyes fixed on King's Champion. The roan, projected to finish in second place, stayed close behind the white filly from the outset. Nevis had no time to think when the filly abruptly stumbled, a move so unexpected, yet so smooth, that it appeared natural. But Nevis had felt the uncoiling of magery, and swiftly murmured an incantation, guiding the filly's legs until she regained her balance in a motion equally smooth and natural. Regaining her confidence, King's Champion swept over the finish line, not a moment too soon, white mane flowing gracefully in the wind.

"Wish you hadn't stopped me from wagering."

Nevis smiled and released a deep sigh of relief at the horse's safety. Cheers from the winners in the crowd turned swiftly to hisses as a harried-looking race official stepped up to the wooden platform, his expression grave.

"The race has been declared invalid." The official waved frantically at the crowd to quiet their protests. "The royal mage adviser, Hugo San Rossi, has just made a serious accusation that sorcery was used to help King's Champion recover from an unfortunate stumble." The official indicated Hugo stepping up to the platform, black eyes scanning the crowds, his whole body radiating irritation.

"Don't look."

"I see him."

"Carmelita—"

"He has an astonishingly bold pair of balls."

"Not many mages in Port Jambi," Lily murmured. "One would guess he's seeking to blame Mage Conarkin, that poor harassed woman, who may even, perish the thought, be a traitor to the crown. Or perhaps Mage Bracken has taken time from her unending hours in the bakery—"

"Don't start."

"Just expressing my opinion."

"Where's he going?"

"Apparently home with Alana. That's my guess, anyway."

"You're probably right. He—" Nevis tensed, green eyes staring straight ahead. "I didn't know he and Slick Hands were friendly."

"What? Oh, damn. Look at the two of them chatting away. Nevis, it can't mean anything. Barry wouldn't be so open about it."

"He's never seen me at the racetrack, so why not?"

"If Hugo's just made a charge about sorcery—"

"He could just as easily think that Hugo bespelled the horse and then helped her along, with me as the implied culprit." Nevis sighed, recalling the black curly strands of hair inside the wig. "There he goes."

"Looks like Hugo just warned him away."

"Does indeed. What's Dev doing?"

"He's very busy writing something down."

Nevis screwed up her eyes. "That's peculiar. He—"

"Come along, Carmelita," Lily instinctively grabbed the mage's arm before she headed in Devlin's direction. "We'd best get home, too, before the crowd turns ugly." Her voice dropped to a whisper. "I'm sorry, old friend. I've probably made it worse by dragging you here."

"Don't be. Hugo would have found another outlet."

The two friends walked unhurriedly in the direction of Lily's carriage out past the clubhouse, not completely surprised to find Brea Kilganor waiting patiently beside the unhappy driver.

The constable eyed the two women. "Looking for a position as an actress, Mage Conarkin?"

"You're not in uniform either."

"I don't wager when I'm on duty. Have you decided to leave the racetrack with your winnings?"

"No winnings or losses, Constable," Lily snapped, still annoyed that Nevis stopped her from placing a bet. "We didn't wager."

"Not even on King's Champion?"

"Decidedly not." Lily headed for the carriage as the driver stretched to open the door. "My partner advised me it would be unethical."

"Because she helped it recover from a stumble?"

"Because she helped it recover from a stumble caused by another mage." Lily waved Nevis inside the conveyance but the mage stood motionless, facing the constable, her stance defiant.

"One mage's word against another's?" Brea crossed her arms, monitoring the troubled expression on Nevis' face.

"If you were standing near that other mage," Nevis said quietly, "then you heard his words about King's Champion." When the constable's expression remained neutral, she added, "I'll also assume you heard about his plans to meet a Cashogi drug merchant in the park two nights from now."

"I heard many things, Mage Conarkin, and I'd strongly advise you to stay the hell away from Alvaron Park at night." The constable pushed away from the carriage, paused, nearly nose-to-nose with the mage. "Tell me why Hugo San Rossi would murder his most reliable Firespark customer? Tell me why Hugo San Rossi would even deal in the illegal drug trade?"

Before Nevis could answer, Lily stuck her bald head out the door. "Hugo San Rossi murdered Adam because he wanted the money from the orphanage. A better guarantee than getting money from a man who was always in debt and never repaid his loans or paid for his drug purchases, despite his thriving business."

When Lily sat back, the constable asked, "And why he would deal in the illegal drug trade?"

"I don't know, Constable. Greed?"

"Perhaps." The constable nodded, absently shoving white-flecked hair from her eyes, taking careful note of Nevis' pensive expression. "And perhaps not. Good day, ladies."

"Good riddance," Lily grumbled as Nevis finally stepped up into the carriage, moments before the driver hastily shut the door in case the constable changed her mind and came back to harass them.

Before the driver had climbed onto his seat, a young guard, the same guard who had interrupted Nevis and Devlin at supper two nights earlier, came rushing up to the carriage window. "Your pardon. One moment, please." The young man's eyes held no recognition as he handed a note to Nevis. "From his majesty."

Nevis hesitated to take the note.

"I'm to wait for an answer."

The mage kept her expression exquisitely neutral, not daring to glance at Lily, as she unfolded the note, Devlin's neat script flowing over the page.

"Deduct the funds I would have won today on King's Champion from the loan. I'll take it out of his hide instead."

A smile broke out on the mage's face, and she laughed aloud. "Tell—" She folded the note carefully and tucked it in her pocket. "Tell his majesty that it's a marvelous idea."

* * * *

"Magic, magic, magic! Please, Nevis, please."

"Mage Conarkin is still eating her supper, and you pests—"

Nevis wiped her mouth daintily with the rough cotton table napkin and lightly touched her sister's arm. "I'm finished."

May Quiddle, wavy brown hair sweetly disheveled, stared at the plate in front of her older sister, a plate, chipped at two points, that looked barely touched. "You're as bad as the children. I don't let them leave the table until they've eaten every last morsel on their plate."

"True, and you shouldn't," Nevis kept her expression diplomatic, a useless effort that her sister saw through only too well. "However, as I had already eaten a short while ago with Lily, maybe someone else might care to nibble on the rest of my sweetened summer potatoes and roast chicken?"

Green eyes scanned the table as one or two of the older boys, busy growing like unrestrained weeds, no less than Teddy, looked expectantly at the mage, though didn't dare voice their desire.

May glanced around the table, made sure that the little ones had filled their bellies, and nodded. "Any volunteers?"

Three hands shot up, one of them Teddy's, and Nevis smiled behind a feigned cough as May muttered at the lot of them, distributing the remains of her sister's largely untouched meal.

While they were busy gobbling up the bonus, May leaned closer to Nevis. "You probably haven't eaten all day," she said quietly, "though I've a feeling you've visited for other reasons."

"Distraction's good for the soul." Nevis cut across May's immediate questions and pushed back her chair. "I'll go distract these hooligans so you can have a little peace and quiet."

Without waiting for her sister's protest, Nevis headed for the parlor, the little ones following right behind as the mage sank to the worn, spotless rug, not surprised to find the smallest red-haired child snug beside her knees, making room for the kitten that bounded free of Teddy's hands.

"Can't wait for dessert, Aunt Nevis," Teddy grinned, wiping his mouth on the cuff of his sleeve. "That new baker brought along a tray of cinnamon cookies and raspberry tarts."

"That new baker?" Nevis glanced at May for confirmation.

"Yes, Clari. She told us she's been baking your breakfast cakes, and, so far, you haven't complained. Seems she heard about the orphanage and thought to bring these hooligans a treat. Not that they deserve it."

"Oh, Ma. Aunt Nevis, have you seen her cane? It's got a wonderful lion's head carved in wood."

"Lion?"

To Teddy's bewilderment, Nevis stared at her nephew in silence, then broke out into a huge proud smile. If Teddy saw a lion's head on Clarissa's walking stick, that spoke volumes for the boy's character, not that the mage was surprised, with the boy coming from such honest, hard-working parents. Clarissa's cane spoke eloquently of others, too, she thought sadly, recalling Adrian's snake and Hugo's fox. Nevis still wasn't quite certain whether her dragon's head was something of which she should be proud or ashamed.

"No, no, I haven't seen it yet. Now, who's ready for magic?"

"Can you make a fierce storm?" One of the boys asked, wiping his mouth on the sleeve of his shirt in perfect imitation of Teddy, prompting a sigh of despair from May. "Teddy said they're as loud as real storms."

"They are, but they're a bit too fierce for this small building. However," she responded immediately to the boy's disappointment, "if Mistress Quiddle doesn't have any objection—"

"Objection to what?" May towered over the seated, sprawled children, a mock frown on her pretty face.

"To taking the children next door to my sorcerous theater on a quiet afternoon and showing them what Teddy's talking about. Fierce storms—" Catching sight of Kimmi's wide-eyed expression, Nevis ruffled her disheveled auburn curls, "It's magic, remember? It's not real."

"But it looks and sounds so real," Teddy said eagerly in spite of his aunt's silent warning.

May glanced at her sister with reluctance. "Then maybe the little ones shouldn't go along."

As those same little ones voiced an incredibly loud and vehement protest, Nevis threw up her hands and laughed. "Stop. Hush. Everyone will go. But not tonight. Give me a few weeks to get my new play started, and I promise you'll have your very own performance."

"You spoil them."

"No, I don't, May. They're going to be completely well behaved or there won't be any private performance. Right?" The responding shouts of agreement overwhelmed May's protest, and she surrendered, laughing, as the mage rummaged in her bottomless leather pouch for a spell.

Nevis pulled out the sphere holding the miniature seals that she had created only days earlier. Keeping it aloft and out of reach, she carefully retrieved the stiletto, mindful of Kimmi's tiny fingers clinging possessively to her black breeches. Touching the stiletto to the sphere, Nevis looked at the miniature seals and gasped, swiftly pulling back the dagger.

"What's wrong?"

Nevis kept her voice calm, expression completely unreadable. "Sorry. Wrong spell."

Before May could interrogate her, Nevis pretended to pull another sphere from her pouch, unobtrusively creating the illusion of a sphere. The mage imitated her usual ritual of triggering the spell with a thrust of her stiletto and concentrated on making a vivid illusion over the heads of the watching children. Resheathing the weapon, Nevis re-created her original spell of dancing, frolicking seals bouncing a laughing, smiling little girl from one to the other. As she extended the illusion spontaneously, only immense control prevented Nevis from shouting her anger and rage at what had so nearly happened. The laughing, innocent faces, so caught in the wonder of her sorcery, would have been helpless at the foul magery she might have unleashed had she not re-checked the spell.

* * * *

Leaving behind the crush of hugs and genuine affection, Nevis carefully packed away the original spell she'd created days earlier and gathered her fury into a finely focused weapon. She borrowed Lily's carriage to take her to the fortress, though not to see Devlin, as any observer might have guessed. Forcing her roiling emotions into an intense calm, she murmured an incantation that swung wide the heavy doors to Hugo San Rossi's private chambers.

"I did hear rumors that the king may have grown weary of you, Nevis. Have you come to whore for me instead?"

Nevis strode uninvited into the mage's parlor, awash with black leather and scarlet velvet furnishings. "You're not my usual type of client." She stopped in the center of the spacious room, eyes fixed on the intensity of his black stare.

"Pity."

"Does Alana know what a cold-hearted bastard you are?"

"For accusing you of using sorcery at the races? By the way, where were you hiding? I searched everywhere."

"That accusation was just an annoyance." Ignoring his question, she pulled the tainted sphere from her bottomless pouch. "I'm talking about this monstrosity."

"Ah," Hugo murmured, his handsome face smiling as he finger-combed thick black hair from his eyes. "You found my little joke."

"Joke?" Nevis stepped forward to throttle the man, restrained her movement at the hungry eagerness in his eyes. "You cursed bastard. If I had unleashed that spell, three seals would have started mauling innocent children."

Hugo sank into one of the leather armchairs, crossed his legs. "If the spell had been triggered—"

"The children would have been maimed, maybe killed."

"Your point?" Hugo lurched back to his feet and advanced toward Nevis, coming uncomfortably close. "If the spell had been triggered, your orphanage would become worthless and your reputation destroyed. Is that what troubles you?"

"Bastard."

"Me? Come now, Nevis. Whom are we really talking about?"

When Hugo crept even closer, Nevis brought her hands up to protect herself from an imminent attack. "Back off, Hugo."

"You're not thinking clearly, Mage Conarkin. Perhaps if Devlin had allowed you into his bed, you might not be so overwrought."

"Perhaps allowing an exotic, foreign woman into your bed—"

Hugo's black eyes narrowed as he swiftly cut off her words. "I value my position as mage adviser to Devlin Graham. The spell was merely a joke, a test, perhaps, to see whether you were paying attention." He shrugged. "Some mages become so complacent when they have the ear of the king. It's my duty as Devlin's mage adviser to make certain your use of sorcery is ethical and responsible. Besides, the children are intact and your reputation somewhat unsullied, though you hardly deserve it."

"Devlin made a serious error when he appointed you to be mage adviser, though it was as much my fault for not seeing your true character. The very fact that you supported your treasonous mentor—"

"I don't know what you're talking about," Hugo said swiftly, again cutting off her words. "Sounds to me, Nevis, you're still angry because your old friend, Adrian, betrayed your trust," his voice was low, brutally ripping open old memories, "and you were left to deal with him when your own mentor deserted you."

Pain flashed in Nevis' eyes, swiftly banished.

But Hugo had noticed and pressed on relentlessly, whispering words of malice that cut into her soul. "She wouldn't have left if you hadn't disappointed her. But she knew you were wrong to destroy him. And so she went away, disgusted and shamed by your actions. Tell me, Nevis, do you desire your position again? Isn't running your foolish little unprofitable theater and sharing Devlin's bed enough for you?"

"A king's ransom wouldn't convince me to take that position again. Devlin's mistake—"

"My father's only mistake was in trusting you." Her presence a clear explanation for Hugo's frequent interruptions and whispered words, Alana Graham stepped from the bedchamber, blonde hair attractively disheveled, belting a black and scarlet silk robe about her slender waist. "You forced my father to say those terrible things the other night about my mother. He hates me because of you."

"He doesn't hate you. Your father's disappointed in you."

"Shut up," the young woman cried, coming into the parlor. "You've caused enough trouble between my father and me, and now you're trying to cause trouble between Hugo and me. There's no other woman in his bed, foreign or local. He told me you'd say that."

Nevis didn't answer, stared at Hugo and nodded. "Good thinking, Hugo. Brilliant, actually."

"Shut up." Alana grabbed Nevis' black shirt and pushed her back toward the door. "Leave us alone."

Nevis walked backward, eyes fixed on the girl's crimson face. "I didn't want you to know about your mother's betrayal. There was no reason to destroy your memory of her, not at this point."

"How incredibly compassionate," Hugo murmured, placing his arm protectively around Alana. "That's the Nevis Conarkin everyone believes to be the real mage. Pity no one but you and Devlin know the truth about your plans to betray Montbasso with the help of Mikaline

Nashat. And Devlin, poor bewildered soul, refuses to believe me. But people will find out, Nevis, and Devlin will have no choice but to punish you or step down from his throne."

Nevis turned her attention away from the mage and stared at Alana Graham intently. "You'll stand here and say nothing when your lover threatens your father's throne? By the gods, Alana, the young girl I knew a lifetime ago had more integrity than the woman I see now. How can you—"

"Nevis, go away. You're growing tiresome." Hugo's voice was bored, though Nevis tensed as his fingers idly strayed in her direction.

"Stay away from me, Hugo, stay away from Devlin, and stay the hell away from the children. If you don't, your cursed life will be worthless."

"Threats?"

"Fact."

"Nevis, really—"

"For the gods' sake, Hugo, your position is the most powerful mage role in all of Montbasso. You've successfully seduced Devlin's daughter into thinking she loves you—"

"I do. Damn you—"

Nevis stepped back from Alana's angry hands. "Fine. That's your choice. You're a big girl, but just you and Hugo leave me alone."

Hugo abruptly lost some of his composure. "Apart from the lies you've forced Devlin to tell his daughter, what other lies do you whisper in his ear when his hands are busy wandering all over your body? And if you believe, Nevis, that I'm the most potent mage in Montbasso because of the position I hold, you're very naïve. But I don't think you are," Hugo spat, black eyes alight with fire.

"Your jealousy is misplaced, Hugo. If you were honorable—"

"What do you know of honor? You—" Hugo stopped, fingers clenched tight on Alana's shoulder.

"I destroyed your mentor," Nevis whispered, "the greatest traitor Montbasso has ever known. Alana may believe what you tell her now, that you didn't know Adrian Bambari was a traitor, and that I'm planning to betray Montbasso as Adrian did with Cashogi assistance, but someday, if the gods are willing, she'll accept the truth." She ignored the hatred in Hugo's eyes, turned to the young woman. "I don't care what you think of me, Alana, but believe that I don't want to see you hurt. I've no cause to wish you harm."

"No cause?" Alana's voice was nearly hysterical. "I tried to execute you only days ago, and I'm sorry my father stopped me."

Nevis shrugged, kept her face remarkably empty, though the girl's words pained her deeply. "I'm not talking about me, girl. I'm talking about you. Hugo San Rossi will break your heart, if not destroy your soul."

When Nevis reached for the door, Hugo hissed, "Are you going straight to Devlin, to complain about me?"

Nevis flung open the door, stood tall and calm, white hair blazing against the midnight black of her clothes. "I fight my own battles, Hugo. I destroyed Adrian Bambari alone, and I'll destroy you, if you leave me no choice."

* * * *

Nevis eased her way past the alert, stiff-necked guard with a spell to ensure the young woman wouldn't notice the door to the royal suite open and shut, nor the mage slip inside. With a silent and disheartened sigh, Nevis adjusted her eyes to the dim lamplight, ebony clothes blending into the shadows, searching the spacious room, until, finally, she recognized Devlin's silhouette on the balcony. From the rigid set to his jaw, Nevis knew he was oblivious to the moonlight shimmering on the river below. Docked between a merchant from Port Cordillero and Port Neeri, the two Cashogi ships were distinct, their white stallion banners rippling in the night breeze.

"Dev—"

Her whisper brought his head around, blue eyes so vulnerable she was beside him in a heartbeat, holding him tight.

He pulled away, fingers resting lightly at her waist. "I didn't want to share my miserable mood with you."

"I always told you that you were miserable without me, but you never listen." She tugged at Devlin's huge hands, callused from sword-play, until he joined her on the stone bench, eyes shut. "I've been think-ing."

Blue eyes snapped open. "Then I'm in awfully serious trouble." Devlin dodged her fist and pulled the mage close, kissing her lips softly.

"I'm serious," she murmured against his cheek.

"I know. Nevis, if it's about Alana—"

"You can't let people know there's trouble between you. Nor," she sat upright, holding his gaze with sheer willpower, "can you stay angry with her."

"My daughter tried to murder you."

"She wasn't thinking clearly. You've got to forgive her."

"Tell me why."

Nevis blinked at his flat tone, and nearly lost her nerve. "She's your daughter, your only child, and she loves you as much as you love her."

"That has no bearing on what she's done."

"It should." When Devlin turned his face away, she added, "There's another reason. When she tried to kill me, she did it thinking it was in your best interest. She also believes I'm a traitor, no better than

Adrian." Nevis grabbed a fistful of silk as Devlin lurched unsteadily to his feet. "Listen to me, you stubborn idiot. Your daughter's been swayed by Hugo into believing me evil and treacherous. Sway her back."

"She's an adult."

"She's a child, who's torn between her father and her lover. Sooner or later, she'll see the truth, that Hugo's the criminal we've proclaimed all along. And when she does, her heart will be broken, and she'll need you."

"She'll never need me." Devlin removed her fingers gently from his arm. "She never has. Ever since her mother committed suicide, Alana turned her heart away from me, blaming me, blaming you. I lost my daughter ten years ago, Nevis. If Hugo breaks her heart, she'll blame you and me for that, too."

Chapter Eight

"If you continue to keep such late hours every night, Mage Conarkin, Lily might recruit you next door to entertain her clientele."

Nevis laughed, unperturbed, as Remo Savanak settled his tall, handsome frame in the chair opposite her desk. "That wouldn't surprise Hugo San Rossi," she answered, not bothering to disguise her bitterness. "To what do I owe this late-night visit, counselor? Business or pleasure?"

"Very late-night visit. You know Lily." Remo rested his shiny boot on the wooden stool beside the desk. "We were walking along the river path, saw the lamplight in your office—" Remo shrugged, gray eyes mischievous. "She sent me to scold, then tuck you into bed."

"Scold, maybe. Too cowardly to do it herself?"

"She claims I'm more diplomatic. I heard what happened at the races. Sometimes, the two of you are enough to stop my heart."

Nevis grunted. "Is that where the scolding comes in?"

"Why bother? You ladies are quite independent minded. You never did tell me about your visit to Adam Museo's home."

"Nothing to tell." Nevis smiled to avoid hurting the attorney's feelings. "I was just doing a little snooping, that's all."

Remo sighed in mock resignation and eyed the open cabinet against the far wall, where Nevis had been working when he'd first interrupted her. "Odd hour for taking inventory, isn't it?"

"Not inventory, counselor. I'm examining each and every sphere in this cabinet."

"You found something else?"

Nevis held up the malevolent sphere she'd planned to use for the children. "I nearly unleashed what I thought to be an innocent, entertaining group of seals in May's parlor this evening." She met and held the attorney's gaze across her desk. "They were no longer innocent, Remo. Hugo San Rossi replaced the sphere with one of his own, making the seals feral."

Remo dropped his boot from the stool, sitting upright. "Are you sure it was Hugo?"

"He admitted it." Nevis replaced the sphere in the cabinet, setting it beside the other tainted sphere, then relocked the cabinet mechanism. She brought her stiletto into contact with the transparent surface of the right-handed sphere, waited until the orphanage came into view, rotated the sphere until she was satisfied all was well on the far side of Alvaron Park. Glimpsing the little red-haired child, thumb stubbornly set in her mouth, peacefully asleep, Nevis smiled and returned to the subject at hand and the patiently waiting attorney. "Hugo said it was a joke, a test."

"Which means," Remo drawled, brushing back strands of neatly trimmed blonde hair, "that you confronted him."

"Correct."

"Any other witnesses?"

"Counselor—"

"Answer the question."

Nevis released a heavy sigh of disgust. "You sound like an attorney."

"I am an attorney. Now answer the question."

"Alana was in the bedchamber listening."

"I won't pry," Remo said softly, when the mage looked away. "I know something happened to rattle Devlin. Lily won't say a word, claims it's not her place to snitch, but I'm worried."

"So am I." Her admission surprised the attorney, more so the following words. "The only reason Lily knows what's going on is because she's aware of some private matters that happened a lifetime ago. Don't be insulted, please."

"I'm not. If I didn't trust either of you, I wouldn't be here. But I am worried. Hugo's playing like a nasty little boy."

"You're not surprised?"

"Sorry to admit it, Nevis, but I am. He's endangering his position as mage adviser to the king. I can understand his financial maneuvering—"

"And bribery or blackmail."

"Yes," Remo admitted readily, "regarding the orphanage and the court decision. Finlay told me that Hugo was putting an awful lot of pressure on Adam Museo about the orphanage."

"To sign over the rights?"

"Yes. And to initiate the lawsuit against you and Lily. But trying to make you out to be in league with the Cashogi trade minister, not to mention Hugo's own dealing in illegal drugs, for the gods' sake, from Cashogi, of all places—" Remo set his boot back on the stool. "He's jeopardizing Devlin's trade negotiations."

"For greed only? No, for—" Nevis stopped short of revealing her thoughts, awhirl with conflicting emotions.

The attorney watched the shift of emotions on her subtly attractive face, pale skin flushed with rising consternation, and said nothing, not until Nevis shut her eyes and rested her head against the back of her chair. She looked so weary, so disheartened, that Remo thought of fetching Lily to soothe the mage's troubled heart or even sending word to Devlin.

"Vengeance," Nevis murmured, fingers clutching the arms of her chair. "I've been a fool, thinking everything has been focused only on me." When she opened her eyes, stared at Remo, it was as though she'd reached a decision. "Can this discussion take place under attorney-client privacy?"

Remo sat upright once more, nodded. Before she spoke again, however, he raised a hand, handsome face solemn. "A moment ago, you didn't want me to know what happened."

"A moment ago, I thought I was the only intended victim. Devlin's reputation is at stake, too."

"Go on."

"Hugo San Rossi was Adrian Bambari's apprentice, a little-known fact." When Remo's gray eyes widened in horror, she explained, "Dev and I made an unfortunate error in judgment, didn't realize the young man had been hiding his true allegiance. We thought him bespelled or just innocent, unaware of his mentor's treasonous leanings. Hugo San Rossi was a damned good actor."

"So it's vengeance for destroying Adrian and his treasonous plot with the Cashogi?"

"And possibly for destroying Adrian's lover, whom Hugo himself held in high esteem. I've often wondered, though I never spoke the thought aloud to Devlin, whether Hugo may have desired her for himself. And failing to gain her as a lover, Hugo chose a substitute who mimicked the focus of his desire, a perfect strategy that allowed him not only vengeance but physical satisfaction," she murmured.

Remo narrowed his eyes, chose his words carefully. "I don't remember anyone else dying at the time that you destroyed Adrian."

"It took several months, and it was suicide, not illness," Nevis said softly, forcing herself to meet Remo's incredulous stare, saw the very moment when the facts fell into place.

"Alana's mother?" When Nevis nodded, the attorney covered his face with his hands. "No wonder Alana despises you."

"So much so that she tried to kill me."

Remo's hands dropped from his face, his expression so appalled that Nevis didn't know how to respond.

"That's what rattled Dev. He was in my bedchamber the night Alana tried to murder me."

Remo shakily got to his feet and paced within the narrow confines of the office. "She blames you—"

"For being Devlin's lover and destroying her parents' marriage. The night she tried to kill me, Devlin told her the truth, that her mother had been Adrian Bambari's lover and that she worked with Adrian to allow the Cashogi dissidents inside our borders."

"Thank the gods you stopped them," Remo said, standing still before the desk, his shadow casting darkness over the mage. "Hugo's planning his own kind of invasion, isn't he? By allowing Cashogi Firespark into Montbasso?"

"You don't know the half of it, Remo. The drug dealing is pure ironic revenge. Adrian—" The mage shut her eyes briefly, pain clouding her features. When she looked at the attorney again, unshed tears shone bright in her eyes. "Adrian was my friend, Remo. We were apprenticed to a master mage together. Somehow, the Cashogi got to him, found his weakness, and addicted him to one of their poisons. He fell prey to their visions of power and greed and promised them the natural riches of Montbasso's land, treasures that their island nation couldn't produce."

"Treasure enough to make them successful as a naval power?"

"And then some, yes. There was no reasoning with him, and it fell to me—" Nevis looked away, shut her eyes again when Remo's hand lightly touched her bowed head. "Anyway, this involvement of Hugo's in the Cashogi drug trade stinks of vengeance. The Cashogi drugs ruined Adrian, but Hugo always blamed me. And now he's using the

Cashogi drugs to sour the fragile relationship Devlin is trying to build between Montbasso and Cashogi."

"And Devlin will look a fool should the negotiations fall apart, and you, a traitor, for plotting with the Cashogi trade minister." Remo's face had gone scarlet with rising anger. "And you, also, a murderer, for slaying Adam Museo and a dozen innocent children."

"Only if I'd triggered the spell tonight."

"Nevis—"

"I'm responsible for any sorcery I unleash. If I were careless, I'd be just as guilty as Hugo. Look, Remo, it's meaningless." Nevis shoved rebellious strands of hair from her eyes. "I can't prove Hugo replaced the spheres. It's my word against his word."

"So you'll not take any legal action?"

"I can't."

"You won't."

"He's waiting for me to do just that." The mage pushed back her chair, stared out the window to the river below, white hair a beacon to anyone watching.

"So?"

"The moment I do, he'll tell the people of Port Jambi that I've run to hide behind Devlin's protection."

"Is that so bad?"

"Devlin's got his own problems at the moment."

"And that's an end to this discussion?"

"Yes."

"Nevis—"

"That's it, Remo. I'm tired. Good night."

The attorney studied the rigid back facing him. "You're a damnably stubborn, independent woman."

"I try very hard." Nevis turned, green eyes soft. "I'm sorry, Remo. I'm not being so difficult on a whim."

"If I didn't know that, Mage Conarkin," he said calmly, "I'd never have agreed to take you on as a client."

"Lily would have made you feel guilty if you hadn't."

"Believe it or not," Remo's smile had subtly turned serious, "I would have had the balls to refuse Lily if I weren't convinced you were honorable. Now go get some sleep." Remo turned to leave, then paused, gray eyes reflecting his concern. "Why don't you spend the night at May's?"

"I'd end up with a bed full of thumb-sucking imps. No, thanks."

"Be careful. Damn it, Nevis, I wish—"

"I thought you were done scolding."

Gray eyes turned abruptly mischievous. "Shall I tuck you in then?"

Nevis leaned over to kiss his smooth-shaven cheek. "If you ever took Lily's words literally, she'd hang you by your balls outside her whorehouse."

* * * *

"I know how you are when opening night gets close, boss, so—"

Expression utterly blank, Simon Masters uncovered a sugar-coated breakfast roll in the shape of a tall woman. Poppy seeds blackened her clothes, with pure white melted sugar to cover the figure's head, and an extra dollop at the tip of one hand to suggest a raspberry sphere. At her waist, was a white sugar stiletto.

"That's an incredible work of art," Nevis laughed, shaking her head in admiration as she examined the cake.

"It is indeed," Simon grinned, presenting a cup filled with extra melted sugar. "Clari made it very clear she didn't want to spoil the appearance of the black clothes, but seeing as you love this horrible concoction, she said you should feel free to spread it over everything."

"A perfect way to start the morning, Simon, thanks." Nevis pushed all thoughts of Clarissa Bracken from her head. "Why are you here so early?"

"Catching up on all the paperwork I never seem to have time to do when we get this close to opening night. Prima donnas shouting at each other, people demanding tickets for nonexistent seats, bedlam in the aisles." Simon ran his skinny hands over his thinning gray hair. "I'll be in my office if you need me. Just yell down."

"I will."

"Nevis—" The stage manager paused in the doorway. "The prima donnas and all the rest of the cast— They'll come through for you. Along with their incredibly inflated egos, believe it or not, they want you to be proud of them."

"I am."

"Word on the street is that Slick Hands' people don't feel that way about him. Wonder why?"

"Simon—" Embarrassed, Nevis toyed with the sugar-headed mage breakfast cake. "Thanks."

"Just doing my job, boss."

"No, you're not. You're doing a lot more. Maybe one of these days, I'll even be able to pay you a decent wage."

Simon clasped his hand to his chest and staggered. "My poor heart couldn't stand it. By the gods— What possibilities." Simon fumbled from the office, leaving his employer with a sheepish grin on her face.

Lost in thought, Nevis stared at the breakfast cake, thinking about Remo's visit and all that had happened the previous day, including her late night chat with Clarissa. Had she been telling the truth?

"Seems the baker still thinks you're innocent."

Startled, the mage glanced up, found Brea Kilganor standing in her doorway, dark blue uniform sharply creased. "Don't you ever knock?"

"Why bother? Incidentally, although the baker thinks you're innocent, Hugo San Rossi thinks you're guilty." Before Nevis could respond, the constable entered the office uninvited, sat in the chair opposite the desk, and hooked one leg over the arm. "He came to visit me, bright and early this very morning, Mage Conarkin, complaining rather loudly about you."

"That contemptible sewer rat. He—"

"Has made a formal complaint against you. Mage San Rossi told me you've been harassing him, played foul at the races, and that you falsely accused him of toying with a spell, one of your spheres again."

"Toying with a spell?" Nevis' face had gone crimson with anger, contrasting so sharply with the pallor of her short-cropped hair that the constable braced herself for an attack of magefire. "Is that how he described what he did?" The mage reached back and unlocked the cabinet under Brea's watchful eye, holding out the sphere she very nearly unleashed at the orphanage. "Do you see what's inside?"

The constable peered intently at the sphere. "Seals."

"Have they teeth?"

"Quite sharp, yes."

"My spell had no teeth, Constable, to keep the children safe. I nearly triggered this spell in May's parlor last evening, maiming innocent boys and girls." She set the sphere on the desk, out of harm's way.

"Nasty," the constable murmured, carefully appraising the rage in Nevis' eyes. "Can you prove that Hugo San Rossi created the sphere?"

"Of course not, though he admitted it to me."

"In front of other witnesses?" When Nevis hesitated, her entire expression gone blank, Brea pressed, "Were there any other witnesses?"

"Alana Graham was in the bedchamber. I assume she overheard our discussion." Nevis' voice was flat.

"Then she would tell the truth before a court of law, wouldn't she?" The constable asked softly, watching Nevis' eyes before the mage turned away. "As heir to the throne, Alana Graham—"

"I'm not in any position to predict what Alana Graham would or wouldn't do under any circumstances," Nevis said tensely, turning back to face the constable. "For that matter—"

"Do you think that by harassing Hugo San Rossi, he'll back off from the lawsuit?"

"Why bother when he's certain of the outcome?" Nevis shot back. "You overheard him at the races, Constable. He's blackmailing the judges to get his way in court."

"Do you think that by harassing—"

Nevis slammed both fists down on her desk, barely missing her breakfast cake. "By the gods, Constable, I'm harassing that man because he very nearly made me responsible for unleashing death and destruction on innocent children who look to me for safety and protection. I'm not the one who started this trouble. Tell Hugo San Rossi to leave me the hell alone. If you want the true measure of him, just see how he's even—" The mage stopped her words, breathing hard.

"How he even what?" The constable asked, getting to her feet, studying with a fair amount of respect the immense control Nevis brought to her shaking hands. The mage's cheeks were flushed with rage as she turned her back on the constable once more. "Keeping dirty little secrets won't help convince me that you're truly innocent, Mage Conarkin."

"It won't hurt me, either, not any more than it already has." Nevis sagged against the window frame, staring at nothing, resigned to the unpleasantness ahead. "Do what you've come to do, Constable. I'll come quietly. Just let me tell Simon what needs to be done here before you arrest me."

When Nevis turned wearily to face the constable, Brea kept her expression impassive, though the mage's disheartened appearance distressed her greatly. "I didn't come here to arrest you."

"Then why'd you come?"

"To warn you." Brea tucked her hands in the pockets of her perfectly creased uniform breeches. "Hugo San Rossi's not quite as proud as you. He's using his position as mage adviser to the king to make demands of me. He's even gone so far as to accuse you of secretly plotting against Montbasso, you and the Cashogi trade minister. A rather peculiar accusation, I might add."

"And you think I should use my position as the king's lover to shove Hugo right back?"

"It's one way to fight."

"Not for me. It's my battle, and I can't fight that way."

"You may very well lose."

"Then I'll be the only one to lose." Nevis studied the constable's unreadable expression and challenged her. "Why just a warning? You could easily arrest me for harassment."

"I need proof, Mage Conarkin."

"Then surely you have it, Constable Kilganor. Didn't Alana support her lover's accusation?"

"Sure she did." The constable's expression, if possible, became even more unreadable. "But you see, Hugo San Rossi didn't have the evidence he needed. The spell he supposedly created." Brea shrugged offhandedly, eyes studiously avoiding the sphere sitting openly on Nevis' desk a few inches away from the carved likeness of Janni and her numerous children. "Since I don't see it anywhere, my guess, Mage Conarkin, is that you destroyed it. No evidence, no arrest."

"Constable—"

"Mind if I look around the theater? Might be I'll find that appalling sphere hiding somewhere." When Nevis stared, speechless, the constable freed her hands from her pockets. "I'll let you know if I find anything."

"Constable—" Nevis' voice was a whisper.

"Don't thank me yet, Mage Conarkin. I might find something worse for which you surely won't thank me."

And to Nevis' mind, she did, when Brea Kilganor reappeared a short time later, holding a miniature portrait in her hand.

"Hans' girl," Nevis murmured, unwilling to say more as Brea shoved the portrait under her nose.

"Same portrait that appeared in Adam Museo's room. I did see that one, too. I didn't just leave it there for no reason. I presumed you'd go snooping." Brea's smile was predatory as she cocked her head to the side, white-splashed dark hair falling rakishly into her eyes. "Odd, isn't it? Look close. Look very close."

"What am I looking at?"

"Her hair. Black, curly, long. Rather similar to what we found in Verdi's wig, don't you think?"

"Shayna Kashi has similar hair."

"Back to Hugo as the guilty party? Why not consider Hans guilty? He's been jumpy enough, hasn't he?"

"Everyone's been jumpy."

"His girl was savagely abused by the murder victim, Mage Conarkin. And the corpse was wearing his embroidered shirt. Was that a slip or was he trying to tell us he's not guilty? After all, if he was, he wouldn't dare use his own shirt. What would we really think? What should we think?"

"It doesn't mean that Hans is a murderer."

"It doesn't mean he isn't. If he is," Brea said softly, challenging the mage, "where does Hugo San Rossi fit in?"

"I don't know."

"You won't say." Brea tucked the portrait deep in her pocket. "Just in case I find Hans guilty, you'd better think about hiring another villain. And soon."

"That won't be difficult." Nevis forced a smile to her lips. "Port Jambi is crowded with villains. Constable—" Nevis met the other woman's eyes. "There's someone else in Port Jambi who knows me and has hair like that."

The constable thought for a moment, shrugged.

"Barry Faddle."

"Slick Hands? Now why would he set you up?"

"I've no idea, but he was awfully cozy with Hugo after he officially challenged the race. Didn't you see the two of them?"

Brea looked past the mage, trying to recall the crowd. "I saw Hugo speaking with the race authority."

"And right after that, Hugo and Barry spoke briefly until Hugo warned him away. Maybe it means nothing," Nevis shrugged, "but I'm getting awfully weary of constantly looking over my shoulder."

"I never thought Slick Hands dangerous, only troublesome. He's too much of a coward."

"That's what I always thought," Nevis agreed, remembering how he backed away from Devlin's reaction to Barry's idea of buying her theater. "These days, I'm starting to question everyone and everything."

"Smart. I've no doubt I'll be back, Mage Conarkin. Enjoy the rest of your day," Brea said pleasantly as though they'd been chatting about the weather.

Nevis watched the constable walk away, feeling more uneasy than she had before her visit. Unsheathing her ivory-handled stiletto, the mage tapped its point against the left transparent sphere on the cabinet door. As the interior of the theater came alive, Nevis rotated the sphere until the room she desired came into view. Satisfied, she pulled the stiletto away, allowing the image to fade, then took the stairs and headed for the cramped room in which the cast and crew kept their possessions.

Hans' drawer was filled with innocuous items, nothing of importance. Nevis started to push the drawer back into its place, but paused at the unexpected sound of crinkling paper. She tucked her finger into the drawer and carefully released a crumpled piece of paper that had apparently been jostled out of place by the constable's searching hands.

Nevis smoothed the creased square and studied the marks. She'd never seen them before, but knew enough to recognize a pawnshop receipt. Tucking the crumpled note in her pocket, she resolved to rescue whatever possession Hans had pawned, not quite sure what she hoped to find.

Chapter Nine

Unable to concentrate, Nevis peered out the window overlooking the Basol River, the silhouette of Brigadier Bridge in the distance. Restless and uneasy, she toyed with the pawnshop ticket in her fingers. Rehearsal had been over for hours, and still she hesitated, uncertain what to do or where to go, until she turned her head in the opposite direction heading toward Alvaron Park. What she saw had her down the stairs and out the side entrance in a heartbeat.

Taking a deep breath, Nevis cautiously approached the two distracted young people wading in the river, trousers rolled up to their knees. "If you're looking for trout, it's far too late in the day, so I've been told."

A duet of startled exclamations loudly accompanied the sound of awkward splashing.

"Hello, Hans, Fani. Lose something?"

"Fani's bracelet. We thought if we were lucky, maybe—" Hans avoided contact with the mage's perceptive gaze, touched Fani's arm in silent warning, or perhaps reassurance, Nevis wasn't certain.

"Mage Conarkin—"

"It's fine, Fani. Nevis knows about us."

Wary eyes peered out uncertainly from long dark curls. "Lily doesn't like Hans very much."

"She likes Hans well enough," Nevis reassured the younger woman. "She simply detests the fact that he uses drugs. As do I. But Hans has promised to stop, hasn't he?" Green eyes darted in the actor's direction, curiosity aroused when Hans' nod was openly distracted. "Hans, you did stop using Firespark, didn't you?"

"Sure, Nevis," the actor said earnestly. "I promised I would. Besides, I didn't seem to enjoy it very much anymore. The Firespark was getting too strong, just a bit too frightening to play with. Something was different."

"Another source?" Nevis asked casually, wondering about the Cashogi dealers that Hugo had been courting.

"That's what Adam told me." Hans looked away, touched Fani's sleeve again when the young woman appeared ready to bolt. "Though I don't know the origin. Doesn't matter, anyway. I'm finished with the stuff."

"Mind if I ask you something?"

Hans looked up at his employer, tried to read her expression, and found nothing threatening. "Go on."

"Where did you meet Adam when you were making a purchase?" Nevis watched the actor's expression, keeping her own amiable. "Just curious."

Hans nodded. "Not far from here. Right in Alvaron Park."

"By the orphanage?" Hugo had mentioned the park, too, and Nevis wondered how long the transactions had been going on. It angered her that Adam and Hugo, both, had bartered poison so near the children.

"Nevis, it's over and done. Adam's gone, and there won't be any more trouble from him." Though Hans was talking to the mage, his eyes kept darting to Fani, who refused to look at Nevis.

"By the gods, if I'd known—" Nevis shook her head in frustration, catching sight of the rolled up trousers, and remembering what had initially brought her running in their direction. "You're right, Hans. Look, if you're searching for a bracelet in the shadows, chances are you won't find it without a bit of lamplight. I can trigger a magefire spell for you and—"

"No, thank you, Mage Conarkin," Fani protested, her face, half hidden behind the black curls, flushed with some emotion Nevis was trying unsuccessfully to interpret. "It was only a cheap trinket I picked up for myself at the craft fair last season. No great loss. Truly."

"It's no trouble," Nevis insisted politely, opening her bottomless pouch and pretending to search for a sphere that would create magefire light.

"Sure it is." Hans waded closer to shore. "It's nearly opening night, and you have a hundred things that need your attention. You shouldn't be bothered over a cheap piece of metal. To be honest, I hated the ugly thing."

His grin was nearly convincing, and Nevis felt inexplicably sad.

She shrugged, hiding her disappointment in the young man behind studied nonchalance. "Call if you change your mind."

"We won't, but thanks, Nevis." Hans guided Fani closer to shore, stepping carefully over slippery rocks. "Enjoy the evening."

"I might," she answered smoothly, wishing she'd didn't have to play games, "if Constable Kilganor doesn't come to arrest me."

Fani glanced up swiftly at the mage, her eyes wide with genuine horror. "But you're innocent."

"She claims she's gathering solid proof against me." Nevis decided to take a chance with the young lovers and schooled her pale features to casual disregard. "And that can't be my ivory-handled stiletto," she said, patting the sheath at her waist as the young people exchanged an uncertain glance.

"No one believes you're guilty," Hans insisted, stepping onto the shore beside Fani, who looked so much like a frightened rabbit, Nevis would have laughed if matters hadn't been so dire.

"You're being naïve, Hans. Given a hint of probable guilt, some interesting evidence pointing in my direction, and a very credible motive—" Nevis shrugged her thin shoulders. "Watch how swiftly people change their opinions. Well, I can't worry about what I can't control, can I? And don't you two worry either. Enjoy yourselves. Hope you find the bracelet." Nevis bade them farewell and strolled along the river path, acutely aware of two pairs of worried eyes burning into her receding back. On the river, the silhouette of Brigadier Bridge came into view once more, rising up and over the swiftly flowing current.

"If you're trying to imitate a deep thinker, don't bother."

Nevis slid an amused glance toward the upper story of the brightly lamplit whorehouse, unsurprised to find Lily Frascat leaning out the window, green feathers snugly tucked into the back of her auburn hair. "Do you spend all your time spying on people?"

"Only people I'm worried about. Or people purposefully searching the rocks along the riverbank."

"About that very point—"

"Come on up."

Nevis entered the alley and headed for the side door opposite the theater. Chappy Markos smiled a warm welcome, waving her up the stairs toward Lily's cozy and inviting private parlor, where Nevis slipped inside and shut the door.

"It looked suspiciously like Fani Sneddle."

"It was. Hans, too."

One scarlet eyebrow shot toward the ceiling, joined by the other when Nevis sighed heavily and sank onto the pillow-strewn couch.

"They've been seeing each other secretly for some time, and— By the gods, Lily, don't shout." Nevis held up a restraining hand. "You never heard any of this idle gossip, understand?"

"Nothing personal about your boy, Nevis, but he uses drugs."

"Used." Nevis stared at Lily until the other woman's feathers stopped bobbing. "That's not the worst part." The mage stretched her long black-clad legs across the plush floral carpet, rubbing the kinks from her knees. "Brea's highly suspicious of Hans, and thinks he killed Adam."

"Because Adam beat Fani?"

"That's her theory. Problem is, the evidence is all circumstantial."

"Care to explain?"

"A lock of dark curly hair was found in the wig. Might be Fani's. Might be Shayna Kashi's. Might be someone else entirely, like Slick Hands."

"Hadn't thought of him."

"Neither had I until the races."

"Hmm." Lily cocked her head toward the window, peering out. "The children are still busy searching along the riverbank."

"For a bracelet, so they told me." Nevis stopped kneading her knees and rubbed her eyes instead, reminding Lily of one of May's orphans. "I'd dearly love a good night's sleep. I feel about three hundred years old right now."

Lily made comforting noises, but didn't lose track of the main conversation. "What about Hans' connection to Adam?"

"He used to buy Firespark from Adam Museo. But that doesn't necessarily mean anything."

"Does it necessarily mean anything that the murdered corpse was wearing Hans' shirt for his role as Adrian Bambari?"

"The constable mentioned that, too. It could mean any number of things, most of them coincidence."

"You don't want Hans to be guilty."

"I don't want anyone I know and like to be guilty."

Lily studied her friend's shadowed face. "Would it make you feel better to know that if Hans wasn't a decent man, Fani would never stay with him?"

"Sure, but if he's decent, then he may very well have gone after Adam simply because he is decent. By the gods, Lily, it's giving me a headache. I don't know what to think anymore."

"I do. I still believe Hugo's behind all this trouble." She waited, got no response from the mage, who'd settled back against the couch, eyes shut. "Remo told me about your discussion last night."

"What happened to attorney-client privacy?"

"I know everything you were trying to keep back from him, don't I? Except that little bit about Hugo having his heart set on Devlin's queen, and substituting Alana for her mother as part of his little revenge."

"It's pure conjecture, which is why I never said anything. It seems a bit silly now that I think about it."

"Not to me." When Nevis didn't reply, Lily said, "I found it exceedingly curious you didn't mention Clarissa Bracken." Getting the expected scowl, Lily tried a different tactic. "Look, Nevis, if Brea Kilganor—"

"Constable came to give me a warning while I was having my breakfast this morning," Nevis interrupted, sitting up, green eyes thoughtful.

"What kind of warning?"

"It was all rather odd. Hugo made a formal charge of harassment against me, but the constable—" The mage shook her head, still befuddled by the morning conversation. "She told me that she needed evidence before taking action on his charge. She told Hugo that she needed to examine the dangerous sphere as evidence, the very one I showed her that was sitting on my desk, Lily, right beside the statue of Janni. And then Constable Kilganor declared that same sphere to be missing mere seconds after I shoved it under her nose."

Lily breathed a sigh of relief. "I was beginning to wonder about her common sense."

"She's doing her job. She had every right to come into my theater and arrest me this morning."

"For harassment, not murder."

"Lily—"

"It's true."

Nevis got to her feet, heard the rustle of paper in her pocket, and gave the madam a very mischievous smile. "Did you enjoy the races?"

Lily eyed her friend with a wary expression. "Why?"

Nevis shrugged offhandedly. "I thought you might want to have a bit more fun tomorrow afternoon."

"Tomorrow night's the meeting in Alvaron Park that Hugo arranged. I wouldn't miss that little scene for all the gold in Devlin's treasury. But what's tomorrow afternoon? Do I dare ask?"

Nevis pulled the receipt from her pocket and showed Lily. "I found this pawnshop ticket."

"I'm even more afraid to ask where."

Nevis slipped it back into her pocket. "Jammed into the drawer where Hans keeps some odds and ends."

* * * *

Far more restless than when she'd started out, Nevis left the brothel and headed toward her apartment at the rear of the theater. With slow, weary steps, she entered the parlor, caught unusually speechless at the bouquet of pure white river lilies surrounded by emerald leaves set in an onyx vase beneath the window.

"Reminds me of you for some reason."

Nevis spun on her heels, even more startled to find Devlin lounging against the opposite wall. "They're beautiful, Dev. Thanks."

"As are you." Devlin pushed away from the wall and caught her in a fierce embrace. "I'm always being so damnably polite in public," he murmured into her hair, "but I don't need to be polite now."

"How rude do you intend to be?"

"Very." He shut the door with his free hand and locked it, dragging her gently into the sparsely furnished bedchamber.

"If your subjects could see you now—"

"They'd be quite pleased. Sit." Devlin urged her onto the bed, kneeling to remove her boots.

"Taking lessons from your valet?"

"Don't be snide. I remove my own boots."

"Even when they're steeped in horseshit?"

"As a matter of fact, yes. Now take off that bothersome thing—" Devlin waved his hands at the sorcerous bottomless pouch at her waist. His unfailing nervousness around her spells always made her laugh, though these days, she couldn't really blame him. "You're frowning."

"No, I'm not." Nevis slipped free of the leather pouch and set the ivory-handled stiletto aside.

"Yes, you are. No pampering until you confess. Is it Hugo?"

"It's everything. Don't scold. That's the truth."

"Brea Kilganor told me that the royal mage adviser made a formal charge against you for harassment. She also mentioned that Hugo accused you of plotting with Mikaline Nashat and thought she should do something about it."

"That woman—"

"Thought I should know, since you probably wouldn't tell me just how nasty and tiresome Hugo San Rossi is becoming." Devlin's expression was every bit as stubborn as the mage's.

"Did Constable Kilganor tell you that she came to warn me and ignored the very evidence she might have used against me, had she believed Hugo?"

One dark eyebrow inched skyward. "Didn't breathe a word."

Nevis shook her head. "Confused the hell out of me, Dev, though I'll admit it was a bit of a relief to hear her slightly more prejudiced in my favor, even if— well, it was probably because of you. Not that that makes it all right."

"I doubt that was her reason." Devlin cocked his head to the side, deep blue eyes studying her face. "Despite her hard-nosed attitude, and maybe because of it, I believe she's as ethical as you. So I seriously doubt she'd be pleasant to you simply because I happen to adore you. In fact, according to Lily, the constable had been growing tiresome. So any change in her attitude means that she's changed her mind about the prime suspect."

"Maybe." Nevis shrugged. "Doesn't matter anyway, Dev. And besides, you're far too busy to worry about such matters."

Devlin's expression shifted to anger as he sat back on his haunches. "When that matter concerns my daughter and heir, who apparently collaborated with her lying lover in accusing you of not only harassment but treason, when her lover could have seriously harmed those children if you hadn't been so cautious—"

Nevis stroked his cheek, tugged gently at his neat trimmed beard. "She's in love with him."

"That doesn't excuse her actions."

"You didn't say anything, did you? Dev?" Nevis grabbed the light wool of his shirt, bunching it in her fist. "If she thinks I came running to you—"

"I didn't say a word." Devlin released her fingers from his shirt, one by one. "But I will say a word, and more than one, when the time is right." He took off Nevis' left boot, fingers shaking with rage. "I haven't said a damned word to her since the night she tried to kill you."

"Dev—"

"Don't you dare scold. When I'm ready, maybe, just maybe, I'll be in the mood to forgive her." Devlin tugged off the remaining boot and tossed it aside. "Maybe. Listen—" His expression changed, blue eyes suddenly lighter, "I've brought something else along." He indicated with a nod of his head a package against the wall that Nevis hadn't even noticed. "The journals."

The journals kept by his queen, with written proof of her romantic and treasonous involvement with Adrian Bambari and their betrayal of Devlin, though there'd never been any mention of Hugo or his attraction to her. Maybe she hadn't known that her lover's apprentice lusted after her.

"Why?" Nevis struggled to sit up, instinct alert. "Has someone been searching your rooms?"

"Not that I could tell. But I've a hunch that someone will. And soon." He shrugged, sat beside her on the bed. "Can you keep them safe for me? At least, until Hugo starts behaving himself again."

"It might seem too obvious to leave them with me. I've a better place." She kissed the tip of his nose. "Lily's whorehouse."

"Brilliant. I'll drop them off—"

"No, you won't." When Devlin looked puzzled, she laughed, though her voice was the tiniest bit uncertain. "If people see you at Lily's, they'll assume you're looking for another whore."

"Damn you, Nevis, I swear—"

"Hush. I was teasing."

"No, you weren't, woman—"

"About your being so rude and uncivilized—" She stroked his face once more, ran loving fingers through his thick dark hair, calming his anger.

Devlin kicked off his own boots, yielding gracefully. "As I was saying, since we're not in the public eye at the moment—"

* * * *

"Aren't you glad I made you keep those costumes?" Glancing in the mirror, Lily adjusted the skin-tone wig over the scarf that covered her auburn hair.

"They're going back to Verdi today."

"You didn't answer my question."

"Yes," Nevis admitted, straightening her own blonde wig from its lopsided fit. "Lily, about those journals—"

"How many times must I tell you that I don't mind?" Lily slapped the ridiculous feathered cap on her head in utter exasperation. "Apparently, I must repeat it one more time. I don't mind, Nevis. And I think Devlin's smart to remove them from his quarters. Besides," the madam smirked as Nevis tucked the stiletto into her ebony boot, without instructions this time, "I assume he delivered them in person."

Nevis straightened up, green eyes daring her friend to comment further. "Your point?"

"I daresay he took great pleasure in persuading you to accept them."

"I didn't need persuading. And besides—"

"Honestly, Nevis, you're a middle-aged and quite accomplished mage, yet you blush like a virgin."

Nevis' skin flushed even deeper, to her utter disgust, though she laughed good naturedly. "Are you quite finished?"

"For the moment. Now come along, Carmelita dear, my carriage awaits your pleasure."

The mage grumbled her way in relatively good humor past Chappy Markos, sworn to secrecy at his employer's antics. Chappy held the door politely, as did the carriage driver, who barely restrained a smile when Lily strode past in her black-and-white-checkered suit. He flashed a small square of paper at Lily as she settled inside the carriage.

"Another receipt?"

"A list of pawnshops in the city, provided by Chappy."

"Good thinking."

"It did occur to me, and Chappy, too, though the dear man would never admit it for fear of insulting the great Mage Conarkin, that you might have thought there was only one pawnshop in Port Jambi."

"I did think there was more than one, but I'd no idea who to ask without arousing suspicion," Nevis admitted sheepishly, straightening the folds of her scarlet skirt before settling back against the seat as the carriage rattled noisily along the cobblestones on McOsley's Road.

"When in doubt about anything questionable in this city, ask Chappy Markos. Now, Carmelita, look sharp. Our first stop is Faulker's Point. It's the closest."

But not the one that provided the answer. The next pawnshop in Milneran's Street was another disappointment, but the third, in the center of Chalker's Hill, gave the two friends something to ponder.

Nevis stepped down the carriage steps, with the driver's assistance, and studied her surroundings, cheap multi-storied buildings crammed close together, shutting out the daylight. "I wouldn't be surprised if Hans lived near here, what with the pathetic wages I can afford to pay him. It's a wonder none of my cast has headed to Barry Faddle's theater troupe."

"They know a decent employer when they see one. Besides, Hans isn't so poorly paid. Stop feeling sorry for him."

"I'll bet he's glad he doesn't work for you." Nevis stepped up onto the curb, avoiding a pile of horse manure, and waited for Lily beside the pawnshop, peering into the cluttered window.

The door screeched on its hinges as Lily pulled it open, both women entering the dimly lit interior, raising a cloud of dust as they passed shelves crowded with odds and ends. Nevis' cough was only part pretense, though she covered her mouth politely so as not to offend the owner.

"Need some help, do you?" A raspy voice echoed from the back of the pawnshop, as an elderly woman, her dress as drab and full of dust as the shop, shuffled her way into their view.

Nevis pulled the receipt from her pocket and handed it over the counter. "My brother asked me to redeem this ticket."

The old woman took the paper, glanced at the number, and nodded. "Your brother, you say?"

"Yes."

"Why not let his woman come running to do his errands?"

Nevis slid a glance at Lily, who shrugged. "That's his business. We do favors for each other."

"Then do him another favor." The old woman smiled, teeth all askew, as she shuffled around to the glass case behind her. She unearthed a rusty key from the folds of her drab skirt. "Tell him not to act so jumpy next time he pawns something. Seemed awfully suspicious."

Nevis kept her expression bland as Lily pinched her arm out of the woman's sight. "Pardon?"

"It was obvious he'd stolen the ring." The old shopkeeper plucked a small gold ring from the open case, a single ruby set within a heart of gold. "And the girl was a bit too obvious she didn't want to get caught."

"Especially when his sister found out he'd taken it," Lily boomed into Nevis' ear, elbowing her hard.

"Filthy swine," the old woman grumbled. "He should know better than to take his own sister's jewelry."

Nevis shrugged, eyes downcast. "It's not the first time."

"Better be the last," Lily declared, her voice a rough imitation of Chappy's deep tones, as she played with a loose strand of Nevis' blonde wig. "Come along, dearie, let's pay the good woman. How much do we owe you?"

"Four silver coins."

"Four silver coins?" Nevis shouted indignantly. "That's all?" She grabbed the ring and slid it back on her finger. "That's an outrage."

"Just think how outraged you'd be if you had to pay more for your own stolen goods," the woman scolded, peering at the disguised mage as though she had not a bit of intelligence in her head.

"Good point."

"Now you'd best go warn that foolish swine to keep away from your jewelry. He should know better."

"I will." Nevis headed out the door into the bright sunshine, relieved that she'd found Gabriella's ring, but saddened at the culprits.

"Will you, really?" Lily asked as they both climbed back into the carriage. "Warn him, I mean?"

"Sure." Nevis shut her eyes and rested her head against the velvet cushion. "In my own way."

* * * *

Waiting patiently until the nervous chatter died down, Nevis stepped gracefully from the wings onto center stage. Her sudden appearance brought a wave of greetings and affectionate catcalls.

"Damnably hard to rehearse without your phenomenal and extravagant special effects," Pepo Daken complained when he caught sight of the mage. "Difficult to imagine the storms and the tidal wave crashing over the city walls—"

"Difficult to keep creating spells to amuse you, Pepo. I needed a break." Nevis smiled to take the sting from her words, and the actor nodded graciously. She slipped past him in Gabriella de la Morsage's direction. Fully cognizant of Hans nearby, within easy hearing, the mage waved Gabriella closer and held out her hand. "Is this gold ring the one you were missing some days ago?"

"Oh, Nevis, yes. That's surely my ring." The leading lady whipped her head around, flaming red hair swirling with her movement. "The very ring that was stolen from me by someone in this theater troupe."

"I'm not quite sure it was stolen," Nevis said quietly, aware that everyone on stage, including Hans, was listening carefully. "I nearly broke my neck a little while ago when I stepped on it."

Gabriella muttered something rude, holding the gold ring up to the burning magefire lamp.

"My foot's not that heavy."

"Just checking." The sarcasm swept right over Gabriella's distracted head. "Where was it?"

"On the floor outside your dressing room. It must have slid off your finger while you were changing costumes."

"Nevis, I'm not careless with my jewelry. I removed it to be sure that I didn't snag the embroidery in my robe. If I had, that lice-ridden creature who designs our costumes would have come screaming at me."

"Can't blame her. Anyway, there it is." Nevis shrugged offhandedly and smiled, green eyes focused, for a heartbeat, on Hans' face. "One more rehearsal, my children, and we perform for your adoring public." The mage headed back toward the left wing but Hans intercepted her, guiding her away from the others.

"Nevis—"

"I trust that was the last payment for any drugs." When the young actor didn't even try to meet her gaze, Nevis sighed deeply. "Hans, I'm serious. Keep your hands away from Gabriella's jewelry and my cash box. If you need a loan, I'll do what I can to help. Just ask me, damn it."

"It wasn't—" Hans stopped his words, only serving to make the mage even more uneasy. "Look, it was important. I needed the money. I had every intention of returning the ring to Gabriella and whatever I took from the cash box. I'm sorry. I'm sorry for lying." He turned to leave but Nevis grabbed his sleeve.

"What kind of trouble are you in?"

"Nothing I can't handle."

Nevis forced him to look at her. "Sure?"

Hans nodded, and she released him, unconvinced. The young man fled from her presence toward the dressing rooms.

"Please don't tell me he really stole Gabriella's ring."

"Wish I could deny it, Verdi," Nevis murmured as the costume designer stepped into the light. "Borrowed it, anyway. He intended to return it."

"Sorry to eavesdrop. I didn't see him standing there until I was nearly on top of you both."

"That's all right." Nevis indicated the sack lying against the wall. "Your costumes. If Lily keeps hold of them, she'll find another excuse to use them. Need help carrying them?"

"No. I can handle the bag. I'm surprised Lily gave them back. She was having entirely too much fun."

"I had to torture her first." Nevis looked back the way Hans had gone. "Keep an eye on the boy, will you?"

"Sure." Verdi grabbed a handful of the sack. "What kind of trouble is he really in? Did he tell you?"

"No." Nevis raked short-cropped white hair from her eyes. "I'm not entirely sure I want to know."

"Maybe I can find out," Verdi said quietly, eying two figures just walking up the center aisle. "Looks like you've got company."

The mage turned, surprised to see Finlay Oscram walking side-by-side with trade minister Nashat. Verdi headed back toward her costume room to give them privacy, but Finlay hailed her.

"Don't leave, Verdi. You and Nevis are just the people we came to see." The banker, conservatively dressed in a dark gray suit but for a lavender cravat at his throat, met the two women at the foot of the stage. His bald head gleamed beneath the flickering magefire lamps.

"Minister Nashat," Nevis shook his hand, not bothering to hide her surprise. "My costume designer, Verdi Casporet."

"The young woman who would hound you without mercy if we didn't agree on a decent price for Cashogi fabrics."

"The very same."

"Some reputation, Nevis, thanks." Verdi grinned, shaking the minister's hand. "Your fabrics are truly exquisite, and I'd love to use them in our theater. If your trade negotiations go well, of course."

"I intend to see that they succeed." The Cashogi minister brushed a hand lightly over his quite short hair, taking a moment to glance around the stage set. "It is also important that I understand the market for my country's goods." He bowed, smiling at Nevis. "And so I convinced Master Oscram to bring me here. In Cashogi, our theaters are not quite as—" The trade minister sought a word that wouldn't insult the mage, came up empty.

"Adventurous? Wild? Reckless?" Nevis laughed. "I understand theaters in your country don't typically use sorcery to create dramatic effects. They're similar to Barry Faddle's theater."

"Yes, and truly it's a pity. They seem so mundane. I greatly look forward to your opening night performance."

"As do I. But I wouldn't be so swift to dismiss theater without sorcery. It forces actors to—" She glanced around to be sure her cast and crew were occupied elsewhere, so as not to offend any sensitive egos, then grinned at Verdi, "well, be less dependent on my sorcery and special effects to create the drama necessary to touch the audience, to make them laugh or cry or feel any number of honest emotions. Although to be honest, I'm rather proud of this particular troupe. They'd do quite well in a non-sorcerous theater, too."

"Don't let them hear your praise," Verdi said, laughing. "You'd have to raise their wages again."

"Not in front of our banker. His heart will stop if he hears such talk."

"Now, Nevis, really. What will Minister Nashat think?" Finlay protested, shaking his head in resigned disgust at their laughter.

"That you are a tough negotiator." The Cashogi gentleman smiled to soften his words. "If you cannot be generous with clients whom you know very well, what hope can a foreign minister have? Particularly one from a country that has not always been on peaceful terms with your own Montbasso?"

"Old history," Nevis murmured, remembering Shayna's awkward relationship to the Cashogi infiltrators caught ten years earlier.

"Yes," the minister sighed, "though still painfully fresh for some."

"Like Shayna Kashi?"

"Precisely. However, Mage Conarkin, if I believed she yet held a grudge against your country folk, I would not have brought her with me on this delicate assignment." The trade minister looked away, and Nevis wondered whether he did indeed have doubts. "Her words to you at the merchants' dinner some nights ago were unfortunate and rather rude."

"Not rude. Besides, we encourage free speech in Montbasso." Nevis nodded her approval when Verdi managed a discreet exit before the minister had second thoughts about his audience. "No harm was done."

"But you are wrong, Mage Conarkin." The minister leaned back against the stage, waving away her offer of a more comfortable seat. "Her challenge was in very poor taste. Your position as adviser—"

Nevis glanced at Finlay, who simply shrugged. "I'm no longer mage adviser to the king. I resigned from that position ten years ago, nearly ten years ago this very day. After I defeated Adrian Bambari," she added slowly, "I asked Devlin to appoint another mage."

"I understand clearly that your advisory position is not the official one. But I also understand that Devlin Graham values your counsel more heavily than he does that of Hugo San Rossi." When Nevis immediately protested, he raised a jeweled hand. "I say these words to you, not because you are Devlin Graham's lover or to cause trouble for you, Mage Conarkin, but truly—" His eyes darted around the theater, much as Nevis had looked earlier, to be sure they were not overheard.

When he didn't immediately answer, Nevis prompted, "If not to cause trouble, then why?"

"Because I regard you highly and wish to share mutual respect and trust." The Cashogi gentleman's expression appeared utterly and genuinely honest, and Nevis decided to take a chance.

"If your words are true, and I mean no disrespect by my words or tone," Nevis said swiftly as his dark eyes narrowed, "then you might be interested in something that's recently come to my attention."

"A test?"

"Perhaps. If you consider my counsel equal to or more valuable than Hugo San Rossi's, your response will be most enlightening." His face a mask, but for a tugging at his lips, gave Nevis the encouragement she needed. "In fact—"

"May I say one thing before you begin, Mage Conarkin? And I say it as another true sign of my good faith. What I said regarding your counsel is precisely what I think. However," the minister's eyes had grown somber, "my companion, Shayna Kashi, thinks highly of Mage San Rossi. In Cashogi, we also encourage free speech and free opinions, but I think my companion misguided."

"And so you place Nevis in an awkward position to speak ill of Hugo San Rossi when Hugo's lover is the king's heir?" Finlay Oscram interrupted, surprising both listeners, who'd nearly forgotten his presence.

"Yes, but not for malicious reasons, Master Oscram. As I said, I regard Mage Conarkin quite highly."

"Why?" Nevis blurted out the challenging question before she actually thought about it.

The trade minister sent Nevis a silent message that she scrambled to interpret, then turned to the banker, his expression grave and courteous. "Master Oscram, please take no offense, but may I speak privately with Mage Conarkin?"

Despite the gentle and polite request, Finlay looked quite offended. When Nevis lightly squeezed his arm, however, the elderly banker nodded and walked toward the main entrance, sufficiently out of hearing.

"I shall have to make immeasurable apologies to the gentleman, but I think it best he doesn't hear what I would say to you."

"Go on," Nevis murmured, caught completely unprepared for the trade minister's simple explanation.

"I heard rumors a decade ago that Devlin Graham's queen was a traitor, yet the people who had the information squashed it to protect a young girl's heart." Mikaline Nashat stared intently at the mage, adding softly, "You have deprived yourself of a well-deserved place at Devlin's side so as not to upset young Alana. Not an easy sacrifice, particularly when someone like Hugo San Rossi spends all his free time discrediting you."

Nevis turned away, felt the minister's fingers touch her arm lightly before retreating.

"I know this fact because my sister was accused in Adrian Bambari's treasonous plot, though unlike Shayna's family, my sister, to my eternal shame, was completely guilty. That knowledge, of the Montbasso queen's betrayal, is known to few still living. For my part, Mage Conarkin," Nashat said earnestly, his voice convincing her of his sincerity, "I've been working toward peaceful trade between the Cashogi people and your kingdom ever since I discovered my sister's appalling part in your troubles. It seems the least I can do to make amends."

Nevis spun slowly to face him. "Does Devlin know?"

"From the very first day I arrived. I could not have kept this secret from Devlin and still negotiated in good faith, though I did ask him not to say anything to you, because I wished to meet you first. You may, of course, tell him of our discussion. You may also," the minister's smile was sad, "research my family history. You may have forgotten the names of those Cashogi individuals involved in the treachery with Adrian Bambari, but they're engraved in my memory forever, a point of disgrace that I am endeavoring to erase."

Nevis raked back white strands from her eyes, absently scratching her head, giving herself a chance to think.

"Devlin has also confided in me that Hugo San Rossi has accused both you and me in a plot to cause trouble for Montbasso. I know that

I had not met you prior to the merchants' dinner," he added dryly, "and so I assume you are just as innocent as myself of these appalling charges. Unless, of course," he smiled uncertainly, "you've been meeting with an imposter aboard one of my vessels."

"Absolutely not, minister Nashat. I apologize for my countryman," Nevis said quietly, studying the gentleman's sincere expression. "And as to what I've heard that might interest you—" The mage paused, wondering just how very much to tell him. "There's something far more solid than Hugo's trumped up accusations that might disrupt the ongoing trade negotiations if the people of Port Jambi ever found out."

The Cashogi minister stood straight, pushing away from the stage, brown eyes locked on her face. "Tell me."

"There are sources in the city already trading with your people. Unfortunately, they're buying Cashogi drugs from one of your ships." If Nevis had had any doubts of his shock or distress, the minister's expression erased them.

"Impossible."

"I wish it were."

"How do you know?"

Nevis glanced at the private box overlooking the stage. "For one thing, the man murdered in my theater only days ago bought and sold Cashogi drugs, specifically a drug called Firespark. Apparently, the deals and the shipments have been arriving by way of Alvaron Park, though I had no idea. Trust me, Minister Nashat, if I knew that Firespark was bought and sold so near my orphanage and those innocent children—"

"I quite understand. Nevertheless, it's not a very good way to reestablish trading between Montbasso and Cashogi, is it? Can you tell me anything more?"

Nevis didn't look away, but met his gaze head on. "I'd rather not. I've no proof, and I'd rather you investigated discreetly on your own."

"You suspect Shayna of involvement."

His matter-of-fact tone left her flustered. "Minister—"

The Cashogi official held up his hand. "If her true opinions go further than her words, then I'd be foolish not to explore the possibility. Trust me, I shall be discreet. I would be sadly disappointed if Shayna were involved in such dealings, Mage Conarkin, because she has been like a daughter to me for nearly all her life. We have grown exceptionally close in the last ten years, ever since her family was unfairly accused and executed. However," brown eyes filled with genuine sorrow, "somehow, and I can't explain why, because even I don't understand, I would not be surprised if your suspicions are correct. It would also seem logical, if her politics went beyond words, that she would try to undermine the negotiations."

"If Shayna were truly involved. If—Minister Nashat, you don't know that, not for certain."

"That is one of the reasons I regard you so highly, Mage Conarkin." The Cashogi gentleman smiled, waving to Finlay Oscram to rejoin them. "You try to give those who would harm you another chance to prove themselves innocent. However," he warned seriously, "it might not be wise to do so with Hugo San Rossi."

* * * *

"You really trust him, don't you?"

Nevis nodded, green eyes scanning the nearly impenetrable shadows along the riverbank as she peered out from their hiding spot between two thick berry bushes. "Not sure why, Lily, but I do."

The brothel owner wrapped her light wool cloak tighter around her stiff, huddled body. "Well, Nevis," she sighed, stifling a huge yawn, "you're usually a decent judge of character. I won't dispute your opinion in this matter. For the moment, anyway, you understand?"

In the dark beneath the moonless sky, the mage grinned, eyes laughing beneath the black knit cap that covered her brilliant white hair.

"What I don't understand is why you didn't tell him about this clandestine meeting between Hugo, Shayna, and the Firespark supplier."

"We have no proof that Hugo and Shayna will show up themselves. And besides, I'd rather have the minister investigate discreetly on his own. He told me he has contacts who can help him."

"I'm sure you're right, but still—"

"How'd you convince Remo to stay away?"

"I told him the ladies needed some privacy to discuss our options."

"Which is why I needed to keep a magefire lamp burning in my parlor?"

"Precisely, though if Devlin shows up unexpectedly—"

"It's audience day again."

"Already?"

Nevis nodded once more, studying the clouds sailing across the sky. It was nearly dawn, and no one had appeared, at least as far as they could see.

"Damn, that wind is unexpectedly cold—"

"Hush." Nevis grabbed Lily's wrist, her face turned expectantly toward the river. "Movement somewhere out there."

"Where's the constable?" Lily murmured, voicing a concern that had already troubled the mage. "I hope she freezes."

"Hush."

The two women sat perfectly still as the unmistakable sound of muffled oars came closer. One burst of light flared, quickly shuttered, then repeated. Nevis strained her eyes in the dark to see where it was directed, waiting for the answering signal. And then saw it, not far from the park bench to their right, between their position in the berry bushes and the darkened theater.

Two hooded and cloaked figures stepped from the shadows and moved quietly toward the riverbank, crouching low. Without warning, the smaller of the two pointed toward the rocks along the shore by the theater. The other figure headed purposefully toward the rocks, stopped immediately by the pointer's panicked grip.

"What's going on?" Lily breathed in the mage's ear. "They're pointing and arguing about something, but I can't see what it is."

"They're—" Nevis suddenly lurched to her feet. "That little fool." She started forward, abruptly caught back by an unexpected restraint that wouldn't loosen its fierce grip.

"They won't dare touch him."

Lily jumped at the sound of Brea Kilganor's sharp voice right behind her. "Touch who? Nevis, what's going on out there?" Bewildered, Lily's eyes darted from Nevis' stony expression to the constable's placid one, then slightly downward to the constable's tight grip on the mage's shoulders.

"It's near dawn, Mistress Frascat. You've been here several hours. It's trout fishing time, though I don't know how the little beast slipped past us."

"Little beast? Constable, if Teddy's in danger—" Lily stood up beside Nevis, followed her stony gaze toward the riverbank, ready to rush toward the rocks and snatch the boy to safety.

"They're signaling the boat away." Nevis didn't dare relax until the two figures crept back from the shoreline, her eyes tracking their progress out of the park and onto McOsley's Road.

"Poor Hugo," Lily muttered, sounding utterly unsympathetic. "No Cashogi Firespark, no winnings from the races, no—"

"You don't know it was Hugo San Rossi," the constable interrupted, dark eyes daring the madam to argue.

"She's right," Nevis murmured before Lily could voice her opinion. "It could have been Hugo, or one of his henchmen. Either way, we didn't see anything that would allow us to recognize him."

"Whose side are you on?"

Nevis started to answer Lily's accusatory question, shook her head instead, and started to walk away from both women.

"Damn it, Nevis—"

"Look, we weren't even supposed to be here."

Brea Kilganor clapped politely. "Excellent point. I wondered whether either of you remembered that pertinent fact."

"As though you'd allow us to forget," Lily grumbled.

"What about the boy?"

"If you tell my nephew there are shady deals in the park, you're inviting him to snoop. Leave him be."

"And if Hugo had hurt him?" Lily snapped, angry at both Nevis and the constable. "What would have happened, Nevis? Tell me."

The mage stared at her friend in silence, then spoke in a tone that chilled Lily's soul. "Hugo San Rossi would have stopped breathing before he ever dared touch my nephew."

Chapter Ten

Nevis glanced down at the sticky, sugar-coated breakfast cake, and wondered idly when she'd bitten off the missing chunk, the piece with the raspberry star. Before she broke off another morsel, still wondering how she'd eaten some of the marvelous cake without remembering, a shriek pierced the silence of the theater, followed in all-too-swift succession by a mewling whimper and shouts of panic.

"It's too damned early," the mage grumbled, pushing back her chair to investigate the bedlam. Her stiletto impatiently tapped the left crystal sphere on the cabinet, letting it revolve until the stage came into easy view, though she couldn't make out what was happening. "It's far too early to deal with adult children." Sighing in resignation, Nevis resheathed her stiletto and shook her head at the carved likeness of Janni surrounded by a dozen children. "How do you manage without murdering them in their sleep?"

When the goddess didn't answer, Nevis left the office and headed for her private theater box, leaning over the wooden rail just in time to see Teddy Quiddle sliding across the stage in pursuit of the black and white kitten. Gabriella leaped out of the way, barely a moment too soon, cursing the boy and his frightened pet.

Murmuring an incantation, the mage gracefully moved her hand. Teddy Quiddle, in a skinny heap on the wooden stage floor, went slack-jawed as the protesting kitten hovered over the pile of garments that Verdi had unwittingly dropped when the assault began and came to land on the boy's flat stomach.

"Out. Now."

"Aunt Nevis—"

"I mean it, Teddy. We've the last rehearsal to survive, and I've no patience this morning. Out."

"But Ma sent me here." The boy gathered the kitten in his arms before the imp could escape. "She said to tell you that inspectors are looking all over the orphanage building. And they're not very polite."

"Inspectors?" Nevis dropped her hand, unaware that it fell lightly atop the ivory-handled stiletto at her waist.

"From the court."

"Tell her I'll be right over."

Before Teddy could sit upright, Simon Masters appeared at the mage's elbow. "Not a good idea, boss."

"Why not?"

"They'll only use it as an excuse to harass you further. You're better off sending Remo over there."

Nevis scratched absently at her hair, badly in need of a trim. "Good thinking."

"That's why you pay me."

"I actually pay you?" Nevis grinned, leaning back over the railing. "Tell your mother I'll send word to Remo. Thanks, Teddy. Now scoot. And take that hideous beast with you."

The boy grinned back, relieved that she wasn't really angry, skinny arms and legs flying out the door to carry out his mission.

"Simon—"

"I'll head over to Lily's. Remo might still be around. It's early enough, I should think."

"Thanks. Why don't you—" Nevis stopped, wide-eyed in dismay, as Gabriella de la Morsage slumped bonelessly to the stage floor without uttering a sound. "By the gods, Simon—"

"I'll get Doc Esteway, too."

The stage manager flew out the door and down the stairs, Nevis hard on his heels. They separated at the bottom, and Nevis rushed to the stage, where Pepo and Verdi were kneeling beside the fallen actress.

"She's still breathing," Verdi said quietly, holding Gabriella's head against her knees, the actress' flaming red hair fanned out around her head.

"What happened? Did she say anything before she dropped?"

Pepo sat back on his haunches. "I thought she might have said something about feeling ill, but that's all."

Nevis joined them on the ground, loosening the actress' tight collar. "Gabriella? Can you hear me?" The actress moaned, and Nevis tried again, leaning closer to be sure Gabriella would hear if she was conscious. "Odd scent."

"What is?" Verdi leaned beside the mage, sniffing the air, trying to decipher the scent. "That smells like—"

"That smells precisely like Firespark," Pepo squeaked, his voice ranging high above his usual tones. "If Hans—"

"Shut up, Pepo," Nevis snapped. "We don't have a clue what's going on."

"Maybe I can help." A slight woman, long blonde hair set in a neat braid hanging over one shoulder, appeared on stage, a duffel bag of herbs and medicinal concoctions dangling from the other shoulder.

Grateful at the speed at which Lily's house physician appeared, Nevis said, "I hope so, Doc. Gabriella said something about not feeling well, then crumpled and fell. And we're smelling the distinct possibility of Firespark."

Setting aside the duffel, the doctor leaned over and sniffed. "Quite right. Potent stuff. Was she a user?"

"Absolutely not," Pepo declared, as though he himself had been insulted. "There are only a handful of degenerates in this theater company, and—"

"Pepo," Nevis warned, not wanting the actor to insult anyone else. "Listen, Doc, as far as I know, Gabriella never used drugs."

"Of course not," the actress murmured, trying unsuccessfully to push herself upright as she started to regain consciousness. "And I dare anyone to ever say that I do use drugs."

"Easy," Doc Esteway cautioned, "you'll get dizzy. Tell me what you had for breakfast, Gabriella."

As genuinely pale and sickly as the actress appeared, Gabriella managed to look guilty. "I didn't. Nevis—" Suddenly, she grabbed the mage's sleeve, her usually rosy face pale. "Nevis, that awful sugar-coated cake was sitting on your desk untouched. Have you eaten any yet?"

Nevis sat back on her haunches, head cocked to the side. "You were the one who stole a piece?"

"I was late, hadn't had time to eat—" The actress shuddered as a spasm hit her stomach. "Doc—"

"Hold on, let's get you somewhere where you can vomit in private." The physician commandeered Pepo to help carry Gabriella off the stage, though she turned to the mage before leaving. "Did you have any of that cake?"

"I was just about to."

"Then go take a look without touching it. I'll be right up."

Nevis grunted, watched the physician haul Gabriella out of sight, barely in time. She headed back to the office, Verdi trailing along behind, desperately trying not to laugh aloud at the unsavory sound of Gabriella's retching.

Though Verdi turned serious once they were alone. "Simon would never have done anything to that cake."

Nevis glanced up at Verdi, both women poised in the corridor outside her office. "I didn't think he would. I may be overly suspicious and looking over my shoulder these days, but I'd never not trust Simon. The same goes for you, Verdi." When the costume designer flushed uncomfortably, Nevis waved away her apology. "The question is, who did tamper with the cake?" The mage reentered her office, unaware of the soft footsteps that approached the open door.

"Don't touch it."

Nevis looked past the costume designer, where Brea Kilganor had appeared, uniform crisp and neat, one hand raised to keep Nevis away from the sugar-coated cake. "I haven't yet. Except where Gabriella broke off a piece, it looks untouched, same as I get every morning."

"Not from this angle." The constable stepped closer to the desk, pointed toward a thin line that ran along the dough. With her dagger, she pried the top and bottom halves apart. "Neatly sliced and coated with Firespark powder."

"By the gods," Nevis exclaimed, staring in horror at the powdery substance dusting both halves of the breakfast cake. "Enough to kill me?"

"I doubt it," the constable said reasonably, adding, "Well, sure, if you managed to eat the whole thing, but you would have smelled it. The likely event is you would have gotten ill."

"Boss?" Simon stormed into the crowded office, thinning hair all disheveled from rushing. "Pepo just told me what happened."

"Why don't you tell us what happened," Brea suggested, a hint of iron in her tone that irritated Nevis.

"Look, Constable—"

"I didn't ask you, Mage Conarkin. I asked Simon."

Distressed, Simon looked to the mage for reassurance. "Nevis, believe me, if I'd known—"

"I know that, Simon. Tell the constable what happened."

Running his fingers over his thinning hair, Simon tried to smooth the frazzled ends. "Nothing unusual. I picked up the cake as I do every morning from Clari's bakery. And then left it here on the desk."

"Before Mage Conarkin arrived?"

"Yes." Simon glanced at the mage, who shrugged.

"Sometimes I'm here, sometimes not. Unfortunately, I wasn't here this morning, so I've no idea if anyone besides Gabriella crept in."

"Could it have been the baker? She's a relatively new arrival in Port Jambi," Simon suggested, unaware that Nevis had wondered the same, sick with dread at the possibility that Clarissa's recent words had been false.

"Perhaps, though my guess is that someone else slipped in during that narrow period of time. I should think someone would notice an old woman and her cane." The constable peered closely at the desk, grunted happily in satisfaction. "Look here." She lifted a strand of black curly hair from beneath the wrapping and held it out for the mage's inspection. "Looks like someone's sending you a warning."

Nevis met her gaze across the remains of the sugar-coated cake, immensely relieved that Clarissa appeared innocent. "Yes, but which someone?" She glanced at Verdi and Simon. "Would you excuse us? Simon, cancel the rehearsal, will you? Tell them all to show up two hours before the performance tomorrow night. By the gods, I hope Gabriella's stomach is settled by then."

"Even if it is," Verdi tossed over her shoulder, "she'll never let you know the truth. You'll have a whining nuisance on your hands for days." She led Simon out of the office, shutting the door behind them.

"What's your theory?" Brea Kilganor sank onto the well-worn chair opposite the mage when they were alone. "Fani? For getting too close to the truth about Hans?" When Nevis didn't answer, she asked, "Shayna? For harassing Hugo? Or Slick Hands? For not selling your theater to him when you were desperate for funds?"

"Could be all or none," Nevis admitted, "though there's another possible reason Shayna Kashi might have done it. I had an interesting chat with trade minister Nashat yesterday."

"Private?"

"Quite. I expressed grave concerns about the possibility of disrupted trade negotiations if the public found out about the sale of Firespark from Cashogi to Montbasso citizens."

Brea stared at the mage, her brown eyes unreadable. "Risky."

"I thought it worth the risk."

"Ballsy." The constable brushed her hands distractedly through her white-speckled black hair.

"It was an even exchange. The minister admitted to me that Devlin warned him about Hugo's accusation regarding my clandestine meetings with the minister aboard his vessel."

"What—" Astonished, Brea stopped speaking as a polite knocking sounded at the office door.

"Come in," Nevis called out, surprised to find Remo Savanak standing patiently in the doorway, impeccably dressed as ever. "Did Simon tell you what happened at the orphanage?"

"He told me quite a few things, Nevis. Good morning, constable. May I join you?"

"If Mage Conarkin doesn't mind, sure."

Remo entered and shut the door, leaning against the heavy wood. "First things first, are you hurt in any way?" He eyed the sugar-coated cake with distaste. When Nevis shook her head, not bothering to say anything further, he frowned. "Suspects?"

"A few. That's not important now. What about the inspectors? Teddy said they weren't very friendly."

"I was too late to talk to them."

"Inspectors?" Brea inquired politely. "From the court?"

"Unfortunately, yes. May Quiddle said they were looking around the building, muttering about fire hazards and other potential trouble."

Nevis sat back, thinking, trying to sort her jumbled thoughts. "There's a rumor going around," she said slowly, gazing evenly at the constable, "that Hugo San Rossi is blackmailing the judges to decide in his favor. You may have heard that same rumor on the streets."

"Seems I did," Brea murmured.

"I'll look into it, Nevis." Remo pushed back from the door. "I've been meaning to do so, anyway, but with all that's been going on, it slipped my mind."

"I'm not your only client."

"Aside from Lily, you're my favorite, and the one deepest in trouble at the moment."

"Is the building a fire trap?" The constable asked, her expression sufficiently pensive to unsettle the mage.

"No more than any other building around this part of town. By the gods," Nevis fumed, "at least it's clean and dry and warm at night. I'd make it into a palace if I could afford it."

Remo leaned over and squeezed the mage's thin shoulder, worried at how fragile she felt. "Seems that every one of those children think of it as a palace already," he said softly.

"Why not ask Devlin Graham for a loan from the royal treasury?" The constable smoothed the well-creased fabric of her uniform breeches, a sly grin revealing crooked teeth. "Anyone else in your position wouldn't hesitate."

"The royal treasury has a hundred thousand demands on it that are far more urgent."

"But you have far more clout."

"I choose my favors, Constable. Same as I choose my battles."

* * * *

"You should have come earlier," May Quiddle smiled, rocking softly in the chair by the cold fireplace. "We had a marvelous trout supper."

"Did you now? Fresh trout?"

"Quite. Teddy caught several today and several days ago, though I don't know when that rascal has the time."

Nevis sank into the opposite seat without daring to answer.

"I did save you a few of the strawberry tarts that the new baker sent over the other day for the children. You left so swiftly that night, without even nibbling on one," the younger woman shot a glance at her sister that was half anxious, half mischievous. "I was worried."

"My heroine," Nevis grinned, rocking her own chair back and forth, and dodging her sister's unspoken query. "I won't refuse now."

"Didn't think you would. Be right back."

The moment May left the clean-swept parlor, a tiny head, long auburn curls loose and wild, peered through the entry.

"You should be in bed."

Kimmi stuck her thumb contentedly in her mouth and sidled up to Nevis, waiting to be picked up. Naturally, the mage hoisted her onto her lap and rocked her gently until the child closed her drooping eyelids.

"Here you—" May stared speechless at the sight, though the little girl's affection for Nevis genuinely delighted the younger woman. "Nevis, really—"

"Hush." The mage stroked the child's thick curls, as her free hand reached for the tart, setting it on the side table. "Sorry about the inspectors today."

"Not your fault. Remo said not to worry, but I can't help it." May wearily brushed dark brown hair from her face, and sighed. "They weren't very pleasant."

"Just doing their job."

"Frightening children?" When Nevis took a spoonful of the sweet dessert and shut her eyes in ecstasy, May asked, "What are we going to do if they decide the building is dangerous?"

"Move the children elsewhere. May," the mage dug out another sweet spoonful, prompting her younger sister to wonder when Nevis had last eaten anything nutritious. "I promise they won't go back on the street."

"But where will they go? Nevis, I've been thinking."

"No wonder you look so tired."

"Don't be fresh."

"Go on."

"Can't you place a spell on the building to repair it, make it better?" Nevis set the spoon aside, eying the empty plate with regret.

"More?"

"By the gods, no, but thanks. Look, May, a spell that broad would work for a limited time. I'd have to keep replenishing it. Besides, the inspectors have already seen the building. My problem with this whole harassment is that not one of us, you, me, or Lily, would keep the children in a building that wasn't safe. This orphanage," Nevis waved her hand around the room, "isn't all that bad. Sure, it needs work, but it's not a firetrap or completely dilapidated and ready to crumble. My crew keeps an eye out for the worst repairs."

"If the inspectors are harassing you, it won't matter. They'll just write up whatever opinion they were told to report."

"Right, so don't worry. Remo said he'll check into things."

"Why is it, Mage Conarkin, that you're always telling me not to worry, and then you go off and worry for both of us?"

"I'm older, and my hair is already white." Nevis stopped rocking and glanced down at the sleeping child. "I'd better tuck her in."

"I'll take care of Kimmi. Go on. I know you're restless." May leaned over and took the sleeping child with practiced ease.

"You're coming tomorrow night, aren't you?"

"Would I miss the opening night of my big sister's new play? I'm just sorry Theo's not home yet. He always enjoys the excitement of your opening night performances."

"We'll run a special one just for the captain when he returns in a few weeks, and make believe it's opening night again." Nevis grinned at the image that just popped into her head. "Gabriella would adore having another opening night."

"Don't be fresh." May kissed the mage on the cheek and held her close. "Get some rest, will you? Good luck tomorrow night. Break a leg."

Nevis stroked the child's soft cheek as she rested against May's shoulder. She crept from the building, taking the river path rather than walking through Alvaron Park. The sound of muffled oars coming closer along the river brought her steps to a complete and sudden halt. Was it possible that Hugo and Shayna had arranged another meeting with the Cashogi supplier? The hour was far earlier than the previous night, but the change may have been deliberate.

Nevis didn't dare use sorcery, instead slipping out of her black vest and tucking it over her head to hide the beacon brightness of her hair. Crouching behind a boulder, she waited out of sight, straining to listen.

Two cloaked and hooded figures darted from the bushes, no different than the previous encounter, and headed for the uneven shoreline after signaling the boat closer. Water lapped along the rocks as the outline of a sleek rowboat appeared. The taller of the two figures waded out to the boat, pulling it closer. Nevis gripped the slick boulder, trying to listen as the oarsman stopped rowing.

"One favor. Only this one time," the man in the boat said. "For my beautiful friend there."

"I appreciate your confidence," the taller figure on land said, his voice no other than Hugo San Rossi. "And won't forget it."

"I won't let you forget it. No payment next time we meet, my Montbasso friend, and mage or no mage—"

"Hush!"

"Well, then, be warned. No payment, and you'll face my very fierce temper. Ask the young lady there about my temper tantrums."

"I believe you, and you won't regret it. I promise I'll have the payment next time. I've found myself a new source of funds, who promises gold the very next time we meet."

"You'd best not be lying." The boatman heaved a hefty sack over the side, careful to place it in Hugo's waiting arms. "Now go, before we're caught. It's too damned early in the evening, and I'm risking the chance that the captain's spies will see me climb back aboard."

"Go on. Thanks."

"As I said, don't thank me. Just pay me."

Nevis listened as the small boat retreated into the shadows, watched Hugo and his Cashogi lady drift back through the park. Only when she was certain they were long gone did she dare leave her hiding spot. She walked back along the river path, Alvaron Park to her left, the theater before her. Along McOsley's Road, she could see the reflection along the street of the light display within the huge sorcerous sphere in the front of the building, and wondered whether Hugo would scrawl nasty words across the sphere again.

* * * *

Nevis had checked and rechecked the extravagant spells she would need for the opening night's performance, trying to push the troubling scene by the riverbank from her thoughts. When she'd reached the building, she was relieved to find nothing smearing the huge sphere, which was busily recreating a fleet of three-masted naval vessels heading out to sea. And so she thought to give herself peace of mind by verifying that the spells were untouched, and whispered a small prayer that Janni would keep watch over her inventory.

Task completed, she sat alone in her private box. The darkened theater was lit only by flickering magefire lamps and a ball of magefire at Nevis' knee, keeping her in the shadows. Grateful for the silence, she sat quiet, startled as two low voices drifted up unexpectedly from the seats below.

"I won't have Nevis take the blame for a murder she didn't commit."

"The constable hasn't arrested her. Hans, be reasonable."

"You be reasonable. Nevis gave me a chance to do some quality acting, and I won't sit here and let her take the blame for something she didn't do."

"I should hope not." Verdi Casporet slid from the shadows onto center stage, hands on her hips, eyes blazing with indignation. "If you know anything to get her out from under the constable's scrutiny, then you'd better speak now."

"Hans didn't kill Adam Museo," Fani whispered, voice uncertain and so very young and vulnerable.

"Fine. But if you know who did, or even a hint of it, you'd better tell the constable, or I'll do it for you."

"You can't. Mistress Casporet, please—"

"Look Fani, I like the two of you, but Nevis' credibility, not to mention her freedom, is on the line here." Verdi crouched down on the stage so she could be closer to the young people. "I heard there was a long black curl on Nevis' desk near the poisoned breakfast cake. If that was your hair, Fani—"

"It wasn't!" The girl leapt to her feet, shaking. "I swear it wasn't." Fani fled from the theater, leaving Hans uncertain what to do.

"Fair warning, boy."

"I didn't kill Adam Museo," he said quietly, though Nevis could still hear his shaken words. "And Fani didn't try to poison Nevis. I swear that's true." Without another word, Hans followed the young woman out of the theater.

"Damn those two—"

"Calm down, Verdi."

The costume designer jumped at the unexpected, disembodied voice that emerged from the gloom of the upper tier.

"Up here."

"A bit melodramatic, Nevis, isn't it?"

"It's my theater. I didn't mean to eavesdrop, but they came upon me unawares." Nevis leaned over, letting the ball of magefire bring her sharp features into focus.

"Fools."

"Frightened fools."

"Nevis—" The designer stared up toward the magefire, trying to see her employer's face through the halo of brightness. "I don't know what to think. I don't believe Hans murdered the man, but they're lying about something."

"I thought the same. Go home, Verdi."

"Only if you promise to stop sitting in the dark and get some sleep."

"Promise."

"You're a pathetic liar, Nevis. Sometimes, anyway."

Nevis listened in the semi-dark of her private box, lit only by the tiny ball of magefire, as Verdi got her things together and shouted a farewell. She listened to the sound of the side door swinging shut, heard it open once more, and took a deep breath as the noise of a cane clicking on the wooden floor came steadily closer.

The sound stopped directly below Nevis' private balcony. "You never liked to sit in the dark."

"I still don't, but sometimes it's useful." Nevis peered over the railing and watched Clarissa Bracken make her way to a seat where she could see Nevis clearly without straining her ancient neck.

"To eavesdrop?"

"And to think."

"Did you think I'd poisoned the breakfast cake?"

"The thought had occurred to me."

Clarissa waved her walking stick in Nevis' direction, letting the younger mage clearly see the dragon on its carved head. "Foolish thought, child. You're the last person I'd wish to hurt. Tell me about Hugo San Rossi," she said, before Nevis could frame an intelligent answer.

"Not much to tell, except that he's as nasty as Adrian became, despises me more than Adrian did, and is doing all he can to ruin my reputation. He's also trying to damage the trade negotiations with the

Cashogi." Nevis got to her feet, the day's events finally catching up to her flagging energy, and turned toward the corridor, pausing as a thought occurred to her. "Did Hugo lust after Devlin's queen?"

Clarissa seemed surprised at the question. "Lust?" the older mage asked quietly. "When I discovered the truth about the affair between Adrian and the queen, Adrian joked with me, said that his young apprentice was panting after her, too. But Adrian never took it seriously." Dark brown eyes stared solemnly up at Nevis. "Why do you ask?"

"Because I think Hugo might have been serious, and having failed to gain the queen's affection, he's gone after her daughter."

"As vengeance?"

"Partly. Though I can't think that desire hasn't played a part." Nevis shrugged, tucked her hands in the deep pockets of her breeches. "Alana is an attractive young woman."

The baker's long silver braid swayed softly along her spine as she stared at the mage's retreating back. "Can I do anything to help?"

Nevis turned around and leaned over the railing, expression utterly empty of visible emotion. "I can fight my own battles, Mage Bracken. I've gotten rather used to doing that."

Without another word, Nevis stepped out of the private box and headed along the corridor to her rooms, determined not to let her old mentor know how much she would dearly love her assistance.

Chapter Eleven

From the wings, Nevis peered out at the restless audience, glanced up toward the royal box, where Devlin Graham waited with eager anticipation, his sapphire velvet jacket a stunning compliment to his eyes. Trade minister Mikaline Nashat sat beside him, then Shayna Kashi and Hugo San Rossi, dark heads very close together.

Alana Graham, who would have somehow blamed Nevis for their seating arrangement, was nowhere in evidence, and the mage wondered whether that had been the young woman's choice or her father's explicit command. If she were a wagering woman, she'd bet on Devlin.

Taking up the best seats in the center of the front row, the flamboyant madam, with her scarlet-tipped feathers and matching gown, was gay and bright beside the two dark-clad men flanking her sides. Both Remo Savanak and Finlay Oscram were dressed fashionably, though in unusually conservative shades for an evening at the theater, and Nevis wondered whether they were unconsciously bracing for trouble.

On Remo's other side, May Quiddle, in a simple velvet dress, sat with hands gracefully folded in her lap, attractive eyes scanning the curtain, no less eager than her ten-year-old son would have been if she'd allowed him to come. As it was, she'd made Teddy promise a thousand times that he would stay at the orphanage with two of Lily's girls, who offered to keep an eye on the children. A few rows back from May, Clarissa Bracken sat alone, wrinkled face peering up at the younger mage's stealthy post, her cane resting beside her arm.

And a few rows behind Clarissa, with an attractive woman on his arm, Barry Faddle preened his drooping moustache, dimples lively as he spoke jovially with those surrounding him. Nevis wondered whether he was inviting the audience to his own theater. She didn't think him crass enough to be mocking her troupe, though after seeing him with Hugo San Rossi, the mage wasn't quite certain what to think.

Had Barry been the new source of funds that Hugo had mentioned to the Cashogi drug merchant down by the river? And if so, why? Was Barry Faddle that foolish to deal with a cutthroat like Hugo? Or was Slick Hands more devious than Nevis gave him credit for, seeking to ruin her reputation and credibility for the sake of profit and greed? Profit, which the peacock didn't really need, if the estimates of his family fortune weren't exaggerated.

The theater was packed, an event that should have pleased her banker, Nevis thought grimly. Although the crowd was apparently looking forward to the performance in the highly popular sorcerous theater, many had come this particular night out of curiosity, simply because of the recent notoriety of the theater's infamous owner. But still, in Nevis' mind, there was something missing.

Or someone.

"No sign of Hans, boss," Simon whispered, gritting his teeth as he waited for the explosion of rage that would transform him into a dirty little street rodent.

But Nevis was far beyond rage, into an emotion Simon never expected. "It's not like him."

"No."

"See that young woman two rows behind Lily, there at the end, to the right, with the midnight curls?" When Simon squinted, then nodded, the mage added, "Ask her, quietly, mind you, where my villain is hiding."

"Who is she?"

"One of Lily's girls. Keep it quiet, Simon, thanks." White hair dared fall into one green eye, and Nevis pushed it back with irritation, watching Simon discreetly approach the girl and speak with her under

Lily's narrow-eyed scrutiny. When Fani's expression shifted from curious to worried, Nevis cursed roundly.

"Problem?" Verdi stepped back as the mage spun on her high black boot heels, long velvet gown a blur of ebony.

"Hans has yet to appear, the performance is scheduled to start in a few minutes, and I haven't a cursed clue what to do."

"That's not like him." Verdi tucked her emergency needle and thread into the pocket of her cotton vest. "After last night—"

"I know. I hope—" But that hope was never expressed as Simon came rushing back, hands running nervously over his thinning gray hair. "Now she's worried, too, isn't she, Simon?"

"Quite. She left Hans some hours ago."

"Where does he live?"

Verdi answered for him, "Only up a quarter of a mile, on the outskirts of Chalker's Hill."

"Near the pawnshop," Nevis murmured, running her own fingers through short-cropped hair, unconsciously mimicking Simon, with utter disregard for its appearance. "Send someone up to see if he's there. Now, Simon. Now, understand? I can delay the performance a short while, but if he's not there—"

When Simon hastened to obey, the mage glanced up at Devlin's box and sighed, swiftly glancing away before he became aware of her scrutiny.

A shriek from Gabriella, followed by a soft meowing, brought another oath from the mage. "Tell that imp that if he and his kitten are not gone from my theater in a heartbeat, I'll turn them both into stupid sheep and sell them to the nearest butcher. And tell him I mean it, Verdi."

"Right away." Verdi made her own escape.

In the audience, Lily Frascat glanced idly at the royal box, saw Devlin's very perceptive blue eyes roam across the theater to where Nevis had still not appeared in her own private seat, thought about Simon's unusual foray into the audience, and whispered in Remo's ear. Gathering her scarlet silk skirts in one jeweled hand, she made her way unobtrusively to the wings, where Nevis stood quietly staring out, arms folded, deep in thought.

"What's wrong?"

Nevis whirled to face Lily. "Hans has gone missing."

"Did he cut his losses and run?"

"If he did, old friend, he ran out on his lady love, too. I don't have a clue what to think." The mage paced back and forth, halted only when the stage manager reappeared, expression completely desolate. "For the gods' sake, Simon, put me out of my misery and tell me."

"The place was empty, a real mess."

"Sloppy mess or vandalized mess?"

"Sloppy. Worse, boss, there were discarded packages of Firespark all over the place. If Hans was using that trash all day, he won't be in any shape to perform, even if you did find him."

"Get the girl up here."

Simon fled the very moment Nevis' expression shifted from worry to magefire-level rage.

Lily didn't flinch, having longer experience with Nevis' moods than the stage manager. "What are you thinking?"

The mage held up one hand, trying out different theories in her mind. By the time Simon came back with the young woman, she still hadn't responded. "Tell her about the rooms," she snapped at Simon.

Fani listened quietly, expression miserable when she recognized the brothel owner beside the mage. Her dark eyes were wide with disbelief at what Simon described. "He's not like that. Messy, I mean. Someone made it look that way, made it look like a pigsty."

"Why?"

Fani averted her eyes from Nevis' cold expression. "People are jealous of his good fortune working in your theater." When the mage snorted, Fani met her gaze. "It's true, Mage Conarkin. Hans does think he's very lucky."

"Maybe. But that doesn't mean people are jealous of him. When did you last see him?"

"A few hours ago. Hans needed some time to rest before coming here. We were up late last night." She looked away again, staring past Lily. "His rooms weren't messy, not when I left them some hours ago."

"And the drugs?"

"Hans stopped using Firespark. He promised you."

"Then answer me this question." Nevis' voice was soft, nonthreatening, though the girl didn't doubt for a moment that she was dangerous. "When he was using drugs, would he have bought and used as much as Simon described?"

A fierce shake of the head loosened a few dark curls. "Never. No one would, not if they had any intelligence. And Hans is smart. Using that much Firespark would kill a person."

"Was he selling Firespark?"

"Never. I swear I'm telling the truth." Color drained from the girl's already pale face, and Fani sank slowly to her knees, prompting Lily and Simon to grab her between them before she slumped to the ground.

"Hush, girl. He'll show up with a head-splitting, awful headache," Lily consoled the young prostitute, helping her back to her feet, "and a huge apology for worrying you and all the rest of us."

"Simon, call the children together backstage, as far as possible from the audience. No need for them to overhear Gabriella's melodrama."

Nevis ran her fingers once more through her hair, this time, attempting to comb it into a civilized appearance. "Don't say a word to them yet. Not a word, Simon, or I promise you, by the gods—"

"Stop threatening the man," Lily scolded, rolling her eyes at Simon in sympathy. "They already know by now that Hans is missing."

"That's all they need to know until I talk to them." Nevis smoothed the front of her ebony gown. "I'll be right back."

"Where are you going?" Lily grabbed her sleeve.

"To cancel the performance."

"You can't."

"Sure I can. I don't have much choice. Look, those drugs—" Nevis caught the girl's attention and debated briefly whether or not to speak openly. "Last night, when I was coming back from the orphanage, I witnessed a delivery of Cashogi drugs. Might be Hugo is having a bit of a lark at my expense." The girl's expression changed subtly to disinterest, and Nevis wondered, still, about the connection to Hugo San Rossi. "I'll be right back."

Nevis headed for center stage and slipped through the opening where the heavy scarlet curtains joined, prompting a rush of curious murmurings from the audience. Green eyes darted upward to Devlin, then slid away, refusing to worry him. She forced a smile to her lips, quite certain he saw right through her well-intentioned effort, and held up a slender hand for silence.

"My apologies for the delay."

Nevis scanned the audience, gaze resting briefly on May's worried expression, then away. A movement in the back of the theater caught her eye, and Nevis recognized the dark, sharply creased uniform of Brea Kilganor.

"An even more sincere apology for canceling tonight's performance."

The mage stood motionless, an ebony, white-headed statue silhouetted against the blood red curtains, listening to the shocked and gossiping murmurs. Once more, she raised her hand. Silence fell immediately.

"One of my lead actors has fallen ill. It would do not only the performance, but even more important, my audience an injustice to proceed without him." She paused, waiting for protest, but they remained silent. "We'll gladly accept your tickets for another performance or grant a refund, whatever you desire."

"Was the actor poisoned?"

Restraining a curse at the rude interruption, Nevis looked up to find Hugo San Rossi smiling, a matching expression on Shayna Kashi's beautiful face. "Taken ill doesn't mean poisoned, Mage San Rossi."

"In this theater, it might." The royal mage adviser laughed, ignoring the deadly look that Devlin Graham didn't bother to hide, despite the presence of Mikaline Nashat. "What was it, Nevis? A bit of your cooking?"

"I don't think the cast and crew would care to have their ills discussed so freely in public," Remo Savanak said smoothly, standing at the foot of the stage at a point even with Nevis' boots.

Hugo's smile was amiable as he leaned over the railing, his rich voice carrying over the curious, excited whispers. "An excellent point, counselor. But the public does have certain rights. Are they aware, I wonder, just what type of woman owns this sorcerous theater?"

The attorney bristled. "I don't—"

"It's fine, Remo. Let him speak. Devlin Graham isn't a tyrant. We still have free speech and opinions in Montbasso."

Nevis' smile traveled from the attorney to Devlin, whose own face was stony. She wished with all her heart that he had followed his daughter's example and stayed away from the theater.

"Go on, Mage San Rossi. Tell my audience, who paid good money for their tickets tonight, all about me."

"I was simply wondering if everyone knew that you had threatened Adam Museo only weeks before he was found murdered in this very box." Hugo grimaced as though he'd found bloodstains on the cushioned chairs.

"Liar," Remo spat, losing his usual serenity.

"Unfortunately, I'm not a liar, counselor. Ask your banker friend, Finlay Oscram, whether Mage Conarkin did or didn't say, and I quote, 'if you win this case against me, Adam, I'll scratch out your cursed heart.' Master Oscram? Do I lie?"

The banker lurched to his feet, bald head and smooth-shaven face flushed with anger. "She did say that, young man, but she also said, and I quote, 'if you win this case against me, Adam, and throw those children back on the street, I'll scratch out your cursed heart'—"

"As though Adam Museo would take such an appalling action," Hugo appealed to the captivated audience, his expression charming, "when his dear deceased father thought so highly of Mage Conarkin that he sold the orphanage—"

"Donated the orphanage," Finlay snapped, losing his patience. "Gave her the building as a charitable contribution to help her set up the orphanage for those homeless children."

"With a whore."

Remo stepped away from the stage, heading for the stairs and Hugo San Rossi's throat, but Nevis softly called his name. When the counselor stopped, gathered his lost composure, Nevis breathed easier, more so when Finlay Oscram nodded confidently in her direction.

"Nevertheless, counselor, it's her word against Adam's that the orphanage was freely given. And poor Adam can no longer defend his own interests, having gasped out his last breath in this very theater box." Hugo scanned the audience, trying to judge their reaction from the eyes riveted on him. "There's another side to Mage Conarkin that most of you don't know. But you'll find out soon enough." Black eyes slid in Devlin's direction, then away, as Nevis remained coolly silent, allowing him the floor. "Rumors are running rampant that she's been secretly meeting with the Cashogi delegates behind the king's back, plotting treachery against you, the people of Montbasso, whom she so professes to serve. I myself saw Nevis Conarkin board one of the Cashogi vessels in the harbor."

Before he could detail the rumors and further insult the Cashogi trade minister, Nevis cut in. "If you should ever need work, Mage San Rossi," she said lightly, "I might hire you for my theater. You're a marvelous performer, so skilled that you even believe your own words."

"I always believe the truth."

"Then you stand by your words and confirm that you have accused me of double dealing with my Montbasso hosts?" Mikaline Nashat stood and faced Hugo, his pleasant face cold as stone.

"You? Of course not, my lord minister. However, it appears that some of your party do not uphold your high standards of behavior. That much, I regret, is true." Hugo shrugged, supremely unconcerned and unaware that Devlin started to speak, stopped only by the warning in Nevis' eyes. The mage addressed the audience again, his smile once more inviting. "I'd be cautious of expecting any refunds for tonight's cancellations. Mage Conarkin is also having financial difficulties. Be that as it may, this evening has suddenly grown tiresome."

Without warning, Hugo murmured an incantation, waved his arms in a display of drama, and vanished from sight, leaving the crowd uneasy at the casual show of sorcerous power.

"I assure you I didn't banish him. If I had," Nevis smiled openly, hoping to prompt a laugh from her tense audience, "it would have been long before now." Relieved at the easy acceptance of her jest, Nevis added, "My cast and crew would ask a favor. We would greatly appreciate your patience in the next few days until we determine when to reschedule our opening night performance. In the meantime, you should enjoy Barry Faddle's theater troupe." She met Barry's eyes over the rows of heads and smiled graciously, enjoying his startled expression. "I understand they put on a marvelous performance." Without resorting to sorcery, Nevis slid back through the heavy curtains, nearly colliding with Lily.

"I've a few ideas about what to do with that bastard."

"I've a few of my own."

"Why were you so gracious about Slick Hands?"

"I wanted him off-kilter. Lily, I didn't tell you all I heard down by the river. Hugo claims to have a new source of funds."

"You think—"

"I'm not sure what to think. Come with me." Nevis gripped her friend's arm and headed toward the waiting cast and crew. "At the moment, I need you to soothe ruffled feathers and egos."

"You might do better with Doc Esteway, judging from Gabriella's murderous expression. She's been plowing right over poor Simon."

"I demand to know what's going on!" Gabriella broke free of the group the very moment she saw Nevis headed their way. "If you don't fire that irresponsible, pathetic, incompetent actor—"

"I may have to bury him."

That caught even the fiery actress off guard.

"Hans has gone missing. There was evidence of Firespark—"

"Nevis, everyone knows he's an addict." Pepo turned away in disgust, earning a fierce nod of agreement from Gabriella.

"He's not addicted, but he did use the stuff. Though nowhere near the amount that was found in his room." When Pepo spun slowly back, she added, "I'm afraid Hans is in real trouble. I've canceled the performance—"

"Canceled?" Gabriella shrieked, clutching her pointed bosom, breath coming rapid, her face and neck flushed.

"Hush and let Nevis speak, or you'll never hear the whole story," Lily gently chided, smiling warmly at the leading lady. "Bad enough you were taken ill yesterday, I know, but this situation affects all of you."

Nevis didn't dare glance at Lily's face. "I'm canceling tonight's performance, and probably a few more nights until we find out what's really going on. We couldn't have a show without Hans anyway, not having an understudy for him."

"If you had an understudy—" Gabriella stopped at the flash of irritation in Nevis' green eyes, instinctively stepping back.

"If I had an understudy for every one of my cast members, I wouldn't be able to afford any of you. That was a decision I made from the first day this theater opened. Maybe it was wrong, but I can't see how a cast can perform well together if a new actor is tossed into the show. It's all or none in my theater." Nevis' cool green eyes stared long and hard at the chastened actress. "If you want the luxury of an understudy, then go upriver to Port Cordillero's sorcerous theater or across town to Barry Faddle. Either way, you'll earn a better wage."

"Nevis, I didn't mean any harm," Gabriella said quietly, cowed for once by the genuine anger in the mage's eyes.

"Boss—"

Nevis ignored both Simon and Gabriella. "In the meantime, you'll all be paid as though you were actually performing," Nevis said calmly, braced for the look of shock on their faces, as wages during a performance were higher than during rehearsals and all the earlier preparation weeks.

A shocked stillness met her announcement, broken by Simon's protest. "You can't afford that. We're barely making enough to cover expenses."

"We'll make do."

"Boss—"

"We'll make do, Simon. Now why don't you all stop in tomorrow as though the show might open? If we're lucky, maybe it will."

Verdi held the mage's gaze. "Anything we can do?"

"Help me find Hans. I'm really afraid he's in trouble."

"And you?" Gabriella flung her unbound auburn hair dramatically over one thin shoulder, though her tone was oddly gentle. "How much trouble are you really in, Mage Conarkin?"

"That's my problem."

"I'm not being cruel."

"I know." She smiled, surprising the actress, and squeezed Gabriella's arm. "I do know." She turned and headed toward her office upstairs, nearly stumbled over Brea Kilganor, whose dark uniform blended well with the shadows.

"Fani told me about Hans' rooms." The constable scratched her white-speckled hair. "And about the Cashogi Firespark exchange by the river."

"He's in trouble."

"I think so, too. But I still don't understand why Hugo San Rossi is involved. If he really is."

Lily joined the two women without waiting for an invitation. "Simple, really. Regardless of who murdered Adam Museo, if Hugo is behind the mess in Hans' room, he's just being malicious."

"You don't know that for sure," Nevis protested feebly.

"No, I don't. But I heard that arrogant man use your theater and your audience as a public forum. He's a contemptible pig." Her trembling scarlet feathers were a clear indication of her indignation.

"What's going on?" Devlin barged into the office, with Remo, Finlay, and May trailing right behind.

"That's no way to greet a struggling theater owner who's just disappointed her eager audience and egotistical leading lady on opening night."

"The gods take the audience and the leading lady, Nevis. What's going on?" Devlin demanded, blue eyes shining with anger. While she explained, he listened, expression growing steadily stonier with every word. "I'll force Hugo to resign as mage adviser."

"You'll do no such thing."

"He insulted the trade minister."

"Who will be gracious and not take insult. Hugo San Rossi would just love you to force him to resign, which is why you won't even consider it. Now hush," Nevis said quietly, grabbing hold of his hands, which were waving aimlessly.

"Much as I hate to agree with Mage Conarkin," Brea Kilganor said dryly, stepping into the conversational gap, "she's right."

"The gods take all of you. I can't just sit here and do nothing."

"Sure you can." Nevis leaned closer and placed a deep, lingering kiss on his lips, promising more and better. "And you will. For my sake. The important thing at the moment is to find Hans Takat. I have serious doubts that the boy engineered his own disappearance."

"While my officers search the area, I'll go look around his rooms." The constable unconsciously touched the dagger at her waist. "Word will spread. Sooner or later, Hans will show up in some rat hole."

"Dead or alive?" Nevis asked, not certain she wanted to hear the constable's true opinion.

"Care to take a wager?"

* * * *

Grateful for the silence, Nevis slipped the stiletto and bottomless pouch of spells from her waist, setting them carefully on the low table beside her bed. A soft knock at her front door brought the ivory-handled stiletto instinctively back in her hand.

"Who's there?"

"Alana Graham."

Nevis bit back an ugly curse and slowly opened the door, alert to danger, not bothering to hide the stiletto from the young woman's view. "You're a little late for the entertainment."

"I heard I missed an excellent performance."

"Was it your idea not to be there? Or did your father forbid you to come to my theater?"

"Shut up." When the mage didn't respond, Devlin's daughter impatiently shoved a loose strand of blonde hair behind one ear, letting the dim magefire lamplight catch the sparkle of her ruby earring. "I want the proof my father talked about the other night, the evidence that my mother was a traitor."

"Did you ask him?"

"I don't need to ask him." Alana's pale face flushed scarlet, making Nevis wonder if she'd had the nerve to ask her father. "If you created the proof from thin air, then you'll have it."

Hiding her weariness and heavy heart, Nevis perched on the arm of her tapestried sofa. "I didn't create any evidence against your mother. I didn't have to. Your mother provided ample proof by her actions. As for having anything in my possession, I don't. Ask your father." The mage kept her eyes fixed on the younger woman's face. "Or are you afraid?"

"Listen, you white-haired deviant—"

Nevis moved so fast that Alana gasped when the mage's lanky body towered over her, the stiletto forgotten in her hand, yet disturbingly close. "I don't have any proof, nor would I give it to you if I did. And I don't care whether or not you believe me."

"I don't," the girl spat defiantly. "My father's a fool if he—"

Nevis grabbed the silken shirt Alana wore beneath the light cloak. "Your father is many things, but he's no fool."

"You have no right to speak about my father."

"These days, I have more right than you." Nevis shoved the girl backward in disgust, slamming her into the wall. "Your father adored your mother until she betrayed him, both as a lover and as a queen. If I hadn't stopped Adrian Bambari—"

"How could I forget?" Alana sneered, blonde hair half hiding her face. "The great and noble Mage Conarkin, now memorializing her great deeds in a play for all of Port Jambi to bear witness."

"I despise the play."

"As though I believe you."

"Ask your father. Damn it, girl, ask your father how I pleaded with him to cast another play."

"And ruin your chances of slipping my mother's supposed betrayal into the last scene?"

"Is that what you really believe? That Devlin and I would destroy your mother's reputation through the performance?" Nevis was shaking with fury and disbelief. "You wouldn't have known the truth either if you hadn't so angered your father the night you crept through my window."

Alana laughed, regaining some of her confidence. "You expect me to believe that you didn't want me to know that alleged truth? Please, Nevis, don't insult me. For the simple fact that I despise you, it's obvious you wanted to tell such a lie about my mother. But it won't work."

"Then you'll break your father's heart by not believing him. I didn't steal him away from your mother. She drove him away by her betrayal."

"Convenient story. It allows you to take the throne beside my father."

"You'll notice I haven't done that."

"Not yet, no."

"By the gods, Alana, I don't want to take your mother's place. I don't want to take Hugo's position. All I want is peace between you and your father."

"Not between you and Hugo?"

"That's not your concern. And truly, that's an impossible task."

"How can—"

Weary from the night's excitement, Nevis lost her patience. "If you love that arrogant, faithless bastard, that's your decision. But don't be naive at his greed and lust for power, not to mention other women."

"Don't you dare—"

"I dare for your father's sake. For my part, you ungrateful child, you can go to the gods. But Devlin adores you, and you're repaying him by breaking his heart. Make your peace with him."

"I tried." The unexpected admission stopped Nevis' pleading. "He won't see me or speak with me."

"Damn idiot." The mage raked rebellious hair from her eyes with tense fingers. "He will."

Fire returned to Alana's eyes. "Because you say so?"

"Because he wants to. Go home, Alana. I'm exhausted and out of patience. Maybe one day, when you've grown up enough—"

The girl's hand slid out to strike Nevis' pale face, but the mage grabbed her slender wrist and held on tight.

"As I was saying," Nevis repeated calmly, "maybe one day, when you've grown up enough into a mature woman, we can have a decent conversation. There was a time, a lifetime ago, when we were able to do that. There was a time," Nevis' eyes were sad, "that you considered me a friend. But until you remember how to behave with simple decency, stay away from me. Go play with Hugo. For your sake, I hope his bed isn't too crowded."

Before the girl could reply, Nevis murmured an incantation. Unharmed, Alana found herself blinking furiously in the silent night, staring up at the empty, darkened theater.

Chapter Twelve

"I thought you might be interested in my little discovery." Brea Kilganor entered Nevis' office uninvited the next morning and tossed a worn leather sheath in the middle of the desk, nearly dropping it on the half-eaten, sugar-coated breakfast cake. "Am I mistaken?"

Without comment, Nevis picked up the sheath, examined the leather. "It's a bit old, don't you think?"

"Quite, with a delightful little nick on the side that matches the jagged spot on the stiletto you pulled out of the river."

"And you found this treasure where, exactly?"

Brea eyed the mage, taking careful note of shadows smudging her upper cheeks. "Chalker's Hill. Surely you're not surprised?"

"You've ruined my appetite."

"I should think it would only improve, if we can come up with positive proof that Hans Takat is indeed the murderer." Puzzled, Brea shrugged. "Takes the pressure off you."

"I wish it were someone I didn't know or didn't like. I wish I understood why he'd even think about murdering Adam. Anger about Fani might prompt a brawl. I can see that. I can respect it, too." The mage ran a finger absently along the carved statue of Janni, admiring the goddess' eternal serenity. "But murder—"

"We'll have to ask Hans. Maybe he showed up during the night." Brea glanced at the sugar-coated breakfast cake and shuddered. "How can you eat that nasty thing so early?"

"On pleasant mornings, it's not a problem. Today—" Nevis sighed, and pushed back her chair. "Even for me, it won't go down smoothly. Now that you've ruined my morning, let's go ruin Fani's."

Nevis led the constable out the side entrance of the building and across the alley to the whorehouse. Knocking lightly on the door, she stepped back as Chappy Markos slid the door open, murmuring, as ever, a polite greeting for the mage, a cool one for the constable.

"Is Lily awake?"

"The woman never sleeps, Mage Conarkin. She's as bad as you. You'll find her in the office." Chappy waved them toward Lily's office on the ground floor of the building, overlooking the Basol River.

"Don't you ever sleep, constable?" Lily challenged, as the two women entered her cheery, uncluttered office, eying Nevis with curiosity. Absently, Lily's fingers reached back to straighten her sapphire feathers.

"We were just thinking the same about you."

"Would I be correct in assuming it isn't a social visit?"

"You would indeed."

Nevis strode past the constable, expression empty, and leaned against the window ledge, staring downstream at Brigadier Bridge. "Constable Kilganor found the sheath that belongs to the murder weapon. In Hans' room," she added softly.

Rather than triumph and relief the constable expected, Lily's face grew genuinely sad. "I'm so sorry, Nevis."

"Me, too. I like the boy, not to mention that I'm going to need another actor. Can we talk to Fani?"

"Of course. I'll bring her in." Lily gracefully maneuvered around the still-standing constable. "Won't you sit?"

"I think better on my feet."

Lily rolled her eyes with immense disrespect and left the office in search of the young prostitute.

"Hugo's involvement is still eating away at me. I'm missing some pieces that you've conveniently withheld." The constable crossed her arms, staring at Nevis, hoping, futilely, to intimidate the mage.

"Lily explained it last night. Hugo will do anything to harass me. You heard him speaking to the audience, slandering my reputation."

"Yes, but why? You've told me only a very small part of the story, Mage Conarkin. It doesn't make sense. His behavior doesn't make sense. He's not acting very intelligently for a mage, though they're so rare, I really have no one but you to compare him against."

"Consider yourself lucky."

The constable went on, ignoring her remark. "Granted, he's mage adviser to the king, but it strikes me that he's pushing Devlin Graham a bit too far. Particularly with that claim about your alleged double-dealing with the Cashogi trade delegation. I confess, I didn't think Hugo would have the balls to mention that in front of Devlin and the trade minister when a theater full of people were listening."

Deciding that staring out the window was preferable to the other woman's cool stare, Nevis shrugged. "He's Alana's lover, so he feels safe."

"If he's behind the Firespark in Hans' room—"

"I doubt you'll be able to prove it. I was hoping that the trade minister would come up with something that would point to Shayna Kashi's involvement in the illegal trade."

"He hasn't had much time. You witnessed a delivery down by the riverbank purely by accident."

Nevis started to reply, stopped when Lily ushered the young prostitute into the room. Fani, too, had shadows beneath her eyes, evidence of sleeplessness, worry, and, perhaps, unrelenting fear.

"Have you found him?"

"Not yet," Brea answered, leaning one hip on the elegantly carved desk. "Have you?"

"Have I?" Fani blinked in confusion. "Hans hasn't sent any word to me. He hasn't—"

"Recognize this?" The constable held up the worn leather sheath, eyes carefully tracking the girl's expression.

"Should I?"

Brea's laugh was forced. "I wouldn't consider hiring Fani Sneddle as an actress, Mage Conarkin. She's a pathetic liar. Maybe Slick Hands might hire the girl in his traditional theater."

"Constable—" Fani pleaded, eyes wild with fear.

"Don't lie to the constable, girl," Lily gently chided, brightly painted fingernails running down the girl's arm. "It will only make matters much worse."

"Hans didn't kill Adam."

"The old woman who owned the pawnshop near Hans' rooms remembered a pair of very frightened young lovers who had stolen a ring, a ruby gem set in a heart of gold." Brea glanced at Nevis. "Mage Conarkin found out about that incident and confronted Hans. Unlucky for your lover, girl, there are several facts pointing to his hand on the murder weapon that killed Adam Museo. Now," Brea crossed her arms against her chest and stared intently at the girl, "tell me the truth."

"Hans didn't do it."

"Not even to get back at Adam for abusing you?"

"Hans didn't do it." Fani was visibly shaking but she refused to say anything further.

Brea tried another tactic. "For a young man who so obviously enjoys working in the sorcerous theater, Hans has nearly ruined Mage Conarkin's reputation. If he's hiding the truth—"

Fani shook her head, eyes pleading with Nevis. "He'd never do that. He respects you so much. Hans didn't murder Adam."

"Then who did?" Brea stood away from the desk, edging so close to the young prostitute that Fani found herself backed up hard against the wall. "Tell me who killed Adam Museo in Nevis' theater?"

"Aunt Nevis! Aunt Nevis! Come quick!" Teddy Quiddle flew into the crowded room, tears running heedless down his flushed cheeks. "The orphanage is on fire!"

Not waiting for the others, Nevis flew past her nephew and headed along the river walk, past the quiet theater, through the lush green of Alvaron Park. She paused in silent horror at the flames shooting out from every angle of the building. Gathering stillness and calm to focus, though it was difficult, Nevis raised her hands to the mocking blue sky and called down a cooling rain over the building that quickly snuffed out the shooting tongues of flame.

"Nevis, thank the gods." Covered in soot, May Quiddle fought back tears of rage and grief.

Nevis didn't reply, simply stared at the smoldering ruins, then turned her attention to the children gathered protectively around May, as though they sought to shelter her as much as themselves. Only the littlest red-haired child dared the mage's cold, distracted manner and stumbled her way to Nevis' side. The mage lifted the shivering child with a whispered greeting and smoothed wild auburn curls from her tear-streaked face. "Are you all right?"

Kimmi nodded, burying her head in the mage's neck.

"Anyone hurt?" Nevis counted heads, touched faces and heads and shoulders in reassurance, as Lily and the constable joined them.

"No. If it had been a few moments earlier, the children would have still been asleep in their beds." May hugged the closest children, ruffling their disheveled hair as Lily busied herself comforting them, too.

They'd had a fright, and it was better that they concentrated on her mothering attention than Nevis' contained rage.

"I don't understand," May said, spreading soot across her cheeks as she wiped away an escaped tear. "It burned so fast. No fire does that. I just don't understand, Nevis. How could it happen?"

"It burns that fast," Nevis said so softly the constable strained to hear, "if it's started by a mage." She hugged the red-haired child, kissed her cheek, and set her beside Lily, only then noticing her nephew, standing forlornly beside his mother, the little kitten held protectively in his arms. She hugged him close, before turning back to May and Lily, her expression and voice empty of all emotion. "Bring the children over to the theater. I'll be back in a little while." She refused to acknowledge the question in their eyes, or the fear.

Brea Kilganor caught her sleeve before she'd gone very far. "Going somewhere, Mage Conarkin?"

Without answering, Nevis headed back through Alvaron Park, her longer strides forcing the constable to double her own pace.

"Mage Conarkin—"

"It's none of your affair, Constable."

"It is, if— Damn it, woman, slow down. If it's arson, and the attempted murder of innocent children—"

Nevis paused, green eyes watching the constable. "I've things to discuss with Hugo San Rossi that you don't need to hear."

Brea didn't blink. "Why would he do this horrendous act? He practically owns the building now. And he needs the funds to buy drugs from the Cashogi."

"He has a new source of funds. Might be Barry Faddle. I can't be sure, but it's something to consider."

"Fine. But listen— I might understand this destruction because Hugo San Rossi can be cruel," the constable admitted, "though I'll deny ever saying that, you understand, particularly to you. What doesn't make sense is why Hugo would destroy a possible source of income. You seem to know why, and I want to understand what I'm—" Brea met her gaze and held it. "What we're dealing with."

Nevis appraised the constable in silence, weighing her sincerity. "It may be simply that I've finally managed to put the seeds of doubt in Alana's Graham mind," she said quietly, refusing to answer any more questions.

* * * *

Brea Kilganor put out a uniformed arm to stop Nevis from opening the door to Hugo San Rossi's suite. "I'll go first, so our intrusion will be legal." At the immediate fire in Nevis' eyes, she added, "I know you don't give a damn about that at the moment, but I do. No sense bringing more trouble on your head."

Nevis grunted, but stepped aside without further argument.

The constable knocked once, then again. She slid a glance at the mage. "I wouldn't mind a little help, but I'll still go in first."

A smile tugged at Nevis' lips as she murmured an incantation and touched the doorknob, stepping back as the door swung open. The constable crossed the threshold, body poised and alert for danger as she stood in the spacious parlor furnished, as Nevis' remembered, in black and scarlet. The mage moved quietly from chamber to chamber, searching, observing.

"For someone looking for a new source of funds," Brea remarked, entering the bedchamber, furnished with elegant wall coverings and satin bedclothes, "he has awfully expensive taste."

"So did Adrian," Nevis murmured, too late to stop the words. She turned away, furious with herself, unwilling to look at the constable.

But Brea wouldn't ignore that slip. "Is Adrian Bambari part of this mystery?" When Nevis stubbornly refused to answer, the constable stepped in front of the reluctant mage, forcing Nevis to look at her. "Mage Conarkin, the more I know, the more I can help you."

"Your job is to investigate arson, Constable, not get ensnared in matters that even I don't wish to be tangled in. Hugo's a mage, and I'm a mage, and you surely don't want to get caught between us when the fighting gets really nasty." At Brea's immediate protest, Nevis added sharply, "My error to speak without thinking first. And for that, I apologize. Now either help me find something to link Hugo to the fire at my orphanage, or let me do it alone."

"Tell me something, Mage Conarkin," Brea drawled, cocking her head to the side, "were you always this difficult?"

"Sure. Ask my sister."

"I will. Now, let's see what we can find."

The two women went their separate ways, searching for anything out of place, anything that might help them connect Hugo to any of the events that had recently happened. But his apartment, though furnished beautifully, appeared unlived in, as though Hugo kept his real life hidden elsewhere.

Joining the constable in the central parlor, Nevis shook her head in disgust. "It's not even as though he's got anything hidden away beneath a spell. I would have sensed that. It's damnably peculiar."

"Would he have another place to keep certain possessions he would want to keep out of sight?" Before Nevis could answer, she took a deep breath, then added softly, "Did Adrian?"

"By the gods—"

"No offense, Mage Conarkin, but—"

"By the gods, Constable, don't you see? He did." Nevis headed back out the door without any further explanation, leaving the constable speechless, and very grateful that the mage hadn't transformed her into a nanny goat.

Brea followed on her trail, alert for signs of Hugo San Rossi. Not far from the corridor leading to the suite given over to the Cashogi delegates, they nearly collided with the trade minister.

"Minister Nashat—" Nevis caught her breath, waved the constable to join her. "Have you met Constable Kilganor?"

"No, not yet." The well-tailored gentleman smiled, though both women could see it was forced. "A pleasure, Constable. Are you investigating the appalling murder of Adam Museo?"

Brea nodded. "Have you an interest?"

"Yes. For Mage Conarkin's sake, yes."

"Something's wrong," Nevis said quietly, touching the sleeve of his light wool gray jacket.

"Yes." The minister glanced swiftly along the corridor. "Is there somewhere we can speak privately?"

"The best place in the whole fortress. Come with me."

Nevis led them through winding corridors, where strategically situated troopers kept silent watch. Before very long, they came to Devlin's study, where the young female guard announced their presence.

"Sorry to bother you, Dev, but we needed some privacy." Nevis came around the huge carved oak desk, piled high with documents, writing implements, and sealing wax, to lightly kiss his bearded cheek. "But you only pretend to be busy all the time, so I know it's not a bother."

"My lord, I apologize. If I had known where Mage Conarkin was bringing us, I would have loudly protested." Nashat looked so genuinely embarrassed that Devlin took pity on his visitor.

"She has no sense of propriety, Mikaline. Don't let it trouble you." Devlin nodded at Brea. "Constable. Intriguing group. Should I let you speak in private or am I allowed to listen to whatever brought you here?"

"If you wouldn't mind, my lord, I would like you to listen, too," Mikaline Nashat answered for all of them.

"Before Minister Nashat tells us what's troubling him, my lord," Brea interrupted politely, not bothering to look to the mage for permission, knowing Nevis would refuse, "you should know that the orphanage was destroyed."

Devlin sat back in his chair, momentarily speechless. "Who was responsible?" he asked softly, not a hint of gentleness in his voice. "Nevis—"

"I've no proof, but a building doesn't burn that quickly under normal conditions." Nevis leaned one hip against his desk. "I believe," she said carefully, "basing it only on my instinct, mind you, that it was started by a mage."

"I'll have Hugo San Rossi brought here in chains. Guard!"

"Dev, no— Listen." She grabbed his sleeve, forced him to meet her gaze. "Tell her to go back to her post," she said softly, hearing the footsteps of the guard behind her. "I'll take care of it."

Angry, Devlin obeyed and, with a muttered apology, waved the guard out.

"I have no proof. Constable Kilganor could have dragged me into prison for Adam Museo's murder without any proof had she not followed the law. You can't act any differently because I'm involved."

"I know that, but damn it, Nevis—"

"Hush." She caressed his cheek, then stood away from his desk to give her attention to the Cashogi gentleman. "Forgive us, minister. There's been an awful lot going on today."

"Yes, I see. And I am most sorry for the poor children. What shall happen to them?"

"They'll be well cared for. My sister won't accept anything else."

"Shall I send word to your sister? She will need many things, and I would like to do what I can to help."

Surprised, Nevis murmured her thanks to the Cashogi minister. She sat on the edge of the window seat opposite Devlin's oak desk, facing the others. "Now tell us your own trouble, please."

"It's trouble that affects you, my lord," Nashat said, taking a seat on the velvet couch, while Brea lounged against the door, quite possibly to prevent anyone from barging in unannounced. "Mage Conarkin had mentioned the possibility of some of my countrymen trading with yours."

"Without your knowledge?"

"Yes, I'm ashamed to admit."

Devlin sat forward. "Does this trouble have anything to do with Hugo San Rossi and the shipment of Firespark that Nevis witnessed?"

"Yes. It also shames me to admit that my companion, Shayna Kashi, is involved, as is some of the crew that came aboard my vessel from Kolmari." Sighing wearily and with deep disappointment, the minister added, "Shayna blames Hugo San Rossi for first approaching her. I'm not certain whether that's true or not. I have doubted her words and her heart for some time, as Mage Conarkin knows," he glanced at Nevis, took heart from her unspoken compassion. "She may very well have approached him first."

"You don't know that," Nevis said quietly.

"No, I don't. Either way, I have proof independent of her lying words. As trade minister, I have acquired dependable contacts in the shipping arena, and my companion's hands are not very clean." Mikaline Nashat bowed his head, the lamplight shining on his close-cut hair. "So far, we've acted with discretion, but I ache to have them all arrested and brought to justice. Most of all, Shayna."

Nevis got up from the window seat and knelt beside the minister, touching his arm. "I'm sorry."

"As am I, Mage Conarkin. Thank you." He squeezed her hand, waited until she regained her seat, and turned to Devlin. "The other trouble, my lord, is that Shayna has disappeared since our heated conversation hours ago."

"We'll find her, Mikaline. My guess is that she's with Hugo." Devlin tugged thoughtfully at his beard, glancing at Nevis and the constable for agreement, which they both gave readily.

"I would expect no special treatment for her. She acted criminally against my country and yours. Shayna's intention was to disrupt the trade negotiations. I would understand if you sent me from your shores in disgrace."

"Would you understand if I continued to negotiate with you?" Devlin crossed his arms, blue eyes alight with mischief.

"My lord—"

"Would you? Or would you think me a weak fool?"

"I would think you a gracious and forgiving monarch. And would even consider some small compromise on a few of our more difficult points," the minister said slowly, a smile tugging at his lips.

"Finlay Oscram will be delighted. And I'll take all the credit." Devlin smiled, then craned his neck to look at Brea. "Does this count as evidence against my mage adviser, at least regarding the illegal sale of Firespark?"

"For that, yes, but not regarding any link to arson or murder." Brea glanced to the mage, uncertain whether to admit their recent snooping. "Perhaps if we find Hans Takat alive, he may be able to tell us something more."

"Dev—" Nevis got to her feet. "Before you confront Hugo, let me take care of a few matters first."

"What matters?"

Rather than argue, Nevis only smiled. "A woman's got to have some secrets, my lord. You should know that by now."

* * * *

"What matters?"

"None of your business, Constable. I've told you that over and over for the last half mile. Weren't you listening?" Exasperated, Nevis stopped a few blocks from the theater, out of breath from the walk, and faced the stocky woman. "I'm not really being difficult, but I have to handle this matter on my own."

"Mage secrets?"

"If that will make you happy, yes."

Clearly unhappy, the constable crossed her arms. "I'm not being difficult either, Mage Conarkin. The truth of the matter is that—" Her expression was peculiar as she stared past Nevis, dark eyes narrowed. "Damn you, woman, I'd rather you didn't face Hugo San Rossi alone. If anything happened to you, I don't want to be the one to tell Devlin Graham."

Surprised, Nevis didn't say anything for a moment, though a smile lit her face. "Under the circumstances, Constable, I very much appreciate that concern. But I still need to do a few things on my own. However—" she raised one hand as the expected protest formed on Brea's lips. "At the races, Shayna referred to a hideaway where Hugo kept his personal riches. She may have just said the words without any real knowledge, and he seemed first to discount her words. I never really thought much of that portion of the conversation, but there was a peculiar tone to his voice. So, Constable—" Nevis paused, eyes fixed on the other woman's face.

"Go on."

"So," the mage continued, "if I do find a potential hideaway belonging to Hugo, I promise to take you along with me when I break into it, just to keep matters legal. Will that satisfy you?"

The constable considered the mage's words, searching for hidden meaning, then slowly nodded. "I'll concentrate on finding Hans." She started to head in the opposite direction, but Nevis gripped her wrist.

"There's Barry. He must have just come from my theater."

"To offer sympathy?" Before waiting for an answer, the constable walked quickly toward the theater owner, crossing his path before he turned the corner and vanished from sight. "Master Faddle?"

"Constable Kilganor. Nevis! I've just come from your theater. What an appalling mess. I'm so sorry. What can I do for the children?" Barry's expression was apparently full of concern, but Nevis had her doubts.

"Nothing, but thanks, Barry. They'll be fine."

"But maybe you can answer something for me," Brea cut in smoothly, keeping careful watch of his shifting eyes beneath the riotous black curls tumbling over his forehead. "There's a rumor going around that you've recently lent Mage San Rossi a bit of funds."

The eyes shifted away from the constable's gaze, didn't dare look at Nevis. The dimples reappeared as Barry tucked his hands into the pockets of his elegantly cut breeches. "Oh, that. Now look here, Constable—" He smiled charmingly at Nevis. "You, too, Nevis, it was a bit of a lark. The mage got into some gambling difficulties. Nothing significant, you understand."

"Do you understand, Constable?" Nevis rested one hand lightly on the ivory handle of her stiletto, saw Barry's eyes dart in that direction, then away, carefully avoiding her eyes.

"Might be that Master Faddle just wants to keep both mages happy. That's my guess." Brea stared up at the theater owner until his dimples vanished again. "He did offer to buy your theater and rescue you, too, from financial difficulties. Why not do the same for Hugo San Rossi?"

"Now look here, Constable—"

"Nothing wrong with playing both sides, Master Faddle."

"I wasn't."

"Seems like you were," Brea nodded thoughtfully. "Seems a bit cowardly under the circumstances. If I were you, I'd be sure to vanish from sight if Mage San Rossi and Mage Conarkin start some serious discussions. After all, if they both ask you for more significant assistance, which side would you choose?"

Barry's face had grown increasingly pale, his mustache drooping listlessly. "It's obvious that Mage Conarkin is in the right," he said quietly, eyes darting all over the place rather than at either woman.

"Well, I think so, too, Master Faddle," the constable said, her tone radiating open disgust, "but I wouldn't want Mage San Rossi to hear me say that if I were you. In fact, I'd be very careful over the next few days."

"Constable—"

"Good day, Master Faddle. Come along, Mage Conarkin. You should check on the children's welfare, don't you think?"

Chapter Thirteen

Nevis paused in the bright sunlight at the main entrance to her sorcerous theater, enjoying the silence, Brea Kilganor beside her. Overhead, the huge sorcerous sphere was lifeless and thankfully devoid of slanderous words.

"Surely it won't be that bad," the constable said dryly.

"Care to see for yourself?" Nevis slid the door open a crack and peered inside at the bedlam that was her theater.

The constable took one peek and laughed. "Well, they belong to you. Look, Mage Conarkin—"

"If we're on the same side, 'Nevis' will do."

"Then so will 'Brea,'" the constable said easily, backing away from the door. "I'll see about Hans. When you're ready to go hunting—" Dark eyes fixed on the mage's face, challenging her.

"I keep my word, Brea. I'll send word when I've found out what I need." She watched the constable head off down the street, took a deep breath, and bravely crossed the threshold into chaos.

"Aunt Nevis!" Teddy came sliding down the center aisle, stopped an inch from the lanky mage.

"Well, Teddy boy, looks like you pests have taken over my theater." She ruffled his perpetually disheveled curls and hugged him close.

"We have." May stepped away from the baskets of food she was unloading and met her sister halfway down the aisle. "But we can't stay here forever."

"You can at least stay overnight, maybe longer. There won't be a performance until we've found Hans." Nevis glanced around the theater, found evidence of juvenile invasion in every corner. "What's that you were doing?"

"Unloading food provisions that Finlay Oscram sent over. Bless the man, he nearly blasted me away when I offered to pay him back." May pointed to where Lily was kneeling center stage, some of the older children beside her. "Remo sent blankets, Devlin sent clothes, and Clari sent sweets. Lily's trying to make sense of a huge mountain of clothes. By the gods, Nevis, even the Cashogi trade minister made a donation of funds to use according to my discretion." May shook her head in astonishment. "I expected help but not this fast or this generous."

"That's because I'm a fierce mage, and they're frightened to cross me," Nevis laughed, distractedly thinking of Clarissa Bracken and what she needed to find out as soon as possible.

"Verdi's been a blessing with the little ones," May broke into her sister's scattered thoughts. She nodded to a corner of the stage where Verdi sat cross-legged, surrounded by all the youngest children, telling them a story. The costume designer glanced up, saw the mage, and waved.

"By the gods, I don't pay her enough."

"Or Simon, either. He's been busy coordinating the deliveries. Neighborhood people have been dropping by all day, Nevis, asking what they can do."

"Why?" Nevis whispered, this time genuinely surprised.

"Why?" May grabbed her sister's arm and shook it. "You can ask why?" When Nevis looked away, May squeezed her arm. "People know that you and Lily are good, decent women, despite Hugo San Rossi's loud-mouthed lies, and they want to help. You can be sure that if Hugo ran this theater, no one would stop in."

"May—"

"I should warn you," May said quietly, as Nevis started toward the stage, "the word on the street is that Hugo started the fire. Don't scold— I didn't say a word, nor did anyone else here. But people aren't stupid. They thought what I did, Nevis. Fires don't burn that quickly, not if they're natural."

"Decided to come and do some real work for a change?" Lily called out, sapphire feathers bobbing gently.

"I thought I got paid to delegate the work." Nevis easily took the few steps onto the stage with graceful movements, stopping by Verdi's circle of children to kneel a moment. "Everyone all right?" When they all reassured the mage, with even the red-haired child, thumb planted securely in her mouth, nodding solemnly, Nevis smiled. "Then I'll let Verdi finish her story." The mage stood up, glanced at the costume designer. "Verdi—"

"Don't say it."

Nevis sighed. "Still—"

"Want to hear the end of the story?"

"No, thanks." Nevis smiled her gratitude and joined Lily and the older children, pleased when one of the boys hugged her in spite of the teasing she was sure would follow. "What's all this mess?"

"His majesty thought that these hooligans would probably need breeches and shirts and shoes so they don't start smelling us all out of the theater," Lily grinned, picking up one little girl's soot-covered stocking and sniffing in disgust. "And Remo figured they'd need blankets. They're all rather excited about sleeping in Mage Nevis Conarkin's sorcerous theater."

"And I did promise them a storm." Nevis laughed as several pairs of eyes lit up. "We'll see. Let's get everything all sorted out first." The mage got to her feet, not surprised to find Lily dogging her footsteps.

Lily waited until they were out of hearing range and physically stopped the mage to confront her. "Well?"

"Hugo wasn't anywhere in sight. But we met up with the trade minister. Seems he has proof of Shayna's drug dealing and the involvement of a few Cashogi sailors. Shayna blames Hugo, and she's gone missing." Nevis shook her head. "Mikaline Nashat is beside himself with grief and anger."

"Poor man. He's probably afraid that all his efforts are wasted."

"Dev reassured him that the negotiations will still go forward. We also met Slick Hands on the street."

"You've been busy."

"I didn't want you to accuse me of dallying," Nevis grinned, pushing shaggy white strands from her eyes. "By the gods, I've got to get this trimmed. Look, Barry admitted to lending Hugo some funds. Brea—"

"You're on a first-name basis, Mage Conarkin?"

"She's declared herself no longer neutral, so, yes. She pretty much made Barry look like a weakling, playing both sides. I don't think he's involved with anything significant. He's too much of a coward."

"I'd agree. What's next?"

"I need to see Clarissa."

Lily narrowed her green eyes in suspicion, jeweled hands rising to her hips. "Why?"

"I suspect Hugo has a hideaway, if not for himself, then at least for his personal possessions. Adrian had one, but I never knew how to get inside."

"And you think Clarissa does."

"I'd wager my theater on it."

Unexpectedly, Lily laughed aloud. "Don't even jest about that, Nevis. We're in enough trouble, don't you think?"

"You're right. Look, can you stay here awhile? I know it's an imposition on your time—"

"Are you the sole partner in the orphanage?"

"No, of course not. But you've got a business to run. At the moment, my theater isn't being used."

"My business practically runs itself. The girls are professionals, Nevis, not like your prima donnas." Lily smiled, squeezing the mage's arm. "Besides, some of them are coming over later to help out. Now go do what you need to do. And Nevis—" the brothel owner was no longer laughing. "Be careful."

"I will." Nevis stepped from the stage, headed for Simon before leaving. "Need help with those boxes?"

The stage manager balanced a box of assorted dolls and games and books on his thin shoulder. "No, thanks. I've got everything covered."

"Simon—"

"If you're going to say something foolish like how ridiculously grateful you are," he muttered, doing a fair imitation of her voice, "then—"

"By the gods, you and Verdi are impossible."

"Then fire us, boss." Simon grinned, shifting the box for better balance. "Now if you've got nothing intelligent to say, would you mind stepping aside before I break my back?"

Nevis shook her head. Knowing the children were in good hands, she set off for the bakery and stepped inside to find Clarissa just wrapping a loaf of cinnamon bread for an elderly customer.

"Mage Conarkin? I didn't expect to see you here."

Mindful of the old gentleman, Nevis smiled. "I came to thank you for the sweets you sent over for the children."

"It's the least I could do. Thank you, sir." Clarissa smiled, waited until the man left the bakery, then stepped to the door and hung the "closed" sign in the window. The walking stick rested beside the counter, its dragon head elegantly carved.

"You never told me what you see on the walking stick," Nevis said quietly, hands tucked deep into her pockets.

"A master mage's privilege."

"Fair enough."

"You've come for more than just to thank me."

"I need your help."

The older mage leaned back against the counter, eyes focused on Nevis' face as though trying to read her heart and soul. "It's cost you a lot to come here and say those words."

Nevis shrugged, as though she didn't care. "I'm not an arrogant fool. I know when to ask certain things from certain people."

"And what do you need to ask of me?"

Nevis stared at a sugar-coated cake, not really even wanting a taste. "Adrian kept a hideaway in the queen's chamber."

"Yes," Clarissa murmured, watching the younger mage carefully avoid looking up. "He did. How do you know about it?"

"Devlin's queen kept a journal. I'd forgotten about it until now." Nevis took a deep breath. "I was never able to get inside."

"And you think I was?"

Nevis looked up, met the older woman's grief-stricken eyes. "Yes."

Clarissa grabbed the walking stick and turned toward the door, her long silver braid swaying gently down her back.

"Clarissa, please— It's important."

"And bringing up old heartache means nothing? Adrian is long dead. What's the point, Nevis? To remind me of my error?"

"By the gods, no." Nevis stepped forward to block the older woman from leaving. "I've many faults, but I'm not cruel."

"You could be, if you believed I'd wronged you, if you believed I betrayed you and Devlin and the people of Montbasso."

"But you didn't."

Clarissa stared long and hard at Nevis. "You weren't so sure of that a few days ago."

"I was wrong."

Nevis' simple statement brought tears to Clarissa's weathered face. "All these years, child—"

"Do you think I've wanted to believe you guilty?"

Clarissa reached out to touch Nevis' flushed cheek. "I always hoped not. Now why are you asking about Adrian's hideaway?"

"Because I think Hugo has one, too. And because Hugo, in his own way, is trying to follow Adrian's example. He's seduced Devlin's daughter, and he's attempting to disrupt Devlin's trade negotiations with Cashogi. Ironically, he's using Cashogi drugs as the vehicle, when Cashogi drugs were the poison that damaged Adrian's ability to reason." Nevis stuffed her hands into her pockets.

"He's also quite busy trying to destroy your reputation."

"I can deal with that. It's when he goes after Dev and the children that I want to strangle him. Who's next on his list of targets?"

"Anyone you care about, child." Clarissa sighed, leaning heavily on her walking stick. "You were right. I did enter Adrian's hideaway ten years ago, found the evidence of his betrayal, and destroyed it."

It was a long, silent moment before Nevis found the voice to ask the older woman, "Why?"

Clarissa's smile was so sad that Nevis reached out to touch her shoulder. "Why? Because, child, if there was no evidence of betrayal, then Adrian couldn't possibly have turned rogue. I denied the truth for a long time, hating you more and more, until I realized how bitter and misguided and wrong I was. And still," she admitted, "still, I needed convincing."

Nevis blinked in confusion. "I don't understand."

"It's not complicated, Nevis. I returned to Port Jambi to find out what I could about you, how you'd grown, whether you were truly a good and decent woman. And nowhere, but from Hugo San Rossi's lying lips, did I hear anything but good. Mind you, there was gossip about the king's lover, but all good natured. I admit that I came here prepared to leave again without saying a word to you." Clarissa smiled, her entire face crinkling with wrinkles. "I'm glad I stayed."

"So am I." Nevis instinctively hugged her, surprising the older woman into tears again.

"Well, now, here's what you need to do to slip into Hugo's hideaway—"

* * * *

Nevis continued to pace before Devlin's huge oak desk until he growled and forcefully grabbed her shoulders to halt her restless movement. She brought her head up to stare at his face. "Wouldn't it be better if Alana weren't there?"

"No. No. A hundred thousand times no." Devlin's blue eyes locked on Nevis' green ones. "If you find what you're looking for, I want my daughter to fully understand the kind of man she thinks she's in love with."

"But Dev—" Nevis paused as the young female guard knocked and entered, Brea Kilganor waiting curiously behind her, then slipped back into the corridor.

"Constable. Thank you for coming so swiftly."

"My lord." Brea nodded at the mage, taking careful note of her tense stance. "How can I help you?"

"By being an objective witness to anything we might find in Hugo San Rossi's hideaway." Devlin leaned one hip on his desk, arms crossed as his eyes darted in Nevis' direction, then away.

"You work fast," the constable admitted grudgingly to Nevis. "Where are we looking for this hideaway?"

"In my daughter's bedchamber." At the constable's raised eyebrow, he added, "Constable Kilganor, you may hear things today that under most any other circumstances, neither Nevis nor I would wish you to hear, but for the sake of objectivity in a court of law—"

"I understand, my lord. And you know that whatever I might hear," she glanced at Nevis' empty expression, "will remain secret."

"If I didn't know that, Constable," Devlin grinned, pushing away from the desk, "you wouldn't be here. Besides, Nevis said I could trust you."

The constable bit back a smug remark at the blazing fire in the mage's green eyes, an expression that shifted to uncertainty, though not, the constable guessed, related in any way to doubts about her own trustworthiness.

"Then let's get this nightmare over with." Devlin paused, cupped Nevis' face in his hands. "It's only fitting that Alana be there."

"I hope you're right," Nevis murmured, stepping back uneasily from his questing fingers.

"What was I thinking to get tangled with a stubborn, sensitive, decent-hearted—" Devlin's sigh was rudely mocking as Nevis rolled her eyes, following her lover and the constable out the door. "Come with me," he told the guard, "and stay posted outside my daughter's rooms. Let no one disturb us, especially Mage San Rossi."

"Yes, my lord."

In silence, Devlin led his party down the empty corridor to the far end, where Alana's suite took up the entire section. The guard stationed herself at the entrance, expression rigid, though her eyes did glance once from face to face.

Devlin knocked hard. Impatient, his fist raised once more, but the sound of swiftly approaching footsteps stopped him from pounding again on the heavy door. When Alana appeared in the doorway and saw her visitors, her face lost all color. Devlin didn't bother to wait for an invitation, but pushed the door back, abruptly gesturing Nevis and the constable inside.

"Poppa—"

Devlin's blue eyes scanned the parlor as though she were a stranger before turning that cool gaze on his daughter. "Have you seen Hugo?"

Alana nervously brushed a strand of blonde hair behind one ear, blue eyes, paler than her father's, darting at Nevis, then away. "Not since yesterday."

"Last night? Did you sleep with him last night?"

At the girl's embarrassed flush, Nevis moved instinctively to touch his arm, decided against it when Devlin's blue eyes slid her way, aware that the young woman caught her arrested movement.

"Did you?"

"No. I—" Her gaze rested on Nevis' face again, and the mage knew she'd guessed right. "I refused him."

"Maybe you're finally learning," Devlin muttered, hands straying absently to his dark beard. "Did you know he burned down the orphanage?"

Genuine horror filled the girl's eyes. "He wouldn't. Even Hugo wouldn't be that cruel."

"We don't have proof," Nevis said quietly, "though the fire was started by a mage. There's no doubt of that, and before you accuse me," she added, "I have an alibi for where I was and whom I was with."

"You'd force anyone to lie for you."

"Not a constable of the city," Brea murmured, letting the girl get a good look at her third visitor, whose uniform was, as ever, crisp and clean. "And I can vouch for Mage Conarkin's whereabouts."

Hugging herself hard, Alana dared a look at her father's face. "Are the children hurt?"

Nevis caught the swift flash of relief in Devlin's eyes that Hugo San Rossi hadn't completely erased her gentle heart. She answered Alana's query when Devlin turned away. "They're fine. But had it been a few moments earlier, they would have been caught in their beds."

"Thank the gods."

"For Hugo's sake, yes." Devlin headed for the bedchamber, trying very hard not to think about his daughter's nightly activities with Hugo San Rossi. "Does Hugo leave any of his possessions here?"

"Here?" Alana followed her father, the other two women trailing her steps. "Of course not. He has his own suite."

"You're absolutely certain?"

"Yes." The girl's eyes were wide, unsure where her father's questioning would lead. "Why are you asking?"

"Because if I find out that you've just lied to me, I'll bring you before a court of law for aiding a man who's broken my law."

Alana sank onto the huge, decadent bed. "What law?"

"I won't even mention the harassment and slander of Nevis Conarkin or the very real probability that he blackmailed the judges handling the orphanage lawsuit and burned down the orphanage itself. But Hugo has succeeded in breaking my trade law, with absolute contempt for his position as my mage adviser. Hugo San Rossi and Shayna Kashi," Devlin noted the tightening of Alana's delicate jaw at mention of the Cashogi bodyguard, as did Nevis and the constable, "have been busy smuggling Cashogi drugs, specifically Firespark, into Port Jambi."

"That's a lie." Alana's hushed protest was feeble.

"The Cashogi trade minister has proof, and Shayna herself has admitted the truth. Unfortunately, both she and Hugo are nowhere to be found."

Nevis winced in sympathy at the expression of betrayal on Alana's face, but she said nothing, listened when Devlin began speaking again.

"We believe that Hugo has created a hideaway in your bedchamber that may very well contain some of his treasured possessions, things that he would prefer kept out of sight."

Alana brushed blonde hair back from her face, looking from one to the other. "That doesn't make sense. I've never seen him do any such thing with any of his possessions. And besides, he's never here when I'm not."

"How do you know?" Nevis asked softly.

"I just do. There's no way—"

"He's a mage, Alana. There are ways he could enter and leave even were you here, and still you wouldn't know."

Fire blazed in the girl's eyes as she struggled to her feet. "So could you. How would I know that you didn't creep in here and create a hideaway, planting evidence to prove Hugo guilty?"

Nevis didn't flinch from the rage in the younger woman's expression. "You wouldn't. All I can tell you is that I didn't."

"Liar."

"Alana." Her name, spoken in Devlin's soft, nonthreatening tone, was enough to silence her insults, though defiance blazed still in her young, desperate eyes. "I'd give the world to see you unhurt, but the truth is, child, that Hugo San Rossi has used you as easily as Adrian Bambari used your mother. And she believed with all her heart that Adrian returned her love. As do you."

Nevis' eyes strayed from the girl's anguished face to the constable's expression, bland but for the involuntary twitch in Brea's jaw.

"Adrian persuaded your mother to fall in love with him. I knew him well, as did Nevis, who was his friend. Adrian wasn't always a rogue. But your mother believed in his cause, listened to his drug-induced ravings, and very nearly brought horrendous trouble and heartache to my people. And for that," Devlin said softly, "far more than her betrayal of my own heart, is why I'll never forgive her."

Alana sank to the bed again, head bowed, not daring to look at any one of her visitors.

"Nevis, if you would?" Devlin crossed his arms, all emotions shoved brutally aside. "Constable?" His eyes met and held Brea's, weighed her reaction, saw, as did Nevis, the regret, and turned back to the mage. "Stand witness when Nevis opens the chamber."

"If there is one," Alana whispered, head still bowed, her face hidden by her loose blonde hair.

No one responded. In the heavy silence, Nevis took a deep breath and faced the empty wall that separated two ceiling-high windows overlooking the Basol River below, where the two Cashogi vessels rocked in their berths. Not far downstream from the foreign vessels, a three-masted schooner waited eagerly at the river's edge for its premiere launch from the Ruskin Shipyards. Another three-masted vessel, two thirds finished, lay just beyond.

Imagining Hugo San Rossi clearly in her mind as though he were standing before her, Nevis closed her eyes, murmured an incantation that eerily changed her external appearance to resemble Hugo. When the transformation was complete, from the top of her head to the tips of her boots, she touched the wall. Opening her eyes, she nearly cried out in relief as the outline of a door appeared.

"Damned unsettling," Brea complained, watching the mage touch the doorknob and pull, opening a door into a room that extended, for all intents and purposes, into thin air over the river. "Too damned unsettling."

Before crossing the threshold, Nevis paused, looked down at the girl, whose expression was bewildered and genuinely afraid. "I'm sorry, Alana." She read the surprise in the younger woman's expression, swiftly banished and replaced by rage. Rather than comment further, Nevis turned her attention to Brea, whose expression was a fine mix of regret, awe, and misgiving. "Coming, Constable?"

"Nevis, you're asking me to walk into thin air."

"I'm asking you to trust me that you'll be walking on a solid floor."

"My lord," Brea Kilganor turned to Devlin, her expression peculiar, fists bunched unusually tight, "when next you consider the wages of the city constables, you might remember this little adventure."

"That's a promise. Go on. I'll be standing out here to pull you both in," his blue eyes laughed at her, "in case Nevis is wrong about the floor."

"Coward." Nevis sniffed in mock disapproval and boldly stepped into the hidden chamber, brightened by scattered magefire lamps. "By the gods, look." She lifted a small package and tossed it to Brea, who'd cautiously edged near, paused, then crossed the threshold with a sigh of relief. Clenching her jaw to keep from shouting out in fear, the constable examined the sack before passing it to Devlin.

"Cashogi writing." Devlin sniffed the package he'd neatly caught and grimaced. "Firespark."

"How do you know?" Nevis' left eyebrow inched upward.

"I distinctly remember that smell from the evening you found your playwright useless and nauseated from the drug." Devlin's expression remained bland, though his blue eyes laughed at her. "As I recall, right in front of me, you ripped off the poor man's shirt, splattered with his Firespark-induced vomit, and threw it away. Unfortunately, it landed in my face."

Nevis blinked. "It did?"

"Indeed. It was all poor Simon could do not to laugh. However, with his mage employer in a rage," Devlin's expression lost some of its neutrality as a smile tugged at his lips, "and precisely on the verge of stinging the poor playwright with magefire to teach him a lesson, Simon didn't dare remark on the incident."

"Smart man."

"I always thought so, though I never understood why he hasn't tried to escape that madhouse and look for a more peaceful job." Ignoring her scowl, Devlin deftly turned the topic back to business. "How much of the drug is in that room?"

"Sacks of it. Same packages we found in Hans Takat's room and Adam Museo's house." Brea's eyes slid in Alana's direction, saw the girl's rigid shoulders, and sighed. "Anything else?"

Nevis' expression was peculiar as she studied a set of documents. "Other than gold and jewels that might do better in the kingdom's treasury, three things of interest. The first—" She held out legalistic papers to the constable. "Validation of old man Museo's donation of the orphanage building to me and Lily. Now completely useless," she murmured, brushing back unruly white hair. "The second." Nevis held aloft a transparent sphere. "My untainted spells that Hugo stole and replaced with his own uncontrolled spells. The last—"

"The last?" Devlin's voice was soft as he watched the play of emotions on her face, saw her green eyes glance with undisguised compassion at his daughter. "What's the document you're holding?"

"Transport papers." When all three observers looked blank, the mage went on to explain, tossing the documents to Devlin,

"Apparently, Hugo plans to book passage on a Cashogi vessel. I don't know when, but I'd expect soon. You might ask Minister Nashat to keep his ships in port until this tangle is over. Might as well keep everything here in case Hugo comes looking for it. Dev," she dared a glance at Alana, then swiftly looked away, "judging from the sheaf of papers attached to this document, Hugo's not planning to travel alone."

Chapter Fourteen

Flickering magefire lamps banished the gloom from the stage, presently covered with sleeping bodies, curled up together like insecure, newborn piglets. In Nevis' private box that overlooked the stage, Lily Frascat, May Quiddle, and the mage were sharing a well-deserved second bottle of wine. On Nevis' lap, thumb defiantly positioned in her mouth, the little red-haired child slept soundly, wild auburn curls streaming over the mage's black-clad arm in sharp contrast.

"Your entire side must be numb," May chided, shaking her head in mock disgust. "Kimmi's sound asleep. Tuck her in with the others."

"She's light. Besides, she was starting to have a nightmare."

"You've a soft heart, Mage Conarkin." Brea Kilganor said quietly, startling the women by her sudden appearance in the doorway. "I suppose I'm one of the last few to find that out."

Lily graciously removed her legs from the cushioned chair to give the constable space to pass by and take a seat. "She's always had that, Constable. You just haven't spent nearly enough time in the neighborhood. So, have you found Fani's young man yet?"

"No, but I've an idea where he might be."

Nevis shifted in her seat when the child stirred, thumb still lodged in her tiny mouth. "Care to share that idea?"

In the soft glow of the magefire lamp, the constable looked weary for the first time since the nightmare had begun. She raked dark brown hair, sprinkled with strands of white, from her eyes and nodded. "Strikes me that if they, meaning Hugo San Rossi and his Cashogi lady, have Hans hidden away somewhere, they'd keep him in the last place people might think to look."

"They'd want to keep the actor hidden away to stop Nevis from running her opening night performance," May said quietly, thinking aloud as she sipped her wine, setting the glass aside.

"Sure, and to keep Hans, if he's the real murderer and not Hugo himself, out of my sight, so Nevis still remains the prime suspect." The constable turned her eyes on the mage. "No ideas?"

"I'm either empty headed or too exhausted, but no."

"None at all?"

"Constable—"

"Must be she's getting crotchety," Lily laughed, "if she's back to calling you by your title."

"And a crotchety mage may very well turn you into a filthy, dis-ease-ridden, long-tailed, sewer rat," May warned, joining in the laughter at Nevis' expense.

"That goes for disrespectful younger sisters and disloyal friends, too," Nevis growled. "By the gods, if you're the people I hold dear—"

"Hush, and let the constable tell us her idea." Lily finished her glass of wine, offered to pour one for the constable, who politely declined.

"The one place that no one would think about," Brea said quietly, "is the only place that makes perfect sense. Adam Museo is dead, and—"

"His house is empty and cordoned off by your official markings," Nevis finished her thought, eyes signaling her agreement. "You might be right."

"If I'm not, there's nothing lost. If I am—" The constable shrugged, narrowing her eyes as she caught the matching eagerness in the mage's expression. "Care to have a look?"

"Not without Chappy Markos, you don't," Lily warned, green eyes darting back and forth between Nevis and the constable. "And don't be so damned proud, Nevis. I know you can take care of yourself, but what if you do find Hans? Chappy can knock him out and sling him over one shoulder as easily as you prick a sorcerous sphere with your fancy ivory-handled stiletto.”

“She’s got a point,” Nevis said diplomatically, slowly getting to her feet and placing the red-chaired child into her sister’s outstretched arms. “Is it a problem for you if Chappy comes along?”

“Not for me.” Brea shot the madam a fierce grin, revealing a row of clean, but crooked teeth. “I may not spend enough time in this neighborhood, this theater, or your whorehouse, Mistress Frascat, but I know better than to tangle with you.”

“I always thought you’d come to your senses, Constable.”

* * * *

The house appeared more overgrown than Nevis remembered from the day not very long ago, though it seemed a lifetime, she’d crept inside and found the black and white kitten. Beside her, Chappy and the constable waited patiently, all three clad in dark clothes, easily blending into the night shadows. The house before them was gloomy and silent with foreboding, sending a shiver up Nevis’ spine, yet the mage felt sure that someone was inside.

“I’m going in first, alone,” Nevis whispered, braced for the argument that came immediately.

“That’s not our agreement,” Brea hissed. “Chappy and I—”

“I can make myself invisible.”

“Then you can make us invisible, too.”

“Yes, but you’d only be clumping along behind me, worrying me half to death you’ll give us away.” When Brea’s dark eyes flashed with irritation beneath the sliver of moon, Nevis added softly, “I don’t sense any magery inside, so I doubt it’s Hugo San Rossi’s presence I feel.”

"You feel a presence, and you still plan to go inside alone? Have you gone completely mad?" Brea restrained the urge to strangle the mage.

Nevis glanced at Chappy, knew that the broad-shouldered, balding man wouldn't disobey Lily's explicit command to shadow Nevis' every step unless he was convinced there was a better way to protect the mage.

"Listen, both of you. I've been thinking all the way over here." Before the constable could voice the tart reply that was clear in her expression, Nevis explained, "Hugo and Shayna can't be staying here or neighbors would see a light and become suspicious. But they might very well stash Hans inside, all tied up, and hopefully still breathing."

"What's your point?" the constable snapped, crossing her muscled arms against her chest.

"That if it is Hans, and it most likely is, all I need to do is take a quick look and signal you both inside to help me."

"Five minutes," Brea muttered ungraciously.

"I'll need more than five minutes just to make my way through his weed-choked forest and find the back door."

"Five minutes, Mage Conarkin."

"Five minutes from when you see my magefire signal from the back fence." Nevis stared at the constable, exhaled when she nodded. "Chappy, I know Lily wants you to tag along like my shadow, but I'd rather you were ready to come rushing in like a tidal wave if I need your help."

One large hand ran thoughtfully over the bodyguard's bald head. "Where will you signal from inside if all's well?"

"The front parlor. If you see a ball of magefire there, creep around along the back and through the open window."

"The window you opened the last time you snooped illegally?" Brea's eyebrow slid upward, enjoying Chappy's silent reaction. "She did, you know. I could have arrested her for that."

"And a lot of other actions. Will you give me my five minutes or must I cast a spell on you both, knocking you senseless?"

"Damn you, yes."

"Chappy?"

"Only five." Lily's man gazed at the mage with somber eyes. "Starting from the back fence."

Nevis patted his bicep through the thin cotton shirt that stretched across his chest. "Thanks."

Without waiting, in case they changed their well-intentioned, fickle minds, Nevis flew across the narrow road and darted into the weeds growing unrestrained along the side of the house. She stealthily made her way toward the back and rounded the corner, found the window she'd used last time, and pushed it open a crack.

Pulling a sphere from her bottomless pouch, the mage pricked it with her stiletto, producing a glittering ball of magefire. Nevis flashed it swiftly for her companions to see, and only then bespelled her lanky body invisible.

Slipping inside, she found the house as filthy and abused as the last time she'd visited, with one exception. In the kitchen, near the back entrance, some room had been cleared. In that space, slumped against the peeling paint of the cracked pantry wall, Hans Takat lay curled on his side, chest rising and falling with soft breathing. Nevis brought the magefire closer, saw the bruises on the young man's face, and cursed. Before touching Hans, she released the invisibility spell, swiftly and carefully walking toward the front parlor, stepping over piles of discarded junk, to signal her waiting companions. That done, she returned to the actor. Anger growing by the moment, she slit the coarse ropes that held him bound at hands and feet, ripped aside the filthy cloth covering his mouth, and scented the peculiar odor of Firespark.

Brea appeared at her side and crouched down beside the mage. "Is the boy still alive?"

"Barely. I don't know how much of the Cashogi poison they poured into him, but his color's bad."

"Doc Esteway can take a look at him," Chappy said, bending to hoist the actor over his shoulder. "Looks like Firespark over there, with the foreign writing."

"Sharp eyes, Chappy," Brea said appreciatively as she reached over to take a few packets for evidence. "Ready to go?" she asked the mage, lightly placing a hand on the other woman's arm when she caught the fury in her eyes. "He's alive, Nevis."

"Barely. And all because Hugo despises me."

"You're forgetting Hans may very well be our murderer."

"No, I'm not. But he belongs to me, and by the gods—" Startled, Nevis sniffed the air, her body tense. "Out. Out now. Go."

"What—"

The sound of crackling wood became suddenly apparent. "Fire. Hugo's setting the house aflame with magefire. Don't argue, or we'll be arguing with the gods in another life."

Chappy raised a hand to catch her attention. "He'll be expecting us to come fleeing out the front or back door."

The mage nodded. "If you go down those stairs, through the cellar, you'll find another set of steps leading into the garden." Nevis sniffed the air again, saw the smoke creeping through the open window, and forcefully shoved Brea and Chappy toward the cellar door. "I'll go out the front—"

"You will not," Brea grabbed her shirt and pulled her along, frustrated when the mage slipped from her grasp.

"I can shield myself with sorcery. And if I go barreling out the front, you'll get the distraction you need to get Hans away."

The constable dug in her heels. "Nevis—"

"I can shield myself. Now go." With one last shove to get them out of her way and onto safe ground, she murmured another incantation and erected a shield. Praying to the gods, particularly Janni, that it would work against the magefire, she tugged her black vest over her head and face, gave herself a running start, dodging the piles of cast-off clothes and other possessions, and crashed through the front window, flying through the scarlet-and-orange flames, shattering glass into the neglected front garden.

Nevis staggered shakily to her feet, braced for assault, but the street was empty and silent, the only sound the crackling flames that had already destroyed much of the building's wooden frame. Hugo San Rossi, if it had indeed been the mage who'd set the house ablaze, had vanished like the wind along the riverfront.

* * * *

"Hold still and let Doc Esteway look at that bruised arm," Lily chided as she paced back and forth in her elegant upstairs parlor, where Nevis sat silent on the couch. The madam glanced at the constable, who shrugged.

"You told me you were erecting a shield to protect yourself," the constable said conversationally to the mage. "That's the only reason I let you crash through the front window."

"It protected me from the magefire," Nevis murmured, not looking at either woman as Doc Esteway, long blonde braid hanging down her back, inspected the mage's thin arms, where scrapes and discoloration had already appeared from her hard fall on the ground when she sheltered her head. "Chappy's not hurt, is he?"

"Just covered with soot and a little singed around the edges, like the constable, but sure, he's fine," Doc Esteway reassured Nevis, eying her patient's melancholy expression. "You're the only one with bruises and cuts. Why, dare I ask, didn't you go out the front door like a civilized intruder instead of flinging your thick head through the window? It's a good thing you moved so fast that the glass didn't have a chance to seriously slice you up." When Nevis didn't answer, the physician asked, "Did the shield help with that, too?"

Nevis nodded, remained silent.

Doc Esteway gently rubbed some soothing ointment on the bruises and wrapped them with a clean cloth. "Lucky you didn't break anything. If you did, who'd want to listen to Devlin Graham? He'd blame me somehow for not being there to catch you with a fishing net." The physician glanced away from her subdued patient to Lily Frascat, who bit her lip, green eyes narrowed in concentration at the mage. "I'll go check on the boy," Esteway muttered. "It'll be hours before he regains consciousness and makes any sense. He's lucky to be alive. I'll let you know how he's doing."

"Thanks," Nevis murmured, shutting her eyes and leaning her white-haired head against the back of the couch.

Brea silently queried the madam if she should leave, but Lily shook her head, surprising the constable. Stroking one sapphire feather as though surprised to find it still intact after the endless day, Lily sat on the footstool in front of the mage, eyeing the other woman's bandaged arms.

"Tell me," Lily said gently, resting one hand on Nevis' bony knee.

"I'm just tired."

"You should be. When was the last time you had a decent night's sleep? Or a nourishing meal beside those sugar-coated monstrosities?"

Eyes still shut, Nevis shrugged.

"It's more than bone weary, old friend. It's heart weary, too, isn't it?"

Nevis kept her eyes shut, knew if she didn't, that if she met the compassion in Lily Frascat's warm, mothering green eyes, she'd do what she so rarely did anymore, not since she'd destroyed her one-time trusted friend, Adrian Bambari, which was to weep endlessly as though her heart would break. Devlin had found her that day ten years past, huddled in a ball over Adrian's dead body, her chestnut hair gone white from one of Adrian's spells gone astray, one of the many scenes that would never appear in Nevis' theater.

Instead, she spoke words Brea Kilganor hadn't expected. "I'm fighting Adrian all over again," Nevis whispered. "It's his hatred, his disregard for the innocent, his greed and jealousy and malice."

"You defeated Adrian. Are you afraid you won't defeat Hugo?"

Nevis' eyes slipped open to find Brea's skin flushed at her daring, but the words weren't meant as a challenge, only as a question. And Nevis read that easily in the other woman's honest face.

"I defeated Adrian, who was my friend, and I destroyed him, and I've always believed I had no choice. But I've always felt guilty. I don't know anymore. And if I don't know whether I did right in destroying Adrian," her voice shook, prompting Lily to grab her fingers and offer what comfort she could, "then how can I know I'll do right destroying Hugo?"

"I leave you alone for a few hours, and you start spouting ignorant words that would make even Teddy ill." Devlin stood in the open door-way, blue eyes afire with anger. When Nevis turned away, he shut the door, knelt beside Lily, grabbed the mage's shoulders, and shook her hard. "You listen to me, Nevis Conarkin, and you damned well listen hard." Nevis' green eyes were so full of sorrow that Devlin nearly lost his nerve in making her see reason. "Adrian Bambari was your friend, and you trusted him. So did Clarissa Bracken, who mentored both of you. And you were both betrayed when Adrian turned rogue, as I was betrayed when he seduced my queen. All of that was horrid enough, but for the gods' sake, Nevis, Adrian betrayed my people when he allied with the Cashogi dissidents. For that, he deserved to die."

And still, Nevis didn't respond.

"I'm sorry," Devlin whispered, "that it was your hand that destroyed him. But that hand was carrying out my command."

Nevis held his gaze. "You never gave that order."

"I didn't have to give it."

"You don't understand." Nevis started to struggle to her feet, but Devlin had no intention of letting her by. He forcibly shoved her back down, oblivious to the quiet astonishment on Brea Kilganor's face. "If you did, you'd never have pressured me to put on the cursed play."

"Then explain it to me."

"Dev—"

"Explain it to me." Devlin sat back on his haunches, prepared to wait. "I'm quite sure Lily doesn't understand either."

The brothel owner said absolutely nothing, though her heart was in her eyes as she thought about Clarissa Bracken, whom Devlin still didn't know had come back to Port Jambi.

"Adrian was a mage," Nevis said slowly, resigned to Devlin's particular brand of stubbornness. "Magery is rare. No one knows why or how the gift is passed on, but it's rare. Damn it, you know this fact."

"I love to listen to you teach." Devlin's words tried to lighten the shadows in her eyes, but he knew it would take more than that.

Nevis started to say something, bit it back. "Because magery is so rare, when a mage goes rogue—" She sighed, ran sooty fingers through her hair, leaving black streaks among the white strands. "When I destroyed Adrian, I destroyed all chance of reclaiming him. Maybe we could have turned him back around, Dev. Maybe we could have created a spell to permanently change his thinking. Maybe, in time, I could have found a way to save him and his gift if we could have just gotten him far enough away from the Cashogi drugs."

Devlin caressed her cheek. "Adrian was hopeless. Even you, with your great and loving heart, would never have been able to reach him."

"But don't you see?" Nevis' cry nearly broke his heart, so rarely did he witness this side of her. "I never even tried."

"And so, you want to try with Hugo."

"Yes. No. I don't know. "

"That's just the answer I expected from a woman who watched her orphanage burn, rescued her missing actor, and crashed through a window to escape magefire, all in one day." Devlin uncoiled and got to his feet, bent to kiss her head, and smiled, blue eyes pleading with her to laugh.

And she did.

"Well, Constable, shall I keep watch on the riverfront?"

"Yes, my lord, if you wouldn't mind. Might be a good idea to take extra care in the fortress, too. I've a feeling Hugo and his Cashogi lady might stop by to get the gold he left behind."

"Dev—" Nevis gripped his shirt. "Maybe you should—"

"Maybe you should let me fight my battle the way I wish, and you can fight your battle the way you wish."

Chapter Fifteen

Simon paused in the doorway to Nevis' office, sugar-coated break-fast cake in hand, and gaped. He tiptoed over the threshold and set the cake gently on the desk, then stepped back, praying he wouldn't wake the mage.

But Nevis was a light sleeper, and stirred, raising her head from the desk, where she'd unintentionally fallen asleep.

"Sorry, boss. I didn't realize you were sleeping."

"I shouldn't have been."

"Did you actually get any sleep last night?"

Nevis rubbed grogginess from her eyes and finger-combed her disheveled hair. "Yes, I did. Not much, I admit. And a warm bath."

"How do you feel? I heard your arms were pretty banged up."

"They feel pretty much like I crashed through a window." Nevis grinned, trying to ease the anxiety on Simon's face. "Any word from the constable?"

"Just now. She said not to wake you if you were sleeping, but Hans is starting to come around. Constable said she'll wait for you before questioning him."

"Then I'd better get over there."

Simon crossed his arms and barred the doorway, eyes sliding to the uneaten breakfast cake on the desk, right beside the carved statue of Janni and her adoring children.

"I'll take it with me."

"Fair enough." Simon stepped aside to let her pass and watched with worried affection as she strode down the corridor, entered her private box to peer at the still-sleeping children huddled on the stage, May and Verdi lying beside them to either side, and departed for Lily's whorehouse.

Nevis slipped out the side door and crossed the narrow alley, frowning at the threatening clouds that promised an early summer storm. She rapped softly on the heavy door and found Remo Savanak waiting in Chappy's stead.

"New job?"

"I needed the extra money." Remo's warm smile didn't disguise his sharp-eyed appraisal of her condition as he kissed her cheek. "Are you well?"

"Sure."

"I'm so convinced."

"Don't be snide. Where's Chappy?"

"Lily decided he deserved to sleep late." Remo tucked his hands in the pockets of his light wool breeches, his question deceptively casual. "Do you want me to listen in on the constable's interrogation?"

"Sure."

"Nevis—" Remo reached out to hold the mage back before she went upstairs, then remembered her battered arms. "Sorry. Nevis, listen—"

"Lily told you about my conversation with Devlin."

"It didn't sound like a conversation to me."

Surprising the attorney, she laughed. "Good point. Remo, I'll deal with Hugo San Rossi and his Cashogi lady."

"I've no doubt of that, Mage Conarkin. I just wish I could help."

"Thanks, but you can't. Not anymore than you're doing just by being my friend and keeping Lily from throttling me." She headed for the stairs, Remo trailing behind, shaking his head.

"Well, look what Remo found in the trash bins along the waterfront."

"Lily, you know you're not supposed to aggravate a mage who's had very little sleep and a nightmarish week," the attorney chided, pointing Nevis in the direction of the bedchamber where Brea waited in the corridor.

"Good morning." The constable, dressed in her usually fastidious style, glanced at the sticky, sugar-coated breakfast cake, forgotten in the mage's hand. "You didn't have to rush over here."

"No reason to hold things up. Is he awake?"

"Quite awake and quite nervous," Doc Esteway said, coming down the corridor. "He's not going to be up and around too quickly. They forced an awful lot of Firespark down his throat. The only thing that kept him alive was the fact that they dosed him in small, regular amounts."

"He was lucky."

"He was. If they had done to Hans what was done to Adam—" The physician shrugged. "I'll tell you one thing, Constable. If the boy killed Adam Museo, then he must have been pretty frightened when they started giving him bits of Firespark."

"Makes sense."

"I always make sense," the physician grinned, turning her sharp eyes on the mage. "How are you feeling?"

"Pretty lousy."

"At least you're honest. If you want something for the pain—"

"I'm all right, thanks."

"And stubborn. Well, good luck. Oh, and Constable," Doc Esteway tossed over her shoulder as she made her way down the corridor, "Fani Sneddle's on her way down to speak with you."

"And here she is," Remo murmured, noting the young prostitute approaching from the opposite direction, dark head bowed, thin shoulders slumped, as she murmured a polite greeting.

Brea opened the door to Hans' room and ushered them all inside. The young actor, lost in a cloud of white bed coverings, opened his eyes at the noise. His gaze darted first to Fani, then Nevis.

"You look like a drunk who lost the brawl."

"Thanks, Nevis." Hans managed a feeble grin, though it never reached his eyes. "And thanks for finding me."

"I had to know if I needed to hire another actor. Look, Hans," she leaned on the window ledge, rested her back against the shutters, the forgotten sugar cake in her hand, "the constable needs to know what happened to you."

Hans looked down at his fingers, tightly gripping the bedclothes. "I know," he said quietly.

"Then start with opening night." Brea positioned herself at the foot of the bed, where she could easily watch both Hans and Fani.

"Shayna Kashi came to see me after Fani left."

"How do you know her?" Brea voiced the question that leaped to Nevis' mind, exchanging a satisfied look with the mage.

"She deals in Cashogi drugs."

"Go on."

"I thought she came to sell me more, though the gods' know, Nevis," he swiftly glanced at his employer, then away, "I told her I wanted nothing more to do with Firespark. But she kept insisting. And I was—" His face flushed, and he refused to look at anyone. "She has a way about her that was convincing, and she surprised me at how strong she was."

"She's the trade minister's bodyguard," Brea said dryly. "She should be strong and deadly."

"She was that and more on opening night. Somehow she managed to get some Firespark down my throat, enough to stun me, and I swear,

Constable, that's about all I remember until you and Nevis found me in Adam's house."

"Convenient memory loss."

"It's true."

"Let's say it is," Brea crossed her arms, kept her gaze fixed on Hans' pale face. "But let's say that maybe you made a deal with Shayna Kashi. Paid her enough to make it look like you were abducted, and plan it so you look innocent of any crime."

"That's not true."

"Then explain why you've been going around thieving from your boss and your fellow actors."

"I needed the funds for something else."

"What else?"

But Hans wouldn't answer, nor would he look up.

"Tell me the truth, boy, and let's get this nightmare done."

"There's nothing more to say."

"Not even when the evidence is pointing to you as Adam's murderer?"

Hans' pale skin flushed, but he shook his head, shaggy brown hair falling into his eyes. "I didn't kill him."

"Everything I've seen and heard tells me you did."

"I didn't."

"Then who did?"

But Hans only shook his head.

Brea took a deep breath, slid a glance at Nevis, who shrugged. "Then I'll have to place you under arrest. The evidence—"

"He didn't do it!" Fani cried, breaking her silence. Long black curls framed her thin face, and Nevis saw the fear in her eyes. "I swear he didn't do it."

"Then who did, girl?"

Fani started to speak, but Hans grabbed her fingers and squeezed. "No. Damn it, Fani, no."

"Yes." The young woman sat on the edge of the bed, her fingers entwined with the actor's. "Yes, Hans. I'm tired of it all."

Brea hardly dared breathe. "Go on."

"Hans didn't kill Adam Museo." Fani looked not at Brea or Hans, but Lily, her young eyes pleading for forgiveness. "I did." No one spoke for a very long time, until Fani broke the silence. "Adam had beaten me badly the week before, and Hans bought me a stiletto to carry for protection. It's a lot like yours, Mage Conarkin, though not intentionally. I hid it in my boot and carried it wherever I went. I was afraid he'd come back and abuse me again."

"Child, I wouldn't have let that happen," Lily said quietly, sinking into an empty chair beside Remo, who took her hand and squeezed gently.

"I know. But you couldn't protect me when I left the building. And I did, went out one evening to meet Hans for supper at the Blackstone Hearth. But Adam found me first, two streets over from here. He dragged me into an alley, slick with garbage and the gods know what else, and tried to rape me. I couldn't—" Fani held her head up high and met Brea's empty gaze, refusing to be intimidated. "I may be a whore, Constable Kilganor, but I have a right to fight back."

"Oh, child," Lily whispered, leaning against Remo for comfort. "Sure you do. You're no less a woman than anyone else."

Fani surprised them all by smiling. "I know. You taught me that when I first came here, and I've never forgotten it." Squeezing Hans' fingers, she continued, her expression relieved. "Well, Constable, I fought back. I didn't mean to kill Adam, only hurt him so he'd be frightened away. But when he leaned over me, I had the stiletto in my hand,

and it slipped into his chest. Then he—" The young prostitute fought back a sob, "Adam Museo collapsed, and I'd killed him."

While she wept quietly, Hans took up the story. "She came to find me at the tavern, and all I could think, Nevis, was that he'd brought you to court and that he'd had some pretty heavy gambling debts. So I thought that if we made it look like a suicide, no one would be the wiser." The actor didn't look away when Nevis nodded. "I never, ever wished to bring trouble on your head. And for all that's happened, Nevis, I don't know how I can ever make amends."

Nevis didn't respond, simply sat there thinking.

"We grabbed the first thing that came to hand that would hide any signs of blood."

"Your beautifully embroidered shirt. You've got a lot to make up to Verdi, let me tell you," Nevis muttered, watching the young man's face, satisfied that he was finally telling the truth.

"I know. We grabbed your flask, too, and your stationery."

"It would have worked if the constable hadn't such sharp eyes."

"And a sharp memory. Since you're telling the truth, both of you, let's go a little deeper. Why did you need the money?" Brea eyed the lovers, saw them exchange a worried glance.

"Here's where it gets complicated." Hans shot a look of apology to his employer. "Someone saw us dragging the body into the theater."

"Teddy?"

"No, Nevis, not the boy. Hugo San Rossi and Shayna Kashi."

"By the gods, they were in the park, weren't they, taking in a shipment of Cashogi drugs?" Nevis stood up, restlessness making her pace, when Hans nodded. "And Hugo was blackmailing you, wasn't he?"

"Yes. I wanted to tell you, but didn't have the courage. I knew there was bad blood between you and San Rossi. It was more than you needed to know, and you had enough worries. Though in the end,"

Hans smiled sadly as he rubbed Fani's cold fingers in his own, "you found out anyway."

"Just another reason to deal with Hugo," the mage murmured, earning a severe scowl from Lily. "Well, Constable, what happens now?"

Brea glanced at Remo. "If the counselor doesn't have any objection, it seems to me that the best thing to do until we know where Hugo and his Cashogi lady are hiding and what they're planning, is to keep Fani and Hans here, where they're safe. I don't want them leaving the building without permission from me or Nevis."

"Makes sense," Remo agreed.

"Unless they haven't been completely honest, I'd guess that Fani stands a decent chance of being forgiven by the court since she acted in self-defense. It doesn't help that the two of them tried to hide the truth, but for the moment—"

Remo nodded, considering the constable's logic. "When matters get a bit calmer, I'll take on their case and see what comes of it. That is, if they'll have me represent them in the courts—"

"Master Savanak," Fani glanced at Lily, then Remo, "we can't ask you to do that for us."

"Why not?" Lily demanded. "If you're telling the truth—"

"We are."

"Let Remo do his job first, and then we'll see what you two have to do in order for Mage Conarkin to forgive you. But in the meantime," she added, "if there's anything you can tell Nevis about Hugo San Rossi, do it now. Because she'll need all the help she can get to bring him to justice."

Chapter Sixteen

Nevis returned to chaos and a sight she never thought to see in the ten long years since she'd opened the sorcerous theater.

Simon met her at the side door, amused at her genuinely baffled expression. And then took note of what she carried in her hand. "Boss, you promised you'd eat that sugar-coated monstrosity."

Blinking, Nevis looked down at the untouched breakfast cake she'd been holding for more than two hours, wondering how it had gotten there. "By the gods, Simon, what's going on?"

"Verdi promised the children she would paint their faces today so they could pretend to be animals or clowns or the gods know what else their imagination might conjure."

"That's not my costume designer surrounded by the children."

"Oh, I know. No sooner had Verdi graciously made that declaration," Simon grinned, tucking his hands in the belt loops of his baggy, unfashionable breeches, "Gabriella flounced in and decided not to be outdone by Verdi, or shall I say, outdone by the 'disgusting lice-ridden woman who wore my wig'."

Nevis muttered under her breath, rubbing her eyes to make some sense of what she was witnessing on stage. "Meaning?"

"Simply this, boss. The great actress, Gabriella de la Morsage, famous not only in Port Jambi, but the entire length and breadth of all Montbasso, and the foreign lands beyond our seas, including Cashogi, has deigned to lower herself and graciously give acting lessons to the children."

"It's too cursed early," Nevis moaned, shutting her eyes as the shrieks of infantile delight, fierce challenges, and loud applause echoed throughout the empty theater. "By the gods, Simon, I don't think I can face Gabriella at the moment. In fact, I don't think I can face her for weeks."

Nevis turned her back on the stage and steered her bewildered self toward the office, shut the door, and dropped into the squeaking chair. Ignoring Simon's fading chuckle, she looked askance at the statue of Janni as though pleading for help, and enjoyed for just a moment the blessed silence.

And only a moment's respite was what she was given. Before she'd taken too many sighs of relief, someone tapped softly on the door. Resigned to unwanted company, Nevis called out for the intruder to enter.

Verdi Casporet, long black hair sleek and shiny along her thin shoulders, never a candidate for lice despite Gabriella's vehement claims, waited behind the half-open door for permission to enter, the red-haired child perched on her hip. "We thought we saw you creep in the side door and then slink away. Some of us," she nodded at the child, "have very sharp eyes when it comes to certain adults."

Nevis laughed, held out her still-bandaged arms to the child, who scrambled eagerly into her lap, throwing skinny arms around the mage's neck for a fierce hug. Immediately after, her thumb found its usual position.

"Can't blame me for fleeing the stage and what was on it."

"No, but I'll admit, I didn't think Gabriella had it in her. Simon and I are rather impressed. She's great with these imps." Verdi earned a bright smile from the child. "We're painting faces later."

"So I heard. Please stay away from Gabriella's costumes."

"You just ruined all my fun." The costume designer leaned against the doorframe, dark eyes watching her employer with a quiet intensity. "Simon said that Hans finally woke up."

"That he did."

"Is he guilty?"

The mage looked away, turned to face the window and the threatening storm clouds that cast deep, unsettling shadows on the Basol River and the fertile farm lands beyond. Not far, Brigadier Bridge yawned open again, allowing two vessels through, both traveling downriver from Port Cordillero.

"I'm sorry. I'm not prying to be nosy. I'm worried about him."

"I know, and you deserve the truth. Just repeat to Simon what I tell you and keep it all between the two of you for the moment." Nevis spun back slowly, stroking the child's wild flame-colored curls. "He wasn't lying, Verdi. Hans didn't murder Adam Museo."

"Thank the gods. Who did?"

"Fani."

Verdi's jaw dropped.

"It was self-defense. She'd taken to carrying the stiletto after Adam beat her bloody. The girl was on her way to meet Hans at the Blackstone Hearth, and ran into Adam instead."

Nevis rested her head against the child's, such a sharp contrast of white brilliance against blood red that Verdi felt inexplicably uneasy, reassured when the mage lightly touched her lips to the top of Kimmi's tiny head, the gesture so natural that Verdi sighed in relief.

"Fani apparently didn't mean to kill him, only scare him away, but unfortunately for Adam—"

"It's his own damned fault."

"I won't argue. Anyway, Hans was scared and concocted a scheme to make it look like suicide."

"They didn't account for Constable Kilganor."

"No, they didn't. Verdi—" Nevis held her gaze. "It gets worse."

Something in Nevis' green eyes filled the costume designer with foreboding, and she knew, before Nevis uttered his name, that Hugo

San Rossi was connected to this unending nightmare. "Hugo?" she whispered.

"And Shayna Kashi. Hugo witnessed the murder and their attempt to make it look like suicide."

"So the bastard— Sorry," Verdi glanced guiltily at the child, but Kimmi was studying the sugar-coated breakfast cake with interest. "Hugo blackmailed him, didn't he? Is that why Hans was stealing from you and Gabriella?"

"Yes."

"Oh, Nevis, I'm sorry. What will happen to them?"

"Brea thinks the court will be lenient. Remo's handling the case, and they'll stay over at Lily's until things quiet down."

"Can I scoot over there later to see him?"

"Sure." Nevis glanced down at the child, watched with a smile as tiny fingers dipped cautiously into the sugar icing.

"Is that anything decent to feed a child before lunch?" May Quiddle's threatening voice caught both Nevis and the child by surprise. The two culprits exchanged a guilty glance before turning back to May, who fought back a laugh with great difficulty. "Nevis, just because you eat that horrible thing—"

"I don't know. Is it so horrible?" Nevis asked the child, scooping a bit of icing onto her finger and presenting it to the tiny lips. When the little girl tasted the cake and solemnly shook her head, May lost the battle and started to laugh.

"Some days I think you're no older than any of them." May shook her own head, mimicking the child, and setting loose brown curls free of the ribbon that held them in place.

"Some days I wish I weren't."

* * * *

Nevis made a swift escape after they'd all gone and slipped out the side door, heading for the river path. The skies were dark, and still the rain hadn't come, but she could feel it along her skin and in her bones, so recently battered by her flight through the window of Adam's house. Her boots led her toward Alvaron Park and past it, and she didn't argue, finding herself standing before the ruins of the orphanage, a sight that brought tears of sorrow, then cold rage, to her eyes. Nevis stepped carefully around the blackened timbers, heart grieving at the singed, broken doll that lay beside the tiny burned shoe. The building had burned so hot and fierce in so short a time that there was barely anything recognizable. It must have been the same when Adam's house burned to the ground, though she had no regrets for that disaster.

"He's getting reckless."

Nevis turned at the unexpected voice. Clarissa Bracken stood only a few feet away, the click of her walking stick silent on the grass.

"He's getting bold and angry and reckless. Just like Adrian."

Nevis shifted her gaze toward the river, heard the distant rumble of approaching thunder. "Hugo's planning to leave Port Jambi the moment one of the Cashogi ships gets permission to leave."

"He won't leave Port Jambi until he destroys you. Only then, child, will he vanish into the night." Clarissa came to stand beside the younger woman, silver braid swaying against her back.

"I won't give him that chance."

"Nor should you. Nevis—" Clarissa raised her walking stick and met Nevis' green eyes without looking away. "I've come to tell you two things. The first is what you always wished to know but I always held secret."

Nevis blinked, eyes darting to the cane, and she nodded. "The image you see?" the younger mage asked softly.

"Yes. I see as you do, child. A dragon's head." The old woman held the wooden head of the cane toward Nevis, letting her eyes see the carved, winged creature. "A magnificent dragon to match yours. I perceive as you do, and my heart lies where your heart lies." Setting the cane back on the ground and regaining her balance, she added gently, "I'm not the enemy."

"I never really believed you were," Nevis murmured, short-cropped white hair tousled by the wind kicking up over the river. Lightning flashed on the other shore, not far from the race stables, as Brigadier Bridge swung shut. "Not in the deepest, darkest part of my heart."

Clarissa gently squeezed her arm, mindful of the neat bandages poking out from beneath Nevis' black sleeve. "The other point is that I admit now something that I never had the courage to accept. You were right to destroy Adrian."

"No." Nevis flushed, recalling her recent words with Devlin, and stepped back as the first drops of rain touched her hair. "I didn't try to save him first. I didn't try to make Adrian see his error."

"Child—"

"I was wrong."

"You're wrong now if that's what you believe."

"By the gods, Clarissa, if you say these things now to confuse me, maybe you are the enemy. Maybe you are trying to help Hugo shatter my defenses."

But Clarissa persisted, brown eyes defiant. "It's what you've wanted to hear from my lips for the last ten years, and now that I admit the truth, you argue with me. What are you thinking?"

"I'm thinking that for the last ten years I wanted you to tell me unconditionally that I made the right decision, to ease my guilt. But I was wrong. And I'm honest enough to admit it to myself now, before I make the same mistake with Hugo." Nevis edged back from Clarissa, heading toward Alvaron Park before the summer storm unleashed its full force.

"Child, think! What will you do when Hugo threatens to hurt you or Devlin? And you know he will. Don't underestimate his malice. What then? Will you try to persuade him that he's wrong to be greedy or to threaten innocent children or to break the laws of Montbasso as though they were nonexistent?" Despite her cane, Clarissa kept up with the younger woman's rapid stride, surprising Nevis. "You can try, but you'll only be wasting your breath. Hugo may not be a victim of the Cashogi drug that wrecked Adrian's mind, but he's a victim of his own cold-blooded lack of a heart. He's ruthless. Look what he's done to Devlin's poor daughter. Believe me, Nevis, your compassionate urging and quiet reasoning won't get you anywhere with Hugo San Rossi. You'd have better luck with a stone wall." The older woman argued relentlessly, ignoring Nevis' firm refusal to listen as the younger woman kept walking. "And in that tiny moment of time when you try to reclaim his soul, Hugo will hurt you and those you love. Mark my words."

Nevis spun on her heels and faced her mentor, heedless of the cold rain streaming down her face and the loud crack of thunder from across the river that shook the ground. "I won't let him." Without waiting for a reply, she fled back through the park and into her private suite behind the stage, soaked to the skin. "By the gods," she murmured, eyes shut against the fear, safe inside her parlor, "I won't let him."

* * * *

She'd been restless the remainder of the day, made ridiculous excuses to May Quiddle for missing supper, promised to make an appearance before the children went to sleep, and escaped to solitude filled with old haunting memories. Before she could face the children with any amount of self-control, Nevis needed calm, and serenity always came with her sorcery. Pulling several fresh sheets of paper from her desk drawer, Nevis forcefully thrust Hugo San Rossi to the back of her jumbled thoughts, letting her subconscious mind deal with the problem.

That accomplished, she thought about one or two ideas for the children that would make them laugh and ease their own frightful worries. Allowing herself to smile, she thought of her sister and how she could use May Quiddle to achieve her objective. First, the mage needed to create a likeness of May, though not so detailed that the woman herself, body and soul, would be caught up in the spell, in the sphere itself, held prisoner until the creator mage released her. That was a danger Nevis would never risk, had indeed, been taught by Clarissa to be ever alert against.

Nevis outlined the slender shape of her younger sister, long dark curls that fell beyond her thin shoulders, a portrait that could indeed have represented any woman in Port Jambi. But to the children, familiar day and night with only one woman who had long dark glossy curls, that woman would only be May Quiddle. Steeped in mischief, Nevis added another object to make the children clap in delight.

Satisfied that she took no sorcerous risk to harm her sister, Nevis murmured an incantation over the vague sketch and waved her hands gently, watching the outlined portrait lift from the page. It hovered briefly over the cluttered desk, becoming solid, until Nevis created the sphere to encase it. She inspected it carefully, took note of the tiny woman inside, and set it aside with a grin.

Immediately, thoughts of Hugo San Rossi intruded, and Nevis recalled the bitter words she'd exchanged with Clarissa Bracken down by the river. Absently, her hands toyed with another sheet of paper while she tried to think what more she could do to trap the mage. To trap him, without Shayna Kashi nearby to help him, so that Nevis could persuade Hugo to give himself up and make amends.

Perhaps it was foolish, perhaps she was being naïve, but she believed that Hugo, who was gifted with mage powers as potent as Nevis' own sorcery, owed it to himself and the people of Port Jambi. And Nevis owed it to her own peace of mind to try and convince him to change, despite the simple fact that everyone considered her naïve and idealistic at the moment.

Nevis tossed aside the quill, only then recognizing what her busy fingers had created while her thoughts were distracted, a heavily detailed sketch of Hugo San Rossi's face, with arrogance and malice staring back at her through his midnight eyes. A shiver swept up her spine, and Nevis took the sheet of paper in her hands, prepared to cast it away. And then the mage reconsidered, laying the sketch back down on the corner of her desk, held unmoving by the carved wooden statue of Janni.

Unsettled by what her hands had accomplished independent of her will, Nevis shoved back her chair and snatched up the sphere, leaving the portrait on her desk until she could think clearly. Seeking distraction, Nevis stormed down the stairway that led to the ground floor, nearly colliding with Lily Frascat, who'd just entered the building through the side door adjacent to her whorehouse.

"Nevis, what's wrong?"

"Not a thing." The mage evaded Lily's persistent questioning by heading straight for the stage, where May was busy, with the help of two of Lily's girls, settling the children down for sleep, resigned to the genuine possibility that Nevis might choose not to appear.

"Well, well." May's hands jumped to her slender hips as she stared at her elder sister in maternal disapproval. "Finally emerged from your cave, did you?"

"I was busy creating a spell for my guests." Nevis came around to the side stairs, practically leaped over them, long legs taking the steps in graceful strides, and plopped on the hard, wooden floor at the edge of the huddled group eagerly anticipating her magic.

"Guests?"

"Sure. Assuming they're ready for sleep," she slid a mischievous glance at her sister, acknowledging the unspoken worry, "I wanted to give them the special, private performance I promised days ago."

"Nevis—"

"She did promise," Teddy piped up, scooting over to his aunt's side, careful of her ivory-handled stiletto.

"I did." Nevis brushed brown curls from his eyes and winked at the little redhead tucked under May's arm, thumb happily in place. "Now everyone has to lie down on their pillows and just look up at the ceiling. And remember what I told you," she reassured the smallest children gathered around Lily's girls, who were no less eager to watch the performance, "it's only magic. It won't hurt you. Nothing in my theater will hurt you. Don't ever forget that."

Satisfied that they were ready, she waited until they'd grown quiet, all eyes eagerly fixed on her black clad arms as they rose toward the ceiling, the edges of the bandages peeking out from beneath her cuffs. Immediately, the stage darkened, the only light emanating from the flickering magefire lamps set in sconces along the sides of the theater.

Nevis opened the bottomless leather pouch at her waist and drew out the sphere to recreate a storm. Teddy gave her room as she unsheathed the stiletto. Nevis held out the sphere to catch the flickering magefire, making sure once more that she'd taken out the right one, and triggered the spell within.

Immediately, a gentle rumble of thunder sounded overhead and behind the false fortress walls on stage, with flashes of lightning branching into smaller bolts across the internal sky. Behind the stage, glimpsed through the windows of the fortress, torrential rain poured down from the portentous clouds, sprinkling the children's faces with cool spray as the water splashed against the scenery. The storm faded and rekindled, shaking the stage beneath their tiny bodies, gathering in intensity before moving off as naturally as a true storm. The heavy rain dwindled to a light mist, while overhead, the clouds across the ceiling cleared, revealing countless stars. While the children craned their necks to see every angle of the summer sky, with shooting stars darting across the heavens like fireflies, Nevis pulled out the sphere she'd created only moments earlier.

Her hand stilled on the sphere as she studied the midnight clarity overhead, lingering thoughts about the hideaway that Hugo had created from thin air in Alana Graham's bedchamber intruding into her restless mind. Once again pushing Hugo away from her thoughts, Nevis triggered the spell and resheathed the stiletto, watching the children's faces, her own anticipation high, as the full moon rose from behind the fortress, then over it. Murmurings gave way to shrieks of genuine delight as the moon, now clear of the building, unmistakably wore the image of a woman with long, dark curly hair, and first one, then another, glanced at May, pointing and giggling. As the spell faded, Nevis raised her arms once more to keep the lighting dim, and stood gracefully at the edge of the huddled bodies. "Sweet dreams," she whispered, bending to touch their outstretched hands and disheveled heads, then stepped down from the stage.

"Was that supposed to be complimentary?"

"Sure." Nevis grinned at her sister, thoughts already far away and leading her steps there as she headed toward the side entrance that led to the alley between the theater and the brothel.

"If you think you're evading me again—" Nevis turned as the sound of Lily's sharp voice emerged from the shadows, green eyes thoughtful beneath their owner's upswept auburn hair. "You've got an awful gleam in your eyes, Mage Conarkin, and I can't say I like it."

"I've been thinking."

"That's what I feared."

"Will you tell May I'm heading over to the fortress for a bit?"

"Afraid to tell her yourself?"

"Lily—"

The madam narrowed her eyes and stared at her friend with suspicion. "Are you going to see Devlin? Maybe get him to rub all that tension from your back and shoulders?"

"Not at first. I need to see Minister Nashat before it gets too late."

"Too late in the evening?"

"Too late to do something about Hugo. Can I borrow your carriage?"

"Yes, of course." Lily made a successful grab at the mage's sleeve. "By the gods, woman, can't you even give me a hint so I won't sit here driving poor Remo mad with worry?"

"It's not altogether clear in my head yet."

"That's what worries me."

Nevis didn't respond and stepped out into the darkness, spoke quietly to the driver, who opened the carriage door to let her inside. Before he'd taken his own seat, a figure emerged from the shadows, uniform well-creased and near perfect, and reopened the carriage door to let herself inside.

"I thought you might want some company."

"Did Lily send you after me?"

"I can't imagine why you should be so suspicious."

Nevis shook her head in disgust. "By the gods, you're all pathetic. Get in. Time's slipping away."

Chapter Seventeen

"Just the two gentlemen I wished to see," Nevis smiled warmly at Finlay Oscram and the Cashogi trade minister, then kept her expression decidedly neutral as she eyed Devlin Graham. "About the third, I'm not so sure."

"Constable Kilganor, always a pleasure," Devlin said politely, ignoring the smile that tugged at the mage's lips. "Have you eaten? We've just finished, but I'll have my chef bring something hot and nourishing."

"No, thank you, my lord. Not for me. Though perhaps—"

"I won't even bother to waste my breath to offer Mage Conarkin a bite to eat, though I'm certain she hasn't thought about eating anything decent or nutritious in the past three days beyond those sugar-coated horrors."

"I did eat yesterday," Nevis murmured, tucking her hands in the pockets of her ebony breeches. "I don't remember what it was, but I did eat."

Blue eyes shot a look of intense annoyance at Nevis, hands twirling an elegant crystal brandy snifter. "Why are you ladies looking for Finlay and Mikaline? Or should I leave the chamber so you can tell them in private?"

"No need to be snide," Nevis said quietly, sitting on the overstuffed arm of the velvet couch opposite the men, while Brea waited beside the door. "You can stay. I'd have to speak to you eventually." A grin escaped, and Devlin snorted, mumbling a mild curse that had Finlay laughing and the trade minister uncertain.

"Don't mind them," Finlay reassured the Cashogi minister. "They're always sniping at each other."

"He snipes," Nevis said, quickly adding, "But we are here for a serious matter, Minister Nashat."

The Cashogi set aside his own brandy snifter and gave Nevis his full attention. "You've found Shayna."

"No. But I might have a plan to lure her into the open. If not Shayna, then Hugo San Rossi." Deliberately not looking at Devlin, she explained, "You know about the transport papers that Hugo kept hidden in Alana's room?"

"Yes. You asked that I keep both my ships here in Port Jambi rather than sending one back to Cashogi as a courier."

"I did." Nevis raked her fingers through her hair, wincing as her stomach rumbled traitorously with hunger. She caught Devlin's blue-eyed accusation, and shrugged, deciding to focus on the matter at hand. "I thought you might announce the ship's departure in two days."

Mikaline Nashat studied the slender mage, saw the shadows beneath weary green eyes and the constant worry that plagued her heart. "Will she really leave the harbor in two days?"

"I doubt it."

"Nevis, what are you thinking?" Devlin's question brought her eyes to his, held them there for a heartbeat.

"If Hugo believes the Cashogi ship is leaving Port Jambi, he'll make plans to be on board. Which means he'll need the gold and the papers he's stashed in Alana's chamber." Nevis got to her feet and stood by the window overlooking the port, at the point where the Basol River opened up to form the broad, deep-channeled harbor. From her vantage point, it was easy to see the two Cashogi vessels and the Ruskin Shipyard, its new schooner waiting for launch. "If we remove those items," Nevis explained, "he'll panic. He can forge papers, but he can't create real gold."

"So he'll go precisely where to find more gold?" Finlay asked, cleaning the remnants of tobacco from his pipe. "Will he steal from my vault?"

"Possibly," Nevis admitted to the banker, "which is why I wanted to speak with you, to warn you. I can place a temporary spell on your vault—"

"Don't bother."

"Actually, it's not such a bad idea,' Devlin interjected, shooting a wary glance at Nevis. "If Mage Conarkin has the time and energy— Mind you, she'd have the energy if she shoved a decent meal down her throat, Finlay. She might be persuaded to cast a spell on your vault and mine, so the people's treasury is untouched." Blue eyes danced beneath thick dark hair, heavily sprinkled with gray. "What say you, Mage Conarkin? Or have I offended your sensibilities?"

Nevis tucked her hands deeper into the pockets of her breeches, a sly smile escaping, a smile that brought Devlin's instinct immediately alert.

"What's your price?"

"I'm canceling the play."

"Nevis—"

"No more, Dev. The play's a bad idea."

Devlin Graham stroked his beard, stared long and hard at the mage. "You really think so?"

"I always did."

"Then why didn't you tell me?" He laughed and ducked as she picked up an embroidered pillow, aiming for his head, caught Finlay's pipe instead as the banker unwittingly raised it to his lips, knocking the unlit pipe to the plush rug.

"Sorry, Finlay."

"Don't be. He deserved that. Sorry to block your throw." Finlay grinned at the mage, reverted to a bland expression when Devlin growled at him.

"If we leave no attractive place for Hugo San Rossi to steal from," Mikaline Nashat politely intervened, "where else would he go?"

Brea Kilganor answered before Nevis did. "Barry Faddle lent him funds a short time ago."

"Then that means," Devlin reasserted his authority, winking at the constable, "that since there's no longer a current play running at Nevis Conarkin's Sorcerous Theater, the good mage, should she find the strength, will have to escort me to a performance in Barry Faddle's traditional, non-sorcerous playhouse."

"I'd be happy to, my lord." Nevis glanced at the Cashogi minister. "As a matter of fact, it's a good opportunity for you to see a performance, too."

"I'd be delighted. In fact," Mikaline Nashat smiled, "I'll even pay for the theater tickets."

* * * *

"Alana, we need to come inside." Devlin kept his voice even, expression empty as he waited patiently in the corridor outside his daughter's suite.

The young woman eyed her father warily, then Nevis and the constable standing directly behind her. "Why?"

Devlin's bland expression lost some of its neutrality. "I don't wish to discuss this matter in the corridor. Nor do I wish to forcibly come into your rooms."

Alana's blue eyes, much lighter than her father's, flashed with a hint of fear, then defiance. She stepped back, grudgingly allowed the three visitors inside. "If you're looking for Hugo, he's not here."

"Has he been here?"

Blue eyes slid to Nevis, then back to her father. "No."

"Are you sure?"

"Poppa—"

"Remember what we told you? As a mage, Hugo may have come here without your knowing it," Nevis said quietly, risking the girl's anger.

"And remember what I told you?" Alana snapped, blonde hair swirling around her head as she strode away from the group in the direction of her bedchamber. "For all I know, Mage Conarkin, you've been here, too. Or have you now come to steal what doesn't belong to you? With the constable for witness to make it legal?"

"Since you put it that way," Nevis shrugged, and followed the girl into the bedchamber, signaling Devlin back, "I suppose I am." She said nothing more, focused instead on transforming her appearance into a mirror image of Hugo San Rossi, a twin of the portrait cast aside on her office desk, held securely by the statue of Janni, whose watchful eyes missed nothing. "Constable?"

Brea muttered a curse under her breath, eying the mage warily, uneasy at the all-too-familiar face of Hugo San Rossi staring back at her. "That's a frightening bit of sorcery."

"But useful."

Distracted, Nevis touched the wall between the windows as she had only days ago. A portal opened into thin air, and Nevis took a cautious step, studying the hideaway for recent signs of Hugo's presence. But the magical alcove appeared untouched, and Nevis stepped over the threshold, heedless of the constable's continual grumbling as she stepped, for all intents and purposes, into empty space.

Nevis picked up the documents that validated her ownership of the destroyed orphanage, in partnership with Lily, and tossed them, along with the transport papers for Hugo and Shayna Kashi, to Brea. The constable caught them and handed them to Devlin. With more care, Nevis picked up the original spheres that she'd created and Hugo stolen, tucking them safely into her bottomless pouch. All that remained were the small gold bars and Firespark that would give Hugo a new start in Cashogi. Nevis looked up and waited.

Standing on the threshold, eying the seemingly solid ground, Brea sighed and took a cautious step closer to the mage. She unfolded a sack that she'd tucked into her belt before leaving Devlin's study and shook it open, holding it wide for the mage. Quickly, Nevis took the gold bars and Firespark from their shelves and loaded the bulging sack until the hideaway stood empty.

"Can you manage that?"

"Easier than standing on thin air." Brea hefted the sack over her shoulder, politely declining Devlin's offer of help as Nevis closed the portal and resumed her own white-haired, female appearance.

Devlin started to leave, but the mage brushed his arm, one gentle meaningful touch that spoke volumes. Blue eyes stared at Nevis for a heartbeat before turning to Alana. "Thank you," he said quietly.

The girl stood silent as her father left without another word, eyes tracking Nevis' retreating back as the mage followed him.

* * * *

"Well, Finlay, that should do it." Nevis stepped back from the immense, ceiling-high vault on which she'd just cast a spell, requiring Finlay's presence alone to open the vault. "For a few days, anyway."

The banker shrugged. "Let's hope that's all it takes to get the bastard out of hiding. You might do yourself and Lily a favor," he suggested, eying both Devlin and Brea Kilganor for their agreement, "and lay a protection spell against magefire on both the theater and the whorehouse."

"Is that the banker speaking or my friend?"

Bald head shining in the lamplight, Finlay scowled. "I can't believe I'm hearing that from your lips, Nevis. What do you think?"

The mage grinned and kissed his smooth cheek. "Both. Come on. The carriage will drop you off at home."

"Don't bother. I can use the walk. It's only a block away." Finlay shook Devlin's hand, nodded politely to the constable. "Devlin, old friend, I don't know how you put up with her."

"I ignore her half the— Oof! By the gods, woman, was that your elbow or your stiletto?"

The mage didn't bother to answer, instead left the building and climbed gracefully back into the royal carriage, the scarlet hawk emblazoned on both doors. "Coming, Constable?"

"I wouldn't refuse a ride to the theater. Someone should tell Lily Frascat what's going on."

"I can do that." Nevis' green eyes looked bewildered until the constable laughed, and then she flushed. "Devlin's not—"

"Devlin probably is."

"Devlin probably is what?" The monarch of Montbasso demanded, as he joined the two women in the carriage as the driver headed for the theater, clattering over the cobblestones of Harbor Road.

"Nothing," Nevis murmured, pale skin still showing spots of scarlet from the constable's unspoken words and the implication of how the king likely planned to spend his evening with his lover. "I was thinking to cast a spell on both buildings tonight. Funny that Finlay should think of it, too."

"Not funny," Devlin took one of her slender hands and held it loosely within his own huge hands. "Finlay's worried, and he's right to be. Hugo San Rossi is a dangerous man."

"He's getting reckless," Nevis said quietly, thinking of Clarissa Bracken and her walking stick, and their contentious words.

"He is." Brea Kilganor stared out the window, thinking. "And so I wonder, Nevis, whether he'll try to leave Port Jambi without coming after you again." She turned dark brown eyes to the mage, fully cognizant of Devlin's own watchful scrutiny. "I don't think so. I believe he'll try to hurt you again somehow."

Nevis turned away, staring out the opposite window at the darkened river as the carriage approached Alvaron Park. Circumventing the park, Harbor Road changed its name to McOsley's Road as it ran through the theater's neighborhood, then returned to its original name further along. Following Harbor Road downstream toward the port itself would lead to the gates of Ruskin Shipyards and the docks wherein lay the Cashogi vessels, merchant schooners, and Devlin's navy.

While Nevis was so distracted, Devlin released her hand and touched her cheek, caressing its softness. Still, the mage said nothing to either Brea or Devlin until the carriage pulled in front of the theater.

"I'll tell Lily what's going on," the constable said, stepping out of the carriage and smoothing her clean, crisp uniform.

Nevis started to follow but Devlin held her back. "You and I must talk after you cast the spells. Nevis—"

She squeezed his hand and nodded, descending gracefully down the carriage steps. Gathering her sorcery together, she crossed the narrow street to the whorehouse, and placed her open palms against the building. Quietly, she whispered an incantation to protect the building

against magefire, stepping back as the brothel glowed with a soft lumi-
nescence that swiftly faded. Without a word, she crossed back toward
the theater and repeated the spell, arms dropping limply to her sides as
the evening's sorcerous efforts took their toll.

"You've been busy," Lily drawled, coming over with the constable,
trying not to stare at her friend's obvious exhaustion.

"Never a dull moment when Dev's around," Nevis smiled, not
bothering to disguise her weariness, knowing that Lily would see right
through any such attempt and scold her mercilessly. And then tell May,
who would, in her own turn, scold her older sister.

"That's entirely true. Hello, Dev." Lily stretched on her toes to kiss
his cheek but the taller man gathered her close for an affectionate hug.
"In front of Nevis? Devlin, really, she'll transform me into a squealing
piglet."

"Nevis is too gods' cursed weary at the moment to notice," Devlin
said lightly, though his blue eyes stared defiantly at the mage, daring
her to deny her fatigue. "I hope you don't object to her spell casting."

"Not at all. Actually, I was going to suggest it for the theater, never
really thinking about my own building."

"If Hugo's going to hurt Nevis, he'll do it anyway he can." Devlin's
voice was somber. "And that includes hurting people whom she cares
about."

"Then you'd best be very careful," Lily matched his tone, checking
to see that her feathers were in place after his enthusiastic embrace.

"I always am, Lily. Now before I tuck the mage into bed," he declared, enjoying Nevis' flush and the constable's restrained grin, "I
want to see what's happening inside the theater. I understand there are
a thousand little monsters in every corner, multiplying by the hour."

Nevis laughed, pulling him toward the door. "Sounds like a thousand, but only a dozen. Come in, but be quiet. They should all be sleeping."

And they were, but for the smallest, red-haired child that escaped May's arms the moment she saw Nevis' white hair. Kimmi scurried up to the mage, waited patiently until Nevis scooped her up, and tucked her head of wild curls onto Nevis' thin shoulder, completely oblivious of the monarch of Montbasso as she stuck her thumb straight into her mouth.

"And here I thought all my subjects knelt at my feet in devoted adoration and awe the moment they saw me," Devlin laughed, planting a kiss on May's cheek.

"When she's older, she'll be appalled."

"I doubt it. Not if Nevis has anything to say about it." Devlin's eyes roamed the theater, taking in the huddled bodies on stage, shepherded by two of Lily's girls. "Need anything?"

"Not at the moment. You've done enough." May squeezed his arm warmly in gratitude.

"Not nearly. We'll get all this sorted out once Hugo San Rossi is in our hands. Until then," blue eyes darted to Nevis, then back to May, "I'd rather the children stay here where we can protect them better. It's no guarantee," he added quietly, running a hand along the child's soft cheek and earning a beautiful smile, "but Nevis cast a spell to prevent Hugo using magefire to destroy the theater. He may still try to harm them some other way, but we can't protect against all eventualities."

"No," May agreed, seeing her sister's weariness as Nevis moved into the magefire lamplight. "But we'll stay alert. He's a mage, but so is my sister."

"Your sister is an exhausted mage. Come along," Devlin took her hand as though Nevis was a reluctant child. "Give the imp back to May before you drop her. You, Mage Conarkin, are going straight to bed."

"I doubt that," May grinned, earning a laugh from Lily and the constable, as she took the sleepy child from Nevis' arms.

"By the gods, you're all—"

"We are, indeed, Nevis." Devlin kissed the tip of her nose and led her from the theater to the private entrance to her rooms behind the stage. "Now sit and let me take off those boots," he ordered, the moment he dragged her into the bedchamber. "But you take off that horrible pouch."

"It's not horrible. Besides, I wouldn't dream of letting the frightened monarch of Montbasso touch it," Nevis teased, ignoring his scowl as she slipped both stiletto and bottomless pouch from her waist.

"I'm not frightened, simply cautious. It's sorcerous, and I'm not a mage. Knowing how your wicked mind works, I wouldn't be surprised if you cast a spell on it to turn a thief into a sewer rat."

Nevis held the pouch in her hand. "Care to experiment?"

"Put that cursed thing away."

Devlin tossed her black leather boots in a corner and pulled down the bed coverings. He reached for the top button of her shirt, honestly intending to tuck her beneath the sheets and leave her alone, but something in her eyes stopped him. "I'm afraid to lose you," he whispered, tracing the smooth pale skin of her jaw. "I'm so terrified that Hugo San Rossi will hurt you when I'm far away and not there to protect you."

Nevis kissed the fingers that made their way to her lips. "I'd rather you weren't there when he does come after me." Before Devlin could protest, she stopped his words with her own finger on his lips. "I'm terrified he'll hurt you, and that I'll be the one who loses you, Dev, not the other way around."

"Then we'll fight him together." Devlin drew her close, kissed the top of her shaggy white hair, remembering with fear how she'd earned that symbol of Adrian's defeat. And suddenly, Devlin was more frightened than he'd ever been, that he'd never hold her in his arms again. "Nevis—"

"I don't know about you, Dev," she whispered in his ear, a sly smile on her face as he waited breathlessly for what she would say, "but I'm not really as exhausted as everyone seems to think."

Chapter Eighteen

"Morning, boss." Simon deposited a sugar-coated breakfast cake in front of his employer and took a seat opposite the desk. Idly, he glanced at the sketch of Hugo San Rossi sitting placidly at the far edge of the desk, held captive by the statue of the goddess, Janni, then away.

"You never sit down. Should I start sweating?"

The stage manager steepled his fingers and rested his chin on top. "I've been thinking."

"Thank the gods, Simon. I was afraid you were going to tell me that Gabriella was going to continue the acting lessons."

"She is."

Nevis nearly choked on the morsel of sweet cake she was busy enjoying. "Simon, she can't—"

"Sure she can. Besides, she's doing a good deed, the children enjoy it immensely, and it makes her feel important." The stage manager sat back in the cracked leather chair and studied his employer's face, features so familiar that he knew when she was weary and when she was worried and when she was hiding either one. At the moment, Nevis was desperately trying to hide both. "Are we canceling the show?"

The mage suddenly lost her appetite and pushed the breakfast cake aside as her stomach knotted.

"You've never been happy about it."

"No, and I spoke to Devlin about it last night. Simon—" Nevis rubbed her eyes like a sleepy child. "I suppose the answer is yes."

"Then here's what we do. The first task is to spread the news to the public and refund all tickets. That leaves—"

"Simon—"

Looking every one of his middle-aged years, Simon Masters drew himself up in the chair. "You pay me to manage your theater and that's what I'm doing."

Resigned to the ugly facts, Nevis sighed. "Go on."

Simon continued on as though she hadn't interrupted. "After the ticket refunds are all distributed, we'll have just enough to pay the cast and crew through the end of the week."

"They were counting on a theater season. I can't just let them go. But by the gods, Simon, at least they could be earning a living elsewhere if I do." Distressed, Nevis fiddled with the breakfast cake, squashing the raspberry star.

"True, but here's what we'll do."

"Morning, Nevis." Verdi Casporet poked her head into the office and eyed Simon. "They're all here."

"Who's all here?" Nevis demanded. "Verdi—" But the costume designer had already left. The mage stared at Simon in bewilderment as he shook his head, muttering words that sounded foul though she couldn't hear them clearly.

"Come on, Nevis. They're all here."

"Simon, who's all here?"

But the stage manager had deserted her, too. Baffled and more than a little irritated, Nevis followed her two employees out into the corridor and peered over the railing of her private box. On stage, the children were still sleeping beneath May's watchful eyes. At the front entrance, Verdi and Simon waited, saw the mage's bewildered expression, and waved her to join them. Cursing and cranky, Nevis arrived at the door, only to find the entire cast and crew sitting on the theater steps.

"We didn't want to wake the children," Verdi explained when Nevis stood at the top of the stairs, motionless, her tall figure casting a shadow along the steps.

"Sit down, boss," Simon said gently, tugging at her arm. "We've got a plan to discuss with you."

Nevis sat warily, eying her employees, one by one, through narrowed eyelids. "It's a little early for you, Gabriella, isn't it?"

"I didn't want this meeting to interfere with my acting lessons." The flame-haired actress gathered her silk skirt around her shapely legs and smiled. "Go on, Simon. Tell Nevis what we've discussed."

"Did you tell her anything?" Verdi demanded, sitting on the step above the mage. "You were in there for a while."

"Not long enough." Simon glanced at Nevis, saw her suspicion, and shrugged. "Boss, listen. We—" Simon's hands encompassed the entire cast and crew. "We figured out that you'd probably cancel the play."

"To be honest," Pepo interrupted, sensuous hands fluttering to his chest, "your heart wasn't in it. From the very moment Devlin Graham demanded you memorialize your gallant act, you've been itching to cancel the play."

"Right," Gabriella took up the tale, "so Pepo and I have been discussing a new plot with our illustrious playwright, who has now sworn off all drugs." The actress fiercely eyed the playwright, who raised both hands to defend himself while nodding vigorously as Gabriella added, oblivious to Nevis' wide-eyed stare, "We'll need a few weeks to get the whole play written, but—"

"Gabriella—"

"Hush, Nevis, and listen." The actress' tone was commandeering, but her eyes surprisingly kind. "After you refund the tickets, there's not much left in the theater's treasury. Maybe enough to pay us for a few days. So here's what we plan to do instead." She looked to Verdi for support when Nevis started to protest.

Verdi tapped the mage on the shoulder. "Until the next performance begins, you're not going to pay any of us. Now just listen to me before scolding— You're not going to pay any of us until the next play is ready to go forward. In the meantime, you have to feed us. That's all you have to do. We've all got a little bit stored by to pay for our room and board. And while these two very talented performers," she nodded her head at Pepo and Gabriella, laughing as they preened like peacocks, "are busy helping the playwright, the rest of us are going to rebuild your orphanage."

Abruptly, Nevis lurched to her feet and walked down the steps, her rigid back to the cast and crew, most of whom had been with her since she opened the theater a decade ago when she resigned the post of mage adviser to the king. Verdi started to speak, but Gabriella raised a hand to keep her quiet. Together, they watched in silence as Nevis hugged herself hard and turned back slowly to stare up at them, green eyes bright with vulnerability.

"I can't let you do that," she said quietly, "though I'll never forget the offer and the generosity behind it."

"Too proud to let us help?" Gabriella demanded, jutting her breasts forward in true dramatic fashion as she set her hands on her shapely hips.

"Too practical to know that you could all be working elsewhere, making decent wages and earning an honest living."

Gabriella pretended to take offense. "You're planning to hire a new cast, aren't you?"

"By the gods, Gabriella, the thought never crossed my mind."

"Then don't argue with us." When Nevis turned pleading eyes to Verdi, Gabriella attacked, gently and effectively. "Seems to me, Nevis, that you went far out of your way not to believe that Hans was guilty of murder. Seems to me you secretly lent Pepo some funds when he got in trouble over the butcher's niece and that you put in a quiet word to Remo Savanak when the innkeeper tried to have me arrested for disturbing his peace and that you sent Doc Esteway to Verdi's mother and refused to let the old woman or Verdi pay the bill, and—"

Nevis raised a hand to stop the outpouring of words, her face flushed with embarrassment.

"Must I go on?"

"I'd rather you didn't."

"I can be here for quite awhile, you know. There's no one in this troupe you haven't helped at one time or other. And most likely, more than once."

"Gabriella—"

"Is it a deal? Because if it's not, Mage Conarkin," Gabriella flounced her bright skirts at the mage, "we're going to do it, anyway."

Nevis stared at the actress, then let her green eyes scan each familiar face, her hands tucked deep in the pockets of her ebony breeches. "All this time, I thought I was in charge."

"Sorry to disappoint you, boss," Simon grinned, getting to his feet and pulling Verdi up with him. "But you were never in charge."

* * * *

Stunned, Nevis left the smug troupe as they disbanded to take on their individual tasks under Simon's organized guidance. She headed straight across the alley to Lily's whorehouse, needing to share this recent revelation. But long before she found Lily Frascat, Nevis Conarkin found trouble.

"What do you mean they're gone?" she demanded of Chappy, staring at the broad-shouldered strongman who let her in the side entrance. "Both Hans and Fani knew they weren't to go anywhere. You knew—"

"Mage Conarkin, you know I'd never let them leave without your permission or the constable's word." Bewildered, Chappy ran a beefy hand over his bald head, glancing uneasily at Lily as the madam came striding briskly down the corridor at the alarming sound of Nevis' raised voice.

"But you did allow them to leave."

"Yes, because you told me you needed them to come with you."

Nevis stepped back from the bruiser, bewildered for only a heartbeat. "By the gods, that means—"

"Chappy?" Lily touched the mage's arm, causing the other woman to jump in surprise. "What has Chappy done?"

Not answering, Nevis headed for the door, stopped in worried confusion, stared at Chappy's unhappy expression, thinking hard. "Where were they headed? Where were they going when they left here?"

"Nevis—" Lily grabbed her sleeve and forced the white-haired mage to face her. "What has Chappy done?"

"He's done nothing. Hugo San Rossi came here, disguised as me. He's taken Hans and Fani somewhere." Frantic, Nevis pushed past Chappy, ignoring Lily's attempts to restrain her until finally the brothel owner grabbed both shoulders and shoved the mage against the wall to keep her still.

"Nevis, before you go racing out of here like a crazed woman, think," Lily chided, pale pink feathers bobbing with every passionate word. "If you're off to find them, take Chappy with you in the carriage. Don't argue, woman. I won't have you go chasing after Hugo San Rossi alone. If he's taken them, then very possibly, and very likely, it's a trap for you."

"I'll get the carriage," Chappy said quietly, slipping out the door before the mage could argue with him.

Lily nodded her thanks, slowly releasing Nevis as the mage gradually brought her tumultuous thoughts under control. "I'll send word to the constable. Where are you headed?"

"To Hans' rooms first, then—" Nevis shrugged uneasily. "I don't know where else to go."

"Then come back here. By that time, Constable Kilganor should arrive. Nevis—" Lily caught the mage back as she tried to leave. "Be careful."

"Sure."

Nevis ignored the madam's blistering oath at her easy acquiescence and stepped outside where the carriage was ready and waiting. Chappy held the door open, jumping up beside the driver once Nevis gave him directions. Alone inside the carriage, Nevis shut her eyes and leaned her head back against the velvet cushions, blaming herself for not anticipating Hugo's trick. The ride was endless and bone rattling as the wheels bounced along the cobblestones, though in reality, it took only a few moments. Yet in those endless moments, Nevis feared for the two lovers and for what she would find, knowing it was her fault.

Once they arrived at Hans' building, Nevis didn't wait for the carriage to stop rolling, but flew out of the conveyance onto the fractured walkway. Chappy followed close on her heels, alert to danger, hurrying to catch up as she approached the unlocked, half-open door.

Nevis paused in the doorway, unwilling to accept the probability of what awaited her. The reality was far worse than she imagined. On the bare wall opposite the front door were eerie words, scrawled in blood, chilling her own lifeblood. Words that left her shaken to her very soul.

"Two bodies for one is not enough."

Bracing herself for what lay ahead, Nevis stepped cautiously through the mess left behind by Hugo San Rossi when he first captured Hans, opened and torn parcels of Cashogi Firespark still tossed and scattered around the cramped parlor. She heard Chappy's sharp intake of breath as he read the words written on the wall, listened as his footsteps followed hers, and prayed to Janni, whose heart encompassed all children, that the two lovers had died instantly. They lay side by side on the narrow bed, naked, facing each other, each clasping within one hand the hilt of a dagger, its point buried to the hilt in the other's chest.

Nevis sank to her knees and wept, oblivious to the passage of time and Chappy's awkward attempts to make her leave. From far away, she heard hushed tones, recognized Chappy's rough, shaken baritone, and the quiet, composed voice of Brea Kilganor as she entered the defaced room.

"Nevis—" The constable crouched beside the mage, touched her arm with grave gentleness. "Come away."

"If I hadn't taken Hugo's gold and forced him to search for funds, he would never have believed that Hans and Fani snitched on him," Nevis whispered, rubbing her wet cheeks with the wrinkled sleeve of her cotton shirt as though to rub away the guilt. "It's my fault they're dead. My fault that I didn't warn them about Hugo's magic."

"It's Hugo San Rossi's fault that they're dead." When the mage only shook her head, setting shaggy white hair astray, Brea's gentle touch gave way to a more intense grip that brought the mage's sorrowful green eyes to meet her angry gaze. "It's not your fault. Hugo wants you to believe that so you'll weaken."

"No—"

"Yes. Don't let Hugo San Rossi win. Don't you dare let that bastard win."

Growing rage slowly replaced the endless sorrow and guilt in the mage's green eyes until, finally, she nodded, accepting the constable's outstretched hand as she regained her feet and her composure.

"Did he have such control over their fears that he could force them to murder each other?" Brea asked quietly, brushing hair from her forehead as she studied the macabre scene. "Or did Hugo murder them himself and make it appear they did so?"

"He probably cast a spell on them and watched them slip the bloody dagger into each other's heart. Depraved and cruel—" Nevis sagged back against the doorframe, her strength nearly all but gone.

"What does his message mean? If he's referring to Adam Museo, that doesn't make much sense."

Nevis shut her eyes, her heart heavy. "That's because he's referring to Adrian Bambari."

* * * *

The two gentlemen flanking Nevis smiled pleasantly at each other over her bowed head, trying very hard not to admit that they were both rather uneasy over what the mage had just proposed to do. Nevis' short-cropped white hair shone bright in the lamplight of Barry Faddle's theater as she proudly produced a crystal sphere from her bottomless leather pouch.

The play had not yet started, and the three of them sat high above the common seats in the private box Barry had vacated for their unexpected appearance for the evening performance. Below them, in the front row, Barry himself, dressed like a peacock, sat preening his drooping mustache, dimples in evidence, at the honor the trio bestowed upon his theater.

Keeping her movements out of sight from anyone who might peer up in curiosity at Devlin Graham's presence, along with trade minister Mikaline Nashat, the mage took a deep breath and unsheathed her ivory-handled stiletto.

"You already had this idea planned," Devlin hissed, staring at the sphere, blue eyes ripe with accusation and more than a hint of worry.

From the moment Constable Brea had sent word of the bodies they'd found, Devlin knew that Nevis was fast reaching her limit of tolerance. He knew she'd take the deaths on her conscience, regardless of whether or not she could have prevented them. And when he and Mikaline Nashat arrived to escort her to the theater, Devlin saw, with sinking heart, just how fragile was the grip holding back her emotions. He attempted to see what lay inside the sphere, grunted when he recognized the miniature figure that so closely resembled his lover. "Admit it."

"Saved me an argument," Nevis countered, trying to lighten his mood with a smile that never reached her own eyes, recalling as she did the grim message in Hans' parlor and the ghastly scene in the actor's bedchamber. Beyond telling Lily and Simon the sad news, she'd spoken to no one since the morning, closeting herself in the privacy of her rooms.

"Mage Conarkin, what if Hugo San Rossi appears and sees right through the deception? What then—" Mikaline Nashat glanced at the monarch for support, found resignation instead.

"You'll be safe," Nevis reassured the trade minister, mistaking his concern, and realizing her error when he looked utterly appalled. "Sorry. I should have realized you were worried about me. I'm a little distracted."

"With good reason," he smiled comfortingly, patting her hand.

"Now, gentlemen, just continue to act naturally."

When Devlin snorted, Nevis placed the sphere in her lap and held the stiletto to its transparent surface. Green eyes slid in Devlin's direction, then swiftly away, unwilling to respond to his undisguised concern. Before he could argue her out of her plan, Nevis thrust the stiletto into the sphere. As the spell took effect, she simultaneously cast another spell of invisibility over her body and gracefully left her seat, watching as a false Nevis, dressed in ebony velvet as the real Nevis was clad, took her place, moving so naturally that the trade minister blanched.

Before Devlin could take another breath, she squeezed his shoulder tight and departed, following the carpeted corridor and then the stairs to the main entrance of the theater. The building layout was similar to her own sorcerous theater, and Nevis made her way through the eager crowd, stepping carefully so as not to bump into an unwitting patron by accident.

Standing at the side entrance, out of uniform, Brea Kilganor waited, dark brown eyes scanning the late arrivals. She mingled with the audience rushing to take their seats, her jacket, breeches, and blonde wig borrowed from Verdi Casporet's costume closet, easily blending into the crowd. At the light touch on her arm, the constable started, then swiftly controlled her expression to stillness.

As the theater lights dimmed, Brea crept quietly down the corridor in the direction of Barry Faddle's office on the second floor. Nevis walked in front of her, unseen, slid the door sufficiently open to let the constable enter, and followed.

"You still think Hugo San Rossi hasn't contacted Barry yet?" Brea whispered, muttering a rough oath as she banged her knee on the sharp corner of the paper-strewn desk.

"Slick Hands looks too calm and relaxed. If Hugo had already been to see him, demanding funds, trust that little weasel to be sweating like a pig." Nevis swiftly looked around, found what she needed. "Can you squeeze into that closet?"

"Nevis—"

"Then I'll make you invisible."

"No, you won't. I'll only end up being stepped on," the constable grumbled, sliding open the closet door and grimacing. "I'll pretend I can fit and maybe I'll convince myself."

"I'll go keep watch. You just listen."

Before the constable could growl a rude reply, the mage crept from the darkened office and leaned against the wooden railing that ran along the entire length of the corridor, allowing her to view the theater space. Across the way, Devlin and the Cashogi trade minister were talking animatedly to each other and to the false mage, more so than Nevis desired, but she knew they'd been ill at ease with her sorcerous replacement, who managed a fair imitation of Nevis' gestures and appearance.

Barry smiled pleasantly to all around him as the heavy velvet curtains rose majestically to the tune of a distant flute, signaling the entrance of the love-struck bard, wandering the countryside in search of his missing shepherdess. Nevis suppressed a grin at the thought of Gabriella's scathing opinion. The grin faded as a somber young man approached Barry, kneeling at the peacock's feet to whisper in his ear. Nevis tensed, caught the theater owner's swift frown before schooling his expression to bland neutrality.

With a quiet word to his companion, Barry followed the young man into the aisle that led toward the side entrance just below where Nevis perched. Alert for danger, the mage wondered if Hugo had appeared, though perhaps it was something else that needed Barry's attention.

Perhaps not.

Without warning, Hugo San Rossi suddenly appeared down the corridor, poised at the door to the theater office, having passed her unwittingly in silence. Shaken by how close he'd come without realizing she was there, and that she'd had no time to warn the constable, Nevis tailed his footsteps, heard Barry rapidly ascend the stairs, and slipped to the side of the corridor to avoid contact with the theater owner.

"Mage San Rossi—"

"I need your help."

Barry's expression lost its neutrality as panic flared in his eyes. "Your pardon, but Nevis Conarkin is here in my theater with her lover, and—"

"That murderous white-haired mage has killed her own actor and his lover, and yet she sits in your theater pretending innocence," Hugo snarled at the theater owner, who stood speechless. "It's true. The news will be all over the streets by morning. Let Nevis enjoy the performance tonight, my friend, but her days of fame and fortune are long past. Even her lover will be forced to take action. I'm the mage to be reckoned with in Port Jambi. The only one."

"If it's true—"

"Why would I lie about something the whole of Port Jambi will know soon enough?"

Barry studied the other man, at the thick dark hair that fell rakishly in his eyes, a gaze so intense that Barry wished he were anywhere but in his presence. "How can I help you?" he whispered, tugging nervously on his drooping mustache.

"I need a small loan. Quite small." Hugo's smile was charming as he ran jeweled fingers down the front of his green velvet jacket. "I shall repay you within the week. In fact—" The mage leaned closer, allowing moonlight from the open shutters to reveal the greed in his dark eyes. "I shall see that you get double the coins you lend me tonight. Unlike Nevis Conarkin, I repay loyalty. Now here is what I need."

While the two men put their heads together, Nevis busied herself murmuring an incantation beneath her breath, a spell to freeze Hugo's movements and allow her to control his body. As swiftly as she completed the spell, holding her concentration taut, the other mage became instantly aware of her threat.

"Traitor!" Hugo's scream, directed at the astonished theater owner, broke the silence in the darkened chamber as Nevis released her invisibility spell, pulling a sphere of magefire from her pouch.

She thrust her stiletto into the sphere to lighten the room and banish the shadows. "Barry's a traitor," Nevis agreed softly as the constable stepped from the closet, "but a traitor to me. Granted he'll plead with me that he was placating you, believing I killed Hans and Fani, keeping you content until help arrived, but that particular tale, I'll never believe."

Barry croaked a protest, fell swiftly silent as Nevis' green eyes glared at him with contempt.

Nevis turned to Hugo. "Why murder them?" she whispered, trying to understand as Brea slipped past her slender form to guard the door and keep Barry from fleeing out of the room. "Wasn't blackmailing them enough? They never did anything to you, never meant anything. Why kill them?"

"Because it would hurt you."

"I've done nothing to you but react to your hatred of me and try to protect the people I love." At the fury in the other mage's eyes, Nevis stepped closer, unaware until that moment that she still gripped the ivory-handled stiletto in her hand. "I've done nothing to you but destroy a drug-crazed mage who demanded justice by his own criminal acts against his king and the people of Montbasso. You're following in Adrian's footsteps, but it doesn't have to be that way."

"So pronounces the great, self-righteous Mage Conarkin," Hugo laughed, the sound almost one of madness. "You should have remained Devlin's mage adviser. You're so damned pure—"

"I'm no such thing," Nevis whispered, holding his fevered gaze for a long, tense heartbeat. "Take your punishment, take what you deserve, and make amends. The court will forgive you if you prove yourself genuine. By the gods, Hugo, don't go on with this madness. Devlin will forgive what you've done if you can prove yourself worthy again. As will Alana," she pleaded with him, trying one last strategy. "Adrian's path was wrong. You don't have to follow it, just because he was your mentor. If Adrian hadn't been so influenced by Cashogi poison, he would have remained true to Devlin and the people of Montbasso. He would have remained true to everything Clarissa Bracken taught both of us."

"Is that what you really believe, Nevis? You poor, misguided, naive soul. Adrian despised Devlin, and he despised you. He—"

"You're lying."

"I never lie about Adrian Bambari, Nevis. You should know that after all these years." Unable to physically move beneath the spell, still Hugo made his hatred clear. "I'd rather be dead than follow your path. So kill me, Mage Conarkin, and bloody your hands. Get it over with. I can see the vengeance clear in your eyes that you won't admit to anyone else, vengeance for the magefires and those two pitiful children, vengeance for turning Alana Graham's friendship away from you, and standing between you and the crown of Montbasso." His voice fell as he added, almost as though he was lost in memory, "Her mother would have been proud of me. So proud. She would have smiled to see what I've done to you and Devlin."

Hugo's whispered words surprised Nevis. His smile was seductive, beckoning her to act, and Nevis wondered if Hugo San Rossi had gone mad.

"I won't kill you," Nevis said so softly, the constable stepped closer to hear. "But I'll grant you justice. Not that you deserve it, Hugo, but because the laws of Montbasso demand it." She turned to face Brea, who tried unsuccessfully to read her empty expression. "Get Devlin, will you?"

Brea Kilganor immediately turned to leave, found the half-open door slamming her back against the wall as a slender, black-clad figure hurtled across the threshold, knocking Nevis to the ground, distracting the mage, and shattering her concentration. Nevis lost control of the spell and watched in dismay as Hugo, his smile triumphant, grabbed Shayna Kashi's arm and vanished them both from sight with the aid of a murmured incantation.

Shaken, Brea regained her balance and stretched a hand to help the mage stagger to her feet. "I'm sorry, Nevis. Shayna came flying through like a whirlwind. That's no excuse, but—"

"Not your fault. She wasn't supposed to be here. And I'm the one who lost my concentration." Nevis brushed at her clothes, green eyes fixing Barry Faddle with open dislike. "A word of warning, Master Faddle. If I hear that you gave Hugo San Rossi or his Cashogi whore one single coin, I'll ruin your reputation in Port Jambi and every other gods' cursed town in Montbasso. The man is a murderer and a thief. Help him in any way, and you'll find yourself in chains."

Brea shoved the theater owner against the wall and out of her way. "And if Mage Conarkin doesn't find you, I will."

* * * *

No sooner had the royal carriage rolled to a smooth stop in front of the sorcerous theater, Lily Frascat emerged from the neighboring brothel, Remo Savanak beside her. From their expressions, it was apparent they'd been waiting impatiently for the carriage to arrive. Nevis stepped down onto the packed dirt of the street, followed by Brea, still wearing her blonde wig, then Devlin and Mikaline Nashat.

Overhead, the sorcerous sphere that graced the front of the theater was alight with fireworks and cannon fire, commemorating Devlin's coronation. The scene shifted smoothly into three-masted schooners sailing upriver, laden with goods. And beneath the sphere, the companions gathered together, their moods subdued.

Though their grim faces told the story, Lily still felt compelled to ask. "He didn't come?"

"He came and went." Nevis straightened the soft velvet vest over her ebony silk shirt, disheveled from disembarking, and rechecked her ivory-handled stiletto, carefully avoiding Lily's eyes.

"It was Shayna's fault," the trade minister explained, crossing his arms and glaring at the mage when she immediately began to protest. "I will hear no more blame of your distraction or the constable's fumbling. The constable was nearly flattened against the wall, and you, Mage Conarkin, were thrown to the ground, both assaulted by my own bodyguard who has turned renegade."

"Minister Nashat—"

"My ship will not sail to Kolmari with tomorrow's tide. The captain will keep a look out for the two criminals, as well as their drug associates." Nashat's dark gaze challenged the mage to argue.

"Thank you." Weary, Nevis raked disheveled hair from her eyes and sighed, though she persisted, "If Hugo disguises them both or keeps them under an invisibility spell until the ship sails—"

"I have told you, Mage Conarkin, the ship will not sail."

"Hugo can bespell the captain to obey his wishes."

"The minister and I have already discussed that particular problem while you were waiting for Hugo to appear," Devlin intervened gently, his handsome, bearded face restraining a mischievous smile as the mage turned cool green eyes in his direction. "I don't always wear the crown for appearance's sake. I do sometimes manage to concoct strategic plans."

Chagrined, Nevis' pale face flushed deeply. "Dev—"

He took her hand and raised it to his lips. "I'll forgive you, my love, considering the appalling stress you're under. Now to ease your worries about Hugo slipping out of port, I've commanded my own ships to blockade the harbor should either Cashogi vessel attempt to leave. They're in position to move swiftly. Will that satisfy you?"

"I'm sorry."

"I told you I've forgiven you. Now go and get some sleep." His hands came up to cup her face and brought her body closer, kissing her lips softly before stepping back. "When this nightmare is over, I'm going to lock you in my bedchamber for several days and nights without interruption."

Nevis' flush deepened further, and Lily couldn't restrain her laugh as the madam planted a kiss on Devlin's bearded cheek. "The two of you are perfectly well suited to each other."

"Don't you dare encourage him," Nevis growled, shoving Devlin away as he edged back for another kiss.

Laughing, he pulled the trade minister along with him back to the carriage. Long after they departed, Devlin's laughter gradually faded on the wind. Embarrassed when she caught the constable's bland expression, Nevis shook her head in disgust and headed for the theater. But Remo Savanak gripped her sleeve and held her back.

"About Hugo—" the attorney hedged, eye to eye with the mage. "He won't go sailing off before he deals with you."

"He had his chance at the theater," Nevis murmured, weary of thinking. "If he wanted to destroy me—"

"He wasn't ready for you," Brea interrupted, pulling the forgotten wig from her head and combing her own white-sprinkled hair into a civilized appearance. "Hugo will be back for you, Nevis, on his terms. When you're not ready for him."

The mage didn't answer, gently released her sleeve from the attorney's fingers. No one followed as she entered through the side door, unsurprised to find Verdi Casporet keeping watch with May over the sleeping children. When the costume designer caught sight of her employer, she left the blanket-covered stage to meet Nevis halfway down the side aisle.

"I've been trying to see you all day," Verdi said quietly, arms crossed against her slender chest, eyes fixed on the mage's shadowed face.

"Problem?"

The costume designer sighed in exasperation. "Problem? Yes, I've got a problem, Nevis, depending on how you answer my question."

Nevis sagged against the nearest seat and propped one boot on a rung. "Look, Verdi, if it's—"

"Are you blaming yourself for Hans and Fani?"

The mage turned away, green eyes scanning the stage, roaming over the mounds of huddled bodies but seeing only the two lovers facing each other, daggers thrust into each other's naked chest.

"You can't carry Hugo's guilt on your own shoulders, Nevis. He's the one who keeps attempting to destroy your life, not the other way around. Unless I'm quite seriously missing something, or maybe I'm just stupid," the costume designer stepped in front of the mage, hemming her in and forcing Nevis to face her, "you seem to be the victim here. Not to mention poor Hans and Fani."

"Not in his eyes," Nevis answered slowly. "Hugo has grievances against me that go back a lifetime."

Verdi cocked her head to the side, letting her long black hair hang below one shoulder. "Are they legitimate?"

"Does it matter?"

"Yes. Are they?" the younger woman persisted.

"They are to Hugo."

Suddenly, Verdi grinned and punched Nevis on the shoulder. "That's not saying much. Nevis, I know you're not perfect, but you're a damn sight more honorable than that arrogant bastard." Her expression sobered as she squeezed the mage's arm. "You're right to grieve for Hans and Fani and seek vengeance if that's what you wish, but no more than that."

"Verdi, no matter what you say, and I'm grateful for it, their deaths are on my conscience. I didn't warn them, or anyone, that Hugo might change his appearance to disguise himself."

"Like I said, Nevis, you're not perfect. Anyone can make a mistake, especially someone who's been running without sleep and rest for days, trying to save everyone she loves." Verdi squeezed the mage's arm gently. "You may not have warned anyone about Hugo's magic, but even if you had, he would have found a way to hurt you."

Nevis' protest faded as a loud boom from the direction of the harbor was quickly followed by a second. The door to the theater flew open, and Brea Kilganor searched for Nevis in the dim magefire lamplight.

"Here, Brea. What was that?"

"Cannon fire down by the docks."

"Cannon fire? By the gods, who's shooting at whom?"

The constable shook her head. "Can't tell. Lily has the carriage waiting if you want to find out for yourself."

"Verdi—"

"I'll tell May you've gone off adventuring again," the costume designer's expression was somber. "You just be sure you're not in the line of fire. I refuse to work for Barry Faddle."

"I'll duck if any more shots are fired." The mage followed the constable outside, found Lily and Remo already waiting in the madam's carriage and joined them as another boom echoed over the water. "That came from the fortress."

"As did the first two, I think." Remo made room for the constable as the driver shut the door and scurried up onto his own seat. "The only foreign ships in the harbor now are from Cashogi, and I can't imagine why we'd be firing on them. There's been no problem with the trade negotiations. Unless Hugo San Rossi is behind whatever trouble's happening in the harbor."

A frown creased Nevis' forehead as she digested the attorney's words in silence. The carriage jolted them along the cobblestones on Harbor Road, bypassing Brigadier Bridge, where curious bystanders stood watching the activity further downstream. Nevis leaned out the open window as they rounded a curve that brought the Ruskin Shipyard into view, the new vessel waiting patiently for its turn at sea.

Beyond the shipyard, the two Cashogi ships appeared, their blue flags, with the brilliant white horse rearing triumphantly, waving in the wind amid a cloud of smoke. Both ships were still docked, trapped in the harbor by Montbasso navy vessels. The middle mast on the nearer Cashogi vessel leaned drunkenly over the side, ropes and canvas dangling down to the water.

No one in the carriage said a word as the conveyance rolled to a stop at a near but safe distance from the ships, easily accessible by foot from their position. The passengers clambered out, one by one, Lily's feathers bobbing with her graceful motion, and stood in stunned bewilderment, watching a troop of cavalry advance on the docked ships. The officer raised his hand, and the troopers halted in a half-circle, waiting for orders. A flash of light from the lead Montbasso vessel in the harbor warned them of signals passing back and forth between the ship and the fortress.

"There's Devlin's carriage." Lily pointed needlessly as the royal coach, its scarlet hawk emblazoned on the door, thundered along Harbor Road, coming from the opposite direction. The carriage braked to a halt, waiting as the cavalry officer approached. "Why isn't Devlin up at the fortress where it's safe?"

"Try telling him that," Nevis snorted, already walking toward the wharf where the Cashogi vessels were trapped, Brea Kilganor close at her heels.

"It would be as effective as telling you to stay here." Lily frowned in annoyance as the white-haired mage shot her a grin over one shoulder without slowing her pace. "Damn fool stubborn mage. I don't know why I bother."

"Hush. I'm trying to listen."

Nevis strained to decipher the shouted commands, green eyes tracking Devlin's descent from the carriage, along with Mikaline Nashat. Nevis and her companions reached the line of troops, who sharply ordered them back. The mage spoke a word with the nearest young guard, who eyed his commander. When the officer recognized the mage, he signaled to the king, letting Nevis catch a clear glimpse of the fury in Devlin Graham's expression. Beside Devlin, standing silent as he gazed up at the damaged Cashogi ship, the trade minister appeared older, as though his spirit had taken a mortal wound.

Devlin waved Nevis to his side, and the others waited outside the circle of troops. His voice was clipped as he explained the situation, skin growing flushed with anger. "It seems that Hugo San Rossi has gone openly renegade," he informed the mage, making his voice carry beyond his troops to reach the Cashogi crew. "He has declared himself traitor to the peace with the help of Shayna Kashi, trade minister Nashat's companion. Hugo San Rossi appeared at the fortress and told my officers to fire on the visiting Cashogi vessels because they were planning an attack on the fortress during the night before heading out to sea." Devlin's blue eyes were hard as he assessed the damaged mast, his gaze evaluating the second ship, which appeared unharmed.

"Hugo informed my officers that I had given the command to destroy the ships, but he thought it best to simply cripple them. I did not give any such order," Devlin roared, his voice shaking with anger. "Minister Nashat and I believe that Mage San Rossi intends to board the undamaged vessel himself and flee Port Jambi. Anyone aiding the mage and his Cashogi conspirator will be labeled traitor to both kingdoms and suffer the consequences." He placed his hand on Mikaline Nashat's arm, spoke quietly with the minister and then turned to the captain of the wounded ship. "My carpenters shall repair the damage to your vessel at first light. We will also make reparations for this unwarranted action. Our kingdoms are not at war." He pointed out to the harbor, where the Montbasso naval vessels were slowly unblocking the entrance to Port Jambi. "I repeat, in front of our Cashogi friends, our kingdoms are not at war."

With Devlin's permission, the trade minister approached his two vessels to confer with the captains and reassure them of the monarch's good faith. Devlin drew Nevis aside, his grip on her shoulder so tight she winced. "Gods' forsaken traitor. I'll strangle him myself."

"I'll hold him down for you. Dev—"

"The problem is that we don't know where he'll strike next. I didn't expect this bit of treachery."

"Nor did I. Frankly, I assumed for a long time that he'd only come after me. But even now that we know he's trying to destroy the peace, we don't know his targets. But we do know he's not finished with you. Dev, be careful."

His eyes lost some of their anger, and he caressed her cheek. "He's not finished with you, either. Nevis, I'll send some of my troops to guard the theater. They'll be able to keep the children from harm."

"Don't. Dev, don't send anyone."

"They'll be able to protect you and the children."

"Not against a mage, they won't. Use them to keep the peace in the city. I'll do what I can for the children. I promised them," she said softly, "that nothing in my theater will harm them. If I can't keep that promise—" Green eyes filled with sorrow as she stepped back from Devlin.

"You're done more for those children than they ever expected."

She touched his arm lightly, felt the tension in his muscle. "Yes, but it may not be enough." Without another word, she turned on her heel and walked back to the carriage, the others following silently in her wake.

Chapter Nineteen

Careful not to disturb the quiet little scene, Nevis crept stealthily along the river path and sat on a flattened rock, watching Teddy struggle with his lively fishing pole beneath the benevolent eyes of Verdi Casporet and the little red-haired child. Instinct warned the child, and Kimmi turned her head, eyes wide with joy at the mage's unexpected presence. When Nevis raised a finger to her lips, the child escaped from Verdi's lap. The costume designer moved instinctively to grab her, saw Nevis, and grinned, letting the child free to scramble onto the mage's lap. Thumb tucked securely in her mouth, the imp sighed, settling down against Nevis' chest, one skinny leg swinging free.

"Here it is, Verdi! Here—" Teddy nearly slipped from the rocks as he staggered back, a defiant trout dangling from his crude hook. With expert skill for such a scrawny little boy, Teddy defeated the trout and turned to Verdi, a triumphant smile on his dirt-streaked face that turned to shock. "Aunt Nevis—"

"Morning, Teddy." The mage stroked the flame-red curls nestled against her chin, enjoying the first sunlight breaking over the horizon. "Is that breakfast?"

"If Ma wants, sure." His grin was precocious, and Nevis returned that contagious smile, though she worried when that grin turned somber. "If I keep fishing for trout, then we don't have to worry about getting food from anyone else."

Nevis bit back her first response and considered his wiry little body, brown curls a riotous frame to a handsome face, the best of May and his seafaring father. "Teddy boy," she said softly, "you don't have to worry about where we'll get food. I promise none of you will ever have to worry about that."

"I know, Aunt Nevis." The boy regarded her so gravely that Nevis wondered when this ten-year-old hooligan had suddenly grown up. "But I want to help. I know you and Ma are worried all the time. And with Pa sailing upriver so much—" Abruptly, Teddy's face flamed in embarrassment, and he shrugged his skinny shoulders. "I just want to help, that's all."

She reached out a hand, and Teddy came closer, letting the mage touch his dirt-streaked cheek. "And your help, like Verdi's help, is what will make us survive. I'd be lying if I said we weren't worried," she quietly responded to his budding maturity, then added, her smile bright, "and I'd be lying if I said I wasn't proud of you. So, Teddy boy, get back to work."

"Yes, ma'am," the boy hugged her close and grinned, a child again, and Nevis breathed a sigh of relief as he snatched up his fishing pole, attention focused once more on the swift-flowing currents.

Verdi cocked her head to the side, eyes unreadable. "That's the problem with you, Nevis," she sighed, feigning despair. "You make people want to help you. To be honest, it's damnably annoying."

Nevis' tart reply never left her lips, as Brea Kilganor, who'd taken to spending the last few nights at the theater, rounded the corner of the building and approached them, her expression grim.

Instinct screaming in her head, Nevis set the child on the ground and nudged her tiny body in Verdi's direction, then got to her feet. "Trouble?"

"Shayna's holding Alana Graham hostage, and she won't negotiate with anyone until you arrive."

"By the gods, they're striking in all different directions. After last night, I thought sure they'd come this way. Verdi—" Nevis glanced down at the child.

"I've got her," the costume designer picked up the red-haired imp, and followed the two women back toward the theater. "Should I tell Lily?"

Distracted, and thinking hard, Nevis nodded, her longer strides making it difficult for the constable to match. "Ask her if we can use the carriage."

"No need," Brea replied, muttering rude oaths under her breath as she struggled to keep up with the mage's long strides. "Devlin's sent horses."

Before reaching the street in front of her theater, Nevis abruptly stopped and faced the young costume designer. "Verdi, tell—" Green eyes scanned the building, the river, searching for something even she couldn't determine. "Ask Lily to send Chappy Markos over here to keep an eye on the children, will you?" She brushed red curls from Kimmi's face, met the constable's narrowed eyes, and nodded, more certain of her decision. "Just in case."

"Be careful," Verdi warned. "Nevis—"

"Oh, and tell Simon," the mage suddenly grinned, trying to keep the younger woman from needless worry, "to keep my sugar-coated cake away from Gabriella's grubby little hands, or I'll fire him."

"You can't fire him if you're not paying him."

"Don't remind him of that little fact." Nevis turned on her heels and strode briskly to the front of the theater where an escort of crown guards waited with two extra horses, the scarlet hawk emblazoned on the saddles.

"Mage Conarkin? The king asked that you come."

She nodded, mounting the fidgety roan in one graceful movement as the constable followed suit with the other horse. They galloped through deserted streets, hooves ringing loudly on the cobblestones, past merchant shops and crowded homes, scrunched together along narrow streets as they moved away from the river toward the center of the city. The fortress loomed ahead, pale sunlight catching on the topmost battlements, the scarlet hawk snapping in the breeze as they raced forward, leaving their horses at the gate rather than riding around to the stables.

Nevis' escort led the two women directly to Alana Graham's suite of rooms, where the door stood open, revealing a scene that nearly stopped the mage's heart. Erasing all signs of dismay from her expression and posture, Nevis drew herself up straight and boldly entered the chamber, not waiting for, nor asking, Shayna Kashi's permission.

Nevis didn't dare look at Devlin or the Cashogi trade minister, both men standing tensely near the door, silk bed robes tied at the waist. Her eyes and complete attention focused on the Cashogi bodyguard. The small woman, clad in black leather, had one well-proportioned muscular arm grasping Alana Graham by the neck, the other touching that slender neck with the tip of her stiletto.

Alana was surprisingly calm, eyes watching the mage as Nevis stood motionless in the center of the parlor. For one brief moment, their eyes locked, and Nevis turned back to Shayna before she lost her nerve.

"I'm here."

"You took your time."

"I don't waste my sorcery in transporting myself as other mages do. I rather prefer," Nevis crossed her arms against her chest, "to keep that sorcery ready for more appropriate usage."

Shayna threw back her head and laughed, black curls swaying sensuously along her back, never loosening her grip on Alana. "Very good, Mage Conarkin. Very, very good."

"Where's your lover?" Nevis ignored the flinch of pain on Alana's face, her expression young and vulnerable, as Shayna confirmed the mage's earlier warnings to Alana.

"Getting things ready."

"To leave?"

"Why stay here? I doubt your monarch will be lenient with either of us. In case you've forgotten," the Cashogi woman said with such pride that Nevis was astonished, "we have broken quite a few of your laws."

"Not to mention damaging your own vessel."

"Only one. The other will be more than ready to sail. And you, Mage Conarkin, won't be able to stop it."

Nevis refused to take the bait. "Leaving soon?"

"Once we've settled a few matters, yes."

Nevis shoved all worry about the children from her expression. "And is one of those matters holding the heir to Montbasso hostage?"

"Since you've managed to frighten Barry Faddle into hiding, and we've no idea where the little weasel keeps his gold, Hugo thought it best to force the girl's father to pay a ransom." Gray eyes slid first in Devlin's direction, then Mikaline Nashat, her young face betraying no remorse. "It makes sense, don't you think, to use the girl one last time, just as he's used her for the last several years?"

"I can understand his reasoning," Nevis said calmly, her heart grieving for the pain on Alana's face, "though I don't see why it concerns me. Devlin Graham's the one to decide whether or not to pay that ransom for his daughter."

"It concerns you, too, now that you've placed the royal treasury under a protective spell. So stop wasting time with idiotic pretense, as though you don't know why you're here." Shayna's eyes betrayed her growing impatience, made evident as she dug the stiletto very slightly into the girl's neck, eliciting a gasp, swiftly stifled as Alana regained her composure.

Nevis didn't blink, ignored the Cashogi woman, and turned to Devlin, whose blue eyes betrayed nothing of his emotions, though they darted once to Alana's face and away. "Shall I release the spell on the royal treasury?"

"I don't give in to bullies who can't stand on their own two feet and fight fair," he said quietly, eyes alighting once more on his daughter's face, some unspoken message, which Nevis couldn't read, passing between them. Though Alana's entire stance, as awkward as it was beneath the Cashogi bodyguard's grip, seemed more confident somehow.

"Then your daughter dies."

"If Devlin Graham's heir and daughter dies, Shayna Kashi, traitor to the Cashogi throne, you'll never leave here alive." Mikaline Nashat, brown eyes unrepentant, stood beside Devlin, shoulders hunched, both hands tucked into the pocket of his silk bed robe as though he were cold. "I promise you that."

"You?" The bodyguard's laugh was rich with mockery. "All the years I've kept you alive and safe, Mikaline, free from nightmares and shadows in the night, calmed your fears, you—" She shook her head again, dismissing his threat. "You promise me that? And expect me to easily frighten? To simply cast aside my weapon and my hostage?" Her laugh was insulting.

"I was never born to be a fighter as you were," Mikaline said with great sorrow, drawing closer to the Cashogi woman, ignoring the sudden curiosity in Alana's blue eyes as she glanced at her father. "I depended on you, relied on your skills, but never," his voice faltered as grief overtook his emotions, "never, did I believe you would turn against your homeland. And against all I have ever believed in."

Shayna studied the minister as though he were a particularly intriguing insect. "A miscalculation I used to my advantage."

"To my everlasting shame, yes."

"To your everlasting embarrassment. Devlin—"

Ignoring the minister's nonthreatening presence, Shayna turned to the monarch, prepared to negotiate. And when she did, the very moment she directed her attention toward Devlin, Mikaline Nashat weighed and judged her miscalculation and snatched the opportunity, moving closer to his bodyguard. Pulling his right hand from his pocket, he plunged a dagger into Shayna's side, catching her off balance.

Desperate and stunned, Shayna tried to hold onto Alana, but the girl elbowed her attacker hard, taking advantage of the wound and thrusting the Cashogi woman away. Shayna stumbled, fell over a wooden stool in pain and confusion, the stiletto slipping from her hands to bounce across the thick rug. Devlin bent to snatch the weapon to safety. Mikaline Nashat, pale face flushed with conflicting emotions, knelt beside her, one hand still gripping his bloodied dagger.

"Finish the job, Mikaline. Kill me," she taunted, daring the minister to further violence. "Execute me as your king executed my innocent family because he believed they had betrayed him."

"I told you," Mikaline said quietly, brown eyes filled with disappointment and regret, "I was not born to be a fighter as you were, nor a traitor to my kingdom. But when forced to act, I will. Your family was innocent, Shayna, for that I'm sorry. Nothing can ever bring them back. But your betrayal wasn't what they would have wished. Your own acts have disgraced your family name." Trembling fingers threw the stained weapon out of her reach, as the minister craned his neck to speak with Devlin. "My lord, if you would keep her under vigilance, I would be grateful."

Devlin moved to signal his guard to deal with Shayna Kashi, fingers halted in mid-air as Teddy Quiddle unexpectedly flew down the broad corridor, skidding into the crowded parlor.

"Aunt Nevis? Come quick! The mage— The one who burned down the orphanage—" Teddy gasped out the words as Nevis held the boy steady. "He's holding everyone hostage at the theater."

* * * *

Beneath the bright, early morning sunshine, Nevis studied the solid exterior of the sorcerous theater, its huge transparent sphere lifeless in daylight, held securely by the carved wooden hands. She knew full well that the building's true value lay not in its artistic purpose but in what the theater held within its sheltering walls, walls that no longer protected the orphan children to whom she'd so recently, and so falsely, promised safety.

Abruptly, Nevis swiveled to face her waiting companions, half of them still in their bed robes. "Dev, it's best if your guards stay outside." When he started immediately to protest, she raised a hand. "It's not their fight. They'll only get hurt for no good reason. It's me Hugo wants."

"He can't have you!"

"No." Her smile was unexpectedly serene, easing some of Devlin's own tension. "And he won't. Trust me. Teddy," she turned to the boy, "I need you to stay outside and keep watch over the main entrance." At the anticipated argument in his eyes, Nevis gripped her nephew's shoulders hard. "I know your mother's in trouble, Teddy boy, and that you want desperately to come inside and help her, but I need you out here. If anyone tries to enter, don't let them in. I'm depending on you to keep us undisturbed. If I'm distracted, I can't concentrate. And if I can't concentrate on casting spells, I won't be able to help your mother."

Trying to determine from his aunt's expression whether she was merely making sure he was safe, the boy finally nodded. "You can count on me."

"I know I can. Now, then, Dev, you and Minister Nashat—"

"Are coming inside, too. Don't waste your breath arguing." The monarch's expression was stubborn, though his eyes showed clear surprise when Alana voiced her own defiant determination, catching everyone off guard.

"I'm coming inside, too." Blue eyes ignored everyone but Nevis, the last ten years of hostility hanging between them as effective as a solid barrier. "Unless you don't trust me."

Nevis squinted her eyes against the glare of the sun, studied the girl's taut expression, and nodded, deciding not to say anything. "Constable?"

"I'll be right beside you, Mage Conarkin. In case," the older woman grinned, revealing crooked teeth, absently scratching her dark brown, white-speckled hair, "there's anything left of Hugo San Rossi to cart away to his majesty's prison."

"By the gods, Constable," Nevis breathed deep, shaking her head in mock disgust. "Lily—"

"I'm not staying outside wondering what's happening in there." Burnt orange feathers bobbed as the madam crossed her arms in challenge. "Besides, Nevis, the children will need some soothing."

Nevis nodded reluctantly, placing her desperate anxiety for the children in a separate compartment of her mind. She glanced at Remo, whose mouth opened to say something, then just as swiftly shut as she turned her attention his way.

"Counselor, I know you're going to demand to come inside, too, waving your fists, but I need you here, at the front entrance, standing just inside the door, to witness what goes on. In case," she added dryly, smiling at Remo's conflicted expression, "we face a court battle over what happens in my theater and any accusations that are later made."

"I seriously doubt anyone will contest what happens today."

"Maybe not. But still, I'd rather have an objective witness, seeing as the constable might be preoccupied. I know you're not really objective," Nevis added, meeting his worried gaze, "but I can trust you to follow the rules of Montbasso justice. That's it. And I—"

"Have I no place inside your theater?"

Nevis turned slowly, only then aware of the clicking of a wooden walking stick along the cobblestones. Clarissa Bracken, long silver braid swaying gently along her back, approached the group slowly, eyes fixed on the younger mage's face, ignoring everyone else.

"It's my battle," Nevis said quietly, tucking her hands deep in her pockets. "I tried to make Hugo listen, but he denied himself a second chance."

"So now you'll kill him?"

"I'd rather not," Nevis admitted, green eyes bright with honesty, her conscience easy, "but I will if I must."

"Fair enough." Clarissa appraised her former apprentice, recognized with relief what she'd hoped to find. "I can help."

"I don't need you to destroy him."

"You may need me to distract him."

"Your pardon," Devlin intervened, utterly confused by the baker's unexplained presence and offer of help that made no logical sense, "but it would be best if you were safe outside."

Instead of addressing Devlin's polite concern for her safety, Clarissa raised the carved head of her walking stick to Devlin's sight, watched in silence as he blinked, face-to-face with the fierce hawk he'd last seen over a decade ago. Slowly, Devlin raised his eyes to meet the older mage's gaze, appraised her appearance and her sincerity and, above all, her loyalty, before turning to Nevis, who nodded slowly.

"Then perhaps it would be best if you came inside," Devlin whispered, his voice reflecting his stunned acceptance.

"Perhaps it would."

Aware of the constable's confusion and Remo's unspoken questions, Nevis glanced apologetically at them both. "A tale for another moment, which I promise to tell you. All you need know right now is that she's a friend." Glancing away from the other woman's gratitude, Nevis took a deep breath. "Let's go, shall we? I want my theater back, or Gabriella will hound me without mercy, spouting pages of poorly enunciated melodramatic lines to punish me."

"Nevis—"

She half turned, saw her bravado reflected in Devlin's own gaze. With a cocky smile, she leaned forward to kiss him deeply on the lips. "I'm looking forward to those days and nights you promised me."

"I kept my bed robe on to remind you," Devlin said lightly, not fooling the mage, whose own heart beat rapidly with fear.

"And here I thought you were all starting a new fashion trend for Port Jambi." Nevis touched his face, shivered at the coarseness of his beard beneath her fingers. Stepping back, she faced the theater and waved Teddy into position. Squaring her thin shoulders, Nevis flung wide the heavy doors.

Though braced for whatever horror she might discover inside, Nevis was not prepared to find the children hovering above the stage, held aloft by sorcery, over a flaming pit of magefire. Her stage was protected from sorcerous elements, Nevis thought ruefully, but not the children, to whom she promised over and over that nothing in her sorcerous theater would ever harm them.

"Has it come to this pitiful point, Hugo? Bullying children?"

Nevis strode with purpose down the center aisle, expression utterly unconcerned, eyes automatically noting everyone's position. May and Verdi, along with two of Lily's girls, Simon, and Chappy, were held roped together at one end of the stage, out of Hugo's way. Their mouths were gagged, but their eyes, peering over the filthy binding, were eloquent with fury. At least, Nevis breathed in relief, they were unharmed.

Hugo San Rossi, flamboyant in a scarlet cape, perched gracefully on the wooden battlement of the stage set, expression bored as he released a huge yawn. Devlin and the trade minister, along with Alana Graham, walked quietly down the left aisle, Lily down the right, with Clarissa Bracken at her side, walking stick silent and hidden, and Brea Kilganor, a short distance from the white-haired, black-clad mage, near at hand, yet out of her way should Nevis need to move swiftly.

"What else is there to do with them, Nevis? I never understood why you cared so about their welfare." One jeweled hand waved effortlessly at the huddled children, setting them quivering as though a strong wind passed by.

Nevis schooled her features to emptiness, knowing that she couldn't allow the terror in Kimmi's delicate face distract her. "It's only something to make the people of Port Jambi think highly of me, a trick you never learned. I'm surprised, quite frankly. Adrian knew how to play that game very well. So well that no one suspected him until it was too late, when the Cashogi drugs finally caught up to him."

"Wasted effort. In the end, all that elegant diplomacy and false compassion didn't help him, did it?"

"No, it didn't. But it might have helped you, since you haven't surrendered to Adrian's weakness. You don't use the drugs, you only sell them." Stance relaxed, stiletto and pouch within easy reach, Nevis shrugged. "I don't understand you. Ten years ago, Devlin appointed you to a place of honor as mage adviser, the highest position for a mage in Montbasso."

"A position you tired of, as I recall. If you hadn't stepped down, Devlin Graham would never have appointed me to that position."

"Devlin might have tired of my advice. You don't know what would have happened, Hugo."

"Nevis, please."

Nevis took a deep breath, continued her argument. "So instead of using the position with dignity and integrity, you seduced Devlin's daughter into believing you were righteous and good after her own mother rejected your affections. And then," Nevis kept her gaze focused on Hugo, heard Alana's sharp intake of breath, not daring to glance at the young woman as the additional insult pierced her heart, "you simply threw it all away. You even discarded the heir to Montbasso. Why?"

"Nevis, I've a ship to catch. Stop wasting my time. Devlin, have you given Shayna the funds she requested?"

"At the moment, Shayna Kashi is a guest in my prison," Devlin answered, blue eyes hard with hatred, "where she will rot, alone and unloved, until she dies for the crime of threatening my daughter's life."

Hugo's sigh was exquisitely bored. "Your daughter was never in any real danger from the woman. Though I did briefly contemplate teaching Alana a lesson, simply to punish her for an appalling lack of skill in my bed." His laughter was cruel, as he added to the mage, "I could have worked in your theater, Nevis, for the exquisite acting I was forced into, letting the young fool believe I desired her."

"You arrogant bastard," Alana hissed, pulling free of her father's warning hand. "I may despise Nevis Conarkin, and she may equally despise me," the young woman shouted, uncomfortably aware of the flash of genuine grief on Nevis' face, "but she was right about you."

"You'll get over your broken heart, my dear."

Alana didn't respond, refused to be baited, until Hugo set the children rocking again. "Set the children free."

"Tell your father to give me the funds I requested, and everyone can go back to bed with sweet dreams." Hugo's hands gestured toward the children, this time sending the huddled group closer to the magefire.

Nevis sheltered her heart from their frightened screams, took a step closer to the stage, murmuring an incantation beneath her breath to transport the children away to safety, but Hugo sensed her movement, felt the rise of her sorcery.

"I wouldn't try that, Nevis. In fact, understand me now, so there's no confusion later. Try to transport the children to safety, and they'll die before they even blink out of sight." Hugo's black eyes bored into her soul, and Nevis experienced pure, burning hatred for the mage and overwhelming terror for the children. "Are we clear on this point, Mage Conarkin?"

"Yes."

"Good. Now, Devlin—"

"I told your Cashogi whore I won't deal with bullies, and I'll tell you the same." Devlin shoved his daughter behind his broad back. "I wouldn't negotiate with Adrian Bambari, and I won't negotiate with you."

"Devlin, really. This bravado is getting tiresome. Maybe this little demonstration will help persuade you."

Hugo stretched a hand toward the monarch, and several things happened at once. Alana broke free of her father's protection and heaved Devlin to the floor, saving him from a bolt of magefire that burned a hole through the wall. Clarissa Bracken raised her cane, and shot a bolt of magefire at Hugo, taking him completely by surprise. Her strike knocked him from the battlement, destroying the wooden structure.

"Brea!"

"Here, Nevis."

"In my office, on the corner of my desk, beneath the statue of Janni, is a sketch of Hugo. Bring it. Bring it to me now."

Without asking questions, the constable fled along the nearest row and up the narrow stairs, fetching the sketch that Nevis requested. In the confusion below, Hugo staggered to his feet, hand pointing with open threat at Nevis.

"She didn't touch you. I did." Signaling Lily Frascat away from her side, Clarissa Bracken raised her walking stick in Hugo's direction, acknowledged his wide-eyed, stunned expression with complete satisfaction. "Now Hugo, let's talk like civilized people, shall we?"

Brea Kilganor slipped back through the rows of seats, caught the tail end of the baker's words. Bewildered, she handed the sketch of Hugo San Rossi to Nevis, who placed it on a chair, out of Hugo's line of vision.

"You were dead."

"Did you really believe that?" Clarissa scoffed, walking stick making the familiar clicking along the wooden floor of the side aisle as she approached the stage. "You're as naïve as my Nevis here, who, at least, understands the meaning of honor and integrity. But you, Mage San Rossi, as Adrian Bambari's so highly promising apprentice," she shrugged, keeping his attention focused on her approach and away from Nevis, "let's just say, I expected better of you. Wasted talent."

Distracted by the old woman's appearance, Hugo stretched out a hand in her direction, oblivious to Nevis' whispered chanting, unaware of the tiny charcoal figure that lifted from the paper, to the constable's slack-jawed astonishment, mindful of the transparent sphere that formed within Nevis' cupped hands. With fierce determination on her face, the white-haired mage concentrated only on Hugo San Rossi, trusting Clarissa Bracken to keep him absorbed in her taunting words, even as Hugo glanced her way, trying to see what Nevis was doing. But Clarissa edged closer, her wrinkled face openly hostile, and Hugo's attention strayed back to the baker, caught in old hateful, pain-filled memories.

"You betrayed Adrian Bambari." Hugo's snarl was bitter. "You betrayed your own apprentice."

"Adrian Bambari betrayed me. And Adrian betrayed you by leading an innocent apprentice down the dark and foul path to greed and treason and murder."

"His path was right."

Hugo raised a fisted hand to strike Clarissa, and magefire erupted simultaneously from both their fisted hands. The older mage crumpled to her knees, having dodged the worst impact, and struggled to release another blast at Hugo, stunning him with her unexpectedly swift reaction.

And in that brief moment when he was bewildered from the force of the old woman's blow, just as Adrian Bambari had been, ten long years ago, when Nevis moved in so quickly to defend herself and wound her friend, unwittingly hitting Adrian with a fatal blow, Nevis moved. Her chanting grew louder as the miniature figure solidified. A few steps away, the constable stifled a cry of amazement at the tiny image of Hugo San Rossi cupped within Nevis' confident hands, a transparent sphere securely taking shape around the image.

On the stage, struggling with fear and recognition of what Nevis had done, and what he could no longer prevent, Hugo stared in horror at the intensely focused white-haired mage. Nevis' hunched shoulders hid the sphere from his sight, but her steady murmuring left him weak and drained as she captured his body and his soul, alive, within the sphere.

And in that moment of triumph, as she held Hugo safely imprisoned, Nevis' concentration shattered when screams echoed through the theater. Instinctively, without conscious thought, she reacted, whispering an incantation that brought the children's drop into magefire to a sudden and complete halt, mere inches from the searing flames. With Clarissa's guidance and support, Nevis gently lowered the children to safety, doused the magefire with conjured rain, and sank to her knees. Shaggy head bowed in utter exhaustion, Nevis clutched the transparent sphere in her trembling fingers, Hugo San Rossi encased within.

Epilogue

Nevis sat cross-legged on the lush green grass just outside the newly completed and freshly painted orphanage building. Surrounded by eager children, the littlest red-haired child snuggled in her lap, thumb securely wedged in her mouth, Nevis eyed her nephew, one white eyebrow raised in query. Cuddling the black-and-white kitten in his arms, Teddy sent his aunt a firm signal, nodding fiercely.

"Now, children. You've all entertained us with the excellent play Gabriella and Pepo wrote for you. And I must say, if you continue to act so well as you get older, I may hire you for my stage. By the time you're old enough," she added, "Gabriella and Pepo will be old and toothless." The mage slid a mischievous glance at her two leading actors, who merely preened at the expected praise, then shook their fists at the humorous threat, earning a laugh from Nevis.

Green eyes scanned the gathered adults, her entire cast and crew, Finlay Oscram talking earnestly to the Cashogi trade minister, both men delighted that the negotiations were behind them and trade had enthusiastically begun, the first shipments of artisan crafts from Kolmari expected within the week, and the first vessel from the Ruskin Shipyards anticipating its launch in the following week. Clarissa Bracken, having pleased everyone's appetite with sugar-coated cakes and raspberry tarts, particularly Nevis' sweet tooth, joined their amiable conversation.

Nevis turned back to the children. "Now it's my turn to celebrate your new soft beds and Aunt May's new kitchen. I promised you a bit of magic, didn't I? I hope you're ready."

A dozen raised voices drowned out May's expected scolding. Beside his wife, Theo Quiddle, handsome in his captain's coat, silenced her words with a kiss, to the children's shrieks of delight. Ruffling Kimmi's wild curls, Nevis lifted the child from her lap and set her beside Verdi and out of danger. Carefully unsheathing her stiletto, Nevis pulled a sphere from her bottomless pouch and held it up to the sunlight.

"You're all certain?"

"Aunt Nevis, don't tease." Teddy handed the kitten off to another little boy, hugging his knees close to his chest. "We've been waiting all day."

"Imagine that," Lily drawled, arm in arm with Remo. "They waited weeks for new beds with bright blankets and soft mattresses, never once complaining, but to go a few days without Mage Conarkin's sorcery—"

Nevis didn't respond, simply smiled and held the sphere aloft. With one swift, sure thrust, she pierced the crystal sphere, releasing a gorgeous panorama of beautiful ladies and handsome men, riding graceful horses across a meadow brilliant with summer wildflowers. Dragons swooped elegantly from the sky, and a rainbow arched across the entire scene, fading as night fell and a million stars shone bright.

With the rising of the moon, the sorcery dissipated, and Nevis, who had already resheathed her stiletto, was smothered with hugs and kisses. Returning their enthusiastic affection, she laughingly staggered to her feet, helped upright by Brea Kilganor, uniform crisp and proper as ever.

"Your audience is never disappointed."

"They're an easy audience to please." Nevis brushed twigs from her ebony breeches. "Easier than the adults."

"Gabriella and Pepo proudly informed me that they coerced your playwright, who's been fastidiously abstaining from Firespark, into penning a magnificent play that will require your quite formidable sorcery and the elegant fabrics from Cashogi." Brea grinned crookedly, dark eyes watching Devlin Graham wander in their direction. "Your next season is bound to be successful. So successful that you can finally start paying them again, so they claim. Even your banker will be delighted."

"I may be able to start paying them wages again, but I'll never be able to repay what they've done for me."

"According to Gabriella, she's rather tired of that old argument." Before Nevis could reply, Devlin had reached them. Brea made a polite excuse to leave the two alone, despite their protestations.

"Well, Mage Conarkin?"

Nevis crossed her arms against her chest and studied his handsome face. "I could use a few more days locked inside your bedchamber."

Blue eyes shifted from mischief to serious business. "About that very topic—" Devlin glanced around, took her arm, and guided the mage toward the river walk. "Nevis, don't you think it's time to stop all that?"

Her steps halted, and Nevis stared up at his sober expression. "Meaning?" she asked softly, not really needing to ask.

"Marry me."

Nevis turned away, blocking his view of her face as she stared hard at Brigadier Bridge. "I can't."

"You won't."

"Dev—"

"Hugo is safely locked away in that sorcerous sphere you created until you can decide what to do with him. As long as you don't release the spell, he'll no longer corrupt my daughter. And besides," blue eyes held her gaze as he turned her back to face him, "she's readily admitted to me that Hugo's a snake and that she'd been wrong to trust him. For that matter, she admitted it to you, too, the very day you defeated him in your theater."

"So she did, but Alana's not ready to accept me as your queen. She may have admitted that I was right about Hugo, but she still despises me."

"She fears you, and she respects you."

"She resents me. Damn it, Dev, I won't marry you, knowing that the girl has forgotten that we were once friends. Alana still sees me as the woman who destroyed her father's marriage. Even though that marriage was destroyed by her mother's own betrayal when she took Adrian Bambari as a lover," Nevis whispered, shaking her head. "Alana may never accept the truth of my innocence and will always hold me to blame for her mother's suicide."

"Should that matter, particularly when you're free of blame?" Devlin demanded, shading his eyes against the slanting sunlight. "Should it?"

"Yes, to both you and me."

"Nevis—"

The mage placed a hand over Devlin's lips and leaned close. "I can't be your queen unless Alana accepts me into her heart. But that doesn't change what I feel for you, Devlin Graham."

Resigned to the fact of her stubbornness, and deciding to press the point at a more advantageous time, Devlin smoothed his beard, blue eyes shifting back to mischief. "And what is that you feel, exactly?"

Laughing, she pushed Devlin away as he edged nearer. "Not in front of the children."

Ignoring her feeble protest, Devlin pulled Nevis close, wrapping his arms around her slender body. "They have to learn sometime."

About the Author

Virginia G. McMorrow has worked as an editor/writer for more than 30 years, after a career in human resources. In her professional capacity, Ginny has worked for business publishers as an editor of books, journals, reports, and newsletters targeted for clients, and now works as a freelance editor/writer. She has also had numerous articles on both professional and writing topics published, along with several short stories. As a playwright, Ginny has had 28 short one acts and one full-length play produced off-off Broadway by Love Creek Productions in a black box theater, as well as two short plays performed on a west coast radio show. She now lives and works in Venice, Florida.

Coming Soon!

VIRGINIA G. MCMORROW'S

MAGE EVOLUTION
THE MAGE TRILOGY
BOOK 3

Mage Evolution, Book Three of The Mage Trilogy, continues the tale of Mage Alex Keltie—her husband Anders the Crownmage, the Barlows, and her dear friend Queen Elena. Five years have passed since the confrontation of the Spreebridge renegade mages, and a new character has entered the saga, four-year-old Emmy, Alex's precious daughter, who possesses mage talents from both her parents. Yet Alex is desperate to protect her daughter, even as a conspiracy sweeping the land takes away all mage powers-even her own.

For more information
visit: www.SpeakingVolumes.us